"Leigh Randall! You're back!"

Leigh watched the woman approach and felt her stomach quiver. Mary Ann was the last person she wanted to bump into her first twenty-four hours home. Well, maybe the *second* last.

"So how does it feel?" Mary Ann asked after Leigh extracted herself from her embrace. "Any qualms about returning to the scene of the...incident?"

Leigh took a deep breath. "That was fifteen years ago."

"But some people still blame you. After all, you were the only one to survive. I guess it was lucky that Spencer McKay saw the boat flip over."

Leigh closed her eyes. New York suddenly seemed very appealing.

"Say, speaking of Spence," Mary Ann began. "Did you hear that he and Jen split up? Years ago."

Spencer McKay. The very last person Leigh wanted to think about. She turned, got into her car and slammed the door.

"I'll call you," Mary Ann said. "I want to know how your life has changed since that night."

Leigh raised the window and drove off. *You have nothing to feel guilty about.* Leigh repeated the phrase until the pounding in her temples ebbed. She didn't know whether to laugh or cry.

How has my life changed? Immeasurably!

Dear Reader,

Island people enjoy a unique and special bond. This bond is forged by the closeness of community and a union of that community against the elements, for islands are always at the mercy of weather.

I first learned about the barrier islands of North Carolina in a *National Geographic* article several years ago. These islands, also called the Outer Banks, are a precarious line of sand and grass strung along the North and South Carolina coasts. Exposed to the relentless Atlantic, they are slowly being eroded by wind and wave and, some experts say, may one day not exist at all.

But the residents of the Outer Banks—and of Ocracoke Island— are a tough breed. History, along with the undiscriminating storms of the Atlantic, taught them to rely on each other for survival. In *The Man She Left Behind*, I have attempted to capture part of the essence of the island spirit. Yet no one could paint a portrait of Ocracoke Island more vividly than those whose families have lived there for generations.

Thanks to Sundae Horn of the Back Road Books shop, I was able to obtain excellent reference works for my research. Because this novel is a work of fiction, I have taken liberties with some of the physical landmarks and geographical features of Ocracoke. And of course, none of the characters in the novel have any connection to any real person on Ocracoke Island.

The people of Ocracoke Island need no outsider to sing the praises of their unique and distinct home. I thank them for the privilege of "borrowing" their magical island for my novel and hope future generations of visitors will continue to share and appreciate Ocracoke's dunes, marshes, wild ponies, marine life and its people.

Janice Carter

THE MAN SHE LEFT BEHIND
Janice Carter

Harlequin Books

TORONTO • NEW YORK • LONDON
AMSTERDAM • PARIS • SYDNEY • HAMBURG
STOCKHOLM • ATHENS • TOKYO • MILAN
MADRID • WARSAW • BUDAPEST • AUCKLAND

This book is dedicated to my two families—
Hess and Carter—with much love

ISBN 0-373-70779-7

THE MAN SHE LEFT BEHIND

Copyright © 1998 by Janice Hess.

Printed in U.S.A.

THE MAN SHE
LEFT BEHIND

CHAPTER ONE

"LEIGH RANDALL?"

Leigh craned her head around. From her perch on the hood of her car, she watched the woman's determined approach and felt her stomach quiver. *Mary Ann Burnett.* A moment before, Leigh had been reveling in the tangy sea air as the ferry churned through the deep blue water of Hatteras Inlet toward Ocracoke Island. The single-deck boat was crowded even for a Sunday with vehicles, cyclists, assorted backpackers and families getting an early start on the tourist season.

When Leigh had begun the last leg of her journey home at the tip of the Barrier Islands, she'd mentally prepared herself for the inevitable encounters with former friends—and foes. But Mary Ann Burnett was the last person she wanted to bump into her first twenty-four hours home. Well, maybe the second-last, she reminded herself, seeing Spencer McKay in her mind's eye.

By the time the woman had bustled around the parked cars and trucks, Leigh had slipped off the hood of the car and gathered a semblance of welcome she didn't feel at all. Mary Ann had been the type of student loathed by all who abhorred social organization; the timid and shy, the aloof and especially the oddball students gave her a wide berth. Even at sixteen she'd been an inveterate matchmaker and gossip; her mission, to link every girl at Ocracoke School with a boy. A difficult challenge, considering the school population seldom topped a hundred kids. But Mary

Ann had the zeal of a missionary and the same self-righteousness.

"It *is* you," she exclaimed, reaching the front bumper of Leigh's car. "I couldn't believe my eyes back there. 'Course I'd heard you were coming home—you know how word gets around on Ocracoke—but I didn't expect to see you so soon." She stretched out her plump arms to give Leigh an awkward hug.

"How are you, Mary Ann?" Leigh asked when she'd extricated herself from the woman's embrace.

"Oh, fine. Getting older, like all of the gang." She gave Leigh an appraising once-over. "You look terrific as usual. Got your hair chopped off, I see. One of those overpriced New York salons?"

Leigh winced. Mary Ann had always been skilled at edging a compliment. She opened her mouth to reply, but Mary Ann saved her the trouble.

"So are you here for long?"

"Not really. Long enough to pack up some things and arrange for the sale of my parents' house."

Mary Ann nodded sympathetically. "Yeah, I heard. Sorry about your mother. It seems a shame to let such a beautiful old Ocracoke home go to strangers, but I suppose there's no point in keeping it, you being in New York and all."

Leigh simply shrugged.

Mary Ann let her large shoulder bag slide off her arm. "Say, this meeting is very lucky for me. I've got a regular column in the *Island Breeze*—you know the kind, one of those human-interest pieces—and I've had a heck of a time coming up with an idea for the next one. My deadline is Wednesday and I think it would be terrific to do an article on your coming back to Ocracoke. How about it?" She beamed at Leigh.

"Sort of 'The Prodigal Daughter Returns'?"

Mary Ann giggled. "You slay me! Still got that sharp

sense of humor, I see. Yeah, you can give me your feelings on coming back to such a small place after— How long has it been?''

''Fifteen years, although I flew in briefly for my dad's funeral ten years ago.''

Mary Ann's face sobered momentarily. Then she said, ''Well, it's been fifteen since I saw you. There's so much to catch you up on—where on earth should I start?''

Leigh felt her mouth work into a tight smile. She had a feeling she wasn't going to get out of the interview. The ride across the inlet took forty minutes, and they'd just left Cape Hatteras. ''Okay. Give me some questions.'' She sighed, hating herself for giving in so readily to the other woman.

''Right! Questions. Here, let me get out a pad and pen.'' Mary Ann plunked her bag on the hood of Leigh's car and poked through it. ''So—'' she flipped open a steno pad, ready to take notes ''— what have you been doing in New York? Insurance or something?''

''I'm an investment banker.''

''Ahhh! One of those fancy-titled jobs. What exactly does an investment banker do, anyway?''

''Make money for people, Mary Ann.''

The woman glanced up at Leigh. ''Is that a lucrative job?''

''It can be,'' Leigh said, refusing to be drawn into a discussion about money.

Mary Ann nodded, but didn't press the point. To Leigh's surprise, she came up with some good questions, often forcing Leigh to take a moment to carefully phrase her answers. She didn't want to raise any hackles on Ocracoke so soon after her arrival.

''Okay,'' Mary Ann said, ''now let me take some photos.'' She stuck her hand into her bag and pulled out a camera.

Leigh was taken aback. The notion that the interview

was going to be in a small but very real newspaper struck home.

"Pictures? Gee, Mary Ann, I don't know about that."

"Come on! Someone as photogenic as you can't be afraid of the camera. And it's not as if your coming home is a secret or anything."

Secret? With a grapevine like Ocracoke's? Not likely.

Still, giving in to Mary Ann had always been much easier than fighting her. The thought reminded her of Jennifer Logan, and she felt her stomach quiver again. Too much was happening too quickly. But what had she expected? Resurrecting the past came with returning home.

So she allowed Mary Ann to pose her for a set of photographs—a couple of her leaning against the ferry railing to stare pensively ahead at Ocracoke Island and then a few full-head shots.

"Okay," announced Mary Ann, lowering the camera at last. "That should do it. Let me look over my notes for a second, make sure I've got what I need. My shorthand gets a bit messy when I rush."

Leigh turned her attention to the bow of the ferry. The dock at the northern tip of Ocracoke was clearly visible. Thank goodness, she thought, surprised at the unexpected rush of anticipation. *Ocracoke Island.* There'd been a time as a teenager when she'd thought she'd never get off the island. And then for the past fifteen years when she'd been certain she'd never return. An oft-repeated maxim of her mother's surfaced. *Never say never about anything in life because you just never know.*

"Leigh? Are you still with me?" Mary Ann was waving a hand across Leigh's line of vision. "I asked if you had any qualms about, you know, reliving the accident and all."

Leigh was grateful for her sunglasses. She stared at Mary Ann and fought to keep her voice neutral. "The accident?"

"The graduation-night drownings. Have you been involved in any other tragedy?"

At that moment Leigh knew she'd underestimated Mary Ann Burnett. Beneath the cheery busybody facade was a steely core. She waited a moment before saying, "That was fifteen years ago, Mary Ann."

"But still like yesterday for some people—for instance, Laura Marshall's mother. How will you feel about seeing her? Or Jeff's parents? Ocracoke is a small place and the chances of bumping into any of those people are good. Are you up for that?"

"I'm not sure what you're asking me, Mary Ann."

"Are you apprehensive about facing those people? Tony's parents left the island, you know. Too many memories, they said."

Leigh fought the nauseating rush of adrenaline. Her mother's advice from years ago came back. *You've nothing to feel guilty about. Take a deep breath and wait at least ten seconds. Look them straight in the eye.* "Why should I feel apprehensive, Mary Ann? I didn't cause the accident."

Mary Ann lowered her notepad onto the hood of the car. "But you were the only survivor, Leigh. Three of your graduating classmates drowned and you were the only one to live."

"There was another boatful of kids who lived. It wasn't just me."

"People said it was your idea to go across to Portsmouth Island after the prom."

"That's not true! I've lived with that lie for fifteen years."

"Then why didn't you ever say what happened? At the trial, you were so vague about everything."

Leigh turned away from the intense expression in Mary Ann's face. She waited ten seconds again before replying. Her voice, when it came, was dead calm. "I was still in shock. Traumatized. Unless you've lived through an experience like that, you can't know. And it wasn't a trial, Mary Ann, only an inquest. We were all to blame for being foolish enough to cross the Sound in a storm without life jackets.''

Mary Ann murmured, "Laura, Jeff and Tony paid dearly for that oversight."

"Yes," Leigh agreed, and fell silent. She could still see Jeff's pinched face from the stern of the fourteen-foot aluminum motorboat. Could see him frantically yanking on the rip cord of the stalled engine and watching the monster wave, birthed by the unexpected squall, rolling toward them. Her last memory of that disastrous night was of Laura's scream as the wave hit the boat, lifting the stern out of the water and sending Jeff flying off into the blackness.

"Lucky for you the accident happened so close to the island. 'Course, you were always a good swimmer."

Leigh sighed. How tiresome to have to explain this again. "I wasn't swimming, Mary Ann. I was swept into shore, or I would've drowned, as well."

"And lucky that Spencer McKay was down on the beach and saw the boat flip over."

Leigh closed her eyes. How much longer did she have to endure these memories? New York suddenly seemed very appealing.

The ferry reversed its engine and eased into the docking site. Crew members clambered over the rail to tie up while passengers returned to their vehicles.

"I'll give you a call if I need any more," Mary Ann said, starting toward her car.

Leigh didn't bother telling her that the phone connection wasn't hooked up. She turned to open her door and was bending to get in when she realized Mary Ann was walking around the front end of the car.

"Say, speaking of Spence McKay," she began, "did

you hear that he and Jen split up? Years ago, it was. Everyone said they wouldn't last, but—''

Leigh got in and slammed the door, pretending not to
have heard. Undeterred, Mary Ann walked up to the window and tapped on it. Leigh started the engine and pointed
toward the windshield. Her car was in the front row and
would disembark first.

Mary Ann was gesticulating with her notebook and
holding up five splayed fingers.

Sighing, Leigh pressed the window button.

''The paper will be out in five days—Friday,'' Mary
Ann shouted over the roar of idling engines. ''There's one
more important question. How has your life changed since
graduation night? Think about it. I'll call you.'' Then she
turned away.

Leigh raised the driver-side window again and switched
on the air-conditioning full blast. At a signal from one of
the crew she shifted into drive and drove off the ferry onto
the Ocracoke Island dock. Cars and other vehicles were
lined up patiently waiting to board. As soon as she cleared
the area, she pulled over onto the shoulder, lowered the
window and filled her lungs with clean salty air.

Nothing to feel guilty about. Leigh repeated the phrase
like a mantra until the pounding in her temples and the
nausea in her stomach ebbed. She didn't know whether
she wanted to laugh or cry. *How has my life changed?*

Immeasurably.

Fifteen minutes later, swinging into the drive of Windswept Manor, Leigh couldn't help recalling native Caro-
linian Thomas Wolfe's famous line. *You can't go home
again.* Maybe he was right, she thought, wondering why
she hadn't simply engineered the sale of her parents home
from New York. But the thought of returning to the Outer
Banks after a fifteen-year absence had been a stronger im-
pulse than reason, even if the decision to take leave from

work had raised more than a few eyebrows in the corporate offices she shared with other bankers.

Leigh turned off the ignition, opened the car door and swung her long legs onto the gravel drive. Once out, she arched her back, easing some of the kinks. Prolonging the moment before she took her first step inside, she looked toward the southern end of Ocracoke Island, where the village curved around the horseshoe of Silver Lake Harbor, known locally as the Creek. Leigh inhaled deeply and slowly turned to face the house. Windswept Manor. *Home.*

The gingerbread trim of the three-story, white-frame house was tinted a neon pink from the setting sun, and the west-facing gable window was ablaze. If Leigh hadn't had such ambivalent feelings about coming back to Ocracoke, she'd have paused to admire the effect. Instead, she leaned into the car for her purse and keys and started to unload the trunk. By the time she'd lugged two suitcases and a laptop computer onto the sweeping veranda, the sun was no more than a crimson band lining the horizon. She inserted her key into the front door with its etched-glass panel and, propping it open with her right foot, heaved herself and a suitcase inside.

Months of dust and stale air assaulted her. She dropped the luggage and hurried from room to room to open windows stiffened with sand and salt. Then she stared at the ghostly hulks of furniture shrouded in covers. *Memories ready to pounce.* She marched about the ground floor, whisking away the tattered bedsheets and tablecloths until the ghosts became plain chairs and tables.

Blessing herself for having had the foresight to get the water and power reconnected, Leigh clicked to life all the lamps and overheads, exorcising all remaining shadows from the house. *But not from my heart.* She chided herself for the thought. *You knew it would be tough, kiddo, so don't go soft after the first ten minutes.*

Satisfied she had everything under control again, Leigh

retrieved her two suitcases and headed upstairs to her old bedroom on the second floor. Nothing had changed much since she'd left it fifteen years ago. The cream counterpane with its faded antique roses still draped the twin bed in her room. The matching dust ruffle had done its duty well, too, over the years. No doubt neither had been laundered since her mother had left to be with Leigh in New York a year ago. Leigh stifled a sneeze and rushed to open the window.

The room was the smallest of the five bedrooms on the second floor, but it had the best view, looking out to the western ridge of sand dunes separating the two sides of the island. Invisible beyond the dunes was Pamlico Sound, the band of ocean separating Ocracoke from the North Carolina coast. But Ocracoke Sound, the channel outside the harbor, was partially illuminated by the sweeping beam of the lighthouse on the edge of the village. Leigh drew away from the window and turned to survey the room some more.

The first eighteen years of her life had been spent in this narrow space, and it was still cluttered with mementos of that time, kept by her parents as if they'd hoped she'd renounce her life in New York and come home. But college, a postgraduate degree and a chance to start at the bottom of an up-and-coming Wall Street investment firm had gotten in the way of that return. Not that she believed her parents ever seriously expected her to come back to Ocracoke. Few islanders returned to stay once they'd left for bigger pastures. *And then there were those who'd never left at all.*

She shook her head, surfacing from the unexpected dive into the past. *Enough already, Randall.* She didn't think she was up to sleeping there her first night back, and besides, the room needed a good airing. Dust and memories could leave together.

Leigh poked around in her suitcase until she found what she needed for the night, grabbed a comforter from the linen closet in the hall, then headed for the door and the couch downstairs. She paused to look back, almost expecting to see her sixteen-year-old self sprawled on the bed, a novel in hand. She smiled, catching her reflection in the vanity-table mirror opposite the doorway. *You're a long way from sixteen, Randall, and right now looking every second of it.* Then something else caught her eye. A photograph wedged into the upper right-hand corner of the mirror frame.

She moved toward it, watching herself in the glass as she did so, her face paling the closer she got. She reached out a hand that trembled slightly and plucked out the photo. It was small enough to have been overlooked all those years. Spencer McKay, with his lanky seventeen-year-old length pressed against her fifteen-year-old self. Six foot something even then, he had one arm draped across her shoulders while he looked down into her laughing black eyes.

Leigh crumpled the photograph and dropped it onto the vanity. Tomorrow, she told herself, everything would go out in the garbage. She switched off the light and closed her bedroom door.

NOTHING IN THE WORLD compared to awakening to the fragrance of freshly brewed coffee. Leigh stretched her legs, flexed her toes back and forth and enjoyed, for a few seconds more, the moment of waking up. Then her legs stiffened. Hundreds of sleepy cells sounded the alarm. *If I've been sleeping, who's made the coffee?*

The balls of her feet pushed against the end of the couch as she levered herself to a sitting position. The living room was in darkness, but splinters of sunlight cut through the gap in the heavy curtains. Leigh could make out the pile of clothes she'd left on the floor, as well as her Day-Timer, which was facedown on the novel she'd cracked open in the wee hours of morning. She swung off the couch, kicked aside the books and struggled to her feet, wrapping the comforter around her.

"Hello?" she called out, her voice a reedy whisper. She called out again, and this time her voice gained volume. There was still no answer, but she thought she heard someone in the kitchen. She padded across the hardwood floor, into the hall and along to the rear of the house.

A short plump woman was leaning over the kitchen sink washing dishes and singing softly. Leigh hesitated, then cleared her throat.

The woman jumped, letting something clatter into the sink. "Mercy!" she exclaimed, turning around to Leigh, standing in the doorway. Her round face flushed, then smoothed into a broad smile.

"Leigh Randall! I hope I didn't wake you up."

Leigh's mind ran through its data bank for a name. "Yes, I mean, no. The coffee woke me up."

The woman glanced behind her. "Heavens, it's all ready, too. Come in and set yourself down." She pulled out a chair for Leigh, who sank into it feeling totally disoriented.

The woman leaned against the counter and smiled. "You don't recognize me, do you," she said. Her tone was friendly.

"It's been a while since I was last home," Leigh explained, playing for time. Then it came to her. "Faye Mercer!"

The smile changed to a wide grin. "Close enough. People get me and Faye mixed up even more these days now that we've both passed forty. Faye's my older sister. I'm Trish. Trish Butterfield now, not Mercer."

"Didn't you used to baby-sit me?"

"No, that was Faye. As I said she's older than I am, though I must say forty is the great leveler, isn't it? And how you've changed yourself! I don't think I'd have recognized you if we'd met on the street."

Trish's smile suddenly vanished. She shook her head sympathetically. "I was very sorry to hear about your mother. And I'm especially sorry I couldn't make it to New York for the funeral. I sent flowers and a card, but it's hard to say what you want to on a card, isn't it?" She paused briefly before asking, "Will you be burying your mother's ashes with your dad's? Ellen was such a lovely person. I'd taken to popping in to visit her before she went to New York."

Too overwhelmed by the memory of her mother's last few months, Leigh only nodded and whispered, "Yes. Later." In her final days Ellen had asked to be cremated and had told Leigh to bury her ashes at a convenient time in the future—preferably next to her husband.

So like her mother, Leigh thought, to be considerate of her feelings even as she neared death. Ellen had known the emotional turmoil that a return to Ocracoke would cause her daughter.

Leigh's smile felt strained. She was bewildered by the chitchat, and her caffeine addiction was clamoring for attention. She glanced at the coffeepot.

"Goodness! The coffee!" Trish swung behind her, opened exactly the right cupboard, pulled out two mugs and rummaged in a plastic grocery bag on the counter for milk and sugar. "You must be wondering how I knew you were here."

"I didn't let anyone know but the Jensens."

Trish nodded. "That was it, you see. Mrs. Jensen got Sammy Fisher to turn on your water and electricity, seeing as how poor old Mr. Jensen couldn't take care of it for you."

"How is Mr. Jensen?"

Trish pursed her lips. "Not good, poor thing. The family's looking for a nursing home on the mainland. He hasn't recovered from his stroke at all."

"I'm sorry to hear that."

Trish waited a respectful moment before continuing. "Anyway, I was on my way to the ferry early this morning and saw your car in the drive. Didn't recognize it as belonging to anyone from the island and then I noticed the New York plates. I figured you must have come in late yesterday."

Another reminder how impossible it was to keep a secret on the island.

"Here's your coffee. I even picked up some doughnuts. If I'd had more notice, I'd have baked muffins for you."

"I'd planned to drive into the village for breakfast, but this is much nicer. Thank you."

"You're quite welcome. Least I can do for Ellen Randall's daughter, not to mention a native islander come home. We don't get many of those anymore!"

Leigh smiled and sipped her coffee. "Mmm, delicious. You said you were on your way to the ferry?"

"I work part-time up in Nag's Head at one of those resorts. I just phoned my boss to say I'd be late. Things are slow yet. The tourist season will pick up soon, though."

Leigh remembered how excited she used to get when guests began arriving at the manor in late June. "Have you worked there long?"

"About ten years. Since my hubby passed away."

Leigh's sympathetic murmur went unnoticed as Trish paused only long enough to refill their mugs. "Is it true you're planning on selling the house?"

No secrets at all. "I hope to. It's pretty hard looking after property from a distance. The past year wasn't so difficult, but now that Mr. Jensen is unable to do it…"

"Yes." Trish sighed. "It'll be hard for him to leave the island."

"I suppose."

There was a long silence. The bond of islandhood linked them momentarily. Leigh's father used to say that islanders were a breed apart. They often had difficulty adjusting to life away from Ocracoke. Certainly Leigh had witnessed her mother's spirit flow out of her right along with her health, which had deteriorated rapidly once she'd left the island to be with Leigh in New York.

Leigh feigned interest in the box of doughnuts and waited for the knot in her throat to dissolve. She wished Trish Mercer, or whatever her name was now, would go.

It was an ungenerous thought, she realized. But the weight of the last year, her mother's chemotherapy treatments and the many trips back and forth to the chronic-care hospice was suddenly and unexpectedly heavy.

She felt a hand press her right shoulder. "I'm sorry, Leigh. All this prattling and you still coping with it all. Forgive me for rushing in, but you know how islanders stick together."

Leigh looked at the woman's kindly face and managed a weak smile. "I do appreciate it, Trish. And thank you for everything you did for my mother in those last few months before she came to New York."

"Not at all. Like I said, your mother spent her whole life helping others here. It was her turn, was all." Trish dropped her hand and went back to the sink.

Leigh watched her, thinking how she'd forgotten so many things about Ocracokers—their loyalty to one another and sense of pride in their unique lifestyle.

"There now," Trish announced, wiping her hands on a towel. "I'll leave you to finish the pot. And I've put the house key your mother gave me on the counter. I won't be needing it anymore and you can always use a spare. Although I suppose you're not planning to stay on?"

Leigh hated to erase the hope in Trish's face, but now was as good a time as any to declare her intentions. "Only as long as it takes me to arrange the sale and pack up what I want to take back to New York."

"Will you be going to the local real-estate office? My cousin runs it."

"I've already been to a place in Nag's Head." Seeing the disappointment in Trish's face, she added, "I thought it would simplify matters if I stopped in on my way down yesterday. I hope I get a chance to see you and Faye before I leave."

"I'd like that very much, Leigh, but I'm afraid you'll have to make do with just me. Faye left the island a long time ago to live on the mainland."

"Well, the two of us, then."

"It would be lovely to see you. You can fill me in on your exciting life these past few years. How long's it been, anyway?"

"They weren't very exciting years, believe me. And it's been ten years since I was here for my father's funeral, but fifteen since I left for college."

"My, how time flies! I hadn't realized it'd been that long."

She was almost out the door when Leigh's resistance crumpled. "Trish?"

The woman stopped, a question on her face.

"I...I was wondering if you could tell me about some of the old gang."

"Of course, Leigh. Give me some names."

"Chris Thompson?"

"He's a lawyer now up in Nag's Head."

"And Jennifer Logan?"

"She's been in Charlotte about four or five years. You heard she and Spencer McKay got a divorce?"

"Yes."

Trish shook her head. "That was a nasty piece of business. I mean, the way Jen just up and took off with their little boy without a by-your-leave. Cleaned out Spencer's bank account and not a word to her grandfather." Indignation rang in her voice.

"I heard some of it from my mother, but we didn't...she didn't talk much about island life after I left."

There was a meaningful silence. Then Trish said, "Yes, well, that I understand."

After a long moment Leigh asked the one question that mattered. "And Spencer?"

"He went through such a rough time, poor man. As if he didn't have enough problems in his life. But it's all worked out for him now. He went in on a fishing-charter business with Bill Cowan about five years ago and has been very successful. We're all quite proud of him."

Leigh felt the corners of her mouth lift in a tense smile.

"Well, enough gossip," Trish declared. "See you in a few days, I hope. Oh—" she paused in the kitchen door "—how can I get hold of you? There's no phone."

"I brought my cell phone with me so I wouldn't need to worry about the telephone hookup. Wait, I'll get my business card." She rushed into the other room and returned with a small white embossed card, which she handed to Trish.

"Ah. Leigh Randall, Investment Banker." Trish beamed. "Don't that sound high-and-mighty!" Then she burst into a hearty laugh, poked Leigh in the ribs and bustled out the back door.

LEIGH FIGURED that Trish's extra-strong brew was responsible for her three-hour cleaning bee that morning, but she had a tiny suspicion it had more to do with avoidance. *I don't need a shrink to spell it out for me or help me deal with it. Just steer me to a mop and bucket.* If she couldn't go to the office to bury herself in work, she'd find plenty to do at the manor. And save herself the cost of a professional cleaner at the same time.

By midafternoon she'd eaten enough doughnuts to resist temptation for the next five years and knew she could no longer put off going into the village. She spent some time preparing herself for the trip, trying on several combinations of the skirts and tops she'd brought. In the end she settled for a peasant-style cotton print she'd purchased in a frivolous moment last summer.

She pulled back her hair on one side with a tortoiseshell comb and, satisfied with her appearance, left by the front door. She started to lock up, but caught herself. *Not on Ocracoke.* She stepped into the brilliance of a sunny early-June day. The balmy ocean breeze seemed to carry the scents of faraway countries. Although the village was a short walk, Leigh decided to drive. She rationalized that she'd need the car for all the groceries, but knew the real reason was that it enabled her to make an easy and quick getaway.

She made a bet with herself on how many minutes would elapse before she ran into old friends or acquaintances, settling on fifteen minutes. But she lost her bet, underestimating the capacity for verbal catching-up the locals had. Every place she went into—the bank to withdraw money, the post office to set up a box number and the gas station to refill for a trip to Hatteras next day—became an endurance test of attempting to attach names to faces she hadn't seen in years.

By the time she loaded groceries into her car, her head was buzzing with tidbits of information and her jaw was aching from repeating her refrain of why she was back and, no, she wouldn't be staying. She was soaked with perspiration, and the impractical plastic shoes she'd bought in New York made her feet throb. And she still hadn't bumped into a single former classmate, not to mention the one person she'd dressed for—Spencer McKay.

She turned on the air conditioner full blast and headed north for Windswept Manor, the last house on the highway before the ferry dock to Hatteras. When she saw a small convenience store just outside the village proper, Leigh impulsively pulled in. The one thing she'd forgotten to buy was a bottle of wine, and she had a feeling the long evening ahead would demand one. She parked next to a beat-up red pickup and went inside.

The cashier directed her to the rear of the store, where the wine selection was stacked on an upper shelf. It contained some surprisingly good choices. While she was debating between a chardonnay and a Chablis, Leigh became aware of the rumble of male voices in an adjacent aisle. Some disagreement about hot dogs or hamburgers. She reached for the chardonnay just as one of the voices rose above the other. She froze. Even after fifteen years, she'd know that voice anywhere. She let go of the bottle and headed for the front of the store.

"Find what you wanted?" the cashier asked.

"No. I changed my mind," she said, pushing open the door and stumbling out into the blinding sunlight. Her hand was on her car door when someone spoke from behind.

"Leigh?"

She swung around into the sun and couldn't see his face. But his voice—the one she'd heard in the store—hadn't changed much over the years. Still deep, still commanding.

Raising a hand to her forehead, Leigh looked up at the man standing mere feet away. Her mouth was dry and black spots bobbed across her line of vision.

"Hello, Spencer."

He shifted to her right under the roof overhang of the store so that she could look away from the sun. His eyes were the same china blue, and the sun-bleached hair was a touch thinner now, but the years had been good to Spencer. Once lean and lanky, he'd filled out in all the right places. Broad shoulders with pectoral muscles that strained against the pale blue T-shirt. His jeans were snug, the way he always used to wear them, and belted across a flat stomach. Yes, Spencer McKay looked better than ever.

The hesitancy in his smile quickly disappeared. "For a

second in there I thought I was dreaming. Just caught a glimpse of your back as you were leaving, but I'd have recognized it anywhere.''

The urge to ask if that was meant as a compliment died as quickly as it had reared its mischievous head. She didn't want to engage in any talk that seemed personal. Before she could reply, a teenage boy came out of the store. He didn't look very happy.

Spencer turned to him. ''Make a choice?'' he asked.

''Hot dogs,'' the boy mumbled. He glanced curiously at Leigh.

Spencer shifted his gaze back to Leigh. ''I was sorry to hear about your mother.''

''Thanks.'' Leigh's voice cracked. She cleared her throat and backed toward her car. ''Nice to see you again,'' she lied, reaching for the door handle again.

Spencer's eyes narrowed. *He always could read my mind.*

''Will you be here long?'' he asked, moving toward her.

She opened the car door. ''Only long enough to pack up and arrange for the sale of my parents' house.''

His right arm shot out as if he intended to grab her. Leigh quickly climbed into the car.

''I didn't introduce you,'' Spencer said, gesturing to the boy just behind him. ''This is Jamie, my son.''

Leigh looked from Spencer to Jamie. Images of Jen flashed before her. Same coloring and build. His eyes were green, too, and right now filled with impatience. Not the disdain she'd seen in Jen's when they'd last met.

''Nice to meet you,'' Leigh said. She closed the car door, turned on the engine under Spencer's watchful gaze and shifted into reverse. As she pulled out of the lot, she gave a brief wave with her right hand and didn't stop shaking until she pulled into the drive of Windswept Manor.

CHAPTER TWO

THE SUNSET PROMISED a beautiful morning, but Leigh scarcely noticed. After a quick supper of sandwich and salad, during which she regretted enormously not purchasing the chardonnay, she closed the front door and walked down the drive to the main road, crossing it to the grassy verge that led to the ocean. Low tide had been two hours ago, and the Atlantic was slowly reclaiming the sandy beach.

Translucent corpses of jellyfish swirled about in the foamy waves, and bits of debris, both natural and man-made, bobbed back out to sea. Flotsam and jetsam, Leigh thought. Like pieces of people's lives. As children she and Jen had concocted wild stories about the tide treasure they'd found. Sometimes their play had spun on long after sundown, and they'd hidden from her parents' calls in the long grasses.

Leigh stopped at the water's edge and looked back toward the road. She could almost see their two heads, one dark and the other blond, peering through the sea grass. It had always been Jen who'd pulled Leigh down, covering her mouth with a grimy hand and whispering, "Five more minutes! Come on! Five minutes!" And of course Leigh had always capitulated. So much easier than enduring Jen's sulking the next day.

A wave swept over Leigh's thonged feet. She moved farther up onto the beach and walked north, away from the village. *Strange, I haven't thought of those games in years.*

She shoved her hands into the pockets of her rolled-up cotton jeans and doubled her strides. *Right. Do what you've always done. Walk away from memories.* The voice in her head kept pace, dogging her efforts to enjoy the sunset.

"Well, ain't you gonna say hello?"

Leigh stopped inches away from collision with a gap-toothed old man grinning up at her from his gnomelike height. She took a step back and flung out her arms.

"Grandpa Sam!"

"That's better, that's better." He stretched his neck and planted a kiss on Leigh's cheek. "When I saw you charging along the beach, I thought a pack of crabs was chasin' you. But I guess you're still travelin' on city time and haven't started walkin' around with your head up, 'stead o' down."

Leigh smiled. "That's about it. How are you? You haven't changed a bit."

"Ah, picked up a dozen more wrinkles or so. You look different. Very…"

"Sophisticated?"

His grin matched her own. "I was gonna say grown-up, but of course you're grown-up now. Haven't seen you since the day you came back for your daddy's funeral. When was that? Ten, twelve years ago?"

"Ten. A long time."

"Maybe for you. For me it's like a week." He paused. "I'm just going back home for a cup of tea. Care to join me?"

"I'd love to, Sam." Leigh fell in step with the old man, veering on a diagonal away from the water and toward the highway. Sam Logan's cottage was perched on stilts just off the road half a mile ahead.

"The sea hasn't taken you away yet," she observed.

"Not yet, though heaven help me, there've been a few close calls."

Leigh grinned. The locals had been predicting Sam's place would be swept away every time one of the frequent storms hit the Outer Banks. But his cottage, considered a shack by many, had survived its precarious location for more than thirty years. Leigh figured the barn-board structure would simply collapse long before any rogue wave carried it off.

As they drew nearer, Leigh saw that Sam's cottage had weathered as well as he had. Everything looked exactly the way she remembered it, down to the red-and-white petunias planted in the whitewashed automobile tires that formed a daisy chain around the structure. She followed Sam up the stairs onto the tiny porch and sat down in one of the rickety green wicker chairs.

"Still the best view on the island," Sam said, grinning.

"Still is," Leigh agreed, taking the cue for her part of the running joke she hadn't heard in years. The third part— *Always will be*—remained conspicuously unspoken. It had been Jen's.

Sam finally pushed open the screen door and, pausing midway through, asked, "The usual?"

"Please," Leigh whispered, recalling suddenly all the peaceful times she and Jen had spent on this porch. She watched Jen's grandfather step inside to brew a pot of his homegrown-peppermint tea.

Joking aside, though, the place really did have the best view on Ocracoke. It was sheltered from the north wind by a string of cypress trees and angled in a way that gave you a panorama of the ocean, including Silver Lake Harbor to the southwest. Some islanders called Sam Logan's place a hovel, but the cottage had a whimsical charm, pieced together as it was with odd-shaped boards and decorated with driftwood, shells and bunches of dried wildflowers. Leigh hadn't yet ventured inside, but a glance told her Sam had probably not redecorated since her last visit.

The screen door swung open and Sam reappeared, tray in hand, one foot propped against the bottom of the door.

"Can I help?" Leigh jumped up, but Sam had already squeezed through onto the porch.

"Still haven't got round to fixin' the spring on that door," he explained. He set the tray down on a varnished wooden crate in front of Leigh. "And who am I kidding, anyway? That door'll be the same next time you visit, though I may not be here to brew the tea."

Leigh's hand was poised over the honey jar. It wasn't like Sam to make that sort of gloomy remark. He'd always prided himself on being active—physically and mentally. "You'd better be," she teased, "otherwise, who'll keep Mrs. Waverly occupied?"

Sam cackled. "Too true, too true. I think tryin' to run me off this bit of beach is the only thing that's kept the old doll goin' all these years."

Leigh hid a smile. The "old doll" was only two or three years older than Sam. When Sam sat down beside her, she raised her mug of tea and said, "Cheers!"

He nodded, reaching for his own cup to clink against hers. "Good to see you again. It's been far too long." He patted her forearm with a hand splotched with sun and liver spots. "Why haven't you been t'see me in all these years?" Emotion thickened the peculiar Cockneylike English accent many old-timers on Ocracoke still had.

Leigh averted her face. It was difficult to believe he had no inkling of the rift between her and Jen. His granddaughter had left a few months after Leigh's own departure for university and, four months after that, had married Spencer McKay.

Perhaps Sam had attributed Leigh's long absence from Ocracoke solely to the pursuit of an education and career, which was fine by her. He'd had his share of problems with Jen years ago. Leigh didn't intend to burden him with yet another Jen story.

"Well, you know how it is," she murmured. "So many things to do. You get caught up in it all." She stopped then, feeling overwhelmed.

After a moment Sam replied, "That you do. And not just folks in the big city, either." He gave a loud sigh. "But take a look at that view and tell me you'd want to be anywhere else."

"For sure Sam, I wouldn't. Nor *with* anyone else."

He glanced away, but not before Leigh saw his eyes glisten. They sipped their tea in silence, watching the last of the sunset. Then Sam plunked his mug down on the wooden crate and cleared his throat.

"She doesn't write to me very much anymore. Jen, I mean. Tried to persuade me to get a phone line, but as much as I wanted to hear her voice, I couldn't bring myself to go that far."

Leigh had to restrain a smile. Sam Logan was certainly an anachronism as far as technology went.

"Maybe you heard she's living in Charlotte now?"

Leigh nodded stiffly. The conversation was making her uncomfortable.

"Well, she got married last summer. That's why her boy is here—young Jamie. Jen's starting a new family with her hubby, and I reckon Jamie thought he was in the way."

"I didn't know," Leigh murmured.

Sam rocked on his chair a bit before continuing. "Anyhow, Jamie came here to live with his daddy, and it seems he's not too happy about that, either." Sam paused again. "I suppose Jen's too busy to keep in touch. No one's heard a whisper from her in the past coupla months. No doubt we'll hear when the little one comes, but I can't be sure..." His voice drifted away.

"And what about Spencer?" Leigh asked. "How is he managing? I mean, with his son and all."

Sam shrugged. "Havin' a heck of a time as far as I can see." He snorted. "That boy is a trial, sure enough. Got in with a wild bunch down in Charlotte and landed in all kinds of trouble. Jen couldn't handle him, is what I think. So after all these years she ups and calls Spence to say his son is comin' to live with him.''

"Couldn't he have refused to take him?"

"Could've I guess, seein' as how Jen had custody. But they made some kind of deal with the court in Charlotte. Jamie got off on probation if he agreed to move here to his daddy's for a spell.''

"*Probation?* What did he do?"

Sam hesitated. "Set fire to an empty building. He said it was an accident and I believe him.'' Sam's voice rose, almost challenging her to suggest otherwise. "None of it's Spencer's fault,'' he asserted. "Other than a few holiday visits years ago, he's barely seen the boy in eleven years. 'Course Jenny was all too willin' to take the money he sent every month. Girl always did know how to survive.''

It was the closest thing to a criticism Leigh had ever heard Sam utter about his only grandchild. Jen's parents had been lost at sea when she was a toddler, and Sam had raised her until she left home to move in with Spencer. And of course everyone in the village had probably clucked knowingly, having blamed Sam for every irresponsible act of Jen's over the years.

"Maybe everything will turn out okay for…everyone,'' Leigh said for want of anything else to say.

Sam patted her on the hand. "You were always so forgivin' of others—especially Jen.''

Leigh flushed. *If only you knew.* "I think I'd better get back before it's too dark to find my way.'' She stood up to leave.

Sam got to his feet—a bit stiffly, Leigh noticed—and insisted she take a flashlight.

"No, no. I'll be fine.''

But he was in and out of the cottage quickly enough for

Leigh to wonder if he'd just been impersonating an old man the whole time. He thrust the flashlight into her hand.

"How long will you be stayin', then?"

"Only long enough to sell the house."

Disappointment swept across his face. "You'll be sure to visit me again before you leave?"

"Absolutely, Sam." Leigh stooped to hug him. They clung to each other for a few seconds until Sam broke away, swiping at his eyes.

"Hey," she said, "why don't you come to dinner tomorrow night?"

"I'd like that, Leigh. And I can get the light back from you then."

Leigh set off along the beach, extinguishing the light once she'd cleared Sam's place. She'd always loved to walk this route in the dark. On a clear night the stars seemed to bounce right out of the sky. In spite of the emotional meeting with Sam, Leigh felt calm and peaceful.

She reached the dip in the ridge of sand dunes where she'd bumped into Sam earlier and paused to remove her thongs. Going barefoot down the slope was easier. When she bent down, she heard a rustling sound from the tall sea oats to her right. She aimed the beam of the flashlight in that direction, but instead of trapping the glistening eyes of a village cat or possum, she caught the retreating form of a two-legged creature. A male, she decided, from the brief flash of T-shirt and jeans.

"Hello!" she called out, but the person disappeared beyond the beam's range. Leigh frowned. Islanders would never ignore a greeting, especially on a dark beach. Perhaps he'd been a tourist out for a stroll, although his stride had been fast and determined.

Leigh continued, replacing her thongs when she got to the shoulder of the main road. Less than a quarter mile ahead, she could see the front porch light of Windswept Manor. The highway out here wasn't lit, so Leigh walked down the center of it. Frogs chirped in the ditches on either side, and every now and then the shaft of light from the island lighthouse strobed across the sky. The stillness of the night had an expectant quality. Leigh could picture so vividly her mother and father rocking on the front porch, holding tall glasses of iced tea dripping with condensation while moths circled the lightbulb above the screen door, that she sucked in a sharp painful gulp of air.

When she was more than halfway to the house, the headlights of a vehicle rounded the curve from the village. Leigh moved over to the right shoulder as the headlights barreled toward her. The vehicle, which was impossible to identify in the dark, roared past, then came to a screeching halt yards down the road and was thrown into reverse.

She debated between jumping into the ditch or jogging ahead to her house. Surely only a madman or a drunk would drive like that along a dark road, and she wasn't eager to meet up with either. But as the taillights neared, the blurred outline became a pickup truck and her anxiety changed to dread. Spence McKay.

Leigh waited while the truck angled closer to the shoulder and finally stopped beside her. Spence leaned out the driver window.

"Leigh."

"Spencer."

"Gawd, I almost ran you down."

Leigh smiled in spite of herself. He'd always had a knack for making his actions seem accidental. "Not quite, but I did consider diving into the ditch for a second there."

Spence's teeth flashed. "Still got that quick wit, I see."

When she failed to respond, he went on, "So...twice in one day. And after fifteen years."

"That's Ocracoke for you," she murmured.

He nodded slowly. "Got that right."

Silence stretched between them. Finally unable to take

it a second more, she asked, "Out for a night drive, are you?"

Spence stared out at the road and sighed. "Nah, it's a long story. I had a bit of a disagreement with Jamie and he left in a huff. I was hoping to head him off before he reached Sam's place. At least, that's where I think he was going."

"I was just walking back from Sam's now along the beach. I saw someone in the dunes. Maybe it was Jamie."

"Probably was. I guess he'll be there by now. No point in driving like a maniac to catch up to him." He paused. "Want a lift to your place?"

"No need. It's just a few yards down the road."

Spence looked at her standing there in front of him in her rolled-up jeans, wisps of black hair struggling out of her baseball cap, and thought she could have been sixteen years old again. He felt the beginning of a familiar ache and was about to say okay when she popped out of sight and reappeared at the passenger door.

It seemed she'd changed her mind. She climbed up onto the seat next to him, and for a fleeting bittersweet moment Spence found himself back in his dad's old pickup, driving down the highway and once again inhaling Leigh Randall's flowery scent. He wanted to say the old line, as well—"Where to? Anyplace special?"

But he knew he wouldn't get her standard reply—"Anyplace is special with you." *Stop torturing yourself, man. You can't relive the past.*

"So," he said, instead, "how did you find Sam? Changed much?"

"Not at all. I mean, other than being a little grayer and more wrinkled, he seemed the same."

Spence backed the truck onto the opposite side of the road, shifted into drive and headed toward the village and Leigh's house. "Reason I asked," he went on, "is that I've been worried about the old guy for a while. Oh, it's nothing I can really put my finger on," he said quickly, catching Leigh's concerned expression, "but he seems deflated sort of. As if he's giving up on life."

"He did make some reference to not being around forever."

Spence slowed the truck almost to a crawl. He glanced at Leigh, thinking she really did look sixteen. Maybe he'd driven through some kind of time warp and he was getting another chance to make things right this time. Back then he'd have extended his right arm along the back of the seat and lightly touched her shoulder with his fingertips. She'd have shifted over until she was against him, her thigh pressing his and the top of her head tilting into the angle of his neck and shoulder, the sweet grassy perfume of her shampoo filling his nostrils. Then he'd put the truck into drive, accidentally brushing his hand against her breast, and say in a hoarse voice, "I can think of a place where we can go...." She'd laugh her throaty laugh, knowing what he meant, and the truck would nose its way along the dark highway and—

"Spencer? I asked you if Sam's been ill."

The steering wheel lurched. "Hmm? Oh, sorry. Not really, but his energy level sure isn't the same. 'Course the guy's going to be eighty this year. But he's been taking the bus up to Nag's Head every two weeks to a doctor, and early this spring, he spent two weeks on the mainland, in Raleigh. Wouldn't say anything about the trip at all, stubborn old coot."

"What do you think?"

Spence heard the worry in her voice and he glanced at her sharply. In the dashboard's glow, her lower lip seemed to tremble. He was overcome with an urge to stop the car, lean over and calm the tremble with his own lips. "I think he's found out something about his health and is keeping it from us."

"Have you asked him?"

Spence snorted. "The old man hasn't changed that much, Leigh. He skirts questions about health and money the way tourists avoid beached jellyfish—gives them a wide berth."

Leigh smiled at the comparison. She'd always thought Spencer had a gift for words. *I was taken in by them often enough in the past.* "I hate to think what life would be like without Grandpa Sam."

"That's odd," he said.

"What?"

He hesitated, then, "Well, considering he hasn't really been a part of your life for the past fifteen years."

The rebuke hurt, but Leigh knew he was right. The truck pulled into her driveway and she whispered, "Stop. I'll get out here." She was almost out the door when Spence spoke again.

"Look, I didn't mean to end things tonight on a sour note. Don't take that comment as a judgment, please. It was just an observation."

Leigh looked up at him through the open passenger door. "I realize that, Spencer. Don't worry about it. But you know, just because I haven't seen someone for a few years doesn't mean I haven't thought about him. Grandpa Sam, I mean," she clarified.

He nodded. "Yeah, I know."

Leigh closed the door and stood where she was as the pickup inched back along the drive. Then it stopped again and Spence stuck his head out the window. "Maybe we can get together sometime before you go back to New York."

Leigh hoped dismay wasn't obvious in her face. "Sure," she said, and waved goodbye as the truck reversed onto the highway.

Once inside the house, she headed straight for the kitchen to make herself a cup of coffee. Then she went upstairs to change. The meeting with Spencer had left her too revved up to think about sleep and in spite of the open window and the balmy breeze, the interior of the house was hot. So she dug in her old bureau and found a pair of denim cutoffs and a tank top she hadn't worn for years.

She went down the hall to her parents' bedroom. Entering it was the hardest step she'd taken since her arrival yesterday. The room was stuffy and dusty, its windows stuck shut with an accumulation of grit. But at last Leigh got them open and fresh ocean air whistled through the room. She could still see her mother hurrying about, plumping pillows and reminding anyone within earshot that guests were arriving "on the hour."

The Randalls had run their home as a bed-and-breakfast ever since Leigh's father, Pete, had decided he was getting too old to brave the Atlantic in his fishing boat. Leigh had been thirteen at the time, and the change in the family's lifestyle had been exciting at first. She'd enjoyed the various guests who'd stayed at Windswept Manor—the name she'd been allowed to choose, based on her fascination at the time for the Brontë sisters.

But later her own responsibilities had grown and the novelty of the bed-and-breakfast diminished. By the time she was sixteen, dating Spencer McKay steadily and preparing for college, she could hardly wait to leave both Windswept Manor and Ocracoke Island.

Poor Mom, she thought. *You had a rebellious teen on your hands at the same time as your husband was showing the first signs of Alzheimer's.* Leigh's eyes welled up.

She sat on the floor beside the bed to go through the stack of photograph albums she'd found in the closet. Some had been passed on to her parents from *their* parents, and the newer ones contained photos of Leigh's childhood. Leigh had been adopted as an infant, and her adoptive parents had always ensured that she had plenty of childhood pictures and shared their own family albums with her as if those stern faces from the past were her own ancestors.

She flipped through one of these, turning the pages carefully but steadily, reluctant to spend too much time poring over them. Better to save that for a winter's day back in New York, she decided. But she stopped at one particular photograph.

She was standing with her parents on the lawn of Ocracoke School after graduation. She was wearing the white Swiss-eyelet dress she'd chosen for the prom and holding the long-stemmed red roses her father had proudly placed in her arms moments before the photo was taken. *How young we all were then! Young and hopeful. Dad still himself, in spite of his frustrating memory lapses, and Mom still strong and proud—always wanting the best for all of us. My Farrah Fawcett hairstyle, newly acquired at the only beauty salon in Hatteras, curling around my beaming face.*

In the right background of the photo, Leigh noticed the lower part of someone's jean-clad leg. Spencer's, she realized. Of course, he'd crashed the ceremony. She recalled the disapproving looks from the teachers and dignitaries—people who'd had enough of Spencer McKay's shenanigans.

Leigh closed the album. All water under the bridge now, as the saying went. It was long past midnight and she was exhausted. She pushed the albums under the bed with her feet and felt them bump against something. She reached over and raised the edge of the mattress sham. The object appeared to be a small leather suitcase. She had to use the handle of the broom she'd been cleaning up with to slide it toward her.

Leigh couldn't recall ever seeing the suitcase before. It was worn, decorated with faded travel stickers partially peeled away. She clicked open the brass fittings and found the case stuffed with a stack of papers, notebooks and receipt books. Also something wrapped in tissue paper. She raised one corner to expose part of a knitted baby sweater. Well, no buried treasure here. She closed the suitcase, pushed it back under the bed and decided to call it a night.

CHAPTER THREE

LEIGH SHOT UP, gasping for air. Her nightie clung damply to her. For a terrifying moment she thought she was underwater, then the blackness abated and she could see the pale folds of curtain rustling in the faint night breeze. Her bedroom. *Home.*

She lay back against the headboard, forcing long slow inhalations of breath to calm muscles and nerves. She hadn't had the dream in years—not since the weeks following prom night. But her mother had coached her well, calmly teaching her the strategies needed to battle the terrors that haunted her nights.

Amazing, she thought, how vivid the dream still was after all this time. Even after awakening, she could see the faces of the gang etched spookily against the arc of their flashlights as they'd stood in a semicircle around her. There were seven of them in all, half the graduating class from Ocracoke School. When the prom had wrapped up, they'd changed clothes and sneaked into two boats for a midnight picnic on deserted Portsmouth Island, two miles from Silver Lake Harbor in the middle of Ocracoke Sound. A storm had come up while they'd partied.

"You're crazy," Jeff had muttered at her suggestion they wait out the storm on Portsmouth. All night, if necessary.

But Leigh had persisted, knowing that because the others had consumed a case of beer, hers was the only voice of reason. "The wind is too strong. You know what the

Sound can be like in a storm. Look! You can hardly see the lighthouse at Silver Lake.''

They'd all turned as one to follow her pointing hand. A pinprick of light flickered in the darkness across Ocracoke Sound.

But after a moment Laura had whined, "I'm not staying here all night. This place is creepy, with all those empty houses and shacks. There're probably rats in them—or even worse!''

Her outburst had clenched the argument. ''So we're going back, right?'' Jeff had said, turning to face the others. They'd all agreed.

When they were finally under way, the small aluminum craft Leigh had shared with Laura, Jeff and Tony following the other boat, Leigh had rummaged frantically for the life jackets, recalling too late how they'd taken them ashore for cushions. She'd dropped her face into her hands and hadn't looked up again until she'd heard Laura's scream. The biggest wave she'd ever seen was heading directly for them....

Leigh brought the edge of the sheet up to wipe her face and neck, already feeling the deep breathing massage the tension away. *I ought to have known that coming home wouldn't be easy.*

It was ironic, she thought. People were supposed to come home to be healed, but in her case, the return only opened old wounds. Spencer McKay's face suddenly floated into her mind's eye.

Leigh sighed. Dawn was already fringing the night sky. Why fight it? She threw back the sheet and drew open the curtains. She'd go for a jog and watch the sun come up. Ten minutes later she was out the kitchen door, savoring the dampness of early morning.

She and her neighbor in New York jogged every second day at dawn. It was a routine that had dragged Leigh out of despair when her mother was dying and one she already missed since leaving the city.

She started out on the main road, but decided to head down to the beach. Slogging through the wild oats and marram grass to the water was difficult, but once she reached the compact sand of the shore, running was easier. As she jogged south, she could see the sky pinkening to her left, across the ocean. The sight reminded her of the times she and Jen had slept out under the stars, awakening to the fuchsia ball of sun edging above silvered waves. The recollection slowed her down. Her mind segued from sunrise to Jen to Sam and then Spence. She pulled a face. *Drop it, Randall. Get your mind on business. Think about why you came home in the first place. To sell the house.*

Yet, only two days home and already the idea of selling was beginning to seem unbelievable. But why? She stopped running and made a slow panoramic survey of the sparkling ocean, the flock of yellowlegs scurrying ahead of the waves, then across to the scattering of cottages swelling into rows of frame houses and shops in the village ahead.

This is why I can't believe I'm selling Windswept Manor, she thought. *Because losing my home also means losing this island forever.* She began to walk, scuffing the toes of her Nikes into the damp sand, flinging clumps of it ahead of her. Then she stopped again, placed her hands firmly on her hips and told herself not to be so sentimental. *There's no one left here for you. Nothing but memories. Your life and future are back in New York.*

The image of her corporate office with its stunning view was a good reminder. She'd fought long and hard for that office and that view. It had taken her almost ten years to get it, along with the very hefty salary and perks that came with it. Now her friends were in New York, whereas she doubted she had a friend left in Ocracoke. Most had left at the end of that summer—after graduation and the accident. By the time the inquest had finished, the rest of her classmates had already begun avoiding her.

Leigh was surprised by the faint stab of pain that came with that thought. *It's been so long and you're still hung up about it. Still carrying the blame.* She shaded her eyes against the glare of the rising sun. The ramps to the public docks lay ahead. It was high tide and she'd have to jog up onto the looser sand to avoid both the water and the ramp pilings. But somehow she didn't feel like running anymore. She headed up at a brisk walk to the main road where it curved into the village.

Fishermen were out, unraveling lines and nets, and calling to one another from the ramps. The familiar sight was reassuring. The village had doubled in size since she'd left, but the boom had more to do with shops and lodging places than actual population. Ocracoke, like all the islands in the Outer Banks, swelled with summer people by late June and shrank to a quiet village by mid-September.

Leigh walked along the shoulder of the road. The number of rental units and bed-and-breakfast places told her she was making the right decision to sell Windswept Manor. Obviously the popularity of the Outer Banks for vacationers had translated into an infusion of money for the locals. She couldn't help but think that, if her parents hadn't died at such relatively young ages, they'd have enjoyed a lucrative retirement from the manor. Leigh's eyes stung with tears. She closed them for a moment and so didn't notice the approaching truck roll to a stop ahead until she'd almost walked into it.

"Whoa! I hear folks in New York City have a blatant disrespect for traffic, but this is Ocracoke an' there's only you an' me on this whole stretch o' road. So what're the odds of you makin' contact with this pickup? Care to lay any bets?"

Leigh had to smile at Spence McKay's exaggerated

drawl. She crossed over to the driver's side. "I'm not the betting kind unfortunately."

Spence lowered his sunglasses to take a good look at her. "Really, though. What are the chances, I ask you, of running into the same person three times in—what? Less than twenty-four hours?"

Leigh grinned. "In New York? Or here in Ocracoke?"

He shrugged. "Wherever. Defies credibility, I think. Maybe we should contact that book of world records publisher."

"You might just have something," Leigh said, laughing.

Spence found he couldn't take his eyes off her. Damn, she was gorgeous. Finally, his voice husky with memory, he said, "I was just heading down the road to get some breakfast at the new bakery-deli place. Care to come?"

"I don't have any money with me."

He waved a dismissive hand. "It's on me. Hop in."

Leigh climbed up into the passenger side, resigned to the fact that her morning run wasn't working out at all as she'd planned and not really minding. "I can't be long," she said. "I've got a lot of cleaning and sorting to do today."

"It's not even six-thirty. I'd say you have time for coffee." He shifted the truck into drive and pulled out onto the road. "Kinda early to be up running," he said.

"I woke up before dawn and thought it'd be nice to see the sunrise. Besides, I haven't done my morning run for a few days."

He glanced over at her. "You run in the city?"

"Every day if I can. Just after daybreak."

There was a moment's pause before he asked, "You go with someone?"

"Always," she said. "The woman in the apartment next to mine is a runner, too."

"That's good. Must be kinda dangerous jogging around New York City."

"New York's probably no more dangerous than any other place as long as you're smart about where you go."

"Still, it sure as heck isn't like jogging around Ocracoke."

"True." Leigh thought about how the city was always alive anytime night or day, with people and vehicles moving about. But on the island there were sections of the route she ran where she might have been the only person on earth. Hard to say which she preferred.

The pickup turned into an almost empty parking lot.

"Is it open?" Leigh asked.

"Better be," Spence said, switching off the engine. "They've been advertising the past few weeks. 'Course I haven't made it until today. Hard to change horses midstream."

"Is the Village Café still in business, then?"

"It is, but Merv and Lou are finding it tough competing with these new places."

Leigh caught up with him in front of the bakery. He'd always been a fast walker. She remembered struggling to keep up as he'd forged a trail through the sea grass or the marsh when she, Jen and he had explored the island.

They paused inside the door a moment, their eyes adjusting to the change in light. A man sat at a table to their right, stirring coffee and unfolding a newspaper. A woman was wiping off the counter that stretched from the cash register to a glass-covered display case. Trays of baked goods were shelved on a tiered aluminum trolley behind the case.

"Mornin'." Spencer's voice boomed around the café.

The woman nodded, motioning into the room with her dishrag. "Seat yourselves. I'll be right with you. Coffee?"

"Please."

Spence stood aside for Leigh to pass. Then, his fingertips pressing gently against her lower back, guided her to a window table at the rear of the café. The gesture reminded Leigh of being guided onto the dance floor at Ocracoke School, the tingling magic of being with Spencer McKay. She shivered.

"Chilly?" he asked as she sat in the chair opposite his.

"A bit." Unconsciously she began to rub the gooseflesh on her arms, but stopped when she caught his grin. Had he read her mind? "The air-conditioning," she said, avoiding his eyes.

The woman brought their coffee and took an order for fresh strawberry biscuits.

"Is she a local?" Leigh asked after she'd left their table.

"Nah. I think she and her hubby came here a couple years ago from Raleigh."

"Yesterday when I was in town, I couldn't believe how much the village had changed. Even the library's gone."

Spence tore open a packet of sugar and dumped it into his coffee. "Actually the library has only changed location. It's in the public school now, and the original building is a museum."

"At least they didn't tear it down."

"True, though it's no longer the smallest public library in America."

Leigh grinned. "I remember bragging about that to summer kids."

"I remember when it was built."

Leigh laughed aloud. "You sound like an old-timer."

"I feel like an old-timer these days," he muttered.

The remark seemed so uncharacteristic of the brash cocky Spencer McKay she'd always known that Leigh couldn't think of a follow-up. Self-doubt or insecurity had never been a part of the Spencer McKay she'd loved. That Spencer—with the strands of golden blond hair teasing his forehead and the quick knowing smile—had seldom failed to win over anyone. Even the toughest teachers at Ocracoke school had often softened the exasperation in their voices when speaking to Spence.

Leigh remembered Grandpa Sam once saying that Spence McKay could charm the skin off a grass snake. She had to admit, once bitten by his charms, she'd not taken long to succumb. She was tempted now to outstare him to see if that old charm still had potency, but instead, she stared into her coffee mug until the biscuits arrived.

They ate in silence until Spence asked, "So you're putting your place on the market?"

Leigh swallowed a mouthful of biscuit and nodded at the same time. "That's why I came to the island," she explained, knowing she'd already told him the day before and feeling a flare of annoyance. *Why else would I have come back?*

"A shame to sell such a beautiful place."

Her annoyance increased. "A worse shame to leave it empty."

It was Spencer's turn to stare into his coffee mug. He signaled the woman, now stacking trays of pastries into the display case, for more. When she'd refilled both their mugs and left, he said, "I guess there's no way you could maintain the place from New York."

The absurdity of the suggestion left Leigh speechless for a moment. Then she replied, "Mr. Jensen has been looking after it for the past year and obviously he can't anymore. There's no point in renting it out because I'd still have to—"

"Come back. To check on it now and then."

"Right. And New York is a long way from Ocracoke." An expression Leigh couldn't read moved across his face. "Besides, there's no reason to come back to Ocracoke now that my folks are gone."

A stain of red crept up Spencer's neck. He took a long sip of coffee before saying, "There's Sam. I know he'd love to have you stick around awhile."

"Sam has his own family," she said, realizing at once how lame and callous the remark sounded.

"Yeah, some family."

The bitterness in the comment silenced her. She was tempted to pursue his lead, but suspected she'd end up on a path to the past she wasn't yet ready to take. So she wadded up the paper napkin and tossed it onto the plate. "I should get back and shower and...stuff."

The bleakness in his eyes held her to her chair. A strand of hair dangled across his tanned forehead. He obviously hadn't shaved that morning, but thanks to his fair complexion he'd always been able to put off that daily task. The weather lines etching the corners of his blue eyes—cornflower blue, she used to call them—and the permanent groove between his thick reddish blond eyebrows did make him look older than his thirty-five years.

But he'll never be an old-timer, Leigh knew. *Not in spirit, anyway.*

"I'll drive you back," he finally said, and headed for the cash register.

His walk was suddenly as familiar as the cutoffs she'd found in her bureau drawer last night. Leigh's breath caught and she had to move, unable to sit and watch the replay of the past another second. She stood up and walked toward the screen door he was now holding open for her. Once inside the truck she thanked him for the breakfast.

"No problem." He turned on the ignition and braced his right arm along the top of the passenger seat while he backed out onto the road. His fingertips brushed Leigh's shoulder and for a moment their eyes connected.

Leigh gave a tentative smile.

"Sorry," he mumbled, and returned his hand to the steering wheel.

Strange how something so trivial could resurrect so many memories, Leigh thought. She stared at his long tanned fingers, the blond hairs on each knuckle. They'd always been working hands, even when Spence was a teenager, and they still bore the callused skin from years of scaling fish, hauling nets and knotting lines. But the nails were trimmed and clean, a personal statement in defiance of work and weather.

Spence had come from a home quite different from the rest of the gang on Ocracoke. His father had been a fisherman like most of the men in the village then, but alcohol had lost him first his wife and then the stability of a home. Everyone in Silver Lake agreed that Spence McKay had more or less raised himself.

Leigh could still remember when Spencer's fingers had first slipped through hers, the night of the Sadie Hawkins dance two years before graduation. They'd arrived at the dance separately. Leigh, who'd come with Jen after her friend had begged her to for days, and Spence, who'd been towed around by a girl in his class. His expression of utter boredom had spurred Leigh to take Jen's dare and ask him for a dance. From the moment he'd halfheartedly taken her in his arms slow-dancing, Leigh Randall had determined to walk home that night with Spencer McKay.

"Something on your mind?"

Leigh glanced up.

Spence smiled. "You looked faraway."

Leigh cleared her throat. "Yes, I was."

"Thinking of New York?"

She shook her head. "Not faraway in miles. In years."

"Ah. Well, I suppose coming home brings back a lot of memories."

That's an understatement. "Yes," she said in a voice as noncommittal as she could muster.

After he shifted into drive he glanced sideways at her. "I hope they haven't all been bad ones."

"Not all of them."

Spence drummed his fingertips against the steering wheel and wished he could think of something clever to say. But he figured he'd already said more than he ought to have. He thought back to a few weeks ago when he'd first heard Leigh Randall was returning to Ocracoke. Seemed like a day hadn't passed since that he wasn't thinking about her. Remembering things—too *many* things—they'd done together, and later, how it had all ended up.

At that point his mind always shut down. Some things, he decided, should not be lived again but laid to rest forever. That was the philosophy he'd adopted long ago. Somewhere around the time he'd grown up—after Leigh left and then Jen. But every now and again his errant mind delved into the past like a wayward child, and memories flashed unbidden before him.

He'd first noticed how beautiful Leigh Randall was about the time she turned fourteen. He'd met up with her and Jen while walking in the marsh. Jen had been chasing Leigh with a cattail, waving it about as Leigh pranced through the marsh grass like a wild filly, her long black hair like polished ebony in the sunlight. From that day, until he'd taken her hand in his at the Sadie Hawkins dance, he'd waited patiently for her.

Sure, he reminded himself, there'd been other girls. A few in Ocracoke—summer girls—and others up in Hatteras. But he'd never let any of those relationships get in the way of that nugget of knowledge deep inside. That one day, when the timing was right, Leigh Randall would be his.

Now here he was on Ocracoke Island—the best place in the world—and once again driving in a pickup truck with the first woman he'd ever loved. *And she's free and you're free. Can it get any better?* he asked himself. His eyes shifted to the right, taking in the set line of Leigh's profile. He sighed. *I hope so.*

"Are those your binoculars?"

Leigh's unexpected question threw him. "Hmm? Oh,

yeah,'' he said, following her pointing finger to the floor hump between them. ''I was out bird-watching just before daybreak. Up in the salt marshes.''

''You? Bird-watching?''

''Is it that incredible?''

Leigh shook her head. ''No, I...I guess not, I just never pegged you for a...''

''Nature boy?''

She laughed. ''There's something geeky about that phrase that definitely doesn't apply to you.''

''Well,'' he drawled, ''I'll take that as a compliment.''

''When did you take up bird-watching?''

''A few years ago.''

Leigh smiled at the brief reply. He'd always hated talking about himself. ''A lot of things have happened since I left Ocracoke.''

''That's for damn sure,'' he said, then, ''Guess we're here.''

Leigh looked up, surprised to see the drive of Windswept Manor so soon. She'd forgotten how very small the island was. ''Thanks for the coffee, Spence. It was... nice,'' she said, searching for a neutral word.

''Yeah. Maybe we could do it again sometime.''

''Sure.'' Her hand settled on the door handle.

''Or maybe I could go running with you—that is, if you want company.''

Leigh frowned. ''Perhaps, though I'm not sure how long I'll be here.''

He raised his shoulders as if to say, ''Whatever,'' and she stepped down from the truck. She was almost at the front door when he called out, ''Good luck with the cleaning.''

Leigh waved and pushed open the screen door. She paused in the shadowy hallway, watching through the screen mesh as Spencer's truck reversed and backed out onto the highway. Beads of sweat dripped down the side of her neck, and she realized she was breathing as if she'd run all the way home.

LEIGH FELT her welcome smile wobble a fraction. She hoped Sam hadn't noticed, but was certain Jamie McKay, lurking behind him in the doorway, had.

Sam clutched his rolled-up Tilley hat, gesturing with it over his left shoulder. "I came by this afternoon to see if it was all right if young Jamie here came along, but you weren't home."

Thrown off by the unexpected addition to dinner, Leigh was at a loss for words. "I'm sorry. I decided to do some shopping in Hatteras and I didn't get back until after four. But that's fine, Sam, the more the merrier. As my dad used to say, 'It just means another cup of water in the soup.' In this case, another handful of pasta in the pot. Come in."

Although she'd been looking at Sam, Leigh had been conscious all the while of Jamie's fixed stare. She moved aside as the two stepped into the hall. Jamie slouched farther into his hooded sweatshirt, hands in his jeans pockets, gaze on the floor. Not a happy camper, Leigh decided.

"Y'see," Sam was saying, "Spence got a call to be in Charlotte for an early meeting tomorrow and he thought he'd best head to the coast this afternoon. And, uh, well, the lad is staying with me overnight and I didn't want—"

"Of course. Jamie's as welcome here as you are, Sam," Leigh said. "I just saw Spence this morning in the village. I hope his trip to Charlotte isn't an emergency or something."

She heard Jamie snort behind Sam, who quickly said, "Not at all. He knew the meeting was coming up but wasn't sure of the date."

"I coulda stayed home alone," Jamie mumbled, "but no one trusts me."

Sam's face darkened. "Enough of that, my boy. You

know the rules. And take that hood off your head—you're inside now.''

Leigh's anticipation of a quiet chatty evening with Sam began to fade. They stood looking at one another until she said, ''Well, I thought we'd eat out on the deck. Come on through to the kitchen and pick up a drink.''

She led the way, listening to the soft squeak of rubber soles behind her. ''I was just finishing up the salad.''

''Can we give you a hand?''

''Thanks, Sam, but I'm almost finished. Let me take your jacket and hat. A beer?''

''I'd never turn down a cold one.''

Leigh smiled at the exaggeration. In fact, he'd never been much of a drinker.

''Jamie? A Coke?'' She turned to the boy, who'd moved farther into the kitchen. He was inspecting the old hand pump at the end of the counter, which contained the newer stainless-steel sinks.

''That pump used to connect to a cistern out back and was the only way we got drinking water when I was a little kid,'' Leigh said.

Without turning around Jamie muttered, ''Yeah,'' and continued to move his fingers along the wooden handle and wrought-iron spout of the pump. Then he pushed his hood off his head and looked across the room at Leigh. For a moment she was lost in the memory of Jen Logan's eyes.

Jamie was a different blond than his father, more platinum, like Jen. And he'd inherited his mother's sea green eyes that could sometimes be as cold as Pamlico Sound in winter. Although he lacked the tall lankiness Spence had had in his own adolescence, Leigh could see that Jamie's build would someday be as muscular as his father's. All in all, he was more Logan than McKay. Anyway, she doubted she'd be around long enough to discover if his teenage rebellion paralleled his father's.

"I'll have that Coke," Jamie said, staring at the floor again.

Leigh's eyes met Sam's across the room. The old man shrugged and headed out through the door to the deck.

When Leigh handed Jamie his drink, the boy said, "So do you use the cistern at all anymore? I can hardly imagine getting water from a pump instead of a tap. It musta been like the Stone Age here."

Leigh tried not to laugh. "Compared to now, it was rough. But later the island installed the water tower—you must have seen it—and there's a desalinization plant, too, to take the salt out. Before the water tower, there were times in the summer when water was rationed."

"Rationed?" Jamie's voice rose in disbelief. "Like it was in the Second World War?"

She smiled at his knowledge of modern history. "I'm sure there are times even now when water use is controlled," she said, then turned to the island counter where the salad fixings were set out and continued her chopping. "I don't suppose," she went on when she realized Jamie was still standing behind her, "you've spent a lot of time in Ocracoke."

"Nah. Me and Mom left here when I was three. I kinda remember some parts. I used to come visit Dad a bit for a couple years after we moved to the mainland, but then I stopped coming."

"Why was that?"

"I don't know." A pause. "My parents weren't talking to each other then. Mom had trouble getting work, so we moved around a lot."

"That must've been hard on you."

When he didn't answer right away, Leigh was tempted to turn around and look at him, but restrained herself.

Finally he said, "Yeah, I didn't like it very much. Hard to make friends."

"Were you able to keep contact with your father during that time?"

Another pause. "Not much. He always sent birthday cards and presents, but sometimes I didn't get them till months later. It wasn't the same."

"I guess that must've been hard on your father, too."

"I doubt it. He sent me those things out of guilt, not love."

Leigh glanced at him this time and saw his red face and darkened eyes. She decided to back off. Adding the last bit of onion to the salad, she took the cutting board to the sink to rinse it. Now Jamie was examining a collection of island photographs mounted on the kitchen wall.

"My father collected those," Leigh murmured. "Took most of them, too."

"Yeah? They're kinda cool."

"He always dreamed of putting them together in a book. Like one of those big coffee-table books." Jamie gave her a blank stare. "Anyway," she went on, "he never got around to it."

"How come?"

"I'm not sure. I'm also ashamed to say I never asked. Maybe he was too busy bringing in the bacon, as he used to say. Fishing is a hard life. I doubt he had much time for recreational pursuits."

"Was he always a fisherman? Like Grandpa Sam?"

Leigh nodded. "Until he couldn't take the life anymore. Then he and my mother ran this house as a bed-and-breakfast."

"*This* house?"

Leigh couldn't help but smile again. The old place *was* a bit run-down. "At that time," she explained, "the Outer Banks wasn't as developed as it is now. People didn't have the choices they do now about where to stay."

"Huh," the boy said, then blurted, "When I'm

grown-up I'm gonna do just what I want to. I'm not gonna settle for second best.''

How did we get on to this? Leigh wondered. She turned away from the sink to take down plates from the adjacent cupboard and tried to think of an appropriate response. Then she said quietly, ''I think that's commendable. People should follow their dreams.''

Jamie stared at her thoughtfully. When she held out the plates, with cutlery and folded napkins on top, he took them without a word and headed for the back door. There, he craned his head around and muttered, ''All the adults I know gave up on theirs. Mom and Dad. Even Grandpa Sam.''

Leigh watched him hold open the screen door with his foot and sidle through onto the deck. She leaned her forehead against the cupboard door and prayed the evening would pass quickly.

CHAPTER FOUR

BUT THE EVENING surprised Leigh in another way.

They'd tucked into their linguini-in-white-clam-sauce with silent purpose. Other than polite requests to pass salad or Parmesan, there'd been little conversation.

Finally, after scraping up the last bit of sauce on his plate with a crust of bread, Sam leaned back in his chair and grunted, "Never eaten clams with noodles before, but I gotta admit, they go together like fries and flounder."

Leigh caught Jamie's eye and he startled her with a wink and a grin.

"'Course," Sam went on, "I hate to see good wine cooked up like that. Belongs in a glass and, yes—" he raised his empty wineglass to Leigh "—I will have another, thank you very much."

"Grandpa!" Jamie admonished.

Leigh got up, laughing. "Never mind, Jamie," she said, giving him a light pat on the shoulder as she walked toward the kitchen for another bottle. "I've known Grandpa Sam a lot longer than you have. You could say I'm used to his ways. If he feels up for another, he can have it."

"What ways? What's this all about? Are ya ganging up on me here?"

Leigh gazed fondly at the wide gap-toothed smile on Sam's face. "Darn right," she said. "Someone has to keep you in line." Then she pulled open the screen door and popped into the kitchen, emerging seconds later with a chilled bottle of white wine.

"Should you really have another one, Grandpa?"

Leigh and Sam turned as one to Jamie, whose face was now serious.

"This is a fine how-d'ya-do when a young whipper-snapper of fourteen takes to giving advice," Sam protested, casting Leigh an expression both proud and amused.

"You're always giving *other* people advice," Jamie said. "Maybe you should follow some yourself."

Leigh didn't dare risk a glance at Sam now. This was dangerous ground Jamie was treading on. But Sam surprised her again.

He pushed his wineglass aside and sighed loudly. "You're absolutely right, Jamie. I've had enough. Can't get across those dunes when I'm under the influence, can I? Might end up in another kind of drink and it'd be a tad too salty for me." He cackled boisterously at his joke.

Leigh put the unopened bottle on the table and sat down. "I've had enough myself," she said. "Besides, I have to get up early in the morning to start working on this place. I'm having an open house in a few days."

Sam sobered instantly. "Ah, my girl, I hate to see this place go the way so many have on this island. Soon there'll be no originals left. They'll all be *summer* people." He spat the word out as if it had a nasty taste.

"What's so bad about summer people?" Jamie asked. "At least they'd be different."

"Different? Aye, they're different all right, boy. And I'm not sayin' that's a bad thing. But when you're only here for two months a year—or even a few weeks—you don't appreciate it the way the locals do. You haven't gone through the hard times together. The storms, the ferry breakin' down an' strandin' you here for days at a time. Water runnin' out and havin' to borrow food or other things from people. There's no bond with the summer folks. That's all I'm sayin'."

Leigh nodded agreement. "I remember the power going off one winter for days. We had to collect all the firewood we could find—and there's not a lot of that on the island. I remember breaking through a layer of ice in the rain cistern, 'cause the desalinization plant's generator wasn't working for a while, either."

Jamie looked from one to the other. "You both sound like..." he hesitated.

"Old-timers?" Leigh suggested.

The boy had the grace to flush. "Not exactly that. I don't know—like pioneers or somethin'."

Leigh grinned. "I think times were a lot rougher when Sam was growing up here, weren't they, Sam?"

The old man nodded vigorously. "Darn right. Water was always the big problem. Sometimes it had to be trucked in—that was before the plant was built." He gazed off into the backyard. "Leigh's mother used to have quite a garden out there, but she worked hard at it. Fought those weeds and marram grass every day. Used water over and over again—from the cistern, the dishes, even the laundry. Huh!" he snorted. "Talk about recycling. People these days act like they invented it. We were a darn sight better at it than anyone today. We reused everythin'."

His lecture finished, Sam leaned back in his chair. He looked tired, Leigh thought. "Sam, would you like some coffee?"

He shook his head. "No thanks. Can't drink the stuff anymore. Bothers my stomach. Comes with old age, I guess. You have to give up all the things you loved so much in your youth." He gazed fondly at Jamie. "Remember that, my boy. Enjoy the young years—but not too much."

Leigh's eyes met Jamie's and they laughed together. "Yeah, right," Jamie muttered. "Here comes the advice again."

Leigh straightened in her chair. The boy certainly had a

disconcerting habit of saying whatever came into his mind. She glanced at Sam, waiting for a sharp retort. But the old man continued to smile affectionately at his grandson. Leigh realized with some surprise that he actually liked the ribbing. He'd changed, she thought. The Sam Logan who'd raised Jen was a lot tougher than this Sam Logan.

"Have you taken Jamie out to Teach's Hole yet, Sam? Shown him where Blackbeard lost his life?"

"Blackbeard? You mean that pirate? Was he real?"

Sam frowned. "Sure was. He and his gang hung out around the Outer Banks when they weren't busy terrorizing the British merchant fleet. Finally met his end right here on Ocracoke Island."

Jamie leaned forward, resting his elbows on the table. "I always thought that was just movie stuff, all those stories about Blackbeard."

"Not all," Sam declared. "The man's real name was Edward Teach, an' there's a spot out past Silver Lake Harbor we call Teach's Hole Channel. That's where Lieutenant Robert Maynard of the British Royal Navy killed him. Musta been some fight. Them pirates and the Royal Navy." He shook his head. "I'd've liked to see that."

"Is he buried here on the island?"

"Somewhere." Sam leaned closer to the table and lowered his voice to a whisper. "But not in any graveyard, I'll tell you that. Some say his head is in one place and the rest of him in t'other, so even his ghost won't be able to come back and haunt us."

"Yeah, right," Jamie said skeptically, but his eyes were round.

Getting into the spirit of storytelling, Leigh folded her arms on the table and said, "I remember my father talking about the time those British servicemen were drowned off the tip of the island. During the Second World War."

"Yep. The church bell was ringin' that night. What a tragedy! All those fine young men—no more'n teenagers.

The village was so taken with the whole event, they even set aside a special graveyard for the men.''

Jamie's eyebrows rose. "Is that what that little graveyard is off the harbor? I was wondering about that place.''

"You've got a lot to learn about your background, young fellow. Your heritage is a damn fine one.''

He so seldom swore Leigh turned to look at the old man. His eyes were glistening. After a moment's silence he said to Leigh, "Well, we'd best be off, my dear. These old bones can't take late hours anymore.''

They pushed back their chairs and wandered around the side of the house to the front. The sun had disappeared below the horizon, but there was still plenty of afterglow. Jamie peered at his watch.

"It's not even nine yet. In Charlotte I wouldn't be in bed until after eleven.''

"Ah,'' Sam teased, "but this here is Ocracoke and we're up with the sun. You an' me are fixin' that hole in the dinghy tomorrow. Then I plan to take you out on the Sound for some mullet. About time you learned how to net mullet.''

Jamie rolled his eyes, but flashed Leigh a grin. She smiled back and raised her shoulders in mock helplessness.

"He's right, Jamie. I plan to be up early myself and to, oh, weed the garden and maybe get a coat of paint on the trim.''

Sam held up a finger. "Don't you be climbing any ladders. I'll have the boy come over—or maybe Spencer, when he gets back.''

"Sam! I'm only kidding. I've been a city girl for too many years. I'll probably sleep till noon.''

They smiled at that—humoring her, she realized. When they'd disappeared from sight across the road and down the slope to the beach, Leigh walked up to the front veranda to watch the remnants of sunset. The evening had turned out much better than she'd anticipated. In spite of

Sam's old-fashioned ideas, his love for Jamie had been obvious. Especially in his tolerance of the almost insolent remarks Jamie often made.

And Leigh had been pleased to see now and then a glimmer of real affection in the boy's eyes for his grandfather. Whatever Jamie's problems had been—or still were—there appeared to be potential for improvement. At least Leigh hoped so for Spencer's sake.

Later, after she'd showered and crawled into bed, her mind returned to Jamie's remarks about his childhood. The picture of his early years wasn't the one she and Jen had imagined when they'd fantasized about their futures. Long before Spencer McKay had taken Leigh into his arms at the Sadie Hawkins dance. Long before Jen Logan had fallen in love with him, too.

Leigh rolled onto her side, punched her pillow into a ball and wished herself to sleep. But her eyes fluttered against sleep like moths against the screen.

"Did I wake you?"

"Hmm?" Clutching the cell phone, Leigh ran her tongue across her dry lips and rubbed her eyes.

"I did. Oh, dear, but it's going on nine-thirty. I hated to let the phone ring so many times, but I was beginning to think I had the wrong number and almost hung up. Sorry about that." A pause. "Oh, it's Trish calling." A brief giggle.

"I, uh, couldn't find the phone," Leigh explained, which elicited a peal of laughter.

"Heavens, I wouldn't have the faintest idea how to even turn one of those things on. Anyway, sorry to bother you so early, but it's my day off and I wondered if you'd like to meet for lunch. That is, if you're not busy?"

"Oh, sure, thank you." Then, embarrassed about her lack of enthusiasm, Leigh added, "'Course I don't have my engagement book handy."

There was a fraction of a hesitation before Trish said, "Oh, well, do you want to go look?"

Leigh smiled. "I'm kidding, Trish."

Another guffaw. "You always were a joker, Leigh, even as a little girl. Faye used to tell me about some of the practical jokes you played on her."

"She did? Gee, I don't remember any myself." Leigh frowned. "But that was a long time ago. Where shall we meet?"

"Meet? Oh! For lunch. Well, there's a new place—a kind of bakery-deli—or there's always Howard's," she said, mentioning one of the island's oldest restaurants.

Leigh closed her eyes. The bakery-deli was probably the place where she and Spence had gone yesterday morning. "Howard's would be nice."

"Great! Twelve-thirty okay?"

"Fine. See you then." Leigh put the phone down on the coffee table and bent over to retrieve the sofa cushions she'd hurled to the floor in her search for the phone. Drained by the energy of Trish's call and her lack of sleep, she slumped onto the sofa, where she'd crashed just before dawn.

Maybe the idea of an engagement book isn't so silly, even for Ocracoke. Two days here and what have I accomplished, other than some cleaning and listing the house for sale? The agent had suggested a few practical improvements to make before the first open house on Saturday.

Leigh took a deep breath and got to her feet with a determined leap. She'd spend the morning sorting out the things she wanted to keep from what could be thrown away. Her bedroom closet was full of boxes of high-school and college memorabilia. There were more boxes in the attic and perhaps in the other bedrooms. The task would take more than a morning, she knew. *But if I'm really lucky, I won't have to spend the whole two weeks here, after all.*

By midmorning Leigh had cleaned out her bedroom closet and started on the attic. The only troubling moment had come when she lifted the lid on a shoe box of photographs, many from early childhood. Leigh, squinting into the sun, her dark hair knotted into two stubby ponytails at each side of her face, with the solemn expression she wore in almost every photo she appeared. She remembered her mother urging her to smile and her father's patience. Poor Dad, she thought. How difficult it must have been for a photographer to have a child who hated having her picture taken.

Then she found several of her and Jen. Jen, who'd never needed encouragement to mug for the camera. Blond hair blazing in the sunlight, Jen pranced and posed in every position a kid could think of—on her hands, midcartwheel, making donkey ears behind Leigh. Later, in the midst of adolescence, there was a demure coyness in the photographs, as if Jen had begun to practice her seduction skills on the camera first. *Before she got around to Spencer.*

Leigh replaced the lid on the box. Her hand held it over the recycling load, then shifted it suddenly to the keeper pile. Sometime she'd go through the box more carefully. Perhaps Sam or even Jamie would like the pictures of Jen. She checked the time, realizing she only had enough to take a quick shower before walking into the village for lunch.

When she pushed open Howard's glass door, noting the new "sports bar" look, Leigh took a few seconds to adjust to the darkness. Then she heard someone call her name and saw Trish waving from a large corner table, around which sat four other women, including Mary Ann Burnett. *Damn.* Leigh pasted a smile on her face and walked toward them.

"I hope you don't mind," Trish explained, "but I thought it would be wonderful for you to see some of your old gang. Mind you, it was pretty hard rounding everyone up.''

I bet. Lunch with Leigh Randall? Gosh, sorry, but I'm terribly busy.

The faces were familiar, but none of the women had been close friends. Leigh nodded politely as Trish refreshed her memory, introducing the other women and ending with Mary Ann.

"'Course you two have already met up. Mary Ann was just telling us about the article. It'll be in the paper Friday!'' Trish beamed.

"I have to talk to you before I send it off. About that last question.'' Mary Ann narrowed her eyes at Leigh. "You know the one I mean?''

How has your life changed since prom night? Leigh was damned if she was going to try to answer that now. She sat down and fiddled with her purse before hanging it over her chair. "Sure,'' she finally said. "Give me your number and I'll call you.''

The expression on Mary Ann's face registered dissatisfaction with that arrangement, but fortunately she didn't press the point.

Leigh glanced around the table. All faces were set intently on hers. They seemed friendly, she thought, although more curious than kind. At first, in the dim light of the restaurant, she'd been unable to attach names to them, but now she began to recall the grades they'd been in and their relationships to other students in her own class. Trish had graduated almost five years before any of them and so had known them all as youngsters. Mary Ann had been in Spence's class along with another of the women— Fran?—and the two others were sisters, one the same age as Leigh and one a couple of years younger.

When Leigh smiled, they broke into a buzz of questions about New York and her career in banking.

"You always were smart at math," one said. "Gee, I don't even know what an investment banker does."

"You spend other people's money," Leigh replied. "It's quite easy and very pleasant."

They all laughed. By the time the waiter had taken orders, the tension had eased enough for Leigh to feel comfortable. The women brought Leigh up-to-date on life in the village—who'd married, who'd left and who'd stayed behind. As she'd expected, most of her peers had left Ocracoke after college and returned periodically to vacation or visit family. They told her about the local environmentalists who were fighting to keep the island from erosion, groups who wanted to promote tourism and others who wanted to keep life in the fishing village as simple as it had always been.

"The place has already changed enormously," Leigh said. "I couldn't believe the number of motels and guest houses."

"But there's still no Laundromat," one of the women put in.

The others laughed. "Who cares?" someone asked.

"Right, you are. We can always use wash buckets and cistern water," Trish said. "If it was good enough for our mothers—"

"Oh, please," Fran moaned, "spare me the island-pioneer bit."

"At least the lighthouse is still functioning," Leigh observed. "It was good to see a familiar landmark that hadn't been altered."

"Yes, and it still manages to save people, too. Imagine all the shipwrecks and drownings this island has witnessed," one of the sisters murmured.

For a moment Leigh was oblivious to the silence that had fallen on the group at this last remark. She'd been checking the bill to determine her share, and when she looked up, everyone else was studying the contents of glasses or coffee cups. Then she recalled the last part of the sentence, sensing at once that it had come out unintentionally.

She decided to ignore it. Lunch had been more enjoyable than she'd anticipated and she didn't want to spoil it. "I hope we can do this again before I go back to New York." The cheerfulness in her voice prompted a round of agreement, and the tense moment passed.

"Will you stay until the house is sold?" Fran asked.

"I don't know. I planned to be here no more than a couple of weeks, and I suppose if I'm lucky things will move quickly."

Trish pursed her lips. "Perhaps. Though the market hasn't been terrific the past couple of years. For cottages and bungalows sure, but for a place as big and..."

"Ramshackle?" Leigh offered.

Trish flushed. "No, I wouldn't have chosen that word. But Windswept Manor is the kind of place that needs a lot of maintenance."

"I know. That's one reason I've decided to sell it. But maybe a big family from the mainland will want it as a summer home."

The others nodded. "Yes," Fran said, "if it's priced right, it may go very quickly. The season hasn't really started yet."

Leigh took her portion of change from the waitress and slung her purse over her shoulder. "Let's hope so."

As the women were leaving the restaurant, Mary Ann took Leigh aside. "Here's my card," she said, handing over a small embossed business card. "Please give me a call before five. Then I can fax the rest of the story in."

"Will I get a chance to read it first?"

Mary Ann hesitated. "I guess I could read it to you over the phone. Unfortunately I'm too close to deadline. You know how it is."

Leigh nodded, though she didn't feel like letting Mary

Ann off the hook. "Over the phone will be fine," she said. When she turned away, Trish was waiting to speak to her.

"I hope you don't have to leave right away. Faye is supposed to be coming for a visit soon and she'd love to see you. Is it possible for you to take a longer leave from work?"

Leigh hesitated. She thought back to the day she'd gone in to see her boss about taking two weeks' leave.

"Take a month," he'd urged. Then, leaning almost conspiratorially across his desk, he'd lowered his voice and said, "To be truthful, Leigh, you look like you could use a long holiday. You've had a tough couple of years and I wouldn't want you to crash."

"Are you trying to tell me something, Reg?" Leigh had managed to make her comeback sound breezy, but anxiety crept up her throat.

He'd shrugged, insisted he was only considering her best interests, but Leigh had left with the sense that some junior workaholic was already lurking outside her own hard-earned and coveted office.

Trish was smiling, waiting patiently for an answer.

"I might be able to swing it, Trish," she said, adding when she saw the rush of excitement in the other woman's face, "but I can't make any promises."

Trish patted her arm. "I'm hoping you'll be here. Now, can we get together later in the week?"

"That'd be great," breathed Mary Ann, who was still lurking about. Before Leigh could reply, the two women swished away to say goodbye to the other women waiting by the restaurant door. She felt overwhelmed and could almost envision the days ahead as one long round of social events. She doubted she was up to it. *More opportunities for more innocent remarks. More memories.* No, she thought, best to stick to her original plan. In and out. Quickly.

"You go ahead," she called. "I want to use the ladies'

room before I leave.'' Leigh waved and turned away to find the washroom. It was downstairs, and on her way in she paused in front of the mirror in the sink area to brush her hair and apply fresh lip gloss. She took her time, reluctant to be offered a ride home when she preferred to walk—alone. Then she headed for the door leading into the toilet section, deciding to make use of the facility, after all. A woman's loud complaining voice stopped her.

"It was, too, Leigh Randall. I'd recognize that raven head anywhere. Didn't I sit behind it for a week at the inquest?"

"That was fifteen years ago, Phyllis. She could be a redhead by now for all we know."

"It was her, I tell you. I'm going to call Trish Butterfield the minute I get home to find out how long she's going to be here."

There was a heavy sigh. "What does it matter now? Let the past go."

"Never!" the other voice hissed. "You wouldn't be saying that if it had been your daughter who'd drowned!"

Leigh stepped back from the door. The familiar sensations of panic were beginning—the pounding heart, the frenzied surge of adrenaline telling her to run, contradicted by the leaden numbness creeping up her legs. Now she could scarcely breathe and next, she knew, would come the terrifying hyperventilation. She forced her legs to keep moving and escaped just as the inner door swung open.

The woman's voice—Laura's mother, must be Laura's mother—was still raving inside, but Leigh willed herself up the stairs to the main floor. *Don't stop. Stay calm. Deep breath. In. Out. In. Out.*

Sunlight streamed through the glass front doors and she stretched out her palms to push, sending the doors crashing against the jambs and raising nearby heads. Leigh stumbled into the parking lot, blinded by light and tears, legs pumping and asthmatic heaves bursting from her chest.

Then someone was at her elbow asking if she was okay and guiding her toward a bench beneath an oak tree at one side of the parking lot.

Leigh sat down and closed her eyes, concentrating on the breathing exercise that she knew would bring everything back into focus again. When she turned to thank her rescuer, all she saw of him was his back as he walked toward Howard's. But it was a back she knew, even in the sun's glare.

"Sit there," Spencer ordered over his shoulder.

By the time he emerged seconds later carrying a large tumbler of ice water, Leigh had herself under control.

"Drink it slowly," he instructed, handing her the glass and sitting down beside her.

"I'm okay now, really."

"Drink."

Leigh took a sip and then held the glass against her face, tempted to pour it down the front of her halter-top sundress.

"Here." Spence pulled a red-and-black-checked bandanna out of his shirt pocket and, taking the glass from Leigh, dipped a corner of the bandanna into it. "It's all right," he said, glancing at her, "this is clean."

Then he squeezed out the wet corner and very gently dabbed at Leigh's forehead.

"Mmm," she murmured, closing her eyes.

"Nice?"

"Wonderful."

He sponged her cheeks and touched each closed eyelid so softly Leigh wondered if she'd imagined it.

"That's terrific. Thank you very much." Her eyes flew open.

Spence held up a palm. "Wait. I'm not finished yet."

Leigh watched him dip the bandanna into the glass again and wring it out. "I'm curious. What's with the bandanna?"

"I always take one when I go out on a charter. Some guys forget to bring a sunhat or they need something to mop up the sweat from a tough catch." He caught the look on her face. "That's why I use a cloth—it can be washed. Now, why don't you rest your head against the back of the bench while I—"

"I'm fine now, Spencer. Seriously."

"Humor me." He pressed an index finger lightly to the center of her brow and tilted back her head.

She felt the damp cool cloth sweep over her face again and then begin to brush down the length of her neck. Leigh held her breath. The bandanna patted the shallow dip where neck and collarbone met, paused and stroked a delicate line of moisture to the top of her sundress, resting lightly at the hollow between her breasts. Something brushed lower, against her breasts. Leigh gasped and shot up.

"Sorry," he murmured. "The end of the bandanna came loose."

Leigh could feel the heat returning to her face. "Well, I think I'll drink some of that water now, if you don't mind."

Spence handed her the glass and shook the cloth loose. Then he extended his other arm and planted the bandanna firmly against the nape of her neck. "The most important spot," he said.

Leigh plucked the scarf away and handed it to him. "Thanks. I'm fine."

"What was it?" he asked. "You stumbled out of Howard's as if a pack of wild dogs was after you. Couldn't be the heat. Howard just got a new air-conditioning unit."

Leigh swirled the melting ice cubes around in the glass. After a moment she said, "I don't know. Maybe something I ate."

Spence narrowed his eyes. She could tell he wasn't buying her story.

"At Howard's? Maybe we should go and report it."

"No! I'm not going back in there."

"Well, they'll want to know if something's off in their kitchen, you know. No one wants a lawsuit from some irate tourist. Besides, I was heading in there myself to meet a client. I just got back from Charlotte and there was a message on my machine about a charter. The guy said he'd be at Howard's for a late lunch. It was a lucky break for me, bumping into you again." He paused and grinned. "Amazing, really. Usually I meet my clients at the marina or my office." He stood up and held out a hand. "Come on in with me, then I'll drive you home."

"I'm not going back inside and I can get home by myself." Then she added in a softer tone, "Thanks, anyway, Spence, but really, I'm all right. This has happened before and I know how to handle it."

He sat back down beside her. "*This* has happened before? What is *this*?"

Leigh cursed herself. Now he'd never let go. He'd chew away at this like a dog with a piece of rawhide.

But she didn't have to answer, after all. The door of the restaurant swung open and two women strode out into the parking lot. They began walking to a car when one of them spotted Leigh and Spence on the bench. She stopped, clutched her friend's arm and whispered in her ear.

The other woman, a plump bleached blonde, pivoted sharply. Her jaw gaped open. "It *is* her! I was right." She looked at her friend and added in a voice deliberately raised, "And look who she's with. My goodness. Doesn't history repeat itself."

Gooseflesh rose along Leigh's arms. She looked down into her lap until she felt the pressure of Spence's arm on her shoulders. Then his finger gently raised the tip of her chin up and toward him.

"Laura Marshall's mother," he whispered. "Keep looking at me and repeat these words—She's a witch…"

Leigh giggled, but her eyes never left Spencer's face.

"That's it," he murmured.

A car door slammed, then another.

"They're leaving," he said.

She nodded, her eyes still fixed on his.

A car spewed a wake of pebbles and sand behind it, gunning out of the lot in a surge of power. Leigh closed her eyes and expelled a sigh.

"Tell me," he said.

But she shook her head. "Not now. Please. I don't want to talk about it."

He dropped his arm and folded up the square of checked cloth. "Guess I'll chase up my client, then. Sure you don't want a ride?"

The offer was tempting, but she still refused. "It's okay. Thanks, anyway." She looked away as he headed into the restaurant.

When Leigh heard the door flap shut, she stood up and stretched. She felt exhausted and wrung out, as if she'd run a marathon. Certainly a gauntlet, anyway. She spotted the bandanna folded carefully on the bench. She picked it up and looked across at the restaurant door, then tucked the cloth into her purse and headed home.

CHAPTER FIVE

THE JUNE ISSUE of the *Island Breeze* lay on the counter. The woman walked past, casually slipped the paper under her arm and continued on outside. Once under the sprawling shade of the magnolia tree on the front lawn, she sat down and carefully unfolded the newspaper. She liked being the first to read the paper, to delve into its pages when they were still pressed and clean. Time often passed luxuriously slowly beneath the tree, and she reveled in the knowledge that she could spend the whole day reading the paper if she wanted to.

But less than five minutes later her hands froze to the edge of newspaper. She stared long and hard at the headline "Islander Returns Home" and then, even longer, at the photograph below. She forced herself to read the article, but knew before finishing it that her first hunch was right. *It's her! It has to be!*

She read and reread the words, smoothing the page until the photograph almost jumped out at her. Then she folded the newspaper up and tucked it under her arm again. She'd have to hide it so no one else would read it and find out. Excitement mounted inside her and she inhaled deeply, remembering the routine and sensing that now, more than ever, she'd have to stay calm. But she couldn't still the warm glow mushrooming in the pit of her stomach. At long last a connection had been made.

My baby. I've found my baby.

"SO WHAT DO YOU THINK?" Mary Ann Burnett's voice crackled over Leigh's cell phone.

"About what?"

"Your interview in the *Island Breeze*."

"I haven't seen it yet, but I trust it hasn't changed since we talked on the phone the other day."

Mary Ann's voice sounded indignant. "I wouldn't do that to you, Leigh. That's the kind of thing big-city journalists do."

Leigh marveled at the way Mary Ann linked the word "journalist" to herself.

"You'll find it's just about verbatim as I read it to you."

The "just about" worried Leigh. "Well, I'll be sure to pick up a copy and let you know. I hope you played down the reference to the accident as I requested."

"Sure did. I mentioned that you'd put the past behind you, blah blah blah, and that you were looking forward to seeing old friends during your brief stay."

Leigh closed her eyes. Blah blah blah. What did *that* mean? "So, you took out that stuff about the inquest?"

A deep sigh. "Yes, yes."

But a hint of vagueness in her voice flashed a warning light. "I get the feeling there's something more," Leigh said.

"Well, I did mention the old friends you'd already seen."

A tiny chill traveled down Leigh's spine. "Like?"

"You know—the gang the other day at Howard's and, uh, Spence McKay."

"You didn't mention his name?"

"Why not? I simply said old friends and then listed them."

"But that makes it seem as if I've been seeing him purposefully."

"You were seen coming out of that new bakery-deli

about seven the other morning. Kind of a weird time to bump into someone, isn't it?''

Mary Ann's voice took on a steely edge, reminding Leigh that the woman had never really been a friend. *I shouldn't have agreed to the stupid interview in the first place.* "I'd been out jogging and, yes, I *did* bump into him. I can't believe this place."

There was a slight pause and then, "Guess you've forgotten how people here tend to find out everything about everyone."

It was Leigh's turn to sigh. "Yeah, guess so."

"I wouldn't make such a big deal out of it," Mary Ann advised. "You went with the guy for two years and then he eloped with your best friend. Surely it must be old news to even you by now."

Leigh swallowed her retort. She hated the way Mary Ann had emphasized "even you," as if she'd spent the past fifteen years pining away for Spencer.

"I think you should take a look at it," Mary Ann said. "It's not as bad as you're imagining. I'll have a copy sent over to you from the office in Hatteras. Do you still have that postal box?"

"Yes."

"Okay, then. And listen, if you run into any flak about the article, let me know."

"What do you mean by flak?"

"Just, you know, in case some people are upset by it."

"For heaven's sake, Mary Ann, you've just told me there's nothing in it to upset anyone. Make up your mind."

There was a nervous titter on the other end of the line. "Sorry, Leigh. The only people who might comment on your return are Laura Marshall's mother and Jeff's parents. Everyone else in the village has basically put the accident behind them. The way you have."

Leigh caught the slight insinuation in the pronoun. She clenched her teeth and decided to ignore it. The article had already been published. "I'll be waiting for the paper," was all she said.

"Good. And listen, give me a call later, okay?"

"Fine," Leigh muttered, wishing you could slam down a cellular phone. Instead, she slumped into the armchair in her parents' bedroom. She rubbed her hand across her face. *Finish sorting through this mess,* she told herself, *and get as far from Ocracoke as possible.* But then the spark of anger rekindled itself, as it had so many times in the past.

Why do they blame me? I begged them to wait out the storm, but they wouldn't listen. And her mother would stroke her brow, shushing her to calmness. *They blame you because you lived and their children didn't. Feel pity for them, not anger.*

But it was anger that fueled her in the aftermath, that kept her spine rigid throughout the inquest, the reproachful looks and the shaking heads. Anger that turned her away from Spencer's apology about the prom fiasco.

Leigh tossed the cell phone onto the bed and stared down at the box of magazines on the floor. She rubbed her face again, rotated the kinks out of her shoulders and upper back and sat cross-legged on the floor next to the carton.

Daddy was such a pack rat! Pete Randall had been loath to throw anything away. Leigh recalled many family clean-ups when she and her mother had removed boxes to the dump or secondhand stores while Pete was out in his boat. Years of *Life* and *National Geographic* magazines, every piece of schoolwork Leigh had ever produced, plastic margarine containers or used stamps—everything was eventually consigned to a labeled cardboard box in the attic. After Pete's death Ellen had most of his collections removed—except for those boxes marked with Leigh's name. Her mother had insisted those be kept for Leigh's own future family, and reluctant to dash her mother's hopes for grandchildren, Leigh hadn't complained.

But now what? Her mother's presence suddenly loomed.

Leigh closed up the box of magazines and shoved it toward the two other boxes destined for a recycling plant. Then she dragged the first of four cartons labeled with her name. *Sorry, Mom, but there's no point in holding on to this stuff any longer.*

The journey into her past took Leigh much longer than she'd expected. She couldn't resist reading every story she'd ever written in elementary school, and the report cards were fascinating. From first grade to eighth, her teachers' comments had seldom varied. *Leigh is a very shy girl… Leigh is hesitant to answer orally, although she is invariably right when she does… Leigh is a serious and observant student.*

The class photos were equally fascinating, but after poring over a couple, Leigh put them aside. The retrospective of changing faces included Laura's, Jen's, Tony's and Jeff's. They'd all been classmates together until graduation, and there they were, mugging for the camera right up to twelfth grade. Leigh held on much longer to a single wallet photo of Jen and her, taken in an instant-photo booth in Nag's Head.

She could recall almost every detail of that day. They'd been fourteen and allowed to take the ferry and bus by themselves up to Nag's Head. They'd gone to a movie, shared a monster banana split and spent the rest of their money in the photo booth. Jen had taken the end of her blond ponytail and draped it across Leigh's upper lip. Leigh had done the same with her own black swoop of hair and pressed her cheek against Jen's. *See? We're twins,* Jen had said. Leigh had laughed until the tears rolled.

Leigh smiled. She tossed the photo back into the box, closed it up and pushed it toward the recycling pile. Half an hour later she'd mercilessly sorted through every carton. Exhausted, she sank onto the cool hardwood floor and stretched out prone. A cold beer was in order, she decided, after such grueling work. She glanced at the recycling pile.

It was far too large to be driven up in one load. Maybe a rental truck would do the trick. *Or I could borrow one. From Spencer.*

The idea of doing so was tantalizing, but Leigh knew she'd never have the nerve to ask. She sighed, rolled to her side to get up and suddenly noticed the suitcase under the bed. *Damn.* She didn't know if she could face any more trips down memory lane. On the other hand, she reasoned, best to get all the emotional stuff out of the way at the same time. She reached out and dragged the suitcase toward her.

Leigh couldn't remember anyone actually using this decal-plastered piece of luggage. The Randalls had seldom left Ocracoke for longer than an overnight stay up the coast on a rare shopping spree. Twice she recalled staying on the mainland when the island had been evacuated during hurricane season. Her father used to say that if everyone in America—he was given to exaggeration—wanted to come to the Outer Banks to vacation, why would the Randalls want to leave? Right, Leigh would mumble, a disgruntled teenager at the time and desperate to see the world.

Well, I've seen a lot of the world and now I'm back in Ocracoke—and surprisingly, not minding it too much. The thought made her pause in opening the suitcase. It was already mid-June, a mere two weeks from the start of the tourist invasion. Yet she felt no urgency to leave and had toyed with the idea of calling Reg to request long-overdue holiday leave.

Right. And stay for what? Another round of reacquainting yourself with old classmates? Avoiding Mrs. Marshall and her friends? Kidding yourself that the past can be relived? Thinking Spencer McKay will be more sincere this time around?

The snap hinges on the suitcase flew up. Nope, Leigh decided. Nothing to keep her here at all. She rifled through the photographs, most of them her baby pictures and some of her parents' wedding. There was a package of letters addressed to her mother, and Leigh thumbed through them, noticing they'd been sent from her father before their marriage. Love letters, she realized, while her mother had been at university in Raleigh. She didn't want to read them, yet hated to throw them away. She added them to the small pile of articles she was saving.

There was another stack of envelopes, yellowed and dog-eared, that appeared to contain insurance policies, old bank statements and even the Randalls' marriage license. Leigh scanned them and tossed them onto the garbage pile. Even Pete wouldn't have clung sentimentally to the license, but would have claimed, instead, that a piece of paper didn't make a good marriage any more than a license made a good driver.

Leigh smiled to herself, remembering the day she'd asked to see her adoption certificate. She'd been about ten and had told her father that a new friend had said she wasn't really a Randall. Pete's face had assumed an uncharacteristically sober expression. He'd pulled Leigh to him, wrapped his beefy arm around her shoulders and murmured, "I can show you that piece of paper, honey. It's tucked away in a safe place upstairs. But that piece of paper is only the legal proof that you belong to us. *It* didn't make you our daughter. What made you our daughter was all those nights your mama and I got up for your feedings, all those times we bandaged your skinned knees, went to your school concerts, taught you how to fish for mullet, took you clam diggin' in Teach's Hole—and every birthday drank a toast to the day you came to us. All those moments packed into these last ten years. That's what's made you our daughter. Not some piece of paper."

And Leigh had hugged him tightly before running outside to tell that girl she really *was* a Randall and didn't need any old piece of paper to prove it. *No, Daddy, you wouldn't worry about my throwing away that marriage license.* When she found the adoption certificate lying underneath the knitted white baby outfit wrapped in tissue paper at the bottom of the suitcase, Leigh couldn't resist reading it before she tossed it, too, on the garbage pile. There had never been any secrets about her adoption, and Leigh had never felt any inclination to pursue her roots. "My roots," she'd once told an inquiring friend in New York, "are on Ocracoke Island and my parents are Ellen and Pete Randall."

She plucked the knitted outfit from the tissue paper and wondered why her mother had saved this particular item of baby clothing out of all the others she must have had. Her mother had never been as attached to things as Pete had, so the outfit must have had a special significance. She held it up, amazed at its size. Hard to believe she or anyone else could have been so tiny. Then she rewrapped it in the tissue paper. If her mother had packaged it up so carefully, she must have considered it important. Leigh decided to keep it.

As she lowered the suitcase lid, Leigh noticed a slight bulge in its interior pocket. She stuck her hand in, pulling out a rectangle of tissue paper and found inside the faded remnant of a powder blue baby blanket.

I don't believe it, she thought. *I haven't seen this in years.* Leigh fingered the worn flannel fabric, vividly recalling every detail of the mystery of its disappearance. The blanket had traveled everywhere with her until she was about to start school. The family of ducks printed on it had almost been obliterated by time, washing-machine cycles and Leigh's sweaty clutching right up to the day of its sudden loss—coincidentally, a week before she first began school.

Years later she and Jen had once compared babyhood stories, and Leigh had confessed to owning a security blanket. Jen had suggested searching the house for the blanket, insisting Leigh's birth mother might have sent it along with her from the hospital. When Leigh had mentioned the idea to her parents, they admitted hiding the blanket prior to her starting school. They also confirmed that Leigh had arrived wrapped in the blanket, which was the reason they'd saved the remaining piece. From that moment on, the powder blue duck blanket had an almost mythical aura to Leigh.

And here it is. Leigh raised the blanket to her face, returning herself to her childhood for a long moment before tucking it back inside the suitcase on top of the baby outfit. It occurred to her she might also have come to the Randalls wearing the white knitted sweater-and-bonnet set.

And if that was the case, perhaps her birth mother had bought or even knitted the outfit. Leigh hesitated, tempted to take the outfit out from its wrapping again. *Not today.* She began to close the lid when she realized there was something else inside the pocket flap. Pulling the flap out, she saw a brown business envelope at the bottom of the pocket. It was addressed to her parents and had as a return address an official-looking stamp that read Bennington Adoption Agency Inc., Raleigh, North Carolina.

Leigh pulled a typed letter from the envelope. She noted the date—April 14, 1980—and began to read. After the introductory sentence, the words seemed to move around on the paper. Beads of sweat dripped from Leigh's forehead. She frowned, trying to take in what her eyes were reading but her brain was refusing to register. She wiped her face with the corner of her T-shirt and climbed onto the bed.

Okay, relax. Let's have a look at this again where the light is better. Leigh propped up the feather pillows behind her back. Sunlight filtered through the filmy curtains. No need for electricity, but she switched on the lamp at her mother's side of the bed, anyway. She didn't want to misread a single word. Then she unfolded the letter again.

Dear Mr. and Mrs. Randall,

The Bennington Agency has recently received an inquiry from the birth mother of your adopted daughter, Leigh. The birth mother is interested in establishing a correspondence with you and her daughter that might possibly, in the future, lead to a meeting.

As you are aware, in spite of the state laws around adoption disclosure, we at the Bennington Agency stand by our pledge to honor confidentiality and privacy of all concerned parties. Hence we will not reveal your address to the birth mother unless you specifically request us to do so. We have reminded the birth mother of the contract she signed at adoption time and she has agreed to abide by your decision on behalf of Leigh.

Should you wish to discuss this issue further with us prior to arriving at a decision, please feel free to contact one of our social workers. Thank you....

Leigh skimmed over the closing paragraph and read the letter a third time. Then she fell back against the pillows, letting the piece of paper flutter to the bedspread. Through the opened window she could hear the roll of waves and distant cries of seabirds. She stared vacantly at the wall opposite the bed where her eyes projected still shots of the letter. Then she rose from the bed like a sleepwalker and went to the window.

The eastern view from the house was one Leigh had looked upon most of her growing-up years. The village and Silver Lake Harbor stretched to the south, while the band of the highway separating the sandy yard of tufted sea grasses from the surf telescoped north, up the island and beyond. The usual view, she thought. Yet nothing seemed usual at all. Colors shrieked and sounds were muted. Leigh ran her tongue over her lips. Her mouth was coated with a dry metallic film.

Every nerve and muscle in her body clamored for action, but her mind was frozen. She wanted her mother, her father. She wanted answers to the questions booming in her head. *Why didn't you tell me? Why did you keep this letter from me? Why? Why?*

She wanted a drink. She fumbled her way downstairs and into the kitchen, finding the refrigerator, cold beer and the kitchen screen door all on automatic pilot. Frosty can in hand, Leigh managed to cross the road to the beach without making physical contact with any object or person and sank onto the first grassy knoll she reached. Then she drank a third of the can in one go and paused to catch her breath, rolling the can across her hot forehead.

The surf broke and crashed before her, its monotonous consistency somehow reassuring. The ocean breeze carried with it the tangy stench of dried eel grass and, somewhere on the beach, a rotting fish. Leigh's heart slowed. She finished the beer, savoring its yeasty coolness, and slowly let the outside world in.

The questions that had been pounding inside seconds ago ebbed to a faint beat. Leigh shook her head. If only there was someone who knew the answers. Her parents had always been so candid and open about the circumstances of her adoption. The letter had arrived in the spring of 1980. *I'd have been fourteen, turning fifteen that July.*

Old enough to make a decision about contacting her birth mother. She remembered a conversation with Jen after watching a talk-show reunion of birth parents and their adopted children. *Aren't you even curious?* Jen had asked. But Leigh had never had the questions that haunted other adoptees. Pete and Ellen Randall had been her parents in every sense of the word and her life a secure and peaceful passage.

Until graduation night, anyway.

The thought made her release the handful of sand she'd been trickling through her fingers and reach for the empty beer can. She stood up and turned around to face the house across the road. For seventeen years the frame house perched on wooden pilings had been a haven of love and tranquillity. A safe place in a world of unsafe places. Memories oozed between its weathered slats. She knew she could summon an event, a moment or even a laugh or tear for every inch of every room.

Leigh brushed the sand from the back of her shorts and crossed the road. From the end of her drive she spotted a cyclist weaving up the slight incline from the village. She squinted, sensing a familiarity about the person. Grandpa Sam!

The bicycle, two full shopping bags in its carrier, wobbled to a stop a few feet away from her, as if Sam had expended all his energy just cresting the small rise from the village. Leigh walked over to him.

"I can't believe you're out riding a bicycle in the hottest part of the day. Sam Logan, have your senses left you, as my mother used to say?"

Sam's red face bobbed up and down. He crossed his arms over the handlebars and leaned into them, gasping for air.

"Stay there," Leigh ordered. "I'm getting my car keys to drive you the rest of the way."

Sam held up a palm. "No…wait…minute…"

Leigh hesitated. He didn't look well. His flushed face was now edged in a chalky pallor.

"Water. Tha's all I need," he finally managed.

Leigh jogged up the drive and into the house. Seconds later she was back, carrying a plastic tumbler of water and her car keys. She handed Sam the water without a word, then urged him off the bicycle and wheeled it up the drive to her car. She stowed the bike in her trunk, along with the bags, noting how heavy they were and realizing what effort they must have cost him in his ride up from the village, especially in the heat. Her thought was confirmed when she saw how unsteady his gait was as he made his way to the car.

Once they were in the car, with the air-conditioning blasting, Leigh said, "Don't tell me you always shop that way. Can't Spencer drive you into town?"

"He usually does, Leigh, but he's been so busy lately I didn't have the heart to ask. Today he was taking out an important client. Spence needs the money, you know. It's a long winter ahead of us."

Too true, Leigh thought, recalling the erratic seasonal flow of cash into the Randall home when Pete was still a commercial fisherman. "Sam—" she turned toward the old man, softening her voice "—you know, I'm sure you could afford the taxi ride back and forth."

His brow knotted slightly, then eased into an expression of resignation. "To be sure I can, but there's no telephone handy. And I won't have one at my age," he insisted.

Leigh shook her head, frustrated. "But even one way, Sam. The hardest part's the ride home."

Sam pressed his lips together and nodded. "Yes, yes, I know. It's difficult to explain. I guess I'm a foolish stubborn old coot. No, don't argue. I know my faults as well as anyone. The good Lord gave me eyes to see and I use them on myself quite a lot—especially now in my old age. Amazing how clear things become the older you get. Ah, well—" he shook his head and gave a tired smile "—that's life for you. Always got one more trick up its sleeve just when you think you've figured it all out."

Leigh pulled the car onto the shoulder at the sandy path leading to Sam's. She knew better than to tackle the path in her car, having once marooned her father's Buick in the soft sand.

"Here, let me get your bike and groceries out of the trunk first." Leigh swung open her door and jumped out. Once she'd leaned the bike against Sam's signpost with its dangling salt-sprayed board that read simply Logan, she retrieved the groceries and carried them down the path to Sam's cottage.

"I can take those," Sam protested, but his exit from the car was slow, and by the time he reached his porch Leigh had deposited the bags inside on the living room table that served as eating place, library and worktable. Sam's housekeeping skills, never laudable, had deteriorated.

From the dirty cups and dishes lying about, scattered newspapers and bits and pieces of tools, Leigh figured that Sam had been living alone too long. When he pushed open the screen door, he gave a halfhearted gesture with his free hand.

"Don't do much entertainin' these days," he said, breaking into a wheezing cackle that ended in a coughing fit. Leigh led him to a chair and got a glass of water from the kitchen.

While he sipped the water, she surveyed the room again, noticing the array of photographs mounted on the walls. They began in one section of wall near his bookshelf, with dog-eared black-and-white photos of Sam and his long-deceased wife—young parents each with a child in arms. Then an assortment of Sam and his fishing buddies standing in front of all the various boats Sam had piloted in Pamlico Sound and the Atlantic. There were familiar faces, but none Leigh could fix a name to.

She paused in front of one photograph—a young Sam with his arm around another man, both holding pipes and wearing squall gear. Nets hung heavy with fish behind them on the bow of a boat—the *Heron,* Leigh could just make out. Pride from a day's fishing glowed in their faces.

"This one here—the other guy looks like my grandfather."

"Why, sure it is! Your Pa's daddy and I were good friends. Mind, he was older'n me, but we fished together a good ten years before his arthritis got to him."

Leigh peered more closely. The resemblance between

her father and grandfather was strong. She wondered if her grandparents on her mother's side looked like Ellen. That set of grandparents had died when Leigh was still an infant, and she'd only seen a few photographs. Pete Randall's parents—native Ocracokers—had passed away when Leigh was in elementary school, but she could still summon memories of them. When she was home, she'd go through her own family photos more diligently.

She inched along the wall, examining photographs of Jen's parents. They were an eccentric couple for Ocracoke, she thought, even in the late 1960s. With their bell-bottom jeans, Nehru shirts and love beads they looked as though they'd been airlifted directly from Haight-Ashbury. Leigh remembered Jen's whispered story during one sleepover.

Her mother had run away from the boring life on Ocracoke and traveled across the country. She'd met Jen's father and had a whirlwind courtship, resulting in Jen and a sudden return to Ocracoke when funds ran out. Jen always said her father had tried to make a go of the local life, but his romantic soul had trouble adapting to a fishing village. Then, two short years after Jen's birth, both parents had been lost at sea in an unexpected storm.

When she reached a big section of photographs of Jen growing up, Leigh stopped. Sam Logan's love for his granddaughter came through in every shot. It was ironic, Leigh thought, that the tragedy that took a daughter from him also gave him Jen. For she doubted that Jen's parents, had they lived, would have spent the rest of their lives in Ocracoke.

The collection of snapshots of Jen and Leigh were familiar. She and Jen had framed or stuck most of them on the wall themselves, tacking masking tape behind each one and arranging them artistically on the painted barn board. Leigh's eyes flicked past them, settling on a bunch at the door she'd never seen before. Snaps of Jen and Spencer just after they'd eloped, judging by their clothes. They must have asked someone to photograph them, and there they were, posing awkwardly in front of Spencer's father's truck outside a motel.

Leigh waited for the quick stab of pain she expected. Instead, she felt a flash of pity for the two teenagers. They looked so eager, so happy. Three years, she thought. Three years later it was all over. She sighed, moving on. By the door frame were a few photos of a blond baby.

"Jamie?" she asked, looking over at Sam. He was still clutching the empty glass and staring vacantly out the window.

"Hmm?" He roused himself to turn toward her. She was truly alarmed by what she saw. His face was gray and slick with sweat.

"Sam!" she cried, "let me take you to a doctor. Right now. Please!"

He shook his head, then pointed an index finger to a chest of drawers opposite the table. "Top drawer. Bottle of pills."

Leigh yanked open the drawer and rummaged through an assortment of greeting cards, buttons, ends of candles and miscellaneous junk. She found a plastic vial of small white pills. Nitroglycerine. She handed him one, which he slipped under his tongue. He'd done this before, she realized. How often?

In a few moments some color returned to his face. "At least let me help you to bed," she said.

The old man didn't argue. Leigh led him to the room behind the kitchen. Sam's bedroom hadn't changed since she and Jen used to bounce on his brass bed. Same old chenille bedspread, too. She pulled it down and tucked Sam in.

"I've made a casserole for dinner, Sam, and I'll go get some for you. Save you the trouble of making a meal. I'll be back in fifteen minutes."

"It's okay," he murmured. "Pills make me drowsy. I'll

sleep now, then get some dinner later. Thanks, Leigh. Go ahead.'' He dismissed her with a feeble wiggling of his fingers.

"I'll be back," she said, closing the door behind her. Then she was outside, running to the car and speeding down the highway. She passed her house, feeling a twinge of guilt about her lie to Sam, but knowing he'd have argued about her fetching Spencer. Her car scattered gravel all the way into Ocracoke village. She wasn't certain where Spencer's fishing-charter office was, but knew the village was small enough to locate it on her own. Two circuits around the Silver Lake Harbor road and she spotted his red pickup outside a squat box-shaped building sided with white aluminum. The sign above the eaves trough read McKay-Cowan Charters. About as eloquent as Sam's sign, she thought.

Leigh parked next to the pickup and pushed open the white screen door. Spencer was sitting behind a desk, feet propped on its Formica top and a sweating can of beer in one hand. Another man sat in a chair opposite and next to the door. Leigh barely glanced at him, heading straight for Spence.

"It's Sam!" she blurted.

He shot to his feet, beer slopping out the top of the can and beading across the desktop. "What? Where is he? What happened?" He grabbed her arm with his free hand.

Leigh stumbled backward. "Careful," she protested, dabbing at the drops of beer on her clothes.

Spencer plunked the can down on the desk and wiped the corner of his mouth with his forearm. "Sorry, you scared the dickens out of me. What's the matter?"

"I met Sam riding his bicycle up from the village. He was carrying two bags of groceries. I think he'd have passed out if I hadn't driven him home." She couldn't keep the accusation out of her voice.

He swore. "Leigh, believe me, I've told him many times

to call me when he wants to go shopping. I've taken him a lot this past year and I will anytime.''

"He said you were out on an important charter." Leigh glanced at the man sitting behind her, then looked pointedly at the cans of beer.

Spencer flushed slightly. "Yeah, well, we've been out all day and now we're back—cooling down."

The glint in his eyes warned Leigh to lay off. She stared down at the floor while the other man got to his feet and mumbled a quick goodbye. Spencer brushed past her to walk his customer to the door. There was a snatch of conversation about money and dates and then the door slammed shut. Leigh didn't turn around.

After a moment Spencer said, "Look, thanks for coming to tell me about Sam. I'm guessing that since you didn't go immediately to a doctor, he must be okay."

She spun around. He stood in front of the door, his thumbs hooked in the pockets of his jeans. The damp splotches in his white T-shirt indicated a hard day's work—or a lot of beer, she thought meanly. The T-shirt strained against biceps earned working out on the boat and stretched across a chest that Leigh had stroked many times one passionate summer. The hard nubs of his nipples poked through the thin cotton fabric. Leigh looked away when she spoke.

"He took a nitroglycerine tablet and I helped him lie down. He was getting his color back by the time I left, but he should be seen by a doctor—soon. Did you know he had a heart condition?"

Spence walked over to his desk, opened a drawer and pulled out a set of keys. "I knew he had a prescription for nitro because I was with him when he had it filled. Back in February. Said he'd had some chest pains—angina— and his doctor warned him to take it easy and take the nitro whenever he needed it."

"I think he's been needing it a lot."

"What do you mean?"

"The date on this prescription was for May, so presumably he's had it refilled who knows how many times."

"Damn. If only the old guy wasn't so private, not to mention stubborn. I've been sending Jamie to see him at least every other day, but I can't get him to move in with us. You've seen his place."

"Yes."

"Well—" Spence flipped the set of keys into his palm "— guess I'd better go check on him."

"I can do that. I mean, I told him I'd bring him back some dinner."

Spence paused in the doorway and grinned. "Yeah? Got a big pot of something on the stove, have you?"

It was her turn to color. His question was a teasing reference to their dating days when Leigh's knowledge of food and cooking had been restricted to opening a can.

Then he gestured toward the door. "Come on. As it happens, I've a pot of chowder on the stove at my place. You follow me. We'll take dinner to Sam together." He pushed open the door and headed for his truck, a sheepish Leigh in tow.

CHAPTER SIX

THE CLOCK IN LEIGH'S CAR read 5:00 p.m. by the time Spencer's pickup turned onto North Pond Drive, a tiny enclave on the shore of Pamlico Sound.

Why am I surprised? He always loved the marshes. Why wouldn't he want to live near them?

Spencer McKay had grown up in a fishing shack near the harbor. Leigh doubted the place was still standing; it had made Sam's ramshackle cottage seem fashionably quaint.

The blue frame bungalow he lived in now was sturdy and well maintained. Recognizing it as an older island place, Leigh bet that Spencer had devoted time and work into its transformation. White-painted rocks edged the flagstone walkway to the porch. A weather vane rotated lazily from the rooftop cupola. No rooster vane for Spence, she observed, smiling at the green-tinted copper heron.

On each side of the walkway he'd planted a strip of annuals and some succulents. Leigh didn't know their names, but recognized them as native to the island. He parked the truck in front of a three-sided breezeway that held a collection of tools and gardening equipment. When Leigh passed the opened side, she noticed everything hung neatly on hooks. Another surprise. Had he always been such a neat freak?

The staircase and lattice barrier around the foundation of the bungalow were painted white to match the eaves trough and window trim. Leigh followed Spencer up the wooden stairs, taking in the thermal picture window fronting the cottage and the handcrafted wooden screen door. Spencer had either paid top dollar for that, she figured, or done the work himself.

He turned when he reached the door and said, "I asked Jamie to tidy the place up when he got home from school, but I can't guarantee anything. You know teenagers."

Leigh raised her eyebrows. "I don't know if I do anymore," adding in a lower tone, "or if I ever did."

He seemed about to say something but changed his mind, pushing open the door with his right hand and allowing Leigh to precede him inside.

Well, either Jamie's done his homework or the place was looking pretty good to start with.

Pine floors gleamed in the late-afternoon sunlight. A partitioned kitchen nook was off to one side of the main room, and on the other side was a short hall that probably led to bedrooms. Leigh's gaze swept from the sliding glass doors opening to a deck facing Pamlico Sound and the marshland fringing it back to the heart of the room—a black woodstove nestled in an alcove of ceramic tiles depicting various seascapes and seabirds. A plump sofa and matching armchair covered in a blue-and-white-striped canvas fabric were arranged in front of both the stove and the view. There were a few pieces of pine furniture, some of which looked like antiques. Braided throw rugs and cushions splashed the room with bold color, but the real focal point, once the view had been absorbed, were the carved wooden birds perched on bookshelves, tabletops and even suspended from the ceiling.

Leigh identified egrets, herons, terns and sandpipers. A plump Canada goose squatted on the ledge of the window fronting North Pond Drive, and she was certain the great blue heron looming in a far corner was life-size. She stood in the center of the room and pivoted slowly, taking in the whole array, then turned to where Spencer stood just inside the door.

"Where did you get these?" she breathed.

He smiled. "Like them?"

"They're...amazing. I mean, upstate these are all the rage, but I've never seen such a collection of really good ones. Where did you get them?" she asked again.

Spence felt his face grow warm. It had been a long time since he'd heard that note of awe in Leigh Randall's voice. He couldn't even recall if he'd ever been the recipient of it. Suddenly he felt uncomfortable. "I did them," he mumbled, heading off to the kitchen to look for Jamie.

When he returned seconds later, she was still in the middle of the living room. "Well, I don't know where Jamie is, but the chowder's all ready," he announced.

"*You* did them?"

Spence didn't know whether to laugh or be insulted by the incredulity in the question. But then he decided that annoyance would be unfair—after all, fifteen years ago he'd never have guessed he had a talent for carving birds, either. Besides, he didn't want to spoil the apparent truce that had occurred since their arrival at his home.

And be honest with yourself, McKay. You could have taken Sam some dinner all on your own, but you didn't want to let the opportunity to spend time with Leigh slip by you.

So he shrugged, assuming a modest expression he hoped looked sincere.

"How and when did you get into carving? I mean, you always were good at art in school, but this—" Leigh stopped, dropped her hand.

"To be honest I can't remember when I started. I saw some carvings in a tourist shop up on Hatteras and decided I could do just as well. It might have been ten years ago. I had a lot of time on my hands in those days."

His face darkened. Leigh realized he was referring to

the period after Jen and Jamie had left him. She had a flash of Spencer sitting by himself night after night, and she didn't like the sensation the image produced.

"Anyway," he went on, breaking the silence, "why don't you have a seat while I pack up the chowder? Then we'll go see Sam. But before we do that I'll phone the clinic and see if someone can drive out to check on him. His specialist is on the mainland, but there's a local doctor who's been treating him for general things the past few years. Make yourself at home." He gestured toward the sofa where Leigh reluctantly sat.

She felt more inclined to look around the room, but didn't want to appear nosy. When Spence left she scanned the shelves next to her, noticing an eclectic library of books and magazines. She couldn't connect the Spencer she'd known with the possessions she saw around her. *What did you expect? Hard-rock posters on the walls, empty pizza boxes and back issues of* Rolling Stone? *The detritus of the early-eighties teen?*

Fifteen years. Leigh sighed, feeling the weight of every year land solidly on her shoulders. She had to admit she probably didn't know Spencer any better now than if they'd never met. Meeting him again was like meeting him for the first time. Either he had changed enormously, or she'd never really known him at all. The realization filled her with sadness. *I devoted two years of my life—more— to loving someone, and for what? Not insight, that's obvious.*

The front door swung open and Jamie ambled in, snapping his fingers to the tune coming from the headset he wore. When he saw Leigh, he did a double take, freezing his one-man rap drill and slowly removing the earphones. The expression on his face abruptly switched from surprise to suspicion.

"'Lo," he grunted.

"Hi, Jamie. Your dad's in the kitchen on the phone—I

think.'' No response was offered, so she added, ''We're, uh, just picking up some food to take to your grandfather.''

Jamie's eyes narrowed. ''Somethin' wrong with Grandpa Sam?''

She hesitated. How much would Spence want him to know? Not wanting to alarm him, she said, ''He's not feeling well. Too much heat and exertion today, I think. He's okay, but we're going to take him dinner and have a doctor see him.''

The boy slowly nodded his head, but there was still a question on his face. Obviously he was wondering why she was there.

''I happened to see Sam riding home from the village, so I gave him a lift. Then called your dad.'' She lapsed into silence, feeling foolish once again. Was there something in the McKay genes that made her babble?

''Where've you been?'' Spencer stood in the doorway to the kitchen.

Jamie met his father's frown with a darker one of his own. ''With the gang. Why? It's just after five.''

''I asked you to clean up.''

''I *did*.''

His voice cracked with indignance. Leigh hid a smile, feigning interest in a magazine on the coffee table.

There was a slight pause, then Spence muttered, ''Okay, so where did you go after?''

''C'mon, what *is* this? It isn't time for dinner yet. What's the big deal?''

''Jamie, there's no big deal. The point is, I have to go out right away, and because you didn't leave a note, I couldn't tell you my plans.''

''So write a note *yourself*.''

Leigh didn't dare look up from the magazine. She bit down on her lower lip. *Whoa,* she thought. *Let's see what Daddy Spence does with that.*

The silence was longer this time and thick enough to cut.

"Your grandfather's not feeling well. Leigh—Miss Randall, I mean—you've met, right?"

Leigh met Spencer's eyes. There was a mix of anger and bewilderment in them. She could see he was disconcerted by Jamie's attitude and felt a rush of sympathy for him. Until she thought of the seventeen-year-old Spencer and grinned.

"Yes, we have. Jamie came for dinner the other night with Sam. And, please—" this to Jamie "—it's Leigh."

"Dinner the other night?" Puzzled, Spence looked from Leigh to Jamie, who nodded. "Oh, when I went to Charlotte. I see." A slight pause, then, "Anyway, Sam's doctor is taking a run out to see him now. I want you to spend the night with him, Jamie— No, hear me out. I don't want him left alone until we're sure he's okay, and I've got a charter first thing in the morning."

Jamie's frown deepened. A rosy flush crept up his neck. "I've made plans to go to Hatteras with the guys."

Spencer walked closer to Jamie. He lowered his voice to a dead-serious decibel level. "One, we haven't discussed any social engagements. Two, I thought we'd agreed that Friday nights would be homework nights. And three, you have a choice—eat here on your own and meet us at Sam's about nine-thirty, or come with us now."

Leigh busied herself with the magazine again. She thought she heard Jamie mutter a curse, but wasn't sure. Spencer headed back into the kitchen and returned seconds later.

"Ready?" he asked.

She looked up and saw him holding a big stainless-steel pot with a pair of oven mitts.

"Well?" he directed this to Jamie, still slouching by the door.

"I'm not hungry yet," he said. "Save me some. I'll get it later at Grandpa's."

Spencer nodded grimly and headed for the door. Leigh jumped up and followed him, pausing only long enough in front of Jamie to say goodbye. When they were standing beside the pickup, Spencer said, "Six months ago he wouldn't have given in."

"He cares a lot about Sam," Leigh said.

"That's what I was counting on." He leaned over and propped the pot into the storage box in the back of the pickup. Then he turned to Leigh. The jaw-clenching lines in his face had eased a bit, she noticed.

"Do you want to come with me now and pick up your car later, or meet me at Sam's?"

"What's number three?"

He laughed. "Thanks, I needed that. Jeez, I don't know…" He wiped the end of his nose with the back of his hand.

Leigh realized then how the incident had upset him. He'd seemed so under control, so tight. It was a character trait she clearly remembered. But the Spencer standing before her now was different, unafraid to show some vulnerability. She had a strong urge to wrap her arms around him. Instead, she smiled and said, "I'll pick up the car later. Whenever."

He nodded. "Whenever. Good." He held open the door for her and then went around and climbed in himself. Reversing and shifting into drive, he headed for the highway.

SPENCER CLOSED the screen door behind the doctor. He stood with his back to Leigh, staring into the night. Finally he turned around. His eyes met hers, then flickered off toward Sam's room. He slapped his palms against his thighs. "Well," he began, and stopped, apparently at a loss for words.

The worry in his face distracted Leigh from the ache in

her own heart. She couldn't help thinking that if they were lovers, they'd be in each other's arms. If they were friends, there'd at least be a reassuring hug.

Spencer forked his right hand through his hair, brought it down over his face, rubbing away the strain of the past hour. He wandered aimlessly about the room, picking up and examining the knickknacks Sam had been collecting for years. He sensed Leigh watching him, waiting for him to speak, but the swelling in his throat was still there. The room was cluttered with so much junk, he thought. Yet old Sam wouldn't part with a single bit of it. Holding on to the things in life he knew he could count on, since so many people had let him down.

Spencer swore under his breath. If only— What? *This is about Sam, not you, buddy.* But he yielded to the thought, anyway. If only life could be replayed. *Yeah, and then what? Do you honestly believe you'd be any smarter the second time around?* He glanced at Leigh out of the corner of his eye. *About one thing, anyway. For sure, about one thing.*

"Look," he finally said, spinning around from the bookshelf to face Leigh. "Let's get some dinner and take it out on the porch. There's enough of a breeze to chase the bugs away."

"Yes. I'm starving."

He walked toward the kitchen. "If we're lucky, there may even be a bottle of wine somewhere." He disappeared, carrying back with him a tray of steaming chowder, two tumblers and a dusty bottle of wine. "I think I gave this to Sam last Christmas. He won't drink alone— an admirable trait, I must say, and one I can't claim myself."

"Nor I," Leigh said. "Here, let me help. That tray doesn't look very reliable." She picked up the bottle, glasses and corkscrew and followed Spencer out onto the porch.

The night sky was breathtaking. The air was so crisp the stars looked as though someone had flung gold dust onto a lustrous mica floor. The dim glow of a lamp inside the cottage provided enough illumination to locate chairs and table, but not enough to diminish the effect.

Still clutching bottle and glasses, Leigh sank into a wicker chair. "It's so unbelievably beautiful." She inhaled deeply. "I haven't breathed such clean air since the last time I was on Ocracoke. Back home the pervading everyday smell is exhaust fumes." She lowered the bottle to the floor and proceeded to uncork it.

"I'm impressed," Spence said. "That corkscrew is as old as Sam, I think."

Leigh laughed. "Well, I've had lots of practice. Talk about drinking alone."

"Oh?"

She shook her head and laughed. "Oh, dear. I realize what that sounded like. I'm not enough of a drinker to make that a problem."

"But you're often alone?"

A long pause. "I guess you could say I'm sometimes alone—by choice," she added. Then she changed the subject. "So, you seemed shocked by what the doctor had to say."

The question prompted a quick return of the pall that had settled over him since arriving at the cottage. Sam had been awake but refused dinner. He drank some apple juice, and by the time Spencer had helped him into his pajamas, the doctor had arrived.

"Yes, I guess I was. I had no idea Sam's heart condition was so serious. He'd always made light of it. Looking back, I can see things now I should have seen at the time. If only I hadn't been so damn occupied with my own affairs."

"You can't blame yourself. We all know how private Sam is about things that worry him. The only people I ever remember getting a rise out of him were Mrs. Waverly and the government.''

"Not to mention the National Park Service."

"Yes, I'd forgotten about that. Are they still trying to get this bit of land?"

"I don't know what round we're in with the latest legal paperwork. Between the Park Service and Mrs. Waverly, Sam's had more stress than an eighty-year-old guy should have."

"It'll be the end of an era if they win the battle."

"Well, they control all the rest of the beaches on the Outer Banks. Think of what it might have been like if the National Park Service hadn't taken them over."

Visions of condos and luxury resorts piled against one another up the coast came to mind. "You're right. It is a horrible thought. Ocracoke is already more developed than I think the island can handle."

"Maybe if you stick around, you could go to an island meeting sometime. See what the new issues are."

It was a subtle reminder, Leigh thought, that her long absence had left her out of the picture. "Well, I suppose someone who'll be leaving soon shouldn't have much input into what the future holds for Ocracoke."

"Yeah," was all he said after a moment's silence. Then, "Anyway, dig into your chowder while it's still hot."

Leigh was grateful for the darkness that cloaked her face. The conversation had struck out on a course she hadn't liked at all. But the soup was delicious, thick with vegetables, tomatoes and chunks of assorted fresh seafood.

"It's wonderful," she murmured. "What seasonings did you use?"

"Some parsley, fresh dill, a sprinkle of oregano and a dash of chili flakes. That's about it."

"Do you like to cook?"

"Yeah, as a matter of fact I do. I guess that surprises you."

"It's been a day of surprises."

He sighed. "That's for sure."

"What will you do about Sam?"

Spence set his empty bowl down on the table between them and reached for his tumbler of wine. "Hopefully persuade him to move in with Jamie and me. Talk to his specialist about this surgery thing."

"The doctor said surgery was a big risk."

"I know, but what else is there? Can you picture Sam as an invalid? Dependent on others for everything?"

"He'd hate it," she agreed. "What's the prognosis if he doesn't have surgery?"

"You heard most of it. 'Not good' is the impression I got out of all the medical mumbo jumbo."

Leigh smiled. He sounded just like her father. "But as the doctor said, he's eighty years old," she reminded him.

"I hate that, you know? Doctors always spout that kind of sugarcoated message, as if age has anything to do with dying. Death comes in many forms to all of us at anytime. Period."

His vehemence startled her. "I didn't mean to sound like a doomsayer. It's just that we have to be prepared. To accept the inevitable."

Spencer reached for the wine and refilled his glass. The bottle hovered over Leigh's glass, but she covered the top with her hand. "You know, Leigh, hearing you say that disappoints me. It really does. You quote those clichés about dying and death when you yourself..." He hesitated.

"What? Should be an expert at it? At dealing with it, like my parents, or causing it? Like—"

"No," he interrupted quickly. "I don't mean that. Let me finish. You heard all the platitudes when you and your mother had to deal with Pete—first the home care, then the nursing home in Raleigh. Then last year you had your mother to nurse and comfort. God knows how you had the strength to go through it all again. I respect and admire you for that, Leigh. I was just trying to say that age has nothing to do with it. In Sam's eyes he loses as much now as if he'd been given this same message at forty or fifty. In his eyes he's still a viable man. Slower perhaps, more forgetful, but still potent.'' Spencer's voice dropped on the last word. After a pause he whispered, ''He's got to go on believing that. He's got to have a reason for getting up in the morning.''

Leigh was moved by his speech. Not only because it was the longest statement he'd ever made to her, but because he said it with such feeling. *A day of surprises, indeed. And as much as I hate to admit it, he's absolutely right.* She put down her bowl and placed a hand on his arm.

''I agree, Spencer.'' She waited, unable to continue without giving in to the emotion that overwhelmed her. ''If there's anything I can do in the short time I'm here to help convince Sam to move in with you, let me know. Right now I guess I should be going home. My open house is tomorrow afternoon, and I still have a stack of boxes to take out to the porch and ferry to the nearest recycling bin.''

''Wait!'' He stood up with her, holding on to the hand on his forearm. ''Jamie should be here any second—he'd better be!—and I'll drive you back to your car.''

''Maybe I should just go straight home, get the car late tomorrow or the next day. I've got a lot to do for tomorrow and I left right in the middle of it.'' Literally, she thought, picturing the adoption-agency letter lying on the bed. The impact of everything that had happened that day settled over her. ''I'm so tired. I think I just need to get some sleep.''

Something in her voice distracted Spence from wondering where the heck Jamie had gotten to. In the splash of light from inside he could see circles under her eyes and the droop of her mouth.

"It's been an emotional evening for all of us," he said. "Just give Jamie another five minutes and I'll have you home in no time."

She murmured something he couldn't hear, then sagged back in the chair. Spence got up, restless, and paced back and forth. He noticed how the logo on Leigh's T-shirt glowed in the dark, making him think of the fluorescent stars Jamie used to have on his bedroom ceiling when he was a toddler. The reminder conjured up an image of Jen, and he pushed it quickly aside.

He looked down at Leigh, curled up in the chair like a little girl. There was a time when she used to curl up on his lap like that. They'd watch the late show on television, snuggling in Pete Randall's old vinyl recliner. On summer nights their skin would stick to the material, making sucking noises as they pulled away. Then they'd erupt into giggling, afraid the noise would attract a parent's attention and, at the same time, unable to stop.

"Are you okay?" Spencer hunkered down in front of her. He was so close he could smell the lingering fragrance of Sam's soap from Leigh's wash before dinner. A strand of hair dangled in the center of her forehead, and he cautiously reached out to smooth it back. When she didn't object, he stroked her forearm with his index finger, whorling the fine dark hairs around and around. She sat so still in the chair he thought she'd fallen asleep—until she emitted a low sound of satisfaction.

He dropped his other fingers onto her skin, tracking invisible lines from the inside of her elbow to her wrist. He paused, waiting for her to sit up and tell him to stop. But her head lolled against the back of her chair and she closed her eyes. Her skin was like alabaster in the moonlight. A tiny pulse flicked a shadowy indentation at the base of her neck.

Spencer placed her upturned hand in his. He leaned over and kissed the hollow scoop of her palm. God, it was all coming back. The cool smoothness of her skin, the taste and scents he remembered so well. He felt a throbbing ache deep inside. How many times had he fantasized about this? Dreamed about what it would be like to place his lips on Leigh Randall again....

He wanted to run his tongue up and down the inside of her arm to see if she still moaned with pleasure. To reach over and touch that pulse between her collarbone with his mouth, then continue his way up her neck to that spot behind her ear that used to make her shriek and beg for more at the same time.

His lips moved slowly out of the hollow up to the inside of her wrist. Bolder now, he traced a line from wrist to the crook of her elbow, flicking his tongue into the dimpled space until the throbbing in his groin was more than he could bear. He raised his lips from her elbow and reached out his arms to pull her to him.

"Dad? Is that you up there?"

Trembling, Spencer leaned onto the porch railing to get himself upright. Leigh swung her legs to the floor and stared up at him, her black eyes big and confused.

"Dad?"

"Yeah, Jamie. We're up on the porch."

"What are you doing? It looked like you were crawling around."

"I dropped my hair clip," Leigh called out.

Jamie was climbing the stairs, his heavy basketball sneakers vibrating the entire porch. "Find it?" he asked when he reached the top.

Leigh couldn't see his face, but she heard the skepticism in his voice. "Yes, he did," she said, and reached back to tie her hair into a ponytail.

"How's Grandpa?"

"Sleeping," Spencer said. "Don't worry about him for tonight. The doctor said he was stabilized and should just get as much rest as he can. I was going to drive Leigh home. Want me to come back and check on things afterward?''

There was a slight pause. Leigh felt rather than saw Jamie look from her to Spencer. "Sure, if it's not too late. Any chowder left?"

"Plenty. Could you store the rest in the fridge for tomorrow? Sam didn't eat at all."

"No problem."

Another pause, then Spencer murmured, "Okay, I'll take you home, then, Leigh. All set?"

"Sure. Night, Jamie," and she followed Spencer down the stairs.

In the car Leigh was struck by a giggling fit. "You know," she said, turning to Spencer, "I couldn't help thinking about the time my dad came out to the truck just when you'd, well, you know..."

He couldn't remember, but he could imagine. Their first sexual explorations had taken place in his dad's pickup in front of her parents' house.

"I did kinda feel like I was eighteen again," he said.

Wondering what might have happened had Jamie not appeared at that precise moment jolted Leigh back to earth. She could still feel the warm rush flowing through her, the tingling of her skin as Spencer's lips had moved up her arm. So close, she realized. She averted her face, staring out the opened window toward the lights of Sam's cottage.

"It's late," she whispered, knowing she was ending a moment that should never have begun.

He drove in silence, taking his cue from her. She felt disappointment, yet relief. When the sweep of his headlights struck her front veranda, he exclaimed, "Is all of that for the garbage?"

"Recycling, if I can. I guess it'll be okay on the porch for now."

"I can bring the truck by when my charter's finished

tomorrow. Then we can pick up your car, and both of us can take a load over to Hatteras.''

''I don't want to interfere with your charter.''

''Nah, the guy said he gets seasick. My bet is he won't make it to lunch.''

He braked the truck and shifted into park.

''Thanks for dinner, Spence. The chowder was wonderful.'' She put her hand on the door handle and pulled.

''I...I hope we can do it again.''

Leigh hesitated midway, one foot on the drive and the other on the running board. *Do what again?* she wondered. *The dinner or the "dessert" they'd had afterward, on Sam's porch?* ''Maybe,'' she said vaguely. ''I guess it depends how fast I sell the house.''

His eyes shifted from her face to the dashboard. She felt a twinge of remorse at the disappointment she'd seen in them. *Best to level with him now, while he's not touching you.*

She moved her other foot down off the running board. ''Thanks again, Spence. I'll see you tomorrow and perhaps then we can talk about...about Sam.''

He continued to stare morosely out the windshield. ''Yeah, sure, okay.''

She closed the door. ''Bye,'' she said, and started up the drive.

Suddenly he poked his head out his window. ''Say, how did you manage that trick with the hair clip?''

Leigh turned around. ''I had it in the pocket of my shorts. Sneaking it out was easy in the dark.''

He gave a throaty chuckle. ''I have to hand it to you, Randall. You always were resourceful.''

''Yep. That's me. Good old resourceful Randall. Night, Spencer.'' Grinning, she walked up the veranda steps, feeling his eyes on her the whole way.

CHAPTER SEVEN

THE LIGHT IN THE HOUSE went out. Time to go. The woman turned on the ignition, and soft strains of classical music drifted from the speaker. Then she rolled up the windows, switched on the air-conditioning and shifted the car into drive. She was glad she'd left as soon as she'd seen the newspaper, driving nonstop and eating takeout in the car. The trip had allowed her that much more time to think, devise a plan. It wouldn't do to go barging in. These things had to be handled delicately and diplomatically. She'd learned that lesson long ago.

She took one last look at the house and aimed the car north on the highway toward the ferry dock. One more night in Hatteras should do. Give her enough time to get everything in place. And then... She smiled. *Soon I'll be with my baby.*

"MS. RANDALL?"

The man standing on the other side of the screen door held a paper bag in one hand and a briefcase in the other. His smile was far too cheerful, Leigh thought, for eight o'clock Saturday morning.

"I thought the open house was this afternoon."

He frowned. "Oh, dear. Sorry, but the agent you arranged this with—Patsy—couldn't make it. She told me ten. Is that going to be a problem?"

"Not if you don't mind helping me vacuum the place."

The smile wobbled. Uncertain whether or not she was putting him on?

Leigh relented. "Just kidding. Come in."

He gestured with his head to the lawn behind him. "I've just put up the For Sale sign, with the Open House banner."

She peered over his head to see a white-and-red sign tilted at a rakish angle. *Reality strikes again.* She held the door while he slipped past. "Seriously," she went on, "I've still got some last-minute moving around."

"Oh?"

She figured Patsy was going to pay big time. "Just some boxes upstairs to come down to the porch. Unless you don't mind people tripping over them."

"Oh, good gracious! That won't do. Of course I'll give you a hand."

Or two, Leigh thought, wondering when his pristine white hands had last done anything more strenuous than lift a wineglass.

He proffered the paper bag. "I brought some breakfast," he offered smugly.

Leigh felt herself softening. *Everyone has a price. Mine is obviously a cup of coffee.* "Muffins?" she asked.

"Danish. Made this morning right in Hatteras."

Ah, maybe I'll move the cartons myself. "Aren't you thoughtful! Well Mr....?"

"Brown. Evan."

"Evan, you just made my morning." She flashed a warm smile. "Come on into the kitchen."

"Usually we vet the house before we list it for an open house," Evan said, following her down the hall.

"Oh, Patsy wanted to!" Leigh asserted, reluctant to get the other agent into further trouble. "But it was a question of time. I only have another week."

He frowned. "Another week? Gee, I doubt we'll sell this place that quickly. It's not the best time, you see. Most

people have already committed to summer rentals or pur-
chases by now.''

"I know. Patsy warned me about that. She also said I
could get someone here to act as sort of a proxy for me.
To sign back any offers on my behalf.''

"True, we can do that. But it seems to take more time
that way—all the back-and-forth business, more paperwork, you know.''

Leigh shrugged. "I may not have a choice.'' She stared
him down.

"I guess if that's the best we can do…''

"Great!'' Leigh gave a dazzling smile. "Now,'' she
said, opening the paper bag, "which coffee is yours?''

Fifteen minutes later Evan had taken off his seersucker
jacket and was carrying boxes downstairs to the porch.
Leigh followed, swooping out on the open swing of the
screen door.

"I think that's it,'' she announced.

Evan was wiping his forehead with a handkerchief. The
motion reminded Leigh of Spencer's bandanna, still folded
in her purse. She'd put it on the hall table so he'd see it
when he came by later.

"Right,'' Evan said, tucking the square of white cloth
into his pants pocket. "Shall we get down to some details
about the house now?''

"I thought I told Patsy everything.''

He summoned a quick tight smile. "I'm sure you told
her what you considered the best features of the house to
be. Now I want the rest of the information—the things I
don't want to be surprised about when I'm showing it.''

He's got you there, kiddo. You've met your match.
"Okay. Well, shall we start with the foundation pilings?''

Later, when Leigh had admitted to a grudging respect
for Evan's attention to the smallest detail, she sat down
with him at the kitchen table. The scent of freshly brewed
coffee filled the room.

"I guess I should have made muffins. Isn't that what they say you ought to do when you show your house?"

Evan pursed his lips. "I don't think the gimmicks make up for a good house. This place—" he made a sweeping gesture with his hand "—is rock solid. Old-fashioned, mind you. And—" he paused dramatically "—no skylights, sunrooms or sauna. The trinity of cottages."

"But there's a deck."

"Yes. Well—" he gave a slight sniff "—I just hope no one wants to have that checked out. How long ago was it built?"

"A little more than ten years. My father was in a nursing home in Raleigh the last year of his life. When he came for weekend visits, my mother wanted him to get some fresh air where she could watch him from the kitchen."

Even waited a respectful moment before continuing, "Anyway, in spite of the obvious inconveniences of old plumbing fixtures and questionable wiring—"

"There's nothing wrong with the wiring!"

"So you say, but I think the fuse box is overloaded. So long as you don't run too many appliances while I'm showing it, we can manage."

"I certainly don't intend to put any money into this place before I sell it."

"I'd never advise you to do so. Only that you may have to settle for less if someone raises the matter."

"I'm willing to come down of course. I've got a job and apartment in New York City. You may want to point out to people that this place is one of the few last private properties outside the village. Everything else is owned by the National Park Service. The beach is right across the road."

"Do you own that land, too?"

"No, but we have right-of-way to it. It was part of the

agreement when my father sold the land next to us to the Park Service. The rest of the beach belongs to the state.''

''That's a selling point, I have to admit. And quite a few people like the…the old-fashioned look these days.''

Leigh closed her eyes. She wondered how her father would have reacted to this conversation. *He'd never be having it, that's how.* She rubbed her forefinger in the groove between her eyebrows. Most of the night she'd tossed and turned, thinking about Sam. About Spencer. About the way she'd felt when he was kissing her. Even about Jamie, wondering how much he'd seen and what he must think of her. She was also starting to get tired of Evan.

A loud rattling at the front screen door propelled her out of her chair and down the hall. She could make out Spencer's blurred outline through the mesh. Her heart picked up speed.

''You're finished already?'' she asked, pushing open the door.

''Yeah, he wimped out before nine. 'Course, I think the partying he took in last night at Howard's might have been a factor.''

''I can't think of anything worse than going out on the Sound with a hangover.''

''I knew I'd be back earlier when I noticed the green tint in his skin after he drank the double-strength coffee I made at five-thirty this morning.''

''Ooh, I never knew you had such a cruel streak,'' she teased. ''Come on in. Evan's here enjoying a regular cup of coffee.''

He halted midstep. ''Evan?''

''The real-estate guy showing my house today.''

Spencer felt the vise clamped on the back of his neck loosen its grip. ''Ahh,'' he said, filled with such relief he decided he'd just paid back any guilt debt he owed his hapless client that morning. He stepped into the hall and, once his eyes had adjusted to the shadows, saw a man standing in the kitchen doorway.

After introductions Leigh said, "Spencer's going to help me take the boxes up to Hatteras for recycling."

Evan's face broke into a big smile. "Wonderful! Then with your permission I'll take a couple of the patio chairs around to the front. It's important for clients to have a chance to appreciate both views."

Spencer helped with the chairs while Leigh ran upstairs to get her purse. She made a quick side trip to the bathroom to check her hair. It was still damp at the back from her shower, but the ends were finally training themselves to curl under. Her hairstylist had warned her that the cut was definitely out, but Leigh didn't care. Fashion trends had always managed to escape her notice until they were on the wane, anyway.

Maybe a touch of lipstick, she thought. She stood back, eyeing her white shorts. Perhaps not the best thing for hauling boxes in and out of a truck. But the shorts fit perfectly and looked terrific with the periwinkle blue halter top. When she turned to leave, a memory flash exploded in her mind.

Laura Marshall and the crisp white tennis outfit she wore to our midnight picnic on Portsmouth Island. That's why there were no life jackets in the boat. Laura insisted on using them for cushions, to protect her white shorts.

Leigh's stomach churned. She waited, holding on to the doorjamb for support. Then she took a deep breath and returned to her room to change her shorts. When she came downstairs minutes later, Spencer and Evan had just finished moving the chairs onto the porch.

Spencer smiled up at her from the foot of the staircase. "I was going to suggest you change your shorts. Not that the white ones didn't look great, but my truck seems to leach oil these days."

"Yeah, I thought the same thing," she murmured. "Black is definitely more appropriate."

"A more dramatic contrast with the blue, too," Evan put in.

Leigh turned his way. "Oh, why, thank you." She caught the grin on Spencer's face out of the corner of her eye. "Um, I'm not sure how long this is going to take, Evan."

He waved a hand. "Don't rush back. We prefer not to have owners around while we're showing the place, anyway. I hope you've locked up any priceless antiques."

"Yeah, right. Okay, then, if I'm not back before you leave, will you let me know later how things went?"

"Of course. I should warn you it's not likely you'll get an offer today. Do you want me to lock up for you?"

"Oh, I don't think so. We never used to worry about that. What do you think, Spence?"

"Maybe in prime tourist season, but not now. Although this place *is* outside the village proper."

"Just close the big door. My neighbors, the Jensens, are down the road a bit, beyond that cedar row," Leigh said.

"Here's my card," Evan said. "If you don't hear from me by Monday afternoon, give me a call."

Leigh was relieved to see that the men had also loaded the boxes into the back of the pickup. "You got them all in!"

"I thought we might as well head right to the ferry, rather than go back to my place for your car. Is that okay?"

It meant spending more time with Spencer than she'd expected. Not that she minded, but the thought of last night's trip down memory lane set off a few warning bells. "Sure, I guess so," she said, climbing into the truck. "Although it kind of ties you up for the day, doesn't it?"

He smiled across the seat from her. "I think I can live with that."

But can I? Leigh tried to appear casual. "Great. So, how's Sam today?"

"You wouldn't even know he'd suffered an angina attack. Up and raring to go. Jamie and I had to practically sit on him to make him promise to stick around his place today."

Spence reversed the truck onto the highway. He glanced at Leigh, her right arm angled on the rolled-down window, wind tossing her hair behind her. She looked so young and beautiful. He could hardly believe fifteen years had passed—until he caught himself in the mirror and saw a line somewhere in his face for every one of those years. Not to mention every one of the mistakes of his youth.

Maybe if he played it right this time, those mistakes wouldn't turn out to be a life sentence. Being thirty-five, instead of nineteen, helped, too. Priorities had gelled; boundaries were clearer. *Except you've got more responsibilities now—Jamie and Sam.* Yeah, he thought, but he could handle it. Spence made himself relax. One step at a time.

For now, it was Saturday. His cares were sitting nicely on the back burner. The sun was brilliant, the sky an aching blue and the woman he'd always loved was beside him again. What more could he ask?

Nothing at all. Just enough time to see if she wants what I do.

Resolved, he gave in to the mellow contentment filling him. It was going to be a great day.

The relatively early hour guaranteed a place on the ferry to Hatteras. "It won't be this easy two weeks from now," Spence said. He parked in the space he'd been directed to by one of the crew, turned to Leigh and asked, "Shall we go up top?"

But she was already out the door, heading for the stairs leading to the passenger decks on each side of the big flat-bottomed boat. He grinned. *Same old Leigh, all right. Still likes the wind in her hair.*

"You know," he said, standing beside her, "I never get tired of this view, though I must have seen it a few thousand times."

"But it's always changing, even in small ways. The clouds, the color of the water, even the shape of the land we pass—so much is determined by light, weather, time of year." Leigh tossed her head, loving the sensation of wind whipping across her scalp. "I love the smells! That acrid combination of salt and fish. Even the diesel fumes from the ferry don't dominate. You know—" she faced Spencer "—after I'd been living in New York six months, I went with a friend on the boat cruise to Ellis Island and the Statue of Liberty. When we were walking through Battery Park, I passed a clump of fir trees that gave off a faint scent of pine. I stopped and breathed it in. That faint whiff of pine was the first natural smell I'd inhaled since arriving in New York City."

She laughed at the absurdity of the incident. "Of course, since then I've discovered some real nature places in the city—little oases of fresh air—but until that moment in Battery Park I hadn't realized how appallingly different the air quality was compared to the Outer Banks."

There was a flush in her cheeks from the sheer joy of looking out over the Sound. Her eyes sparkled and Spence wanted to kiss her so badly he had to turn away, lean over the railing and fake an interest in the water.

Finally he said, "Nothing compares to life on the Outer Banks, that's for sure."

"Why didn't you ever leave Ocracoke? When you were a teenager, going to the mainland was all you talked about."

Spence uttered a derisive snort. "Yeah. When I was a teenager, I thought I knew everything." He looked quickly at Leigh, then back out to sea. "Having a kid when you're barely out of your teens is a sobering experience. Sam got me a job working for one of the fishermen in the village, and after a couple of years of that, old man Cowan took me on in his charter business. It was the break I needed. Better money, better hours and the work wasn't so damn hard.'' He turned again to Leigh. "I don't know how Sam and men like your father did it. Especially in the days when commercial fishing boats weren't as well equipped as they are now with all the high-tech stuff.''

Leigh nodded and Spence swung his gaze back to the water of Hatteran Inlet.

"Anyway, to make a long story short, I practically took over the whole business. Cowan is really just a silent partner now. Once I had an investment of that kind on Ocracoke, there was no way I'd ever leave. Besides, by then I'd grown to appreciate the island and village life. Things are…simpler here. Our wants and needs are—'' he paused "—basic. No, more than that. Uncomplicated.''

Leigh looked at Spencer as he stared out over the railing. She'd never in her life considered him an uncomplicated person, and she didn't altogether agree with his take on life in the Outer Banks—certainly not on Ocracoke. Her experience here after graduation night and later, in the world outside, had taught her there were no simple conclusions to make about places and people.

"But then,'' he went on, standing upright and once again turning toward her, "I suppose you've experienced a different perspective, having gone to college and living in New York.''

The blue of his eyes assumed a neon quality in the bright sun. They were the same eyes Leigh had gazed into with longing and adoration for two years, but they signaled something different now than they had then.

"Have I struck a nerve?'' he asked.

"Hmm?''

"You seemed lost in thought.''

"I was. Thinking of you back then."

The smile in his face disappeared. "I was a kid back then."

"A nineteen-year-old kid."

"Not at the beginning. Not when we started dating."

Leigh smiled. "We were both kids. I only turned sixteen the July after the Sadie Hawkins dance."

"When it all began," he said almost wistfully. "I remember your mother threw that big 'sweet sixteen' party."

"And I was so embarrassed! I didn't even want to go."

"No, we wanted to sneak off and go to a movie in Hatteras."

"But the party turned out to be fun."

His smile returned. "Yeah. It was."

After a moment's silence Leigh said, "We've both changed a lot. Gotten older—"

"Wiser," he put in.

"Yes," she murmured. "I like to think so." She leaned her forearms on the railing and looked ahead to Cape Hatteras, looming into sight.

"But there's no reason we can't reminisce and enjoy each other's company. As adults and friends," he quickly added.

The awkwardness of his proposal tugged at her. "No reason at all," she said, straightening and looking him in the eye.

A smile stretched across his face.

"LUNCH?" SPENCER CLOSED the truck door behind him.

"I'm starving," Leigh admitted. "And by the time we wait for the next ferry..."

"Not to mention the forty-minute crossing," he said.

She laughed. "You don't need to twist my arm when it comes to eating, believe me."

"Great." He shifted the truck into drive and pulled out of the gravel parking lot where they'd deposited Leigh's cartons in the rows of recycling bins. "I know a little place up by way of Kill Devil Hills, if you don't mind the drive."

"No commitments," she said. And realizing it, felt wonderfully free. Much later, after they'd eaten stony crab at the family-run café outside Kill Devil Hills and stopped for homemade ice cream at yet another tiny out-of-the-way place driving back along the highway, Leigh decided the day had been one of her best in a long long time.

"I don't know about you," Spencer sighed, switching off the truck's ignition after he'd turned into his driveway, "but today was..." He searched for a word.

"Cool? Awesome? Rad?" she suggested with a grin. "Or are those still the in words for teens these days?"

"'Fantastic' was the word I was looking for. Damn fantastic."

Leigh returned his smile. "That's a good word. Yes, I'd have chosen that word, too."

"Good." Spence couldn't take his eyes off her. There was a glow about her that instinct told him had a lot more to do with spending the day with him than with being in the sun. It had been a day of connections, he realized. Every word, every joke, every accidental brush of skin against skin had created an immediate and charged connection. And he was still riding high on the day, still giddy with the thrill of rediscovery the day had given him.

Rediscovery. Another good word, he thought. Because that was the way the past few hours had unrolled, revealing new facts about Leigh Randall, as well as sketching in long-forgotten details. But here he was, at the end of that glorious, *fantastic* day, and he couldn't let go of it. He wanted it to go on and on.

"Well, guess I'd better get home and see if there've been any offers today," Leigh said, averting her face and reaching for the door handle.

Disappointment was bitter in his mouth. Was that what

she'd been thinking while he'd been looking deep into her eyes, sending the message his voice couldn't utter?

He yanked the keys out of the ignition and followed her out of the truck. When he joined her at the driver side of her car, she paused, playing with her car keys. Reluctant to open the door and drive off? he wondered. Or just thinking of the safest way to say goodbye.

But then she beamed a heart-stopping smile at him and he didn't wait to analyze it. He simply placed his hands on her shoulders and gently drew her to him. He moved his hands around her back, pressing the hollow between her shoulder blades into him, feeling the softness of her breasts against his chest. He lowered his face to her hair, inhaling its flowery scent, then brought his hands around to cup her head while he placed a line of soft kisses across her brow. He felt her arms wrap around him, then she tilted her head back as far as his hands permitted and parted her lips in invitation. He accepted and brought his mouth to hers.

She tasted of raspberries and cream and the minty gum she'd bought somewhere on the trip home. He shifted his right hand to the dip of her lower back, pushing her hips into his groin. He wanted her so badly he ached. When she pulled back, he felt empty.

"Spence," she whispered.

Her voice sounded shaky and he knew she hadn't wanted to pull free.

He stared into her eyes, urging them to stay fixed on his. But they flickered toward the ground, the car door and back to the ground. Anywhere but on him, he thought.

She opened her car door and got in. "I'll call you," was all he said as he closed the door after her.

She nodded and backed out the drive. She straightened the car out to head for the village, but then braked and reversed.

Spencer stood watching, puzzled.

Leigh rolled down her window. "You can't call me—not unless you know my cell-phone number."

"Got me there," he said.

"How about dinner tomorrow night? My place?"

"Sounds great."

"Okay. Bring Jamie. Bye."

Spencer waved. *Jamie*. Ah, yes, he thought, back to the real world.

When he stepped inside the front door, the pulsing bass of a rock number pumped out from behind Jamie's closed door. He tapped briskly, then pushed open the door. Jamie lolled on his unmade bed, flipping through a sports magazine. Schoolbooks littered the bed and floor, along with a week's laundry—clean or dirty, Spence couldn't have said. He motioned to the CD player, but getting no response, strode over to turn it off.

"Hey!"

"I need to talk to you. Didn't you see me standing in the door?"

"Yeah, I saw you. I saw plenty."

"What's that supposed to mean?"

Jamie flung the magazine onto the floor. His face was bright red. "You and Leigh. Jeez, can't you make out in private?"

Spencer felt his own face flush. "We weren't making out," he protested, then hated himself for rushing to defend his actions. "I kissed her goodbye. Don't you ever do that on your dates?" It was a mean gibe. As far as he knew, Jamie had never had a date.

But the shot went over Jamie's head. "Some kiss," he muttered. "Good thing no one was outside to notice. Jeez."

Spencer thought he'd better let the matter drop. He sensed there was a lot of complicated emotion behind Jamie's outburst. Instead, he cleared a square of the bed and sat down.

"How's your grandfather today?"

"Same as when you left him this morning. Before you took off."

Spencer pursed his lips. Hmm. Did Jamie feel slighted at being left out? "And how was that?"

Jamie heaved a great sigh. "You know. Like Grandpa Sam. Itching to get up and about."

"That's a good way to put it. Did the doctor call here?"

"Yeah, said he wants you to telephone Grandpa's specialist as soon as possible. Said he called the dude himself, told him about the attack and all."

"Okay. Anything else?"

Jamie shrugged. "Nope. That was it."

Spence started to leave the room, then turned to ask, "Has it been a long day?"

Another shrug. Then, "Not much doing here, that's for sure."

It was Spencer's turn to sigh. "Look," he said, "how about catching a movie up on Hatteras? We could go somewhere for a bite after. Maybe talk a bit about the summer. You know, make some plans."

Jamie scowled, but Spence saw a glimmer of interest in his eyes.

"You mean talk about getting a job."

Jamie made the word sound like an obscenity. Spence smiled inwardly. "There are jobs…and then there are jobs. I don't necessarily mean working for me on the boat. But you know, some kids have had the good luck to get part-time work with the National Park Service looking after the herd of ponies."

Jamie's head shot up. "The wild ponies here?"

"What's left of them. They're not wild by the usual standards because they're penned in to protect them. But there may be something available."

Jamie's mouth twisted. "I bet it takes clout to get a job like that," he said.

Spencer wondered what had made him so cynical at such an early age. *Was I the same?*

"Come on," he said, "pick up your clothes and stash them in the laundry basket. We'll pop in on Sam on the way."

LEIGH WAS SCARCELY aware of the drive home. Snippets of her day with Spencer zapped across her mind like a pixel sign. She figured the subliminal messages were a warning, rather than an advertisement. *Go home. Keep clear. Danger zone.*

She laughed at herself. Drama had always been Jen's forte, not hers. Leigh had preferred the blunt mathematical correctness of truth and honesty. Which, of course, accounted for her unwillingness to bend the truth in any way. A promise was a promise. A declaration of love, a declaration of love. Simple enough, she'd thought. Then why had it all unraveled so easily?

She pulled up in front of her house. Leigh sat for a moment arguing with her inner self. *It all fell apart fifteen years ago. Who knows why? Who cares? Give it up and go on.* She'd been giving herself the same lecture for years. *Right, so when are you going to start listening?*

The For Sale sign in the center of the front yard was a good reminder of the temporary aspect of her return to Ocracoke. *Time to quit playing games with the past, kiddo. It can't be relived in any way and even if Spencer has changed, what happened then is stamped forever on your mind.*

She got out of the car and by the time she reached the porch, she'd already decided to cut short her stay on the island. There was no reason Evan couldn't act as sales agent without her.

Speaking of Evan, she thought, pursing her lips, why hadn't he closed the main door? Not that it mattered much in Ocracoke, but you never knew when some undesirable type might pass through.

Annoyance at Evan bloomed as she proceeded into the kitchen and found the coffeemaker still on. The man had even left his unwashed mug and spoon on the counter! Obviously her initial judgment of him had been way off base. He wasn't nearly as fastidious as he'd appeared. Leigh put her bag on the table and headed upstairs to shower and change.

She'd been waiting for Spencer to suggest something for that evening, but now felt relieved he hadn't. She doubted she'd have been able to decline; at least, not if he'd fixed those baby blues on her the way he had just before he'd kissed her. That kiss. Warmth crept back into her system at the mere thought.

His mouth definitely hadn't changed, but his technique seemed more—Leigh searched for the word—sophisticated? *Nah, makes him sound like a lounge lizard.* How about restrained? She frowned. Yes, that seemed a bit more like it. *And I'd add a little patience and a dollop of confidence. 'Course, he had that in spades when he was seventeen going on eighteen.*

Leigh left the bathroom and walked down the hall to her bedroom at the rear of the house. She paused in the doorway. Something different here. Her brow wrinkled. *Must be my imagination.* She walked to the vanity to stare at herself in the mirror. She smiled, replaying the kiss one more time.

Then the smile disappeared. Leigh blew out a lungful of air. She might as well be sixteen all over again, judging by the giddiness, the tingling, the light-headedness. Even her resolve to keep him at arm's length, determined on the drive home, was as weak as it had been years ago. *One touch, one kiss, and it's game over.*

Leigh sank onto the edge of the bed and lowered her

chin onto her cupped hands. *Brother,* she thought. *You've got trouble.*

Maybe she'd call Evan tomorrow to arrange his handling of the sale for her. No. Tomorrow was Sunday. *And Spencer is coming for dinner.* Leigh moaned. If she was lucky, Jamie would come, too. A fourteen-year-old would make a good buffer. Leigh kicked off her sandals and pulled off her halter top. Turning her head, she eyed the closet and paused.

That was what it was, she realized. When she'd first stood in the doorway, she'd had a sense of something different about the room. The closet door had been left open, probably by someone seeing the house. She finished undressing and slipped on the terry-cloth robe hanging on the hook behind her door.

When she opened the top drawer of her bureau to get clean underwear, she gasped. Someone had been rifling through her lingerie. She was beginning to feel like Goldilocks. Leigh yanked open the other drawers. Every one but the last had been rummaged through. Some attempt had been made to pat things down, but none of the little piles were symmetrical. If she hadn't sorted through these just the other day, she realized, she'd never have noticed.

Her cell phone downstairs rang. Leigh tied the bathrobe sash and ran to get it.

"Ms. Randall? Evan Brown here."

"Aha! Just the person I wanted to speak to."

"Oh?"

"I think someone's been in my house."

"Quite a few people, actually."

Evan the joker. "I should have said, in my drawers."

"In your *drawers?*"

Leigh counted to ten. "I think someone was looking through my chest of drawers—at my clothes and things."

"Good heavens! Why would anyone do that?"

"That's what I've been asking myself. So far I haven't come up with any answers. Can you help me out?"

"Are you certain about this? I mean, I was with the clients all the time. Well, except maybe once when I was in the washroom."

"I'm pretty certain, Evan. I just cleaned everything out a couple of days ago, and it was obvious as soon as I opened the drawers. Everything was a bit messed up."

"Just a bit? So we're not talking vandalism here, right?"

"Heavens no. It's just that the little piles of clothes look as though they've been moved." She heard his sigh of relief.

"So it may be that the drawers got jiggled somehow and shifted things a bit inside."

"We haven't had an earthquake, Evan. And you didn't close the big front door and...oh, the coffeemaker was still on and your cup was left on the counter."

"What? Hold on here, Ms. Randall. When I left, the door was closed and everything was shipshape in the kitchen. Do you hear me? Shipshape."

Evan sounded so indignant Leigh decided to drop it. What did it matter, anyway? "Evan, I'm not going to lose any sleep over it, all right?"

"Is anything missing?"

"I don't think so, but I haven't really looked carefully. I'll call you back if I find anything missing."

"Call the police if there is. Ms. Randall, I apologize. This has never happened to me when I've shown a house. Seriously, I was with people every minute."

"Except when you..."

"Well, a few seconds maybe."

Leigh already regretted raising the issue. "Were there any offers today?"

"No, but some promising clients. A young family who want a summer home, a couple who were thinking of the place as a business investment, and there was an older woman who said she and her husband were interested in a retirement home.''

''It's a bit big for a retirement home,'' Leigh said. ''My parents couldn't manage the upkeep.''

''That's what I thought, but she still seemed quite fascinated with the place.''

''Maybe she's the one who opened my drawers and my closet.''

''Oh, dear, I might have opened the closet myself. Good heavens I—''

''So now what?'' she interrupted.

''We wait. How about another open house in, say, three or four days?''

Leigh closed her eyes. *So much for my plan to leave earlier.* ''Fine. I'll make sure I'm here for that one.''

There was a brief silence until Evan set a date, his nose clearly out of joint, and rang off.

After her shower Leigh methodically went through all the cupboards, closets and drawers in the house. Nothing seemed to be missing. The boxes of mementos she'd decided to keep were stacked in her parents' bedroom, and the leather valise was still under the bed. Who would want old photographs, anyway?

After a late dinner and an evening in front of the television, resurrected from an upstairs closet, Leigh headed for bed. Someone had certainly been in her house that afternoon after Evan had closed up. Perhaps Trish. She seemed to have a penchant for making herself at home in other people's houses.

Leigh switched off her bedside lamp. The music of the night filled the room—the whack of moths and June bugs against the screen mesh, the muted roar of the incoming tide and the wind, gaining momentum in the treetops be-

hind the house, whistling under the curtain hem. She settled into the hollow of the mattress and let her mind slip
back into the afternoon—the sun, the sky and, most of all,
the kiss.

land the house, whistling under the curtain hem. She settled into the hollow of the mattress and let her mind slip back into the afternoon—who got hurt, the why and, most of all, the what.

CHAPTER EIGHT

"GRANDPA SAM?"

Leigh tapped on the edge of the screen door. She waited, then crooked a finger through the handle, propping it open with one hip while she sidled through, holding aloft the casserole dish and bag of groceries. She tiptoed into the kitchen, noticing at once that someone had tidied and cleaned and placed the food on the table.

"Sam? Are you awake?" The faint sound from his bedroom urged her toward it, her heart racing with fear.

But Sam was sitting up in bed, leaning against a stack of pillows. His smile was wan, almost apologetic. As if he shouldn't be caught sick in bed.

"There's my girl!" Sam croaked. The smile spread into his eyes and Leigh bent down to hug him as gently as she could.

"I won't break, you know," he chided her. "Clear those magazines from the armchair and bring it close enough so's I can feast me eyes on ya."

"Sure. Hey, I didn't know you were into home decorating," she teased, noticing some of the magazine titles.

"Ah," he sighed, "what am I to do with all that stuff? There's more in the living room, too. Books I've never even heard of. Dishes of this and that in the pantry."

Chicken-rice casserole flashed in Leigh's mind. "I'm afraid I've joined the parade—sort of. I brought dinner and a few things from the convenience store."

"Nobody's thought to bring me a cigar and a good bottle of port."

Leigh smiled. "Thank goodness *some* people have common sense."

"I don't recall you havin' that hard streak in you when you were younger." Sam's face looked stern, but there was a twinkle in his eye.

She leaned across to pat his hand. "How are you, Sam? Seriously?"

"Well, if everyone would stop pesterin' me about my health and droppin' in for a social, I'd most likely be up and out fishin'. As it is…"

"So the news has hit the island grapevine."

"Seems like." Another sigh. "Even had old Mrs. Waverly come by."

"Did she ask if you were ready to sell?"

Sam sniffed. "Nope. In fact, she said she hoped I'd be here another ten years at least so's the two of us could protest against all the newfangled ideas comin' down the tube from the National Park Service."

"What stuff?"

"All that environmental poppycock. Ha! In my day, people never had to feel guilty about earnin' a livin'. We fished exactly what we needed to dry and salt for ourselves, and we had just enough to heat our houses and feed us through the winter. We knew how to keep our boats and engines clean, and we never took anythin' from the sea we couldn't eat or sell." He stopped to take a breath that turned into a coughing fit.

Leigh reached for the glass of water on his bedside table and held it for him while he sipped. Sam fell back against the pillows, his open mouth sucking in gulps of air.

It was then that Leigh knew he was more ill than she'd thought. He looked almost as bad as her parents had in their last weeks. Sadness overwhelmed her. She didn't want to think of Ocracoke without Sam Logan.

"I hear you're entertainin' tonight."

That grapevine! "Yes," Leigh murmured. "Spencer and Jamie are coming to dinner. And you'd be coming, too, if you were feeling better."

Sam coughed again. He sipped some more water and paused. "Glad to see Spencer getting out. He's lived like a hermit for too long."

"That's difficult to believe. There aren't that many eligible bachelors in Ocracoke, I'm sure."

Sam's cackle rolled into a spasm. Leigh raised his pillows and put the water on the table. When he was finished coughing, he continued, "I think you're on a fishin' expedition, my girl."

Leigh's face warmed. "You always were good at reading people."

"Only some people. I'm afraid I missed the warnin' signs about my own granddaughter." He paused, then said, "When Jen left, Spencer just about went wild looking for her and Jamie. Drove up and down the coast to see every friend and relative I never even knew we had." He paused again, taking a few breaths.

"Maybe you should rest, Sam."

He waved a hand at her. "Got to get this out now before it's too late. After a few months Spencer got a letter from Jen tellin' him she was applyin' for a divorce."

"He must have been shattered."

"Yep. But I doubt it was 'cause of her. He loved that boy."

"Why didn't he try to get custody?"

"He got himself a lawyer—spent what little he had—only to find out he didn't have much chance unless he could prove Jen was an unfit mother." Sam paused again for breath. "He'd never do that. And don't get me wrong, Jen loves Jamie, too. These troubles with the boy—they didn't start until after she remarried. By then he was a teenager and used to havin' her to himself. Poor boy. First he lost his daddy, then his ma. No wonder he's all con-fused.''

Sam lapsed into silence. Leigh pictured Spencer driving up and down the coast of North Carolina searching for Jen and Jamie. He'd never been one to give up easily. Even after the prom-night accident and the inquest, he'd tele-phoned or come around to her house so many times Leigh's mother refused to lie for her anymore. After Leigh had left for university in Chapel Hill, the telephone in her dorm had rung so often the house mistress had complained.

Persistence had been his second name, until the last time he tried to contact her. He'd traveled all the way to Chapel Hill one stormy night in late October. Leigh had persuaded her roommate to tell Spencer she was at the library. But he'd stood outside in the driving rain under a willow tree, hunched into his windbreaker. She'd watched him through a gap in her curtains for almost an hour.

All she could think about was the image of Spencer and Jen at the prom, entwined in each other's arms, and then later, the scene in the ladies' room where she'd confronted Jen.

''You had your chance, Randall, and you blew it. Spen-cer's had it with you and your big thing about leaving the island to go to college. He wants to be with me now.'' Jen had flashed a triumphant smile. ''You go with the others to Portsmouth. I've got better things to do.'' Then she'd sashayed out the door.

So instead of running to him that night in Chapel Hill, Leigh had locked herself in the bathroom and cried. Later she'd written him a long letter, explaining why she couldn't see him. He'd never replied and never called again. A few weeks later he and Jen eloped.

''Funny how things turn out,'' Sam murmured.

Leigh raised her head. From the expression on Sam's face, she guessed he'd been delving into the past, too.

He looked across the bed at Leigh. ''I always figgered

you an' Spence would be the ones to run off together, not him and Jen. I mean, Jen had been itchin' to leave Ocracoke most of her life, so I was expecting her to take off right after graduation. She could have gone to some college—even with her grades—but she never wanted to apply. Wouldn't talk about her plans at all. Came as a complete surprise to me when she an' Spencer run off.''

A surprise to me, too. Although, be honest—was it? After that night didn't you guess that Spence would head right back to Ocracoke and Jen?

''Anyhow, what's done is done.'' Sam sighed wearily. ''I reckon everyone is happier now for how it all turned out. What do you think?''

Leigh ducked her head, picking at loose threads in Sam's blanket. She let his question hang in the air until he sighed again.

''That's what I reckoned. I got a feeling Jen is the only one who's happy about how things ended up. But then, like I said before, Jen was always a survivor.''

Leigh clasped Sam's hand in hers. ''We're all adults now, Sam, and capable of planning our own futures. Don't worry about us.''

''I worry about Jamie.''

''Don't. Jamie has two parents who love him very much. There are lots of kids who don't have even one.''

''Well,'' he sniffed, ''you're right about that, I reckon. What are your plans, then?''

''Oh, sell the house. Go back to New York.''

''No temptation to stay longer?''

''What? Here in Ocracoke?''

He pulled a face. ''Ain't that bad here, is it? You managed to have a wonderful childhood and all.''

''I didn't mean I don't love Ocracoke, Sam. It's just that—'' she searched for the right words ''—I've outgrown it.''

''Gone on to bigger and better things?''

"Well, *different* things."

"And any special person in your life back there?"

Leigh smiled. "I have some good friends, but no love interest. Talk about a fishing expedition!"

His grin was sheepish. "Guess that's a no, then, though I can't imagine why."

"It's been great coming here to see all of you, but to be honest, Sam, I don't think one can turn back the clock. Coming home again is...okay, but definitely not the same. Everything's different."

"'Course it is! Why'd you expect otherwise? Life goes on. All that stuff. Don't mean it can't be tried again. That you don't get another chance."

Time to change the subject, Leigh decided. "Perhaps. Listen, Sam, before I go, is there anything I can get you? More water? Juice?"

Sam scowled. "Nope. Unless you got a bottle of port in that bag of yours, don't bother."

"No way." She leaned across the bed to kiss his cheek. "I'll be off, then. Got to prepare a good dinner for tonight. I hear Spencer has become quite a gourmet chef."

"Don't know about *goor-may,* but he's darn good. Maybe if you stick around longer, he'll cook for you at his place."

Leigh smiled. "Stop matchmaking!" She stood up. "I'm sure Spence will drop by later this evening on his way home."

Sam shook his head. "Get Jamie to do it. That'll give you two more time."

"Sam!"

"Not matchmakin'," he protested. "But I'm sure you both have some talkin' to do. Things to clear up. You know—" he stumbled, catching the look in her eyes "—from the past."

"As you've just said, Sam, the past is gone. Why bother?"

"Because, my girl, it's damned hard to get on with the present—forget about the future—if you're draggin' the past along with ya."

Leigh slung her purse over her shoulder. "And what makes you think I'm dragging the past along with me?"

"I see it in your face, Leigh Randall. I hear it in your voice every time you say Spencer's name—or Jen's."

"I think you're seeing too much, Sam Logan. And now goodbye. Get some rest." She moved toward the door.

"Wait."

Leigh stopped, but reluctantly. She didn't want to hurt Sam's feelings, but he was encroaching on some dangerous territory. Couldn't he see that?

"Hear me out. Indulge an old man, and one who's known you since you were a babe. You've got to lay all those ghosts to rest and soon. Don't play with time! You've got to stop blamin' yourself for that stupid accident. Fifteen years ago you were all young and reckless kids."

But not me. Never young and reckless. Just weak.

"Ain't no one blames you for that trouble. No one but a sad lady who most likely feels guilty about something else."

Laura Marshall's mother, he meant. Leigh could remember Laura complaining about her mother's overprotectiveness. There'd been many quarrels in the Marshall family, and Leigh had been privy to some of them. What Sam had implied made sense, given Mrs. Marshall's inability to cope with her daughter.

"That may be, Sam. But I've only been back in Ocracoke a week and sometimes I have the feeling no one's forgotten what happened, even if it *has* been fifteen years."

With obvious effort Sam raised himself from the pillows. His face was red with the strain.

"Sam, don't get up!"

"I'm not," he panted, using his elbows to prop himself. "Maybe there's too much pussyfootin' around the whole thing. People are *bound* to be reminded if you get that stricken look on your face every time someone even hints at it."

A pulse of annoyance throbbed at her temples. If it wasn't Sam speaking... Then Leigh recalled the moment at lunch a few days ago when a simple comment about the lighthouse had dampened the party. Granted, she'd managed to laugh it off, but perhaps her face had revealed what her voice had not. Perhaps Sam was right. Perhaps she herself had kept the tragedy alive long after everyone else had finished with it.

Then again, maybe not. Maybe Sam's the one who can't see. "Sam," she said, looking down into the wizened face upturned to hers, "I think you'd better get some rest. And don't worry about me. I'm quite capable of taking care of myself."

He fell back against the pillows. "I'd like to believe that, Leigh." He gave a feeble wave. "Go now. Send the boy over later. Give his daddy a break."

Leigh closed the bedroom door softly behind her and leaned against it for a long moment before she felt able to move.

"SURE I CAN'T HELP?"

"Never the first time. It's a house rule."

Leigh reached up to put the clean wineglasses into the cupboard. When she turned around, Spencer was still hovering in the doorway leading to the deck. He wore crisp tan chinos and an emerald green polo shirt that enhanced his fair hair and deep tan. He looked like a model for some men's magazine.

The thought surprised her. Spencer McKay's good looks had always been a fact of life during Ocracoke schooldays.

But they'd been less refined, almost...snarly. One could never be certain just how far he'd go to prove a point.

And now—she gave him a sidelong glance as she walked over to the sink for a glass of water—his attractiveness stemmed not just from his age, but from life experiences that had added character to his face. Gone was the "dare me" look in his eyes, replaced by...what? Leigh couldn't tell and she didn't want to be caught staring.

"You're quiet," he observed.

Only on the surface. Inside, things are bubbling away as usual.

Leigh shrugged. "I'm worried about Sam. He seemed so frail today and yet barely a week ago he was his old self."

"You mean that night I ran into you on the highway?"

She laughed. "Yes. My welcome back to Ocracoke."

"Talk about heart attacks! You practically gave me one. I hope you don't make a habit of prowling around after dark."

"Even if I did, this is hardly New York City." Leigh put the empty glass on the counter. "Want to take your coffee out to the deck?"

"Sure. Jamie was certainly impressed by your dinner. He said it was 'cool,' which in his book means a five-star rating."

"I'll take that as a compliment, though I've never heard Thai food called 'cool' before."

Spence grinned. "I guess for a kid raised on burgers and fries, it was."

"Milk?"

"Please. No sugar, though."

Leigh took the carafe from the coffee machine and filled the mugs. When she handed Spencer's to him, he clasped it, along with her hand. Reluctantly she lifted her eyes to his.

"I'm worried about Sam, too. But I don't want to spend

the rest of the evening thinking and talking about him. Besides, Jamie's gone over to his place now, and that'll make Sam happy. He adores the kid.''

She smiled. ''Yeah. And Sam wouldn't want us worrying about him, anyway.''

''You're right, he wouldn't,'' Spence said. He pulled her by the hand out the screen door to the deck.

The sun was just lining up for its descent into the western end of Pamlico Sound, and the white plastic chairs on the deck glowed a faint rose. Spencer led her to a chair and took the one next to her. If Leigh had been sitting with anyone else, she knew contentment would be oozing out her pores. But she could feel Spencer's eyes on her, sense them peering over his coffee mug watching her every move. Expectation hung in the air.

''Did I tell you that Evan had some interest in the house yesterday?'' She made her voice sound breezy and animated, but didn't look his way.

Spencer clinked his coffee mug down on the metal patio table. After a long pause he said, ''No, you didn't.''

The air around Leigh seemed to thicken. She drank more coffee, but it tasted bitter and she set her mug down next to Spence's. When she pulled her hand away, Spencer grabbed it.

''Look.'' His eyes glimmered with an emotion she didn't care to translate. ''I want you to see something. Come on. No, don't ask any questions.''

He led her around to the front of the house to his pickup. She held back, looking at the house.

''It'll be all right. We won't be long.''

Leigh didn't find her voice until the truck had reversed onto the highway. ''Spencer, where are you taking me?''

He held an index finger to his lips. ''Shh. Trust me, okay?''

She thought of the old Spencer and his impulsiveness. *Maybe he hasn't changed that much, after all.* The truck zipped along the road toward the harbor—the Creek, as everyone called it. She guessed where they were heading as soon as the marina came into sight. Her hand clamped on the door handle.

"Spence..." she warned.

"Shh. Not a word. Promise."

It wasn't a request, but a command. Beads of sweat broke out on Leigh's upper lip. She could feel her heart expanding in her chest. When the truck squealed to a halt at a line of parked cars across from the docks, the thudding in Leigh's temples accelerated to a drumroll.

"Spencer! Please!" She clutched his forearm as he took the keys from the ignition. "Why are you doing this?"

He placed his hand on top of hers and pressed. "Because someone has to, Leigh, and it might as well be me."

"This is ridiculous. For heaven's sake! Stop playing amateur shrink! Take me back home *now*."

That last word almost got to him. Not what it said, but how it was said. The shrill, almost frightened ring to it. Too late, he realized. He had to go through with this. He brushed her cheek with the back of his hand. "Come on, Leigh," he whispered.

He jumped out of the truck and reappeared instantly at her side, pulling her out and down the boardwalk to the line of boats, bobbing in the early-evening breeze. They stopped in front of an old but well-maintained white-and-blue Chris-Craft. Spencer began untying the bow line.

"Go aboard," he ordered, but Leigh stood shivering on the dock until he came up behind her and, cupping her elbows in his palms, helped her onto the boat. He untied the lines and got aboard himself, then started the engine and reversed out of the slip. When he had the boat headed out of the harbor, he looked back at Leigh and motioned for her to come up front.

She sat down gingerly in the worn leather seat next to his. It swiveled at her touch, and she reached out for the ledge beneath the windshield, steadying herself. She was afraid to ask where they were going. Knew, anyway. As sure as she recognized the dry mouth, racing heart and breathlessness of her panic attack, the landmarks of the Creek materialized before her as if they'd never been absent from her life. As if this evening was happening fifteen years ago. A night much like this, she realized. Balmy golden sunset and the water a deep smooth jade. Until later, when the wind picked up and whipped it into some unrecognizable beast....

Leigh licked her lips, working them around the words ready to erupt from her mouth. "Spence?"

"It's okay, Leigh. We'll watch the sunset and then go back. Trust me."

"It's just that...I haven't been..."

"On a boat for fifteen years."

She nodded.

He reached out a hand and tilted her face toward him. "Then it's about time," he murmured, dropping his hand and turning his attention back to the steering wheel.

So she held on to the ledge with her fingertips, watching the water of Ocracoke Sound slice by the boat as it raced the setting sun for Portsmouth Island. Twenty minutes later the island appeared, backlit by the hot-pink sunset. Spencer slowed the boat, letting it coast toward an inlet, and then he cut the engine.

Without a glance at Leigh he moved to the stern and cranked out the anchor. Then he sat down next to her and placed his arm around her shoulders.

"If we're lucky, we might see the green glow," he said.

Leigh felt the breath ease out of her in tiny spurts. She relaxed her grip on the edge of the bench. "Have you ever really seen it?" she asked.

His eyebrows raised in mock hurt. "What are you suggesting? That I've made up something that's been well documented all over the world? The green glow of a sunset at sea?''

In spite of herself, Leigh smiled. ''Doesn't it only happen in the tropics? Or below the equator or something?''

''It happens wherever there are people who believe.''

A laugh burst out of her. His hand squeezed her shoulder. ''That's the Leigh I remember,'' he said.

Is it? What exactly is *the Leigh you remember?* The question swirled around her mind, but she clenched her lips, keeping it inside.

''So,'' he went on, staring ahead at the outline of deserted Portsmouth Island. ''Did you know that the government is resettling the place? Seems like there's a movement afoot to revitalize the Outer Banks. Maybe rebuild or restore what's there and let a few people come back.''

Leigh looked at the the curve of inlet. A mere twenty-minute ride from Ocracoke, Portsmouth had attracted not only fishermen and sailboats, but sometimes teenagers in search of adventure.

''Looks innocent enough, doesn't it?''

''What do you mean?'' She turned to Spencer, realizing for the first time how very close he was.

He shrugged. ''It's just a pretty island with a few old buildings. How could it have had such an impact on your life?''

Leigh's jaw dropped. Anger sizzled deep in her gut. She forced herself to wait, then said, ''How can you possibly ask that question?'' Her arm swung out in a crazed arc that included the island and the bay. ''That place reeks of memories. I...I can almost hear the clanking chains of all the ghosts that haunt it.''

''And haunt you.''

Her mouth closed. She nodded dumbly. ''And me,'' she whispered. ''There's so much you don't know. You weren't there!'' The exclamation pitched in accusation.

''I should have been.''

Leigh met his gaze head-on. "Yes. You should have been. I wanted you to be there. The day before the prom I asked Mary Ann Burnett to give you a note saying I'd wait for you at the lighthouse. I wanted to patch things up between us—to ask you to take me to the prom, after all."

"I never got any note from Mary Ann," he said, surprise in his face.

She sighed. "It doesn't matter now, anyway. If only—"

"You couldn't have changed what happened either way, Leigh."

"No, of course not. But…"

"What?"

"Maybe the other kids would have waited it out."

"You didn't make the storm happen and they didn't want to wait it out. They made a decision. They chose not to listen to you."

"I should have made them!"

"What could you have done?"

Leigh shook her head. Tears welled in her eyes.

"Take a deep breath, Leigh. Slowly."

She took the tissue he held out. It reminded her of the red-and-black bandanna, and in a confused non sequitur, she murmured, "I have your bandanna at home. On my hall table."

"Better?" he asked, ignoring the remark.

She nodded and blew her nose. "Yes. Thanks." She looked across the water at the island. "I remember so many details."

"Tell me."

"I haven't talked about it in years—not since the inquest. And then I went over it all so many times I thought I'd be sick."

"It's been fifteen years."

"A long time." Leigh sighed again. "I don't know where or when plans about the midnight picnic all started. I can't even recall whose idea it was to go to Portsmouth after the dance. At first, when people started saying how it was my idea and I was the only one to survive, I was outraged. I tried to fight the rumors for a while, but later I just gave up. There didn't seem to be any point.''

''Or perhaps insisting on the truth didn't fit in with your scenario.''

''What do you mean?''

''Taking the blame,'' he explained.

''You make me sound pathetic.''

''Not pathetic,'' he murmured, tracing the frown lines across her brow with his index finger. ''Valiant, maybe even idealistic. Trying to make their deaths more noble, perhaps, by taking all the responsibility. I was at the inquest, too. I heard it all. You let them assume all kinds of things about that night. Why didn't you set the record straight?''

''What *is* the truth, anyway?''

Spencer moved his finger down to the tip of her chin and turned her face to him. ''You tell me,'' he whispered.

And she did, beginning with the fierce argument she'd had with Spencer a week before the prom.

''Looking back,'' she said, ''I can see I wanted everything my way. Stop grinning at me like that or I'll never finish! You didn't seem to care that I was leaving Ocracoke at the end of the summer. Whenever I wanted to talk about our plans, you'd always walk away or shrug me off.''

''Because the thought of you leaving tore me apart.''

''But I was only going off to college. People do it all the time.'' Her voice dropped to a whisper. ''Lovers do it all the time. Separation isn't the end of things.''

''I had my own insecurities, Leigh. Believe me, the way I behaved was the complete opposite of what I was feeling. I figured you'd meet some smart rich guy in Chapel Hill and that'd be the end of it. Of us. Sure, I went along with what you said about coming home on weekends or visiting you in Chapel Hill, but I knew after a couple of months you'd meet—" he paused "— someone else. It was inevitable as far as I was concerned."

"But you never gave it a chance. You acted as though you didn't care at all that I was going."

He gently touched her lower lip with the tip of his index finger. "Leigh, I cared so much I had this dull ache in my gut for months. I was afraid to talk about it in case—" he gave a small laugh "—I burst into tears."

"If only you had—" she breathed out slowly "—things might have been so different." She caught the look on his face and laughed. "Seriously, Spencer, we were such fools. Both of us. Then when you said you didn't want to go to Portsmouth for the midnight picnic, I lost it."

"You sure did. I was shocked at the names you called me," he teased.

She sobered. "I was unbelievable, wasn't I?"

He shook his head. "Just hurt."

"And afraid."

"Afraid?"

"Of losing you," she said. "So of course, I responded by pushing you away—right into Jen Logan's arms, as it turned out."

Spencer looked away. "That's where *I* lost it," he muttered.

"What do you mean?"

"I always knew she had a thing for me. At the end she wasn't even trying to be subtle about it."

"I guess I was the last to know."

"You were preoccupied with—"

"—going away to college."

"Yep. When you said you wouldn't go to the prom with me, I got my dad's truck and headed for the highway. Just drove—all the way to Nag's Head and back. Jen was waiting at my place. You must have told her about the fight. She...she was very sweet."

"I'll bet." The tone in her voice drew him back to her. "Why couldn't you see through her?" Leigh asked.

"I don't know. Guess I didn't want to. When I heard you'd decided to go with Tony to the prom, I asked Jen. Later, after the accident, I tried to explain everything to you, but you weren't listening."

"I was such a self-absorbed fool," Leigh murmured. "And you even gave me a second chance. At Chapel Hill," she explained at the question in his face. "The night you drove up to see me. I was there, hiding in my room."

Spencer shook his head. "We were a couple of fools, all right." He pulled her to him, tucking her head into his chest and holding on as tightly as he could while her sobs tore at the calm night.

CHAPTER NINE

LEIGH ROLLED OVER, blinking her eyes against the stream of sunshine filling her bedroom window. For a moment she was lost in the no-man's-land between sleep and awakening. The dream hangover was so intense that reference points seemed only vaguely familiar. *Where am I?* quickly floated into *Home.* Leigh found the sensation oddly pleasant. *Home.*

Somehow the apartment in New York had never felt like home. She stretched out her legs and wiggled her toes under the white cotton sheet. The curtains at her open window fluttered weakly in the early-morning heat. Another perfect day in paradise, she thought. *So why the rush to leave?* Leigh smiled, ignoring the internal doomsayer. *Maybe I'm not in such a rush anymore,* she told the voice. *Not after last night.*

The return to Ocracoke in the indigo twilight had been slow and dreamy. She'd sat in Spencer's seat, enveloped in his warm arms, while he'd stood behind her, steering the boat. She'd rested her head against his chest, feeling a comfort and safety she hadn't felt since she was a child.

When they'd docked, neither spoke a word until Spencer pulled the pickup into her driveway. She'd glanced over at him and asked, "Will you come in?" And he'd replied, "If you want me to."

"I do," she'd said, extending her hand to touch the side of his cheek. They'd both known the invitation hadn't been for coffee, and as soon as they were in the hallway, they wrapped their arms around each other and walked upstairs. Like an old married couple, she'd thought.

At the top landing he'd said, "Let's go to your room. I had fantasies for two years about sneaking into your bedroom one night and making love to you."

"While my parents slept down the hall?" Leigh pretended shock.

"What can I say? I was a full-blooded teenage male, pumped with sexual longing."

"Yet we waited almost two years before—"

"Yes," he whispered. "And I remember everything about that first time."

"We weren't very original. The back seat of my dad's Buick."

"Where else could we have gone in Ocracoke? Not to a motel."

"The dunes," she reminded him.

"You never liked the dunes. The grass prickled."

Leigh gave an embarrassed laugh and playfully pushed him away. They stood in her bedroom doorway, staring at the narrow single bed.

"Hmm," he said. "Are any of the guest rooms made up?"

"No, but my parents' bed is."

"Really?"

She looked down, fiddling with the buttons on her sleeveless blouse. "It made me feel more at home. You know what I mean? As if they were just down the hall."

Spencer drew her to his chest and buried his face in her hair. "You're—"

"Don't say 'sweet,'" she warned.

He pulled back to look into her eyes. "Wonderful. Amazing. Irresistible." He lowered his mouth to her brow and pressed a line of kisses across it. "Tempting." He moved his mouth down the bridge of her nose to its tip, paused, then covered her lips with his. After a long moment he murmured, "Delicious."

"Come on," she said, escaping from his arms to pull him out the door and along the hall to the master bedroom.

"Seriously?"

"I think my folks would approve," she replied, and once they were in the room began to unbutton her blouse.

"Wait," he said. "I want to." He undressed her slowly and, when she stood in front of him, ran the palms of his hands lightly over every part of her.

"You make me feel like you're buying a new car or something," she tittered, but the awe in his face silenced her.

"I'm remembering you—how you felt, what you looked like. Your skin, your beautiful breasts…"

Leigh extended her arms. "Come here. My turn."

By the time she'd finished slipping the second pant leg off his foot, he was fully aroused. She took his hand and led him to the bed, drawing back the cotton coverlet and sheet with one strong flick of her wrist. Then she turned to him.

"You feel just like you did when you were nineteen," she breathed into his ear as he lowered her onto the bed.

A TINGLE WORKED its way up her body again as Leigh lay under the sheets, recalling Spencer's every caress. It had been a long time since she'd felt so alive and so desired. He was a different lover than he'd been at nineteen. Slower, more sure of himself and wanting to please. When he'd left hours later, Leigh was certain she'd been glowing in the dark.

She smiled and threw back the sheet. She had a feeling the day was going to be like no other since her return to Ocracoke.

Fresh from the shower half an hour later, Leigh was searching for coffee filters when the telephone rang. She'd taken the cell phone into the kitchen with her, hoping Spencer would call early as he'd promised. She had to hide the disappointment in her voice when Evan said hello.

"Sorry to call you so early," he began, "but I wanted to be sure to get you before you left for the day."

Leigh tightened her grip on the phone. "Did you get an offer on the house?" she asked, crossing her fingers that he hadn't.

"Well..." he drawled, "not an offer but a definite show of interest. My answering service got hold of me yesterday because the same person called several times. Seems this lady is mighty drawn to your house."

"The lady who came to the open house?"

"That I don't know. We didn't exchange names on Saturday."

"Didn't you just ask her?"

"I did ask her if she came to the open house on Saturday, and all she said was that she'd seen the house."

"That makes it pretty obvious, then. I mean, how else would she have seen it?"

"Yes, that's what I figured. Anyway, she must have asked a million questions."

"Even after seeing the house?"

"Strangely enough, most were about you."

"About me?"

"And about why you were selling."

"That's weird."

"Not really. Sometimes people think the reason might have to be connected with something about the house— you know, that it might be sinking into an old landfill site or whatever."

"There's nothing wrong with this house that—"

"—a can of paint won't fix," he finished.

"Yes."

"That's what I told her. But she was very interested in

your family—how long you'd been there, when your folks died and so on.''

"What did you tell her?"

"Ms. Randall, there was very little I *could* tell her. Simply that your parents had died, you lived in New York and were only here long enough to sell the place. End of information.''

"Good," Leigh murmured. "That's creepy, don't you think? Asking all those questions about me?''

"It's odd, but it may have just been her way of making conversation.''

"Making conversation? She's buying a house, isn't she? Not attending a cocktail party.''

Evan laughed. "That's good. I like that. Anyhow, not to worry. Only reason I called is that she said she'd get back to me about seeing the house again. Will you be in today?''

"Yes." She thought of Spencer. "If I do go out, I'll leave a key with the neighbors—the Jensens—the place down the road toward the village?''

"Right. That's it for now, then. Thought any more about your return to New York?''

"I...I'm not sure. Perhaps I will stay here a bit longer. I've got a lot of holidays saved up," she explained. *Idiot. You don't have to make excuses to the real-estate agent!*

"Then you'll be available. Good. Did we agree on another open house?''

"This week, you suggested.''

"Okay. What about Friday? We'll get the weekend traffic, too. And I'll send out flyers to places up the coast. Mind if I write it up as a possible bed-and-breakfast?''

"Of course not. That's what my folks used it for in the last seven or eight years of Dad's life.''

"Fine. If I hear from that woman, I'll call you. Do you have an answering machine?''

"No. I don't even have a phone except this cell. Here

in Ocracoke we leave messages on doors and with neighbors.''

"Pretty inconvenient if you're calling from off the island."

"That's Ocracoke. Part of its charm."

"If you say so. Hmm, well, if I don't get hold of you and she wants to see the place, mind if we just drive out there?"

"Not at all. As I said, I'll leave a key with the Jensens."

When Leigh hung up, she decided to find an extra house key and leave it on the hall table so she wouldn't forget it. If Spencer called with plans for the day, she'd be all ready. She paused in her rummage through her purse.

What if Spencer doesn't call? Silly girl. Of course he would. *What if he's busy today?* A distinct possibility, given that he wasn't on holiday as she was. *Still, be prepared.* For what? A royal summons? Leigh groaned and covered her eyes with her hand. She was behaving like a teenager. Worse. She had the feeling she'd have acted more cool—as Jamie would put it—at seventeen.

Leigh took the key and headed into the hallway. Coffee could wait. She placed it in the center of the table and hesitated. Something different here. What? There was the little brass dish her mother had bought years ago and used for spare change and oddments. The brass letter holder Dad had given Mom for Christmas one year. Her car keys.

Then the image of a folded red-and-black checked bandanna came to mind. Spencer's handkerchief. Where was it? Leigh looked under the table, pulled open the drawer and searched every inch of hallway before deciding Spencer had noticed it himself and picked it up. She returned to the kitchen for coffee and to wait for Spencer's call.

HE WAS ABOUT TO HANG UP the phone when she answered. At the sound of his voice she gave a little intake of breath that made him smile. So, he told himself, he hadn't had to try three times before gathering courage to call. Maybe she'd been waiting all morning. *Right. And maybe she was just running to the phone.*

"Spence."

She said his name as if she were savoring a piece of Belgian chocolate. Spencer felt a tingle zip up his spine. "I meant to call sooner," he explained, "but I had some urgent phone messages to get to when I arrived at the office."

"That's okay."

Her voice sounded husky and faraway. The cell phone. Instinctively he lowered his own. "Listen, I...I hope you had no regrets this morning."

There was a pause long enough to raise the hairs on the back of his neck. Then she said, "No regrets," and he ached to reach through the telephone and wrap his arms around her. For a moment he couldn't think of anything else to say. His mind teemed with scents, touches and whispers in the night.

Leigh Randall at thirty-two was twice the woman she'd been at seventeen. He'd be hard-pressed to identify the exact nature of the difference. Her skin, amazingly as silken; curves more voluptuous, fitting the planes of his own body perfectly. The heat was there, as it had been fifteen years ago. But then it had been uncontrolled.

The real change, he decided, was in her responsiveness. The strong confident enjoyment she displayed at his touch. The lack of fear.

"Are you still there?"

"Huh?" Spencer shook himself. *Get a grip, fella.*

Her throaty laugh sent another sizzle up his backbone. He wiped his face with his free hand. *Gawd, it's going to be a long day.*

"Yeah, sorry. Listen, something's come up. Nothing bad, but important. A priority." He was babbling and screwing up. "Sam's specialist called and wants to see him right away. Thing is, I can't take him in the pickup. He really needs to be lying down. So the clinic is sending an ambulance for him. Jamie's with him now until the ambulance comes. The doc wants to run a few tests in Raleigh.... Sorry, what's that?''

Damn. The house. ''So when is this woman supposed to come about the house? Oh, it's not definite.'' Relief swept through him. Time, he thought. All he needed was more time to sort everything out. ''Leigh, the thing is...I may not get back to Ocracoke until tomorrow. I've canceled my charters for today and tomorrow morning just in case. But I'll call you when I'm back. No, don't be silly. It's my turn for dinner. Tomorrow night? Great.''

He hesitated, wanting to find just the right words. But imagination failed him when he needed it most. ''Look, I'll be thinking of you all the way to Raleigh and back. Take care. Bye.''

He replaced the receiver on the cradle and wondered why he felt like such a jerk.

LEIGH STARED at the phone lying on the kitchen table. For a sophisticated piece of technology, it could be hopelessly inadequate at times. She'd stammered and stumbled her way through the conversation like some geeky adolescent taking her first call from a boy. She emptied the rest of the coffee into the sink. Obviously Spencer wouldn't be popping round to share it. The day loomed disappointingly empty in front of her.

But it demanded occupation. Anything to get her mind off last night. *I'll save that for tonight when I'm lying alone in bed, thinking of Spence—thinking of me. Yeah, sure. Or maybe he's busy thinking of Jen. No, no, get real, Randall. That's over. Has been for a long, long time.*

Leigh wandered into the hallway, stopping at the table and mirror to see if she looked any different from yesterday. Because she certainly *felt* different. She stared at herself. Same black hair, tied in a messy knot at the moment; same nose, eyebrows thick and arched. Long lashes framing dark eyes—pieces of coal, Pete used to call them. Nothing much to rave about or turn heads—unlike Jen. Leigh smiled.

Who cares about Jen, anyway? Not you, she reminded her reflection. *After last night, the things he said? The things he did?* Leigh shivered. She touched her lip with the tip of her index finger, tracing its contours the way Spencer's tongue had. Closed her eyes. Felt the current play up and down her spine. Her eyes flashed open. *Okay. Find something to do.* A make-work project to take her mind off last night's make-love event. She gave herself one last glance, deciding that the pallor of an all-night session required a workout and turned to head upstairs. But something at the corner of her eye stopped her. Craning her neck sharply to the left, she caught the blurred image of a person standing on the other side of the front screen door. *Watching her.*

Leigh jumped. She walked slowly to the door, putting together the outline of a woman the closer she got.

"Have you come about the house?" Leigh asked through the screen.

"The house?" The woman looked behind her, seeming to notice the For Sale sign for the first time. "Oh. Yes."

Leigh pushed open the door. The woman was about her own height. Her dark brown hair was pulled back in some kind of knot, and her hazel eyes were fixed on Leigh's. In her early fifties, she might have been an attractive woman if she wasn't dressed so soberly and wore a little makeup. She didn't return Leigh's smile, but stared as though trying to memorize details of her face.

"Evan said he'd call to let me know you were coming. Is he with you?"

"Who's Evan?"

Leigh was beginning to wish she hadn't opened the

door. Perhaps the woman wasn't there about the house, but rather soliciting something. "The real-estate agent. You *have* come about the house, haven't you?"

The woman nodded slowly. "The house caught my eye, yes. It's a beautiful place. Shame you're selling it."

Leigh waited. When the woman didn't continue, she said, "I assume you're here alone."

Another nod. The eyes still hadn't moved from Leigh's face. She was starting to feel uncomfortable. "I guess it'll be all right to let you in and show you around. Evan told me you had some questions about the house." *Not to mention its owner.*

"Please. I'd like to come in. I've come a long way and it's very hot today."

Leigh held open the door while the woman stepped into the foyer. "Perhaps you'd like a cold glass of water before I show you around?" Leigh suggested.

"Yes. That would be wonderful."

Leigh hesitated, then stuck out her hand and said, "I'm Leigh Randall, by the way. This is my parents' home, but, well…" she stammered under the woman's gaze, "I'm the owner now."

"I know." The woman nodded again, then seemed to remember her manners. She extended her own hand and added, "Janet Bradley's the name."

Her handshake was firm and confident, though her palm was damp. Leigh withdrew hers and surreptitiously wiped it across the back of her shorts. "Why don't you come into the kitchen with me? We can start the tour from there."

She led the way along the short hall, past the entrance to the dining and living rooms. "The staircase splits the house, as you can see. The kitchen is behind the dining room and leads out to a deck."

"It's lovely and cool," the woman murmured.

"The house rarely heats up. There's a lot of cross-ventilation upstairs, as well as high ceilings. We seldom needed a fan, even in the hottest part of the summer. The breezes from the ocean and the Sound across the back keep it cool.''

"You've lived here all your life, then?"

"I grew up here, but I went to college on the mainland. After graduation, I got a job in New York City. I've lived there for the past seven years.''

"So you live there now?"

"Yes. Well, this is the kitchen," Leigh announced, stepping aside for her. "You can see it's fairly modern. I must admit the work was done about twenty years ago, but everything's in good shape. My father was a real handyman.''

"He *was?*"

The emphasis in the question made it sound as though Ms. Bradley knew otherwise. Leigh studied her as she scanned the room. She didn't appear to be as interested in the room as Leigh had expected. When her eyes landed back on Leigh's face, Leigh swooped over to the sink.

"I'll get you that glass of water. The island has a water-desalination plant now, but when I was small we still used the cistern out back. Here. You'll find it surprisingly cold.''

The woman took a tiny sip. Then she smiled. It seemed a genuine, if hesitant smile.

"It is good," she agreed, and placed the glass on the table without drinking any more.

"Well, then," Leigh slapped her hands against her thighs. A little too heartily, she thought. "Would you like to see the rest of the house now?''

Janet Bradley shook her head. "Not yet. Would you mind if I just sat here for a moment?" She pulled out a chair and sat down before Leigh could reply.

Maybe she walked from the ferry and is suffering from

neatstroke. That would explain her odd manner. "Do you have a car? Or did you walk?"

A single eyebrow lifted. "Heavens no! I have a car. Well, it's a rental, really. Won't you sit down, too?"

In my own house? Don't mind if I do. The woman's behavior was beginning to get to her, and Leigh could hardly wait to call Evan on the phone. Why hadn't he come with her?

She sat across from the woman and was about to comment on Evan's absence when Janet leaned across the table and said in a conspiratorial whisper, "Actually I haven't come about the house."

Leigh straightened in her chair. Gooseflesh sprung up along her forearms.

The woman plunked her beige leather purse onto the table and unclipped it. She poked through the purse until she retrieved a folded segment of newspaper. Then she carefully spread it out on the table. It was the article Mary Ann had written about Leigh's return to Ocracoke for the *Island Breeze*. Leigh stared down at it, seeing it for the first time, and then looked back up at Janet Bradley.

"I don't understand," she said.

"This is how I found you," the woman explained. "I couldn't believe my luck. I mean, I've been looking for so long and then suddenly, there you are. Staring up at me from the newspaper I read every month."

The hairs on the nape of Leigh's neck stood up. She glanced around the room. Where had she left the darn cell phone?

"I can see I'm going a bit fast for you," Janet said. "That's always been a problem of mine, I'm afraid. Assuming people can read my mind," she added, and smiled.

It was a brighter warmer smile. More of a take-charge smile that set Leigh at ease. The woman was strange, but not crazy, she decided. "I admit to being a tad confused."

"I did call about the house, but to be honest, I'm not really interested in buying it."

"Oh?"

"I should have written or telephoned, but sometimes these things are better said in person, don't you think?"

"What things?"

Janet's brows raised in surprise. "Why, reunions."

"I still don't get it. Who's being reunited?"

The smile became a little less assertive. Janet leaned back in her chair. After a moment she said, "I've been looking for you for a long long time, Leigh. It's been...very difficult, to say the least. So when I got my copy of the June *Island Breeze* and went over it until I was certain it was you, I knew I'd have to move very cautiously. That's how these things have to be done, you see. Carefully, so's not to upset the parties."

Leigh pushed back her chair and crossed to the sink. She poured herself a glass of water, tempted to dump it over her head to clear her mind. She took a long drink, then counted to ten. More composed, she returned to the kitchen table but didn't sit down. If she stood, perhaps the woman would get the hint and cut her bizarre story short.

"Okay," Leigh announced. "You saw the article Mary Ann wrote. She's an old friend," she explained at Janet's puzzled expression. "The reporter who did the story. And when you read it, you recognized me."

"Yes!"

"Where have we met? That's the part I haven't got yet."

Janet shook her head vehemently. "We haven't met. Today's the first time!"

The excitement in her voice slowed Leigh down. *Don't blow up*, she warned herself. *This woman really seems thrilled to have met me. Heaven knows why.*

Leigh put the empty glass on the table and folded her

arms across her chest. "You've lost me again," she said, not bothering to hide her impatience.

"I made inquiries at the real-estate office about the house to get directions. And to make sure it was really you. You see—" her voice fell to a stage whisper "—I knew you were somewhere in the Outer Banks and always knew the Randalls had adopted you, but I just never had the chance to follow through on my investigation."

"Investigation?"

"My search. For my daughter. For *you*."

The kitchen tilted. Leigh pulled out the chair and sat down. She rubbed her temples with her fingers, trying to erase the pounding. She reached for the glass, but it was empty. *Water isn't what you want now, anyway.*

Janet Bradley's smile was sympathetic. "I'm sorry. It is a bit of a shock. There doesn't seem to be any normal way of doing this sort of thing."

Leigh looked across the table. She took a calming breath and said, "You think I'm your daughter. Is that it?"

"You *are* my daughter. I gave birth to you almost thirty-three years ago. At the time I was only a girl myself. Too young to bear the responsibility." A frown darkened her face. "Your father left before you were even born, and my own parents wanted nothing to do with me. That's how things were in those days."

The words flew at Leigh, but made no sense. "What makes you think I'm your daughter?"

"You were adopted by Peter and Ellen Randall."

She could have gotten their names from anyone in Ocracoke. Slow down, Randall. "What...what papers do you have?"

"Papers?"

Leigh shrugged. "Papers to prove you're my mother."

Janet gave a sad smile. "They don't give you papers, my dear. You only sign them. The adoptive parents take the papers. Surely you have them?"

Leigh's mind made a quick replay of the past week. She'd tossed the adoption certificate onto the pile of stuff to go to the dump, hadn't she? She groaned.

"Are you all right?" Janet was asking. "I know this has been a bit of a shock."

Leigh felt her eyes narrow. *I'm not ready yet to say you're my mother.* "What did you think when you didn't get a reply to your letter?"

"The letter?"

"The letter you sent to the adoption agency. Years ago, to say you wanted to make contact with me."

Janet ducked her head. She reached for her purse and put it on her lap. Leigh waited while she flicked through it, then brought out a tissue. She blew her nose and dabbed at her eyes. When she raised her face to Leigh again, the tip of her nose and her eyes were red.

For the first time a feeling of pity pulled at Leigh. *Whoever she is, she obviously wants to believe I'm her daughter.*

"What did you think when you received the letter?" the woman countered.

Leigh swallowed hard. The unexpected question threw her. "I...I never received it. My parents did, but I just found out about it the other day."

Janet reached out a hand to pat Leigh's forearm.

"At the time it came—the spring before I turned fifteen," Leigh went on, "my father was in the first stages of Alzheimer's. We didn't know it then, but my mother obviously knew something was seriously wrong with him. I...I'm certain she couldn't bear to have the complication of..." She hesitated.

"A birth mother appearing on her doorstep."

Leigh uncovered her face and raised her eyes to the woman across from her. For a moment compassion linked them. "Yes," she murmured.

"Could I see the letter?"

What harm could it do? Leigh asked herself. Even if the woman wasn't her mother, she was certainly sincere and caring. They'd have tea and chat and then she'd be on her way.

"It's upstairs in the master bedroom." Leigh got unsteadily to her feet and gestured toward the door. In the hall she led the way up the staircase, pausing at the top landing for Janet, whose pace was slower. When Janet caught up to her, she passed Leigh and continued on down the hall toward the front of the house and Leigh's parents room.

"Did you come to the open house?" Leigh asked from behind. Janet knew which was the master bedroom.

The woman stopped, hesitated and then turned round to look at Leigh. "Not the open house," she said. "But all these old homes have a common design. The master bedroom is always at the front."

Leigh cocked her head. "Hmm. I guess you're right. Never thought of it before. Anyway—" she brushed past Janet who was hovering in the bedroom doorway and got down on all fours beside the bed "—my mother stored important things in here," she said, and dragged the leather valise into the center of the floor.

Janet sat down on the edge of the bed and watched Leigh unsnap the lid and begin to sort through the contents. "Did she keep the blanket in there, too?"

Leigh slowly lowered the lid. A roaring sound filled her ears, and when it cleared, she was able to ask, "What blanket?"

"The blanket you went home from the hospital with. The one I wrapped you in before I…I signed you away." Janet lowered her face and dug the tissue out of her purse again.

Leigh couldn't take her eyes off the woman perched so casually on her parents' bed. *What's happening here?* The question spun through her brain like a deflating balloon.

Finally Leigh's mind shut down. She couldn't assimilate anything. The action played out before her all on its own. A sense of utter lethargy overwhelmed her. She felt devoid of movement, power, even feeling.

"What's the blanket like?"

Janet tucked the used tissue into the pocket of her dress and smiled. It was a dreamy remembering kind of smile that took her back to another era. "It was a pale blue. Some people would call it powder blue, but when you think about it, what kind of powder is blue?"

Leigh struggled to keep pace. "I...I don't know."

"And there were yellow ducks—babies—following a mother duck." She frowned. "Was the mother duck yellow, too, or brown? Because, of course she should be brown."

Leigh nodded up and down, back and forth—as erratically as Janet spoke, she thought. She took in a gulp of air, forcing it around the lump in her throat. "And do you still have the piece?"

Janet's head pivoted down to Leigh's upturned face. "Piece?"

"The corner. It's always been missing a tiny piece of the corner and my mother—Ellen—used to say my birth mother had kept it. As a reminder."

Janet covered her face with her hand. Leigh waited patiently, restraining herself from rushing to her side.

"I left it at home," was the hushed reply. "I...I suppose part of me decided I'd probably be disappointed all over again."

"Would you like to see it?" Leigh asked, raising the valise lid once more.

"Please."

And when she pulled it out from the bottom of the suitcase, Janet cried, "That's it! That's your ducky blanket." Then she burst into tears.

Leigh pushed the valise aside and crawled over to the edge of the bed. She pulled herself up and enveloped Janet Bradley in her arms.

CHAPTER TEN

LEIGH CLOSED THE DOOR behind Janet and, after the woman's car had backed out the drive, swung round and fell against the frame. She blew out a lungful of air, flapping the strand of hair that had been dangling across her forehead. She felt spent, exhausted. Bone tired, as Mom would say. *Mom*. She wanted her mother. She ached for her. Only her mother would understand the flood of confusion, the upheaval of emotions that she was experiencing.

She flipped on the porch light, even though the full darkness of night had not yet fallen. Suddenly it mattered to her more than anything that the world—people out there—should know someone was home at Windswept Manor. *Home*. She walked aimlessly through the ground-floor rooms, almost the way she had a week ago when she'd first arrived. A week ago. Hard to believe so much had happened in seven days.

But she was too exhausted to make a mental list of the events. Her mind was scarcely chugging back into gear, even now that Janet had left. She and Janet had chatted, drunk two pots of tea and then shared a pizza delivered from the village. She'd invited Janet to stay the night, but the woman had insisted on returning to her motel in Hatteras, giving Leigh more time, she'd said, "to get used to things."

That was one way to put it, Leigh mused, though she'd have chosen something more dramatic, if she could have found the appropriate description. But her brain wasn't functioning except at a basic level after spending all that time answering, almost like an automaton, Janet's many questions about her childhood. And when it had been her turn to do the asking, her unreliable mind went blank. Horses bolted from the stable, as her dad would have said.

Leigh switched off the lights on the ground floor and strolled out onto the back deck to sit, cloaked in the comfort of night. She poured herself a glass of wine, and her analytical banker's mind began to kick into action as she contemplated the afternoon.

Once Janet had warmed up, her strange mannerisms disappeared. Her conversation, except for a tendency to digress, was animated and interesting. She was especially enthusiastic talking about her pregnancy—her only one, she confessed—and the events leading to the adoption. She'd never met the Randalls, but had seen a photograph and liked their appearance.

Leigh's head was swimming with new names and new family connections. By the time she'd finished a second slice of pizza, she was wrung out, unable to take in any more information. Janet insisted on leaving so Leigh could get an early night. And Leigh, even knowing she couldn't, had solemnly agreed to go right to bed.

She downed the last of the wine. If only Spencer was here to help her sort out the emotional confusion of meeting her birth mother. *Or perhaps he'd only add to it.* She wondered what he'd say when he heard the news and guessed his initial response would be skepticism, as hers had been.

No, she thought, going over the scene yet one more time. Janet could have learned everything from records or gossip, but not the part about the blanket. Who else knew about the blanket? Her parents and Jen. She was certain she hadn't even mentioned it to Spence. Baby blankets didn't exactly rate high in teenage girl-boy talk.

Just the opposite. The topic of babies had been taboo, the very idea striking cold fear in her. She grinned, recalling the first of only three times she and Spencer had made love as teen sweethearts. The experience had been mostly a sweaty grappling in the back seat of Pete Randall's Buick. It was the spring before graduation and Spencer had just turned nineteen. They'd both been paralyzed with fear for weeks afterward, until Leigh discovered she wasn't pregnant. Looking back, she was amazed she'd had the courage to try it twice more. But Spencer always had the magic touch. His grin alone had been sufficient persuasion.

Leigh stood up. Time to call it a night, she thought. Or try to get some sleep. She closed the French door leading to the deck and tidied up the remnants of dinner. Glancing at the chair Janet had been sitting in, she could almost see her still there, a crumpled tissue clutched in her hand as the story of her life—and Leigh's beginning—eked out word by word over the long hot afternoon. She walked into the living room, extinguishing a lamp she'd forgotten. The picture window was speckled with moths that even sudden darkness couldn't budge, so Leigh tapped briskly on the window.

"There's another light, guys. Just over there on the porch." As she pulled back, she caught sight of a jeans-clad leg stepping onto the veranda. She reached the hallway just as someone started banging on the frame of the screen door. *Spencer?* Anticipation propelled her across the floor. But the outline behind the door was too small for Spence. Leigh slowed down. The porch light beamed a bright yellow orb over Jamie's head.

"Jamie?"

"Yeah. Sorry to bother you, coming by so late and all. I saw your light still on and figured you might be here. Everything's okay, you know. You look kinda worried."

"I admit to a flash of concern. Come in." She released

the catch and held the door open as he brushed past. "Is your dad still in Raleigh?"

"Yeah."

He wore a striped cotton T-shirt over his jeans. Although the night was sticky, he rubbed his hands up and down his arms, warming himself. His blond hair was slick with perspiration, and Leigh noticed tiny beads of it strung along his upper lip. He looked around the foyer as if checking his bearings.

"Are you all right?" Leigh asked.

He just nodded. She closed the door and turned off the veranda light. Except for Jamie's labored breathing and the steady whack of insects against the screen, all was silent.

"Hungry? I've got some leftover pizza."

Another nod. Leigh motioned for Jamie to follow her into the kitchen, wondering when exactly her very peculiar day was going to end.

"Coke?"

"Please."

Ah, manners. A good sign. "You want the pizza heated up?"

"I like it cold."

"Yeah, me, too. Besides, it's been sitting out for a bit, and room-temperature tonight is about the same as the microwave."

"Pizza sucks in the microwave."

"No kidding! Best is straight from the fridge, when the cheese is all hard and bumpy."

Jamie grinned. He took the same chair Janet had used and pulled the tab on the pop can. He drank long enough for Leigh to wonder when he'd had his last.

"Been working out?" She was teasing, but gestured to his damp shirt.

He ducked his head to focus on the top of the Coke, and Leigh decided she'd said the wrong thing. She plunked the rest of the pizza onto a plate and set it on the table in front of him. *There goes breakfast.*

He looked up then. "Sure you don't want any?"

She waved a hand and waited. After he'd wolfed down one slice, come up for air and chugged another swallow of Coke, he was beginning to resemble his old self. *Oh, to be fourteen again,* Leigh thought.

"Great," he said between bites. "How'd *you* like the pizza? Not bad for poky old Ocracoke."

"And they even deliver."

Jamie nodded solemnly. Leigh figured he'd missed the irony of her comment.

"I'm locked out," he blurted.

Leigh blinked. "Locked out?"

Jamie pulled a face. "Dad told me to take a key when I left this morning to wait at Grandpa's for the ambulance, but I forgot. When the ambulance came, there was a lot of commotion. He didn't want to go—you know what Grandpa's like."

Leigh nodded. "Uh-huh."

Jamie shrugged. "Then I forgot to tell Dad I didn't have the key. He locked up Grandpa's place and followed the ambulance, taking that key, too."

"So you can't even go to Sam's."

He shook his head.

"And friends?"

After a moment he mumbled, "None available."

"Well, I certainly have lots of room here." She waited while he mulled this over, knowing that was the very reason he'd come to her door.

"I don't want to put you to any trouble," he murmured.

"No more trouble than handing you sheets and a pillow." She kept her voice light.

He thought some more, then said, "Thank you," topping it off with a smile. He returned to the pizza with more decorum and less enthusiasm this time, finally leaving the

ast slice on the plate. "I'm actually kinda tired already,"
ie said.

"Me, too. Would you like a bed upstairs or the couch
lown here?"

He frowned. "Maybe the couch. That way I won't dis-
urb you at all."

"Fine. Follow me and I'll let you have the first
hower."

He wasn't much of a talker, she thought, leading the
vay upstairs. Especially compared to Janet, who hadn't
eemed to pause long enough for air. And he obviously
elt uncomfortable crashing at her place—someone he'd
mly met twice before. Leigh figured he must have been
lesperate for a place to stay.

After she'd handed him towels and steered him toward
he bathroom, she took sheets and a pillow downstairs and
nade up the sofa. Then she locked up, tidied the kitchen
igain and headed upstairs. They bumped into each other
n the landing.

Jamie was still damp from the shower and full of apol-
igies about staying the night. He turned awkwardly and
ackled the stairs two at a time, shaking the framed paint-
ngs and photographs lining the wall. Leigh shook her
lead, went into the bathroom and swore softly. Towels and
in uncapped shampoo bottle littered the floor. A puddle of
vater remained in the bottom of the tub, where the fallen
topper had trapped it.

As she bent down to tidy up—again—she thought of
en doing this for the past fourteen years. It was a sobering
mage, the more so because Jen had always been com-
iletely incapable of cleaning up after herself, let alone oth-
rs. The fleeting insight amused Leigh, but also produced
seed of admiration for her old friend. She'd been so
young when Jamie was born. It couldn't have been easy,
ven with Spencer.

The thought segued into one of Janet, obliged to hand

over her infant just days after the birth. Leigh shuddered. The experiences of the two women had been very different, but they'd both been dealt a challenging blow at a young age. She wondered suddenly if she'd have been as capable as they had. *What if Spencer and I...?*

Well, we didn't, she told herself sharply. She flicked off the bathroom light, leaving the hall one on for Jamie as she'd promised. Too tired to read, she crawled into bed and turned out the lamp. What was that feeling she'd had this morning?

Oh, yes. That the day was going to be like no other since her return to Ocracoke. *I can't argue with that,* she thought, and immediately fell asleep.

THE TELEPHONE. Once the noise registered, Leigh extended an arm and fumbled around on the night table until she located the cell phone, all the while blessing her foresight in remembering to take it upstairs with her.

"Leigh? Sorry to wake you. Spencer here."

His voice was clipped, almost urgent. Before she could mumble a hello, he went on to say, "This is probably a dumb question, but would you happen to know where Jamie is?"

Leigh unglued her lips and pulled herself up to lean on her elbow. "Spencer. Sorry. Just waking up. Yes, he's here."

There was a sharp intake of breath followed by a silence. Then, "Well, that's a relief. Jeez. I could strangle that kid."

"He didn't have a key."

"He *forgot* his key. I swear he'd forget his head if he wasn't always admiring it in a mirror."

"He came around about nine last night," Leigh said. "He seemed pretty upset. I'm sure the experience was... well, enough punishment."

"Ha!" Spencer snorted. "Wonder how long he'll remember this lesson. Anyway, thank you for taking him in. It was a long shot, but I was hoping he'd be there. I've spent the last hour trying to find him.''

"Spence—"

"I—" he blurted at the same time.

"Go ahead," she said.

"I was going to call you, anyway. Just to…to check in and see how things are going. Give you an update on Sam."

"How is he?"

"Okay. Ornery as usual. Insists he's made a full recovery and demanding to be discharged. But the doc wants to run him through a few tests, then fiddle around with his medication. Get it right, I guess. He'll be here a few more days."

"At least that'll force him to stay in bed where he should be."

"That's what I said." Spence paused. "I've got an appointment this afternoon in Charlotte about Jamie. Something's come up."

The hesitancy in his voice made her wonder if he wanted to discuss it or not. Finally she asked, "Anything I can do?"

"Nah. Just keep your fingers crossed. Thing is, I haven't even mentioned this to him yet, but…well, seems like Jen's new husband has declared an intention to legally adopt Jamie."

"What? Can he do that?"

"I don't know. My lawyer says only if I'm not considered a fit parent or something. I guess Jen's hubby—Rob's his name—figures if he adopts Jamie, they'll be one big happy family once the baby comes."

"That's crazy!"

"That's what I think. I mean, couldn't he and Jen figure out that's why Jamie was giving them such a hard time? 'Cause he was so damn *un*happy with them?"

Leigh held the phone away from her ear. His anger had raised his voice a few decibels.

"Anyway, as I said, I'll be pleading my case before a judge this afternoon and then, I guess eventually, he'll want to talk to Jamie."

"The poor kid." Leigh sighed.

"Yeah, as if he doesn't have enough to sort out. Look, don't breathe a word of this. I hope to get back to Ocracoke later tonight. Would you mind…"

"I'll be happy to keep an eye on him."

"Well, he doesn't really need a sitter, but since he's locked out and probably has no money…"

"I have lots of food."

Spence laughed, but she could hear the relief in his voice.

"Probably not enough for a growing teenager." There was a brief silence and then, his voice deeper and lower, Spence said, "I owe you big time for this, Leigh."

"Darn right," she said. "Wasn't that going to be dinner?"

"Ah, yes. Was it tonight?"

It was Leigh's turn to laugh. "Forget it, Spence. I think you have enough on your mind right now. Besides, who knows when you'll get back? Another time. Seriously."

"You…you're being good about this, Leigh."

That's me, all right. Good old Randall. "See you later, then?"

"Yeah. Thanks again."

Leigh plunked the phone down on the table. She realized she hadn't even mentioned her own news. Well, there'd be plenty of time for talk when he got back later tonight. Then she muttered a curse. Who wanted to talk, anyway?

JAMIE COULDN'T DO enough for her. After the biggest breakfast Leigh had ever cooked—much less witnessed anyone eat—they spent the rest of the morning cleaning the attic, then hauling out boxes of stuff Leigh couldn't bring herself to toss in the garbage.

"I can see I'm definitely going to have to hire a big moving company to take this stuff to New York. Problem is..."

"No place to put it when you get there?"

"You said it!"

Jamie stood back to inspect the pile of cartons. "Too bad you can't just leave everything here. You know, like sort of keep this as a summer home. Then all this stuff would be here for you when you came back for a holiday."

The innocence of youth, she thought, looking at the eagerness in his face. "That would be nice," she said and hating to dampen his optimism, added, "The problem is, really, I can't keep up the place from New York. It's just too much work and too much money."

"I could do it! Seriously, Leigh, my dad wants me to get a job and I could do it."

Leigh was touched by the zeal of his proposal. She smiled. "Jamie, that's incredibly thoughtful of you, but I think it would be too much. Even for you. And then, you have school starting in September, right?"

He scowled. "I hate school. I'm so glad summer vacation's started."

Something in his voice advised her to swallow the platitude perched on the edge of her tongue. One of the few things she could recall hating in her adolescence was the way adults readily came up with phony advice that kids knew they'd never follow themselves.

"I have an idea," she said, instead. "How about packing a lunch and hiking through the marshes to where the wild ponies are? I haven't seen them in years. In fact, I haven't even been to the other side of the island since I got back. Interested?" She saw the glimmer of excitement flare in his green eyes before she'd even finished.

"All right!"

"AND LEIGH FOUND a place in the fence where we could slip through to get a closer look at them."

Spence shot an amused glance at her. *Leigh?* But Jamie wasn't slowing down for comments.

"We musta seen about ten mares and stallions and two foals. They were just wandering around, eating that wild grass. A couple of them pranced into the surf just to cool off. They were so...so..."

"Cool?" Spence asked.

"Nah. More than cool. Way more than cool. Awesome."

Spencer set his cold beer on the patio table. "When I was a kid, they still roamed free. But then the highway was finished and too many of them were getting hit by cars and trucks. Plus, the number of tourists skyrocketed."

Jamie nodded. "Yeah, that's what Leigh said. It seems a shame to fence them in, but hey, 180 acres is still a lot of space to wander around. Anyway—" he slugged back the rest of his soda "—we had a great time. Didn't we, Leigh?" He grinned across the table at her. She was sitting next to Spencer.

Leigh again. Spencer was beginning to feel like the odd man out. But he didn't mind the sensation. He certainly liked the enthusiasm he saw in Jamie's face. It was the first genuine emotion—other than hot anger—he'd seen in his son for months. Everything else had been an apathetic indifference.

He crumpled up the empty wrapper on his plate. He'd returned just before the dinner hour, bringing burgers and fries with him, to find Jamie and Leigh relaxing after their all-afternoon hike around the salt marshes and woodlands fringing Pamlico Sound.

Leigh looked at him, their grins connecting at Jamie's tale. It was the most she'd heard the boy speak. He'd been so quiet for most of the hike that at times she'd had to turn around to see if he was still following. But when she'd asked him if he wanted to return home, his vehement *no* spurred them on for another hour and a half until she was the one begging to come back another day.

"The ponies will still be here next week," she'd said, to which he'd softly replied, "Yeah, but you might not be." She'd turned away, feeling the sting of tears and decided that, next to Sam's, that was the best homecoming remark she'd heard since her return to Ocracoke.

Now Jamie was standing up, thanking her for the great day and the sleepover and extending a polite hand, which Leigh firmly shook. Then he left, off to a movie in Hatteras with a friend; he'd be staying at his friend's place that night, he told Spencer, making Leigh wonder where this friend had been last night. Then she bustled about, picking up the remains of dinner because she suddenly felt shy and awkward alone with Spencer.

But his hand shot out to clamp onto her forearm. "Sit down," he said, softening his order with a heart-lurching "please" that made her go all wobbly in the legs. Must be the big hike today, she told herself, although she knew otherwise.

"You've made quite an impression on Jamie. I haven't seen him like that for...I hate to say it, but for years. Since he was a little kid."

"It's only because I'm a neutral party. You know—unconnected with any family issues or..."

"Problems?"

He sounded bitter. "I didn't mean that, Spencer. I'm just a novelty—something new and different in his life. If I were staying longer, that would change, too."

Spencer forked a hand through his hair. "Yeah, you're right. Maybe I'm jealous. That's the Jamie I've been searching for since he came to live with me."

"He's also a teenager. Even if you'd never lived apart, he probably wouldn't be much different than he is now with you."

Spencer waved a dismissive hand. "I know, I know. Gawd, I've been telling myself that for months. I guess the heat is on now with this adoption thing."

"Are you feeling scared about it?"

"Damn scared. I've lost too many people in my life." He stared ahead into the yard. "First my own mom, when I was about ten."

"I never met her."

"Nope. She'd put up with enough of my pa's drinking and took off. Too bad she didn't take me with her." He cocked his head at Leigh and flashed a weak grin. "But then, I'd have never met you."

There was a long silence that Leigh desperately wanted to fill, but words failed her. She pushed around some crumbs on the patio table and didn't dare meet his eyes.

Finally he continued, "Then I lost you and a few years later my son."

"And Jen," she put in, almost out of perversity.

"Not Jen. I never had Jen. After the first few months of marriage, I couldn't even pretend anymore. I...I wasn't very nice to her. I feel bad about that. But—" he uttered a cynical laugh "—she paid me back in full. I reckon we're even now."

Despair swept over Leigh. "You can't put the past back together," she whispered, staring down at her lap.

"No. I wouldn't want to, not now. Now I'm...hoping to make something new." He reached out a hand to angle Leigh's face his way. "All the way to Raleigh, and then Charlotte, all I could think about was you. What I'm trying to say...I'm not getting this out very well, but the way I used to feel for you—nothing's changed. Not for me. And I need to know—how do *you* feel about all...about Sunday night?"

She hated herself for hesitating, but emotion churned through her sluggishly. "I...I don't know, Spencer." She paused at the disappointment in his face. He was expecting something more from her, but she wasn't certain she knew what that something was. "So much is happening so quickly. It's difficult to take it all in, much less make sense of it all."

"I've loved you my whole life, Leigh. The other night when you were talking about the last time you saw me standing outside your dorm, waiting for you to come out—I wish you could have known how I felt, driving back to Ocracoke. I knew my life was over. That it wasn't going to turn out the way I'd thought for those two years we were together."

Heat rushed into Leigh's face. She clenched her hands, shoving them into her lap under the table. Spencer stood up and pulled her out of the chair. He folded his arms around her and murmured huskily, "Let's change the course of our lives. Right now." He rubbed his cheek into her hair, inhaling salt spray and jasmine shampoo, and buried his face in the crook of her neck.

Leigh tugged on the back of his head, gently raising it to hers. She cupped his face in her hands, said, "I've tortured myself with this fantasy a thousand times," and planted her mouth firmly on his.

MUCH LATER, deep in the still of night and after they'd roused themselves to make love again—but more slowly this time, luxuriating in the sense of time without end— Leigh told him about the visit from Janet Bradley.

Spencer was lying spooned against her, his cheek resting on her bare shoulder. He rolled her toward him. Her face was pale in the spill of moonlight from the open window. "You really think she's your mother?" he asked.

Leigh sighed. "I don't know, Spence. She knows things I can't explain otherwise."

"Like?"

"First the blanket. And she knew stuff about my dad's

family—how they settled here in the early 1800s. She knew that my mom's parents were from the mainland...''

''Couldn't she have found that out by questioning some of the locals?''

''I suppose. I can't explain it. Her story about the adoption just rang so true.''

''Maybe she has a good imagination.''

''But what would be the point in making it up? What does she have to gain by pretending? It's not as if I'm an heiress or something.''

''You've got this house.''

''She wasn't even interested in the house.''

''Why now? How did she explain linking up with you now?''

''She said the article revived all her lost hope. That's exactly how she put it. *Lost hope.* Said she gave up after she didn't get a response to her letter.''

''What letter?''

''The letter she sent just before I turned fifteen. The one I found in Mom's bedroom. Didn't I tell you about it?''

''No.''

When she'd finished, Leigh said, ''If Mary Ann hadn't written that article about me, Janet would never have shown up.''

''You're right. Still, it does seem damn coincidental. And you've really got no proof.''

''Just the proof of what my heart tells me, Spence. If you could have seen the expression on her face when I pulled out that blanket...''

Spencer nuzzled the nape of her neck. ''Mmm.'' He gave a low growl. ''I'd like to see the expression on your face when I start doing this....'' He nibbled a dainty track along the base of her neck, then angled toward her breast.

Leigh's laughter bounced around the room and then ebbed into the breathless whispers of lovemaking.

CHAPTER ELEVEN

"WAKE UP!"

Leigh groaned and rolled onto her back. One eyelid fluttered open. She saw Spence's face hovering over her and begged, in a voice that cracked, "Please! I can't take any more."

He grinned. "Neither can I. I'm not nineteen again."

"Thank goodness."

The grin shifted. "What's that supposed to mean?"

Leigh threw a pillow at him. "'Cause we'd be here all day, silly, and I've got things to do."

He straightened, zipped up his jeans and bent to retrieve his shirt from the floor. "I'll say you do," he said, gesturing with his head to the doorway.

Leigh pushed herself up on her elbows. "What do you mean?"

Spencer inserted one tanned arm into his shirt and then the other. Leigh watched the last of the golden hairs at the V of his neck disappear as he buttoned. She sighed. The night was really over.

"I think your friend is here knocking on the front door. I peeked out through the bedroom window."

"My friend?" Leigh ran a thick tongue along her dry lips.

Spencer returned to the edge of the bed. "Sure you're okay? What is it? Can't be a hangover, not from two beers."

She pushed herself up to sit cross-legged. The sheet fell

away and Spencer murmured, "You have beautiful breasts."

Leigh smiled encouragement, arching her back slightly.

"Here," he said, throwing her blouse at her. "Put this on or we'll be leaving Janet what's-her-name standing pounding at the door all morning."

"Oh, no! What's she doing here now?" Leigh wailed. "She was supposed to phone today." Leigh slipped into the blouse and began to button it.

Spence was fumbling with a pair of socks. "Maybe she couldn't wait to see you. If we're lucky, she's bringing breakfast."

Leigh got out of bed and tiptoed to the door. "I don't think she's the breakfast-bringing type."

Spencer was staring at her again.

"What?" She looked at him from the bedroom door, hands on her hips and a knowing smile on her face.

"Hmm?" Then he grumbled, "Hell of a way to wake up. So who's getting the door?"

"I will. She doesn't know you." Leigh reached for the robe swinging from the back of the door and tied it around her. "I'll stall her at the front door so you can sneak down into the kitchen and get coffee started."

Spencer shook his head. "I don't believe it. You're not seventeen."

"And aren't you damn lucky I'm not," she countered, swaying out of the room.

HE SAW THE WOMAN'S face fall in disappointment the instant he stepped into view from behind Leigh, and his hackles bristled with annoyance. *If she wanted Leigh to herself, she should have called as she'd promised.* But Spencer extended his right hand at Leigh's introduction and released the woman's damp one as soon as he politely could.

Leigh had been right, he noticed. There were no paper

bags of coffee or doughnuts in sight, only a beat-up black leather Pullman standing on the veranda. Spencer frowned and decided to make himself scarce.

"I'll put some coffee on," he said, turning to Leigh and raising a quizzical eyebrow, which she ignored. By the time they joined him in the kitchen, he'd drunk his first cup.

Leigh seemed nervous. She was wringing her hands and gesturing to a chair at the same time. "Guess what?" she asked, her voice unusually loud.

Spencer set down his empty cup and stared at her.

Without awaiting a reply Leigh said, "Janet's going to be able to stay with me for a few days. Maybe even a week."

Spence looked at Janet, who gave a smile he found ingratiating. *Must have been some conversation in the hallway.* He simply nodded, not trusting his voice. Complications were springing up all over his plans suddenly, and he didn't like it one damn bit.

He pushed his chair back and got to his feet. "Guess I'd better go pick up Jamie at his friend's." He looked meaningfully at Leigh, whose face had become unnaturally still. "See you later?" he asked, heading for the door.

"Wait! I'll walk you out." She shot after him, clutching his forearm just as he reached the front door. "Spencer! What's gotten into you?"

"I think you'd better go slowly with this mother thing, Leigh. What do you know about that woman?"

"Please. Trust me. It's just that she can't afford to stay in the motel anymore. She was going to go back home— to Elizabeth City—and I don't want her to leave so soon, Spence. Can't you understand that? I want to get to know her more before she just walks out of my life."

"Leigh, if she's really your mother, she won't be walking out of your life. Maybe she should go back home for a little while. Give you a chance to..."

"To what?"

He shrugged. "Do some checking. Find out if she's really who she says she is."

Leigh stepped back. "I want her to stay. I'd like her to get to know you and Jamie. And Sam, too, when he's back. I can always check her out later. What's the harm in having a houseguest for a few days?"

Spencer moved toward the door. "Just be careful, okay? She looks a bit odd to me."

"What do you mean?"

"I'm not sure. But she has a strange look in her eye."

Leigh poked him in the shoulder. "And I used to think I was the fanciful one."

He grinned, running the tip of his finger along her jaw. "As I said, be careful. I'll call you later." He pushed through the screen door and took the veranda steps in one leap.

JANET BRADLEY looked forlorn standing in the middle of the bedroom, her suitcase clutched in one hand.

"In here?" she asked.

"If you don't mind..."

"I don't mind at all. I feel honored you want me to have your parents' room."

Leigh smiled reassuringly. "I think that's what they'd have wanted, too. Why don't you get organized while I have a shower, and then we'll take a spin around Ocracoke."

"All right. But I hope I haven't put you to any trouble, dear. With your boyfriend and all."

Leigh stopped midway through the door. "Spencer and I are good friends."

Janet's shoulders lifted in a small shrug.

Leigh added, "I know this must be as overwhelming for you as it is for me..."

"Yes, indeed it is. And the thing is, Leigh, I'm really a

very shy person. Back home I don't get out much at all."
Then she startled Leigh by walking right up to her and
lightly touching her cheek with one hand. "I'm so very
happy now that I've found you."

Leigh closed the bedroom door behind her and leaned
against it for a moment. *I don't really know her,* she
thought, and wondered why on earth she'd asked a stranger
into her home. *But she's not a stranger and you'll know
plenty about her—in time.*

LEIGH FIGURED they'd covered all twelve miles of Ocracoke Island by lunch, stopping twice—once for iced tea
and once for a closer look at the lighthouse, which Janet
found fascinating.

"It's the oldest working lighthouse in North Carolina,"
Leigh boasted. Seeing Ocracoke through a newcomer's
eyes revitalized her own sense of the past; the fact that
Janet appeared to love the place was a bonus. Somehow it
mattered that Janet like Ocracoke, although Leigh couldn't
have explained why.

When the car pulled into the drive of Windswept Manor,
Janet said, "You must have had a wonderful childhood
growing up here."

"I did. It was and still is an idyllic place for children.
We could basically roam as free as the wild ponies did at
the time."

"Then I did the right thing."

Leigh glanced at Janet next to her on the seat. She was
fiddling with the clasp of her handbag. She raised her gaze
to Leigh's, her eyes brimming with tears. "Giving you up,
I mean. There's no way in the world I could have given
you a childhood like that in Elizabeth City."

She's my mother, Leigh thought. *She* must *be.*

"SAM'S COMING HOME in a couple of days," Spence announced as soon as Leigh picked up the phone.

"How is he?"

A long pause. "Not great, but okay. The doctor said that at his age the best they can do is regulate his medication. Try to get him to rest and so on."

"Then he's not going to be able to stay by himself."

A heavy sigh from Spence. "Yeah, I know. I've been thinking and making plans all morning. 'Course, none of it will amount to much if the old guy refuses to cooperate."

"You'll have to make him."

"Right. Easier said than done."

"What can I do to help?"

"Thanks for asking, but not a heck of a lot. I'm hoping to persuade Jamie to stay with Sam for the summer—if he refuses to move in with me right away, that is. Once fall is here, I don't think I'll have any problem getting Sam to move. There's no way he's going to spend another winter in that place of his."

"How about if I clean up for him? Before he returns."

"That'd be great. I'm fully booked the next two days, so I was planning on giving that job to Jamie, too."

"Well, I doubt he'd be much improvement over Sam as a housekeeper."

Spence's husky laugh made her smile. She wished he'd come to the house, rather than telephone. But then—she glanced at Janet rocking in the wicker chair on the front veranda—perhaps out of sight was also out of frustrating thought.

"So—" his voice trailed off momentarily "—is she still there?"

Leigh knew whom he meant. "Yeah."

"For how long, do you think?"

"I don't know for sure. At least until the end of the week." Leigh thought she heard a muttered curse on the other end.

"And the end of your holiday?"

"I almost forgot. I called my boss, Reg, this morning, and he's given me more time. In fact, almost as much time as I want."

There was a sharp intake of air and then, "That's terrific. That more than makes up for...for everything."

When Leigh hung up moments later, she wondered what he'd really meant to say. Although she thought she knew.

BY THE TIME they'd finished dinner, Leigh had learned a lot about her birth mother. The bottle of wine they shared had loosened Janet up, and she'd told Leigh so much about her own childhood that Leigh's head was whirling.

When Leigh took the tray of coffee out to the patio, Janet murmured, "I can't tell you how happy I am. I feel a contentment I haven't felt for years."

Leigh patted her hand.

"Did you ever hear the story about how you were named?" Janet asked.

Leigh sat up in her chair. This was one childhood memory she hadn't mentioned at all since Janet had walked into her house. "You tell me."

The woman smiled. "Is this some kind of test?"

"Perhaps," Leigh said, returning the smile.

"When I was a young girl, my all-time favorite movie was *Gone with the Wind*."

Leigh tensed. She was pretty sure she knew where Janet was heading.

"And my favorite star was Vivien Leigh, from the movie. When you were born, you were so beautiful with that black head of hair and eyes. I named you Leigh, after the actress."

"And?" was all Leigh could manage.

A tiny smile flit across Janet's face. "To make sure the Randalls knew that was the name I wanted you to have, I wrote it on a piece of paper and pinned it to your sleeper."

The breath Leigh had been holding escaped. Ellen had

often talked about the note with the name "Leigh" printed on it. This was the piece of the story she'd never had of course. The story Janet had just told was the whole puzzle put together. Overwhelmed, Leigh couldn't speak for a long moment.

Finally she asked, "Did you also knit the baby outfit I came home in?"

In the splash of light from the kitchen, Janet's face paled. "You still have it?"

"My mother kept it."

"Ellen."

"Yes," Leigh affirmed. Then, out of loyalty repeated, "My mother."

Janet stared down at her lap, then finally up at Leigh. "I hope someday... Well, it's too early for that, I suppose."

Darn right. Tension fell between them, until Leigh felt herself relenting. Janet was only saying what was in her heart. "Would you like to see the outfit?" Leigh asked.

"Another time, dear. I'm feeling very tired. It's been a long and full day. My back, you know. Flares up. An old injury from my nursing days." Janet rose from the table. She began to pick up dishes to take into the kitchen.

"Don't do that. Go to bed. There's plenty of time for dishes tomorrow."

"Yes, there is time, isn't there? Now. Good night, then." She turned to walk through the opened French door, then paused. "I knitted that outfit myself, you know. Bought the wool with some money I'd saved and knit it under cover of darkness so my folks wouldn't find out. They were that upset," she explained, sighing. "It was made out of a great deal of love, Leigh." With that she went inside.

Leigh sat so still and so long her legs cramped. When the banging on the front door roused her, she had to practically hobble through to the front of the house. Spencer was standing on the other side of the screen door and he looked grim.

"Sam?" she asked, hand at her mouth.

"Nope." He hesitated on the porch, then stepped inside at Leigh's gesture. "Jamie. I don't suppose you've seen him or heard from him? Heck of a long shot, but…"

"I haven't seen him since yesterday. Why? What's happened?"

Spence swore. He pawed at his face with his right hand while the other jiggled his truck keys. "I just got in from my fishing trip about half an hour ago and found the sheriff waiting on my doorstep." He took a calming breath, shaking his head at the question in Leigh's face. "No accident or anything. Nothing that normal!" He snorted cynically. "It seems that an old shed on the edge of the village, down near the riding stables on Pond Road, was purposefully set afire tonight."

"They don't think…"

"Yeah, as a matter of fact, they do." He lowered his head, flipped the keys around a few times, then finally looked up and announced, "And so do I."

He held up a hand at Leigh's protest. "It's got Jamie written all over it, dammit. Apparently the night before last the guy who owns the shed caught two kids running out of it. He wasn't concerned until they acted so suspiciously. He chased them, but couldn't catch up. One of them was Jamie and the other, a buddy of his, name of Shane. When the guy checked out the shed, he found matches."

"Maybe they were just having a smoke. You know how kids experiment."

The look Spence shot her pitied her naiveté. "They could have lit up a cigarette anywhere, Leigh. Why a shed off the beaten track? Nah, he also found a can of lighter fluid and some rags. They obviously were there to start a fire."

"But why would they do that?"

"For fun! Who the hell knows? I'm so mad at that kid, I could—"

"Spence, Jamie was with me that night. That's when he showed up at the door and said he was locked out. He spent the night on the sofa!"

"I thought of that. But the sheriff said this happened early, around eight-fifteen. When did Jamie show up?"

Leigh thought back to Monday night. Janet had left at dusk, so it must have been at least eight-thirty or nine. "I'm not sure. About nineish. But Spence, he seemed too casual to have done anything like that. Wouldn't he have been afraid?"

Spence's shrug conveyed his skepticism. "Maybe not."

Suddenly Leigh could see Jamie standing at her front door, sweat beading his face and soaking his T-shirt. He'd obviously been running. She decided to keep that to herself for now. "What are you going to do?"

"I promised the sheriff I'd bring Jamie to the station as soon as I found him. The thing is, Leigh, that fire tonight could have spread to the horse stables. The guy who owns the place might not have discovered it in time. Or he could have been injured putting it out. He'd already started on it when the volunteer fire brigade showed up. My Gawd, I don't even want to think about it!"

"Spence, why don't you come in for some coffee? Then we can both go out looking for Jamie. Maybe we should check Sam's place."

"It's all locked up, but anyone could easily break in. That's a good idea. Forget the coffee, Leigh. I'm going straight there."

"I'll come, too."

"What about...you know?"

"Janet?"

"Yeah. Is she asleep? Won't she worry if she wakes up and finds you gone?"

"I won't be that long. I'll leave a note on the kitchen table. Just a sec."

Spence watched her disappear into the darkness at the back of the house. The floorboards creaked overhead. He tensed. Then he heard a door click shut upstairs. Had Janet been listening to them from the landing? But why not just call down, see what the commotion was about?

He swore silently. How he wished he could turn back the clock and make last night play all over again. No trouble with Jamie and no Janet.

THE TRUCK TORE down the road. Leigh was grateful for her seat belt, but held on to the door handle, anyway. Now was no time to quibble about Spence's driving, but did he think they were teenagers again and had to make her curfew? She glanced at his profile, highlighted by the illumination from the dash. It was set and determined. She pitied Jamie. The receiving end of that anger must be daunting.

Spence didn't say a word until the truck hit the ruts by the side of the track leading to Sam's. "Why don't you go on to Sam's while I check the beach and the dunes?"

It wasn't a request as much as an order. If the situation hadn't been so serious, she'd have been tempted to salute. Spence shoved a key at her and Leigh jumped out of the truck to run down the trail to Sam's. She took the stairs carefully in the dark, stumbling once against a watering can that clattered past her down to the sand. When she reached the porch, she felt her way along the railing until she came to the door. Fortunately there was enough moonlight on the door to pinpoint the lock. She'd just inserted the key when she heard a sound from behind.

She froze, then heard, "Leigh? That you?" and wheeled around to see Jamie step out of the shadows.

"You scared me, Jamie. Are you okay?"

He made a harsh sound that was half sob, half laugh.

Leigh turned the key and pushed open the door. "Come on in, Jamie. Your dad will be here in a minute and...well, we need to talk. Obviously."

The boy didn't move. "I didn't do it," he whispered.

"I know you didn't," she said.

"He won't believe me."

The bitterness in his voice warned her to tread softly.

"Why not give him a chance to decide that?"

There was a long silence. His breathing, tense and ragged, paced her own. Then he moved closer, out of the darkness. She held out a hand and led him into the living room. When she turned on a lamp, she saw he'd been crying.

"Have you eaten anything tonight? Want something to drink?"

He shook his head and stood still in the middle of the room.

"Where's Dad?"

"Out looking for you on the beach and in the dunes. He'll be here soon, I expect."

Jamie began to pace restlessly. At one point he started toward the door and Leigh's throat constricted. How could she stop him from leaving if that was what he intended to do?

"Jamie, I don't know exactly what happened tonight—or the other night when you came by my house."

He swung sharply about at that, but kept silent.

"And it's been a long time since I was a teenager living at home with my folks. But what I do know is that you can't run away from things. They have a habit of tailing along after you—sometimes your whole life. Believe me, I know." She sat down on the edge of Sam's rumpled sofa.

"When I was almost eighteen, I went with a bunch of kids by boat to Portsmouth Island. No big deal, right?" She uttered a sarcastic laugh. "Yep, that's what we all thought. Except we took along some beer and we weren't real careful about running lights or life jackets or even the amount of gas in the engine.'' She stopped then. *What if Jamie misses the point of this morality play?*

But he sat down on the arm of the easy chair next to the door.

''It was our graduation-night celebration, a prom, and we thought a night on Portsmouth would be a blast. It's been deserted for a while and there are a lot of scary buildings and things still there.''

The expression in Jamie's face told her he wouldn't have thought them scary.

''At least that's what one of the girls—Laura—said when I suggested we camp overnight. You see, we'd spent a while drinking and partying and so didn't notice the wind had come up. Come up pretty fast, in fact. You know what the Sound can be like?''

He nodded gravely.

''Ever been caught in a flash storm? A line squall?''

A negative shake this time.

''Even Grandpa Sam would have found it a challenge. He told me that afterward. To make me feel better, I guess.''

''What happened?'' Jamie asked.

''We had two boats with us. I wanted to stay until the storm ended—all night if we had to. The others—they thought I was afraid. And you know what, Jamie? I was. Scared to death. So scared that when they insisted, I just went along with them. Even when we realized we'd left most of the life jackets behind.''

''And?''

''A line squall came up out of nowhere. One of those monster winds that drives the water in a huge long wave. We were more than halfway across the Sound when the wave swamped the boat. I...I was the only one to survive. I don't remember much about that part. The other boat made it back to Ocracoke all right. But three of my friends didn't.''

Silence fell thick and heavy on the room. After a while Jamie asked, ''Were my parents there?''

Leigh shook her head. ''No.''

''What happened later?''

''There was an inquest because of the deaths. I had to go and give testimony.''

''It wasn't your fault! *They* were to blame, not you!''

Leigh winced at the idealism in his declaration of her innocence. ''I was never officially accused of anything of course. But—''

''Some people didn't agree.''

She locked eyes with him. He was quick. ''Some people didn't. And I blamed myself, too, Jamie. For a long long time. I really thought I could have changed what happened.''

His upper lip curled. ''That's silly. You couldn't have. Man, what a crummy thing to happen to you.''

Leigh was both touched by the sentiment and amused by its form. ''The whole point of that sad little tale, Jamie, is that I spent a lot of years thinking I could avoid dealing with it by pretending it never happened. But all I did was drag it along with me wherever I went.'' She paused, then added, ''Your dad helped me to see that, just the other day.''

''Dad?'' His voice rose in disbelief.

At that moment the screen door swung open and Spence stood in the doorway. He wasn't smiling. Nor did he raise his voice when he spoke to Jamie. ''Shall we go, then?''

When his truck pulled into Leigh's drive, he followed her to the front door. ''Thanks, Leigh. I'll call you tomorrow.''

''Wait! Spence, I don't think Jamie did it.''

A faint sardonic smile flashed across his face. ''If thoughts were wishes...''

"Listen to him first before you come to any conclusions. Do that for me. Please?"

"Sure. And I'll ask the sheriff to do the same." He turned to leave.

"It's good advice, Spence."

His face looked too tired for the glow of anger in his eyes. "Perhaps it is. I just wonder why you feel you should be offering it. I mean, maybe I haven't spent the time with Jamie I wanted to, but he *is* my son. To take care of and...and cherish in foul weather, as well as fair."

Leigh's face burned. Tears stung her eyes, but she persevered. "Maybe you need the opinion of a third party, someone neutral, who's not—"

"Emotionally involved?"

She flinched at the sarcasm in the remark. "You're twisting my words," she protested.

His face softened then. He shook his head, giving up on the conversation. "Okay, Leigh, I'll listen. And you do the same for me. When it counts."

He headed back to the truck idling in the drive. Leigh waited on the porch until it backed into the night, taking with it two pale faces staring fixedly ahead.

By the time she crawled into bed, she was spent—physically and emotionally. She lay in the darkness, wide-eyed and thinking, all night long.

CHAPTER TWELVE

"HOW ABOUT LUNCH?"

Leigh hesitated. Trish Butterfield might be too much for Janet to take her first full day in Ocracoke. "Ah, I'm not sure, Trish. Can I get back to you? See, I've got a house-guest here—"

"No kidding? Anyone I know?"

Now wasn't the time, Leigh decided. Besides, she guessed that telling Trish would be the same as telling the whole island. And that wouldn't be fair to Janet. She made her excuses and got off the phone as quickly as a person could speaking to Trish Butterfield, promising to call back later in the week.

When she told Janet, the easing of lines in the woman's face told Leigh she'd made the right decision. Later that morning Leigh telephoned Spence's office in the village but got no answer except for his machine. She duly recorded her message and hoped that he and Jamie had cleared the air last night.

By eleven she was beginning to feel restless and asked Janet if she'd like to drive into the village. "I'd like that," Janet replied. "Maybe I could pick up a newspaper, too."

"Sure. Though I think the *Island Breeze* only comes out once a month."

"Yes, it does. We get it way up in Elizabeth City."

"Really?" Leigh asked, preoccupied with a note she was leaving for Spence in case he dropped by.

"Well, of course. That's how I knew about you. Don't you remember?"

Leigh glanced up at the sharpness in Janet's voice. *She's under as much strain as you are, Leigh.* Yet it was a reminder that perhaps, as Spence had implied, Leigh was moving this whole birth-mother thing along too quickly.

She turned back to Janet, standing in the door frame, and summoned a cheerfulness she wasn't quite feeling. "Are you ready, then? I've left a note for Spence in case he drops by. There was a problem late last night—with his son," she explained when she saw the question in Janet's face.

"Have you and Spencer been dating?"

Dating? Funny word that. Reminiscent of movies and holding hands in coffee shops. "Not exactly." She searched for the right words. What could she say? *We used to be lovers and we are once more?*

"It looked like you'd been together a long time."

Leigh headed for the front door, reluctant to have Janet see her face. "Probably because we've known each other for so many years," she said breezily, and held the door for Janet to pass through. But on the short drive into town Leigh realized that a complete stranger had picked up the current between her and Spencer and guessed accurately about its significance.

The car pulled into the parking lot of the Ocracoke general store. "I've got some things to get here. Any particular request for dinner tonight?" Leigh asked.

"No, don't go to so much trouble, Leigh. How about if I cook?"

"If you like. I was also thinking of asking Spence and Jamie."

"Oh."

"Do you think that might be too much?"

Janet smiled timidly. "It was so nice last night, just the

two of us. And I've been thinking I should go home in a few days."

"Really?"

"I've got a house to run, too."

"But no job to go to, right? I mean, you mentioned last night that you were on a disability pension for your back."

"Oh, yes. That's right. But I'll have mail to check and so on."

"Is there a neighbor who could get your mail? Maybe send it to you?"

"I suppose. Why?"

"I just thought, since I rearranged my leave from work, that you...we would have more time together."

"Would you really like that?"

Leigh smiled at the enthusiasm in Janet's voice. "Yes," she said, "I would. Come on. Let's get steaks. We haven't had a really special celebration dinner yet. Just the two of us."

"That would be wonderful. I haven't had steak for years. Pension, you know."

The store was full of locals and a few tourists, although Leigh knew by the end of the summer the population of seven hundred in Ocracoke would triple. She sent Janet off to get some wine and headed for the butcher counter. Trish Butterfield was standing in line.

Leigh gritted her teeth and took her place a couple of people behind. It didn't take Trish long to notice her in the hubbub of island greetings and catching up on local news.

A few heads turned when she cried out, "Leigh Randall!" but Leigh was pleased to see that, after polite nods, most of the customers returned to their own conversations. Trish bustled back to stand in line with Leigh. "What a coincidence!"

"In Ocracoke? Hardly," Leigh murmured.

Trish dug her in the ribs. "You are droll, aren't you."

She peered over Leigh's shoulder. "So, are you alone or with company?"

For a moment Spencer came to mind, but then Leigh recalled the morning phone call. "Oh. My friend is here somewhere."

"Good. And how's the house selling coming?"

"We're having another open house Friday."

"Tomorrow?"

"Is tomorrow Friday? Already?"

"Funny how fast time goes the older you get. Even in Ocracoke!" Trish laughed merrily. "And we used to think things moved at a snail's pace here." She got serious then and leaned closer to whisper, "Have you heard about young Jamie McKay? Charged with arson?"

Leigh pulled her head back. "He was?" No wonder Spencer hadn't phoned. He'd probably been talking to lawyers all morning. She suddenly felt sick to her stomach.

"He and Shane Robertson. They apparently burned down Sy Haygood's shed. Caused a lot of damage, not to mention scaring the poor horses in the stable farther down the lane. I heard they just about rampaged they were so panicked."

Leigh wasn't sure she'd be able to stand there much longer listening to this. "No doubt the truth will come out soon," she said in a flat tone. But there was no slowing down Trish.

"No doubt. Guess you'll be the first to hear that part, eh?" Another poke in the ribs. "Or is it unfounded rumor that you and Spencer have picked up again?"

Picked up what? Leigh wanted to ask. Instead, she feigned interest in the rows of meat on the other side of the glass display.

"Okay, I won't push you on that one. But we all think it's terrific."

We? This was the negative side of island life, she realized. Events speculated on and plans made, all without participants' knowledge.

"I got a bottle of red and one of white," a voice announced from behind Trish's broad back.

Trish whirled around. Janet was there holding a wire basket with two bottles. She looked from Leigh to Trish, just realizing she'd interrupted a conversation. *Good timing,* Leigh thought.

"Trish, this is my...my friend, Janet Bradley. Janet, Trish Butterfield. Trish and her sister used to baby-sit for me way back when."

Trish beamed at the other woman. "Nice to meet you. So are you a friend of Leigh's from New York?"

Janet glanced at Leigh. "No, I live in Elizabeth City."

Trish frowned. "Then are you a relative of Leigh's mother?" She turned to Leigh. "Wasn't your mother from Elizabeth City?"

Leigh nodded vaguely. "Close by. Uh, Janet's an old family friend," she added, hoping that would satisfy Trish.

"Well, it's nice to have people come and visit. Especially since you'll be selling up and taking off again, right? Though maybe you've altered your plans now." There was a knowing grin and another elbow jab.

Leigh stepped closer to the head of the line. *Maybe we'll forget the steaks.* A glance at Janet told her she wasn't enjoying the talk, either. Besides, Leigh was desperate to get to a phone. Why hadn't she brought it with her? *'Cause this is Ocracoke, silly, not New York. You'd stand out like a sore thumb.*

She'd just given her order to the butcher when she heard Trish say from behind, "My sister lives near Elizabeth City. She's coming for a visit on the weekend and I hope you and Leigh will be able to meet her. She and Leigh haven't seen each other in years. I know Faye will be excited."

Leigh took the paper-wrapped order from the butcher

and turned around to the two women. Trish was prattling on, oblivious to the strain in Janet's face.

"What's this about Faye?" Leigh asked.

Trish moved to her place, gave her order and then repeated, "She'll be here maybe Saturday. I hope we can all get together sometime."

Leigh smiled, feeling more generous now that she was leaving the store. "I'll be here for sure. Though I'm not certain about Janet." She looked at Janet, who was picking something off the front of her blouse.

"Oh!" Janet glanced up then, her face a greenish tint in the store's neon light. "I'm not sure about my plans. Perhaps…"

Leigh looked at Trish. "Well, give me a call when she gets into town." She backed toward the door and waved.

"I will," Trish promised. "And you give me a call when you hear how Sam Logan's doing."

Leigh nodded. *She's definitely got all the latest news.*

On the way home, Janet was subdued. When Leigh switched off the engine, Janet murmured, "Why did you introduce me as your friend?"

The question took Leigh by surprise. She thought she'd been doing Janet a favor by the discreet introduction. "You probably noticed that Trish Butterfield is one of the island gossips. I just assumed you'd want your privacy respected."

Janet reached out a hand to Leigh's, still clinging to the steering wheel. "Thank you for that, my dear. But you know, I'm very proud to be your natural mother." Then she opened the passenger door and headed for the front door.

Leigh watched her retreating back, tall and resolute. She shook her head. It seemed as though she couldn't get anything right anymore.

THE DAY DRAGGED. Leigh wandered the house, distracted by thoughts of Spence, Jamie and Sam. Entertaining Janet

was difficult. Most of the filling in the blanks of their pasts
had been accomplished. And it was clear to Leigh that,
though they might tell each other the stories of their different lives, there was no bond of shared experiences to
link them. *She's my biological mother, yet she doesn't feel
any closer to me than a stranger.*

Leigh warned herself not to have such high expecta-
tions. She knew that only time would make Janet seem
like her mother, although she also knew in her heart she'd
only have one real mother—Ellen Randall. It was an important distinction and one she wouldn't forget.

Evan's phone call broke the monotony. He wanted to
arrange details about the open house the next day. Leigh
assured him she'd be available and then told him that the
woman who'd made so many inquiries about the house
was staying with her as a guest.

After a brief silence Evan said simply, "I'm dumb-
founded."

Leigh had to laugh at his reaction. "So am I. But it's a
long story, and if there's a chance tomorrow, I may tell
you some of it."

By early evening Leigh was ready to call Reg to say
she'd changed her mind about staying, after all. She wondered how people managed to survive in a place as small
as Ocracoke all year round. Then she caught herself and
smiled. *You spent your whole childhood here, kiddo, and
your parents most of their lives. Everyone managed to find
plenty to do.*

At last Spencer called. "You've probably already
heard," was the first thing he said.

"Trish Butterfield."

"Say no more. Well, Jamie's back home now. The
judge kindly hustled the bail bond procedure through, but
it was dicey at first, given Jamie's record."

Leigh closed her eyes. She didn't know whom to feel more pity for—Jamie or Spencer. "Anything I can do?"

"Sam's place?" was the tentative reply.

"Omigod! I completely forgot. I'll go over there right now."

"No, wait'll the morning. He won't be home until afternoon sometime."

"Okay. And...how's Jamie?"

She could almost hear the shrug. "Scared, I suppose. He's not saying much, only that he didn't do it."

"Do you believe him?"

An explosive exhalation. "I want to believe him, but I can't figure out why he isn't explaining what happened. He doesn't say a thing."

"Well, hopefully he'll talk more now that he's home. It must be terrifying for a kid to go to a police station and have people questioning him."

There was a pause. "You must know about that."

"You're right. Funny, I'd forgotten about that part of graduation night. Didn't you drive me to the police station?"

"Yep. When the wind came up, I headed down to the Creek. I knew you hadn't come back from Portsmouth, because I hung around after I took Jen home. Then I saw the first boat come back, and as soon as it docked, I realized you were on the other one. I was about to get into the boat myself and go out after you, but someone was screaming. It was so dark and the wind was roaring, I could hardly see a thing."

"We swamped just before we hit South Point," Leigh whispered, picturing it all again in her mind.

"You were real lucky 'cause you were carried to shore almost right in front of where I was standing on the dock. I just jumped into the water and pulled you out."

Leigh could hardly speak. "You saved my life."

"I wouldn't put it that way. You'd already been swept into the harbor. I just followed after and—"

"Pumped me dry and stopped me from getting hypothermia."

"I think you had some of that, anyway. You went to the sheriff with me, but he took one look at you and sent you on to the clinic. He asked me to go with him and some other islanders to look for the others, but..." His voice dropped away.

You never found them. Not that night, anyway. "Why didn't you talk to me like this years ago?"

"You weren't talking to me. Remember?"

There was a slight edge to his voice. "I was horrible to you. You must have hated me."

"No, never. And you have to stop hating yourself."

His advice replayed itself through the night. Leigh knew Janet sensed something was wrong, but she had no desire to relive the whole story again so soon. Instead, she told Janet that she was anxious about the open house and allowed her to help her pack up some of the mementos she planned to take back with her to New York.

"Then your decision to sell and stay in New York is final?" Janet asked.

Leigh glanced up at her, surprised at the question. "Of course. Why?"

"I just thought that your newfound friendship with Spencer and my turning up might—"

"Janet." Leigh clasped the woman's hand. "I have an important job in New York and an apartment. We'll still keep in touch when I'm back there and when you've returned to Elizabeth City."

"Perhaps. But it won't be the same." She looked around the living room. "This is such a beautiful home. I've always dreamed of living in a place like this."

The wistfulness in her voice stilled Leigh's response.

Then Janet said, almost shyly, "Especially with my daughter."

The words bounced around in Leigh's mind into the early hours of the morning, until she finally fell into a fitful sleep haunted by curling black waves and the unforgettable sound of distant screams.

"SHE DIDN'T COME to the open house, I'm certain of it," Evan declared after Janet left the room.

Leigh rolled her eyes. *Who cares?* she thought. "It doesn't matter, Evan. You said she was the one who phoned you."

"I said she *could* be the one," he clarified.

"Whatever. The thing is—and this is amazing—she phoned about the open house because of the article in the *Island Breeze*." She explained to a mystified Evan how Janet Bradley came to be a guest at Windswept Manor.

After she'd finished, she could see him working his face into an appropriate response. "Kind of coincidental, wasn't it?" he ventured.

Leigh decided that would probably be the normal reaction until she had more concrete proof to flash before cynics. She vowed to contact the adoption agency after Janet returned home. Any sooner, she thought, would be an affront to the woman.

"Of course it is! Coincidences do happen in real life. And now I have to pop out for a short while. Okay if I leave you for a bit? I've got a favor to do for someone."

"I'll wait till you get back to report on anything that happens. How negotiable do you want to be about the asking price?"

Leigh thought for a minute. "I can't really drag this on, in spite of the extra time from work. I'm willing to come down three thousand, maybe four, if there's a quick closing date."

"Righto." He nodded, then took a pencil from his briefcase and was making notes on a pad when Leigh left the kitchen.

Janet was nowhere in sight, but Leigh had told her about the cleaning job at Sam's. "I'd come and help, dear, but the back, you know," she'd said.

Leigh had commiserated, although she was grateful for the chance to be alone. The last two weeks had been so jammed with people and events the time passage seemed more like months than days. The knowledge made her realize how much of her life in New York revolved around work, punctuated by the solitude of weekends and holidays.

When she arrived at Sam's, she picked a bouquet of flowers from the annuals lining his walkway. She stooped to retrieve the watering can where she'd kicked it last night—*only last night?*—and then let herself in with the key Spence had insisted she keep when they'd parted.

In spite of the mess, the cleanup took a mere hour because Sam's cottage was so small. She opened windows to air it and changed the sheets on the bed. The flowers she placed in a glass of water since there were no vases or jars available, and then she cleaned out the fridge. She almost wept when she pulled out her own casserole, still wrapped in foil, and tossed it into the garbage with the other offerings. What had Sam been eating?

She was glad Spence had decided Sam would move in with him at the end of the summer and suddenly had an urgent desire to stay the whole summer, too. Something at the back of her mind warned her it might be Sam's last, and she hated the thought of leaving. For a minute she toyed with the idea of having Sam move into Windswept Manor, where both she and Janet could take care of him, but she pushed the notion aside almost at once. Although Janet was a nurse, she didn't seem to have that empathetic nursing gift.

By the time she'd finished cleaning, Leigh had almost

decided to stay longer in Ocracoke. Perhaps—and a pang of disloyalty attacked her—she wouldn't tell Janet until after she'd left for Elizabeth City. Then she'd have Sam to herself. The idea appealed to Leigh. She wasn't related to Sam, but there was an island bond between them that outsiders would never understand. It occurred to her that the same bond linked her with Spencer, which explained, as Janet had pointed out, why they'd seemed so close.

She locked up, leaving the windows open to continue airing the place. From the bottom of the stairs she took one last look at the Logan cottage where she and Jen had spent so much of their childhood. Her heart glowed with memories.

EVAN WAS STILL TALKING to a couple when she returned home. He waved casually, and when he didn't gesture for her to join them, Leigh headed upstairs to grab a quick shower. The door to the master bedroom was closed. Leigh frowned. Perhaps Janet was napping, although Evan had asked for all the rooms to be open for inspection.

After her shower Leigh went looking for Evan downstairs. He was packing up his things.

"How did it go?" she asked. "I hope you didn't need me for anything."

"No, no. No questions I couldn't answer." He seemed to hesitate.

"But?"

He pursed his lips. "Your...mother? She stayed in her room most of the time. Said she had a headache and I had to *tell* people what the master bedroom was like." Annoyance pitched his voice. "The most important room in the house, next to the kitchen, and I couldn't show it. People need to see the bedroom, Leigh. Not...*imagine* it."

Leigh swallowed. *Brother. What next?* "Look, I'm sorry, Evan. Janet must have had a terrible headache, because she'd agreed to vacate the room and sit on the veranda all afternoon. I even took out her favorite chair and a stack of magazines.'' She heard her own voice break with frustration with this last weak disclaimer.

Evan rolled his eyes and sniffed. ''That wasn't all,'' he said.

Leigh rubbed her temples, feeling the start of her own headache. ''There's more?''

''Just before this last couple came—I knew they weren't serious, that's why I waved you on—there was a bit of a lull. Janet came downstairs—as if she owned the place, but that's another matter—and asked me what you were asking for the house.'' He looked expectantly at Leigh.

Her head was swimming with Evan's start-and-stop reporting style. ''And?''

Another sniff. Disdain now, rather than irritation.

''Then when I told her, she asked what you'd settle for.''

''I give up,'' Leigh said, shaking her head. ''What are you saying, Evan?''

''I'm saying she made an offer on your house.''

''*What?*''

''That's what I said to her, too.'' He giggled.

''Gawd, what's going on?''

''My thought precisely. However—'' he made a flourish with his hands and snapped the clasps of his briefcase ''—that is your problem, I'm happy to say.''

Evan headed for the door, turning around once more to announce, ''And she quoted the price you were willing to settle for!'' He fluttered his fingers. ''Toodle-loo! Call me tomorrow when you've recovered.''

Leigh stood staring at the empty door frame until she heard the whap of the screen door. Then she ran upstairs looking for Janet.

By the time she knocked on the bedroom door, Leigh had counted to twenty—one for each step and five for the hallway—so when the bedroom door was finally cracked open, she was a bit calmer.

"Leigh!" Janet exclaimed in delight. "I thought it was that agent. He's a very rude man, you know."

Leigh took a deep breath. "He was upset that the room wasn't available."

Janet's smile vanished. "I'm sorry, dear. I know I promised, but I had such a migraine and you weren't here. He wasn't at all sympathetic and I just had to lie down. Come in." she motioned with a hand and walked back to the bed.

The covers were pulled back and the pillows indented. Obviously she'd been resting. Leigh said, "It's okay. Can I get you anything? Pills? Hot-water bottle? Ice pack?"

Janet swung her legs back onto the bed. "No, dear, I've taken my medicine. Now it's just a matter of waiting till it works."

"Why don't I make more iced tea?"

"That would be nice, thank you. By then, I should be well enough to come downstairs and sit on the veranda with you. Is the open house over?"

"Yes." Leigh turned to leave the room.

"I hope I didn't inconvenience anyone. Or ruin a sale for you."

Leigh paused. "No, but Evan said you'd made an offer on the house yourself. I thought he must be mistaken."

Janet waited a moment before responding. "I did, my dear. Maybe we can discuss it at dinner. I think it might be the answer to our dreams!" she exclaimed.

"I don't understand," Leigh murmured. She knew her mouth was gaping but couldn't help herself.

"Our dream of staying together."

Leigh took a step forward. "Janet," she began, changing what she'd planned to say at the stricken look on the woman's face. "I'm not selling this place for the money.

I don't need the money. I just can't maintain it from New York.''

Reassurance spread across Janet's face. "I realize that, my dear. That's why this is so perfect. I've always wanted a house like this, and you get to keep your childhood home with all its memories. And," she added triumphantly, "you also have a permanent vacation home.''

Leigh backed toward the door. It all sounded so convincingly right she couldn't think of a rejoinder. "We'll talk about it at dinner," she blurted, and closed the door behind her.

On her way downstairs she couldn't shake the feeling of being sucked up in some kind of vortex. Why did she feel as though everything was out of control? Because it was, she told herself. At least, out of *her* control.

Leigh headed promptly for her cell phone and took it into the kitchen with her, closing the door behind her. She slumped onto the cool tile floor and called the first person her bewildered mind plucked from a list of random names. Spencer.

CHAPTER THIRTEEN

HALFWAY THROUGH her telephone call to Spencer, Leigh got the very clear message that he wasn't a hundred percent with her. She heard his rundown of events for the day, including the important fact that Jamie was given a court-imposed curfew and ordered to stay with his father.

"There goes my plan to have Jamie spend the summer with Sam," he said. "Maybe you can help me persuade Sam to come here."

Leigh listened to him complain about Jamie, who still remained "mute and sullen. Even with the two-hundred-bucks-an-hour lawyer I've hired!"

When finally he came up for air to ask how she was doing, his reaction to the news about Janet's offer on the house was disappointingly flat.

"Frankly I don't know why you're so upset. I mean, it does seem peculiar, but she's given you some pretty good reasons why she did what she did. You don't have to take the offer, you know."

"That's not the point, Spence. It puts me in a weird position. If I don't take the offer, what kind of person am I? If I do, it'll mean..."

"What will it mean? Spell it out."

"I don't know. She'll be, you know, like *here*," Leigh said.

"Here, as in Ocracoke?"

Leigh closed her eyes. The irony in the question was all too obvious. "Yes," she whispered.

And as she'd expected, he added, "Isn't that what you wanted? To have her become part of your life? Didn't you lead her to believe that when you asked her to come and stay with you?"

At that point Leigh wished she'd never called him. "Coming to stay for a few days isn't the same as...as moving in."

"Maybe it is to Janet Bradley. I hate to say I told you so."

"Then don't. I called for advice, even sympathy, though heaven knows I probably shouldn't have expected that."

"Come on, Leigh. You're being unreasonable. I'm only pointing out to you that, yes, Janet's put you in an awkward position, but she must have good intentions. She believes—and you can deny it, but it's clear to me—that you've accepted her as your mother and want her to be part of your life."

His unexpected defense of Janet surprised her, but she pushed her point. "Even if my mother was alive and well, I wouldn't be living with her. I'm going to be thirty-three next month and I don't want to live with someone who could be my parent. You know what I mean."

A loud sigh. "Yeah, I know what you mean. I've got a fourteen-year-old going on thirty who feels the same."

Leigh couldn't help but laugh. Suddenly her anxiety seemed very unimportant. "What should I do?"

"My real advice is to try to get her out of your house as soon as you can." He waited and then said, "The advice I think you *might* consider would be to ask her to withdraw the offer and hint that you'll make some kind of arrangements to see her—wherever—in the future. Be as vague as you can. Obviously she's the kind of person who takes things very literally."

"I think so, too, and I've already suggested something like that."

"Right." A deep yawn and then, "Look, I gotta go.

Dinner's ready and I was up most of the night. I'm headed for the sack as soon as we've eaten. Jamie and I are leaving for Raleigh at daybreak to pick up Sam. Can I call you when I get back to the island?''

"Please." The word was heartfelt. "Give Sam and Jamie a hug for me." She clicked off the phone and sat staring at the tile pattern for a long time.

What she'd really wanted him to say was that he'd come over. But he had more than his own share of problems, and he was correct when he'd said she'd probably led Janet to expect more than she was ready to offer at the moment. Still, she thought wistfully, a few minutes snuggled in his arms would be wonderful.

She heard Janet call her and she stumbled to her feet. *Tonight I'll have a little chat with her, maybe take Spencer's advice.* Leigh grinned. *That'd be a first.*

"I DON'T WANT to pressure you, but I just had another offer on your house this morning. About one hour ago, to be precise."

"What time's it now, Evan? I just woke up."

"Oh, dear. Sorry. It's now ten-forty-eight and the second offer was made about nine-thirty." A meaningful sniff traveled over the phone line.

Leigh shook her head. What had she done to deserve a real-estate agent with attitude? "A *second* offer?"

She could almost see him rolling his eyes heavenward. "Your mother, or that woman staying with you—whoever—made the first offer, remember?"

"But do we have to consider it a serious offer? I mean, *really?*"

"Oh, she was dead serious when she made it."

"Well...just ignore it. What was this other offer for?"

"I can't just ignore it, Leigh. I do have a code of ethics, you know, not to mention a license I'd like to hold on to. Have you talked to her about it yet?"

Leigh had an impression of standing in front of her math teacher, homework incomplete. "I...I haven't had a chance. I started to last night," she said lamely, "but she has this annoying habit of sidetracking you when she doesn't like where the talk is headed. I've noticed a few things about her in the past couple of days."

"Well, living with another person tends to gel first intimations, if you know what I mean."

Leigh wasn't certain she did, but mumbled agreement.

"Then there isn't much I can do here until you turn down her offer or she withdraws it."

"Evan!"

"My hands are tied."

"I'll talk to her right after breakfast."

"You had all last night."

"I know, I know. She kept relating all these stories about distant relatives. I come from a family of scoundrels, to hear her rave on."

"Lucky she didn't bring her photo albums."

"Yes." Leigh shivered. "Though I've got plenty here. She's working through them—very slowly."

"Hide them. Have your talk and get back to me by midafternoon. No later than three-fifteen," Evan ordered.

Leigh promised and put the phone back on her night table. This time she wouldn't allow Janet to change the subject. She couldn't face Evan otherwise.

But an hour later, after a discussion over coffee, Leigh wondered why she'd worried so much about Janet.

"Of course, dear. If you think other arrangements can be made for the two of us to see each other, then by all means, go ahead. I only wanted to make things simple for both of us, and my idea seemed the obvious solution."

Leigh could only stare at her in mute admiration. Janet's negotiating skills and resilience would go far in the business world, should she ever decide to enter it. And because she felt such relief at the way Janet had responded to her

talk, she was completely unprepared for her closing remark.

"I have some business to take care of back home, and
I'm afraid it requires more than a phone call. Would you
mind terribly if I left for a few days?"

Leigh was surprised, but mainly at her own lack of disappointment. The notion of having several days to herself
again—especially with Spencer returning—was very appealing. She worked her face into an appropriate mixture
of dismay and encouragement.

"How will you get there?" she asked, recalling that
they'd returned Janet's rental car the day she'd arrived
with her luggage at Windswept Manor.

"Oh, I can take the bus," she said.

But one look at Janet's pinched mouth prompted Leigh
to ask, "Would you like to borrow my car for a few days?
No, really," she said, forestalling the protest. "I don't
need it to get around Ocracoke. I insist."

And by midafternoon Janet had left. Leigh called Evan,
leaving a message on his machine that Janet's offer had
been withdrawn. Then she spent the remainder of the afternoon poring over old photograph albums. Odd, she
thought, that looking at these with Janet had seemed almost an invasion of privacy. *As if I want to keep my life
here separate from any life I have with Janet.* She tried to
ignore the inner voice that questioned such a feeling. *If
you really felt right about everything, why can't you feel
comfortable about mingling the past and the present? Ellen and Pete would be thrilled for you.*

But would they have so readily taken Janet Bradley into
their home? That was the question Leigh could no longer
avoid.

"I WAS JUST THINKIN'," Sam said, looking happily around
the room, "how darn important it is to have a family.

Lying here in me own bed again, havin' all of you with me, there's nothin' like it, I tell you.''

Tears stung Leigh's eyes. She was standing at the foot of Sam's bed, with Jamie perched awkwardly on the edge and Spencer leaning against the door frame. What Sam had uttered about family had really hit home. But he'd been referring to his own family and she wasn't part of it. In fact, she no longer had any family at all.

Except for Janet. Somehow that wasn't consolation enough. She envied the three of them.

After a decent interval she said, "It's good to have you back with us, Sam. And now...I ought to leave. I have a few things to do."

"Oh, I hoped you'd stay. Maybe we can get Spencer here to bankroll dinner for us. I hear the charter business is picking up now. What do you think? Some clams and fries from Howard's?"

"Cool!"

Sam smiled. "There you go. Jamie's all for it. What do you think, Spencer?"

Leigh didn't trust herself to turn around. She'd been avoiding eye contact with Spencer ever since she'd arrived. He'd telephoned earlier to invite her over to see Sam; the call had been terse and businesslike, as if he'd wanted to relay a message and get off the line as quickly as possible. Something was definitely on his mind.

"Sure, I'd be happy to drive over to Howard's and pick up dinner. How about it, Leigh?"

There was no way she could gracefully decline. Besides, the eagerness in both Sam's and Jamie's faces was enough to persuade her that, if she wasn't family, she was definitely welcome. "I'd love to stay," she said.

While Spencer and Jamie drove into the village to pick up the food, Leigh kept Sam company. The strain of the trip from Raleigh was taking its toll. He drifted off a few times, awakening at last to drink some fruit juice and listen to Leigh's account of the past few days. She didn't want to burden the old man with her problems, so purposely kept the story brief.

"You say you've no paper proof that this woman is your birth mother, and I agree with you that perhaps she never received any herself years ago when the deal was done. But what does your heart tell you, my girl?"

Trust old Sam's radar. "I don't know, Sam. I suppose I want to believe it's true because I'm all alone now and...and it would be nice to have a family."

"You have us, Leigh. We're your family."

"Thanks, Sam, I needed to hear that. But you know what I mean. If she is my mother, then I want to get to know her."

"It does seem possible. Like you said, she knows all that stuff about you. Stuff no one else could know. Maybe your misgivings have something to do with, you know, your feelings of loyalty to Ellen and Pete."

"Maybe, but you know, Sam, in my heart they're my parents and always will be. They made me who I am. I'd just like to learn about my biological parents in case I ever get married and have children."

"No 'in case' about it," he harrumphed. "And if I have anything to say about it, you'll hitch up with the one you were meant to years ago."

Leigh was rescued from a response by the noisy arrival of Jamie flying up the wooden porch steps and bursting through the cottage door.

"Dinner's here!" he called.

Leigh and Sam exchanged smiles. "Do one thing for me, Leigh. Help patch things up between that boy and his daddy."

From the way his daddy is acting, I doubt I'm a candidate for the job. Leigh patted Sam's hand. "I'll do what I can. You know how stubborn he can be."

Sam's eyes twinkled. "That's why I asked you. You're a good match."

"I'm not sure I like the implication of that, Sam," Leigh teased. "But I'll see what I can do. Just can't promise anything."

"You can promise me one thing."

Leigh turned in the doorway. "What's that?"

"Not to run away anymore."

Leigh bit down on her lower lip. "I'll do what I can, Sam," she whispered, and headed out of the room to find Jamie.

Later, after they'd loaded their plates and joined Sam in his room, perching on extra chairs, Leigh was filled with a contentment she knew she ought to preserve in her mind. She glanced around the room and at the men she loved. *Yes, it really does feel like family.*

LEIGH WAS ALMOST RELIEVED when Spencer informed everyone he had some phone calls to make at his office. He and Jamie would spend the night with Sam. Leigh insisted on staying behind to help clean up.

"I can give you a lift home on my way into the village," Spencer quickly offered.

"Thanks, anyway, but I'd like to spend some more time with Sam," she countered, feeling slightly guilty about dragging poor old Sam into the fray.

The screen door flapped shut behind him. Two could play at the avoidance game, she thought, watching his ramrod back move down the stairs. But she had a hunch she'd see him again before the night ended. His face had bad news written all over it.

When the kitchen was tidy, Leigh peeked in at Sam and found him already fast asleep. She closed the door softly behind her and joined Jamie on the porch. He was sitting on the top step, gazing pensively out across the ocean. The sun had dipped below the horizon, but dusk had not yet become deep night. The air was still, heavy with moisture and the salty aftermath of low tide.

"Mind if I join you?" she asked, and sat next to him without waiting for an answer.

He glanced at her, then away, focusing on a callus on his thumb.

Leigh waited. After a few minutes she said, "It's so quiet and peaceful here. In New York, there doesn't seem to be any part of day or night that's absolutely silent."

"I can't imagine that," he said. "Even in Charlotte, nights could be real quiet. Too quiet."

"The older you get, there's no such thing as too quiet."

"You're not old!" Jamie scoffed.

"No, but once you get out of your twenties life seems to demand more settling down."

"That's not the same as being *old*. You know, like having old ideas and attitudes."

"True. Although my parents often didn't understand what my friends and I were up to, they never put us down. Maybe because they'd learned to be less judgmental than their own parents."

"My parents aren't really like that, either. 'Fact, my mom says she can't point a finger at me because she was no angel when she was a teenager."

Leigh laughed. "That sounds like your mother, all right."

Jamie turned to look at Leigh. "You an' her used to be best friends, didn't you?"

Leigh glanced away. "Did she tell you that?"

"Yeah, she talked about you a lot. Always about how Leigh Randall was so smart and popular and stuff. I kinda got the feeling she was a bit jealous."

Leigh felt her throat swell up. "Actually Jen was a lot more popular than I was. Everyone liked her because she was always cheerful and game for anything."

"It's funny to think of your folks being kids," he murmured.

"Yes," she said, then taking a deep breath, added, "and they weren't much different from the kids today. We did lots of crazy things. I bet Sam could tell you some wild stories."

Jamie grinned. "Yeah, he has. A few, anyway, about my mom and dad. None about you, though. Guess you were the good one, right?"

Leigh flushed. "I suppose that was the image I had, but believe me, Jamie, I wasn't any better than anyone else."

After a moment he mumbled, "Yeah, but I bet you didn't get blamed for stuff you didn't do."

"I can't remember, but I'm sure I did sometimes. I know I blamed myself for a lot of things I *didn't* do, and I think that's just as bad."

"Like that accident you told me about the other night?"

She sighed. "Yes."

"That was tough."

"Yes, but it wouldn't have been so tough on me if I hadn't kept everything inside. I was afraid to talk about it with my friends because I thought they blamed me. But now I'm not so sure. Maybe they just didn't want to talk about it because they were afraid to hurt me. Because I kept so quiet about it."

"That's only natural."

"At first it was, but later it became something else. I don't know how to describe it, but I do know I ought to have talked about it. To anyone. Silence is not a good thing, Jamie. It makes people draw the wrong conclusions. It puts up barriers between people."

A night heron swung low over their heads, squawked and flapped toward the marshes.

Finally Jamie said, in a voice so quiet Leigh had to lower her head to hear him, "It wasn't even my idea, you know. Shane came up to me and said he heard I used to set fires. I was real ticked off. Like, that was a dumb thing I did last year, but I did it because I wanted to get back at...at people I thought had deserted me. Since then, I realized what a jerk I was. No wonder everyone was fed up with me.'' He played with the callus on his thumb again. ''Anyway, I told Shane that was all in the past and to take a hike. Then a few days later I found this letter for my dad.''

He paused. Leigh guessed what was coming next.

''It was from some lawyer in Charlotte telling him I was going to be adopted by my stepfather. I couldn't believe it.'' Jamie turned to Leigh, his eyes red with tears. ''I mean, like my stepfather's okay—he's not my favorite person, but I don't mind him. We kinda get along but...he's not my dad!''

Leigh wanted to put her arm around him, but was afraid he might stop talking. Instead, she gave a quick nod and said, ''Your father wouldn't let that happen, Jamie.''

''I don't know that, do I?'' he wailed. ''He hardly ever talks to me, and when he does, it's always to give me an order or a job.'' He uttered a short sarcastic snort.

''I know he can be like that, but I think it's because he's afraid.''

''Afraid?''

''Believe it or not, yes. He's not good at talking about his feelings. He never was, even as a kid. Has he told you about his childhood?''

Jamie hung his head. ''Yeah,'' he muttered. ''His mother took off and his father was a drunk.''

Leigh winced at Jamie's cynical tone. ''He told you that?''

''Well, my mother did once. He never really talked about it. Just gave hints about it.''

She waited a moment before saying, ''Then your mother and he split up when you were very young. I know that hurt him.''

"It did?"

"Yes. Is that so hard to believe?"

"I don't know. He just seems so tough sometimes. Always in charge and in control, you know?"

Leigh could barely talk around the lump in her throat. "I know. But he has another side, too. You have to look for it, though. And you may have to be the one to speak up first."

"He wants me to tell him about the fire."

"Of course he does."

"Thing is, I couldn't. Because I'd have to tell him I nosed around in his mail and saw the letter."

"That's a small thing, Jamie. He wants to talk to you about the adoption, but he's afraid."

"Dad afraid? Like, I don't think so."

"He's afraid of losing you all over again."

"He tell you that?"

"He did."

Jamie rubbed his face. Then he stood up and leaned against the porch railing. "Shane brought all this stuff over to the house. He showed up almost right after I'd seen the letter. Lousy timing. I was feeling...bad. Real bad. Shane dragged me over to old man Haygood's shed. I don't know why he wanted to torch it. He said he just hated the guy. I think Shane's a bit weird." Jamie paused, wiping his forearm across his nose. "Anyway, the guy musta heard us 'cause he came tearing in there mad as a bull. We took off, but he musta recognized us. Two nights later Shane went again, but by himself. He didn't even talk to me about it 'cause I told him I didn't want to even see him again. And I haven't!" His eyes met Leigh's. "I swear!"

"I believe you, Jamie. But you need to tell your father and the sheriff."

He ducked his head. "I don't want to rat on Shane."

"Shane should get some help. He shouldn't be allowed to set any more fires."

After a while Jamie said, "Yeah, I guess you're right."

Leigh stood up and held out her arms. When Jamie stepped into them, she closed her eyes, thinking how lucky Jen was.

LATER THAT NIGHT, long after Leigh had left Sam's cottage and headed wearily for home, a loud rattling at the front screen door woke her. She knew it was Spencer and was tempted to let him stand on the veranda until common sense drove him away. She lay in bed a few moments longer. The rattling continued.

Common sense has obviously deserted him. Leigh climbed out of bed and threw her robe around her. She swung open the big etched-glass door.

"It's not that late," he offered by way of apology.

"It's midnight."

"Didn't I say I'd drop by later?"

She shook her head, realizing at the same time how much better she was getting at reading his mind.

He frowned. "I thought I did. Anyway—" his face brightened "—here I am. I just came from checking on Sam and Jamie. Both are sleeping soundly."

She raised an eyebrow. "And so was I."

"Aw, jeez, guess I've blown it again. Sorry about that." He shuffled his feet. Stared down at the veranda a bit and then raised his head.

It was his nineteen-year-old grin all over again. Leigh felt her heart do its seventeen-year-old flip. She pushed open the screen door. "Come on in, Spence," she said, and turned without another word toward the kitchen.

"Coffee?" she asked when he pulled up the chair at the table.

"Decaf?"

"I don't think I have any."

He mulled this over. "If I have regular, I'll be up all night."

She ignored the knowing look he shot her way. As if he didn't mind being awake all night if he had something to occupy him. Or someone.

"Then you'd better have herbal tea," she said, smiling inwardly at the flicker of disappointment in his eyes. *Does he think he can just show up any time of day or night, dismissing the way he acted earlier?* No, she decided. It was too reminiscent of the old days. *Except that then, I was foolish enough to overlook his shortcomings.*

"So it'll be herbal tea. Just as well. I have an early charter."

Leigh busied herself brewing the tea, reluctant to sit on a chair across from him and get down to the business that had been troubling her all day: his behavior. She wondered how long it would take him to get around to the subject.

But he surprised her. "I actually came by because there's something I have to tell you."

His opener didn't bode well, she thought. "There's something I have to tell you, too."

"Oh?"

"At least, Jamie has something to tell you in the morning."

"Did he talk to you?"

"Yes."

"About the fire?"

"Yes, but he has to tell you what happened himself."

"I appreciate that. And I appreciate whatever you did to...to make him change his mind."

"Does it bother you? That he told me?"

Spence thought for a minute. "I guess I feel a bit let down. But the important thing is, he's opening up. I can understand why he might have chosen you."

She nodded, acknowledging the compliment and gaining some assurance from it. *Would he say something like that if he was about to tell me he couldn't see me anymore?*

Leigh poured the tea and sat down. She concentrated on spooning honey into her mug.

He sighed. "Thanks for that, Leigh. What I wanted to talk to you about...well, it's hard to begin."

She was afraid to look him in the eye, but forced herself, almost daring him to proceed.

Spence waited, took a sip of the hot tea and then made a show of blowing on it. He wished she'd find somewhere else to rest those big black eyes. Damn. He gazed down at the spoon in his hand, flipped it back and forth and then lifted his head to meet those eyes again. "When I was in Raleigh getting Sam discharged, I made a few phone calls to Elizabeth City. I have a friend there on the police force." He waited for Leigh to say something. "I asked him to make a few inquiries. To, uh, check out Janet."

Her eyebrows squiggled together in a frown. She sat very still.

Spencer pushed on. "He did that, but couldn't find any trace of anyone by the name of Janet Bradley. None at all."

Her eyes never wavered from his face. The cool unblinking stare unnerved him. It also annoyed him. "I did it as a favor, Leigh. I thought someone should check her out. And there's no such person as Janet Bradley."

"You mean, you didn't *locate* anyone by that name."

He shrugged. "Same thing."

"No, it isn't." Her voice rose on the last word.

"This friend of mine suggests we hire a private detective to find out if she really is who she claims to be."

"If she's Janet Bradley? Or if she's my mother?"

"Aren't we talking the same thing here?"

Leigh's hand slapped the table. "No, we aren't. There could be any number of reasons Janet Bradley's name isn't in the Elizabeth City phone book, Spencer."

"Not just the phone book!" He could almost feel his

blood pressure rise. "He checked tax records and birth registrations. No Janet Bradley anywhere."

"Maybe she changed her name."

"Then it would have to show up somewhere."

Leigh turned sideways in her chair and crossed her arms. She refused to look at him. "I'm very upset that you just went and did this without talking to me about it, Spencer. It was presumptuous of you."

He couldn't hold back a grin. "You always were one for big words." Then he leaned closer to her, softening his voice. "Leigh, you have a right to be angry at me. I accept that. I should have talked to you about it, but it was an impulsive thing. I was hanging around this waiting room with nothing to do. I saw the phone and—"

"And you always were impulsive," she retaliated. "Acting as though you ran the show. Never having to confer with anyone. Never having to accept responsibility."

"What is this? Are we talking about Janet or about how I behaved when I was a teenager?"

Leigh fluttered a hand in the air. "I don't know. I don't know what we're talking about." She folded her arms on the table and lay her head on them.

Spencer's stomach heaved. *What's happening here? It's not supposed to go like this.* He reached out a hand to the crown of Leigh's head. She didn't budge. "Leigh, I'm sorry. I'd never intentionally hurt you. You know that, don't you? Because you *should* know it by now. Especially after the last two weeks. After…everything."

Silence. He withdrew his hand. "And isn't it better to find out the truth about Janet now?"

She lifted her head. Her eyes looked tired and red-rimmed. Shadows had suddenly appeared beneath them. "I don't know the truth about anything anymore, Spencer."

The admission hit him in the solar plexus. *Does that*

include the other night, too, when we... He wiped a hand across his face. The sick feeling in his stomach persisted. He had to leave. He pushed back the chair and struggled to his feet. From the doorway he looked back one more time. "Leigh?"

But she refused to look at him.

Is it happening all over again? he asked himself. Then he smacked the palm of his hand against the door frame and left.

"NOT AGAIN," Leigh moaned.

The front door clattered. She roused her head to see the clock. Barely nine. Spencer was out fishing. Couldn't be Evan, she thought. Janet? She moaned again and slumped back onto the pillow. Janet was not a person she wanted to face after the night she'd just endured. But the noise was increasing, instead of going away, so Leigh staggered out of bed where she'd fallen, robe and all, hours after Spence had walked out.

Drained of energy, she cracked open the front door and peered blearily through the screen. Jamie.

"Leigh! Something's wrong with Grandpa. He won't wake up. Can you call for help?"

Leigh unclasped the screen door and pushed it open. "Come in, Jamie. The phone's on the kitchen table. You call while I get dressed." She ran upstairs.

By the time she'd thrown on shorts and a T-shirt, grabbed a slurp of water from the bathroom faucet to finger-brush her teeth, Jamie had made his call. He was bobbing impatiently from one foot to the other and sweat beaded his brow. He'd been running hard.

As they headed for the door, Leigh realized she would be running, too. Janet had her car. She swore softly and followed Jamie down the drive. By the time they reached the lane leading to Sam's place, she was gasping for air. The faint wail of a siren drifted up from the village.

THE MAN SHE LEFT BEHIND

"Volunteer fire," Jamie panted. He took the porch steps two at a time and was inside and standing beside Sam's bed when Leigh reached the bedroom doorway.

She looked across the room at Sam. His head lolled on the pillow; his mouth was slack, lips edged in blue. Too late. Too late. She moved slowly toward the bed and felt the first roll of pain hit, curling upward into her chest and throat, filling every part of her.

"Oh, Sam," was all she could say. Leigh held out her arms and Jamie tumbled into them, holding on tightly while his body heaved with sobs.

CHAPTER FOURTEEN

LEIGH WAS STILL HOLDING Jamie when the volunteer fire
truck arrived. They were pushed aside while two men ad-
ministered CPR. Within minutes Sam's tiny cottage
teemed with people attempting to revive him, including
Sam's local doctor, who'd been summoned from the medical clinic. But to no avail.

At nine-forty-eight Sam Logan was pronounced dead.
Leigh took Jamie onto the porch while people bustled
about inside. The sense of hushed urgency had gone, along
with the strong indomitable spirit that had been Grandpa
Sam. Leigh knew that hours from now the full significance
of that loss would hit. But for now she was only aware of
a yawning emptiness.

"I feel strange," Jamie whispered, sitting next to her in
a wicker chair. "Kind of like I'm floating in a big black
pool. I see everything around me—I can hear the surf,
those guys inside and stuff—but it's like nothing's touching me."

"Is this the first time you've lost someone close to
you?"

"Yeah. I can't even imagine life without Grandpa Sam!
I didn't see a whole lot of him most of my life 'cause my
mom and I were always moving. But he always wrote—
every week! Did you know that?"

"No, but it doesn't surprise me. There aren't many people like Sam in this world."

"Nope." Jamie sighed.

Silence stretched time, so that when Sam's doctor came onto the porch, Leigh visibly jumped. She thought everyone had left hours before. He took her aside, suggesting Sam be left in his own bed until someone from the funeral home in Hatteras arrived. He'd taken the liberty of calling the nearest one and hoped the family wouldn't mind. Leigh nodded, half-aware he'd included her in his reference to family.

When the fire truck pulled away, Leigh said, "Jamie, we can go to my place and wait for the funeral people and your dad, or wait here. What would you like to do?"

"I want to stay here with Grandpa. Is that okay?"

"Of course."

"When's Dad coming?"

Spencer. "Do you know when he's expected back?"

"Sometimes he's out all day."

"Does he have a shortwave radio on the boat?"

"Yeah, I think so."

"I'll see if someone can contact him." She pushed open the screen door and went inside. Then Leigh remembered Sam had no telephone and she'd left hers at home. She also realized that because she'd been away from Ocracoke so long, she had no idea whom to call. She didn't even know who Spencer's friends were. Overwhelmed by these obstacles, she plunked down on the sofa and wept.

Then Jamie was sitting next to her, patting her shoulder and comforting her. When Spencer swung open the screen door moments later, they both looked up, teary-eyed, their arms around each other.

"Where is he?" Spence asked, his voice tight with pain.

Leigh pointed to the bedroom.

When Spence returned, his face was drawn. He seemed calm and in control, Leigh noticed, except the end of his nose was red and his voice husky.

"The doctor called me as soon as the clinic was notified by the fire department. He had the number of a buddy of mine with a shortwave. Fortunately I wasn't far out." He stopped, seeming at a loss for words, and stared down at the two of them.

Leigh stood up. "I think you two may want to be alone for a while. Sam's doctor said he contacted a funeral home in Hatteras and someone would come soon. If you want to, you can wait at my place."

Spencer rubbed his hand across his face. "I think I'll stay until the hearse gets here." He glanced at Jamie. "Son, would you like to go with Leigh?"

"I'd like to stay with you—if that's okay?"

"Sure." Spencer smiled at Jamie. Leigh had a sense that he wanted to hug him as readily as she had but didn't know how. She moved toward the door.

"Leigh!" Jamie called. He was standing next to his father. "Thank you for helping me. For coming with me and taking charge. I was too scared to think straight."

She smiled. "So was I, Jamie." She placed a hand on the door.

"Leigh?"

This time it was Spencer. His face was tight, almost closed. Yet she saw warmth in his eyes. "Yes?"

"I want to thank you, too. For being there for my son—and for Sam."

The pull of his eyes drew her away from the door. She dropped her hand and took a step forward. But then Jamie blurted, "What about Mom? We have to call Mom."

Leigh stopped. The glow in Spencer's eyes extinguished. He shook his head and looked down at the floor. Then he muttered, "Yeah. I'd better call your mother."

Leigh slipped out the door.

THIS WAS THE UPSIDE of village life. The way people rallied around in a personal crisis or tragedy. Leigh remembered the same quiet parade of casseroles and well-wishers immediately following the accident that had taken the lives of her three friends fifteen years ago. It wasn't until just before the inquest that the rumors and whispers had begun. The hints that Leigh Randall should been more assertive in her efforts to prevent the others from leaving the island that night. Even that the stunt had been her idea. *The downside of village life.*

Leigh sighed. She took the tin of cookies, smiled and uttered an automatic thank-you. She'd been acting as unofficial hostess for Spencer all afternoon, receiving cards, flowers and food for the impending funeral reception tomorrow. Spencer and Jamie had followed the hearse to Hatteras to discuss arrangements for Sam's funeral. Although final decisions would not be confirmed, Spencer told Leigh on the phone, until Jen arrived from Charlotte.

"She's not sure about flights yet," he'd said. "I was wondering if you'd go to my place later today. People have already started calling and sending things, and I have too many things to do."

So Leigh found herself sitting on Spencer's deck in the late afternoon, looking out over the Sound, but not really seeing it, and answering the frequent knocking at the door. She noticed quite a few raised eyebrows and fielded some indirect inquiries about why she was there. But in spite of the curiosity, Leigh had the impression that most people accepted her presence and some even shyly welcomed her back to Ocracoke.

She busied herself stowing food in the freezer and setting aside the rest for the funeral reception. Spencer had informed her that Jen would probably want her grandfather buried in Ocracoke's small cemetery. When the telephone rang just before five, Leigh rushed in from the deck. Spencer had said he'd call back.

But the voice on the other end was female.

"Spencer?" There was a bewildered note to the word, as if the caller was confused by Leigh's breathless hello.

Leigh knew the caller. "He's...he's not here right now," she stammered.

"Oh. Who am I speaking to?"

"It's me, Jen. Leigh."

"Leigh Randall?"

And Leigh had to smile. *Do you know another Leigh?* "Yes. I've been back in Ocracoke for a couple of weeks now. I thought you might have heard."

There was a stifled exclamation. "No one tells me anything these days, I'm afraid. So you know about Grandpa?"

Leigh hesitated. Obviously Jen knew very little about the circumstances. "Yes, Jen, and I want to tell you how sorry I am. Sam was a very special person."

"I know he was, although some people think I haven't appreciated him."

The bitterness in the remark surprised Leigh. Jen had always been happy-go-lucky. Sometimes self-centered in her pursuit of pleasure, but always cheerful and optimistic.

Jen added quickly, "Anyway, no point crying about it all now. Will you tell Spence my flight gets into Hatteras about seven and I'll be in Ocracoke about nine? I'll be alone." She stressed the last word, hesitated and said, "I hope I'll get a chance to see you?"

"I suppose. I'll be at the funeral. Would you like to hold the reception at my place?"

There was a slight hesitation before Jen murmured, "That would be nice. Thanks for the offer, Leigh."

After they hung up, Leigh sat in the chair a few minutes longer conjuring up a picture of Jen Logan. But the only picture she could summon was of eighteen-year-old Jen, and the image was, oddly enough, still daunting.

Leigh was unprepared for the last callers of the day. She was getting ready to walk home, exhausted by the monotony of the small talk and most of all by the impact of

Sam's death. It was time to go home, close the door and be alone with her thoughts.

She didn't recognize the couple standing in the doorway, but knew from the mix of facial expressions that they recognized her. After she thanked them for the plate of brownies, she was about to close the door when the woman spoke up.

"You don't remember us, perhaps. It's been a long time. We're Jeff's parents."

Leigh couldn't move. The familiar sensation of breathlessness began to expand up and around her chest. Her mouth went dry and her mind blank.

The woman gave a tentative smile. "We heard you were back in Ocracoke. Will you be staying long?"

She shook her head. Then she ran her tongue over her lips and found her voice. "Only until I sell the house."

They both nodded. Jeff's father said, "That's a shame. Too bad you can't stay longer."

The comment whirled around Leigh's mind. She looked from one to the other. Their smiles were hesitant, but sincere. "I'd like to stay longer," she ventured, "but I'm not sure yet what my plans are. Everything's a bit up in the air—with Sam and all."

More sympathetic nods. Then Jeff's mother reached out a hand to Leigh's, still clamped on the plate of brownies.

"We want you to know that we wouldn't have a problem if you stayed longer. It's nice to see you again. And it's especially nice to see Spencer looking like a human being again."

Jeff's father laughed at that. There were smiles all round. Leigh thanked them and waved goodbye when they left. After closing the door, she leaned against it, weak-kneed. Then she smiled. *The upside of island life.*

THE TELEPHONE CALL came while Leigh was taking a tray of sandwiches into the dining room. Someone in the kitchen, where the cell phone was, let her know.

She placed the tray on the table and wove her way through the clumps of people chatting, holding teacups and eating in every available space on the ground floor. A sea of black, with flashes of white shirts, flooded Windswept Manor. Sam had been a much-revered resident of Ocracoke Island.

Somewhere in that sea bobbed Spencer, Jamie and Jen like net floats cut adrift, Leigh thought. Coming together momentarily and then cast apart by another wave of conversation or new arrivals. Throughout the funeral and now here, in her own home, Leigh had purposely kept in the background. She'd performed every task quietly, seeking the reassuring comfort of the kitchen or her bedroom upstairs whenever she felt overwhelmed.

Trish Butterfield had rallied a handful of village women to work in the kitchen, leaving Leigh few tasks other than carrying and removing dishes. Jamie had smiled wanly a few times. He looked very grown-up in a suit, and the outfit and circumstances had instilled a quiet and considerate responsibility that Leigh knew must have made Spencer proud.

Jen's appearance in the church had caused a stir. People had swarmed around her, greeting her with the respect that a granddaughter of Sam Logan's deserved. Spencer and Jamie stood next to Jen the whole time, offering her arms of support and helping her into and out of cars and buildings. Leigh had felt a small tug of envy. Other than a curt hello and a thank-you for helping out the day before, Spencer had seemed to be avoiding her.

When she reached the telephone, Leigh ran up to her bedroom with it. Five seconds into the conversation she was grateful for the privacy.

"Ms. Randall? The Bennington Adoption Agency here, Eleanor Irwin speaking. I'm returning your mother's call."

"Pardon?"

"Your mother called us yesterday and didn't leave a return number. I assumed she was still living in Ocracoke and so I dug out our old file for the number."

"I don't understand. My mother's dead."

Static filled the line. Then, "Oh, dear. I'm terribly sorry. I'm a bit confused. You see, we had a call yesterday from an Ellen Randall. She identified herself as your adoptive mother and said you were interested in contacting your birth mother. My secretary took the information, but the phone number she was given was out of service."

Leigh sat down on the bed. "My adoptive mother passed away last year. I don't know who could have called you." But she had a good idea. Her heart was pounding so hard she could scarcely hear the woman on the other end.

"Well, this woman knows a lot about you. She said we'd sent a letter years ago advising her that your birth mother wanted to make contact. And we had. Later I looked up the file and found the original inquiry logged by my predecessor."

"What else did she say?"

"She said that at the time, you were unable to proceed because your father had just been diagnosed with Alzheimer's."

Leigh closed her eyes. Janet, of course. She knew everything, thanks to Leigh's blind trust. "And?"

"Well, then she said you were interested now. I must admit I was surprised that she was the one to call and not you. That was my first indication that all was not...well, right. When I told her that you had to contact us, she got very annoyed. And rude. When I explained that because you were an adult now, we could only handle the inquiry with you, she calmed down a bit and said she'd have you write a letter. I suggested you telephone, but she said you were returning to New York and would be too busy. That also seemed peculiar to me.''

Leigh uttered a harsh laugh. ''I'm not surprised. The woman who called is not my adoptive mother. I'm not sure who she is, but she claims to be my birth mother.''

''What name did she give you?''

''She said her name is Janet Bradley, but—'' Leigh thought back to Spence's revelation about his own inquiry ''—I doubt that's her real name.''

''Well, I can tell you that Janet Bradley is not the name of your birth mother.''

Leigh expelled the breath she'd been holding. ''Thank you for calling. I appreciate it.''

''While I have you on the line, are you interested in making contact with your birth mother?''

Unprepared for the question, Leigh couldn't speak. The woman went on, ''The reason I'm asking is that I see there were a few more inquiries after we sent you that letter. I don't know why they weren't passed on to you or your adoptive parents.''

Or perhaps they were. Leigh's reply came without thought. ''Yes,'' she blurted, then without saying goodbye she turned off the phone and rushed to the master bedroom. She got down on her knees, raised the hem of the sham, pulled out the leather valise and lugged it onto the bed. Her fingers fumbled at the clasps. She pushed away the thought she couldn't bear—that Janet had taken more than the letter.

Yes, it was still here—the ducky blanket. And yes, the baby outfit. Leigh rifled through the rest of the papers and documents. The letter from the agency was gone. Leigh lowered the lid. She couldn't understand why Janet had taken only the letter.

Unless she plans to come back, not knowing the agency would call me.

Leigh felt sick to her stomach. Spencer was right. How

could Janet possibly be her birth mother? Would a real mother behave like this? Sneak around? Lie? She crossed her legs on the bed, pressing her hand to her forehead. How she wanted someone to be here. To hold her tightly and love her. To surround her with the comfort and safety only a family could bring.

"Are you okay?"

Leigh's head shot up. Jen stood in the doorway.

Even in mourning and clearly pregnant, she was beautiful. The long blond curls had been layered into a flattering style, and her petite frame balanced her pregnancy delicately. The black dress she wore was fashionable enough to serve as regular wear afterward. Leigh had to admit she looked good. Very good.

"Come in," she said, and Jen stepped hesitantly into the room where the two had spent many a rainy afternoon.

Jen looked around, remarking how little things had changed. Leigh could only murmur, struck dumb by Jen's very presence. She felt like a kid again and realized for the first time how familiar the sensation was. *Have I always felt intimidated by her?*

Jen sat down in the rocking chair in front of the bay window. Leigh smiled. She had a flash of Jen at twelve, rocking imperially while she ordered Leigh about in one of their many pretend games.

Jen returned her smile. "It's good to see you again, Leigh."

"Really?" The question popped out meanly.

But Jen's skin had always been much thicker than Leigh's. She ignored the jab and rocked some more.

"Thank you for what you've done for Jamie," she said.

Leigh frowned. *What have I done for Jamie?*

"Spencer told me how you helped clear up that whole mess. About the fire," she explained.

"Ah. Well, I didn't really do anything, Jen. Jamie wanted to talk and I was there."

Jen smiled. "Still the self-effacing Leigh, eh?"

Leigh's face burned. *The sting of the glove. What have I done to deserve this?* "I don't know what you're talking about, Jen."

Jen laughed. The familiar tinkling laugh, but throatier now. "You know, I don't think people change, do you?"

Leigh's head was spinning. Talk with Jen had always been a meandering route through moods and bursts of creative energy. "I like to think they change a little bit," she finally said.

Jen's smile vanished. "Yeah, probably you're right. A bit—some more than others. Do you think Spencer's changed?"

It was a typical Jen question. Loaded. "We've all changed," Leigh said evasively.

Another laugh. "Yes, the same old Leigh. I think you prove my point that people don't change. You and Spencer. He's still very much the old Spence—just under the surface, mind."

Leigh pushed the valise aside. The conversation was becoming a little too bizarre. She started to get off the bed.

"Do you still have the ducky blanket?" Jen asked.

Leigh stopped. "Yes, I do. You remember it?"

"Of course I do. You talked about it so much. That and how you got your name. Those stories were very thrilling to me—my imagination got to work overtime."

"You always did have a great imagination," Leigh said.

A cloud drifted across Jen's face. "Yes. I always used to have a lot of things." She looked out the window.

Leigh studied her profile, pensive and almost sad. She recalled the few things Jamie had mentioned about growing up. What kind of life had Jen ended up with?

"You have a family," Leigh pointed out.

Jen's chewed on her lower lip. She looked across the room at Leigh and smiled. "You're right. I do. And a husband who really loves me and—" she patted her swollen abdomen ''—a little one on the way. A new beginning. We all need them, you know.''

Leigh glanced down at the suitcase. ''Yes,'' she murmured, ''we do.''

''It took a lot of years,'' Jen went on, ''but I finally got mine. 'Course, it's not quite the future I expected fifteen years ago.'' She gave a breathless laugh. ''Still, it's a new beginning for me and I think it'll be okay.''

Just okay?

As if reading her mind, Jen said, ''I mean, my new hubby, Rob, is a lovely man. Very good to me. He adores me. But...''

''But?'' Leigh had to ask.

''He's not Spencer, that's for sure.''

''What do you mean?''

''He's not fun and exciting the way Spencer used to be. Daring and outrageous.''

''Spencer was fun and exciting?'' *Moody and reckless perhaps.*

''In the beginning he was.'' Jen leaned forward in the chair. ''I'm sure you don't want to talk about this, Leigh. Lord knows, it's hardly the time or place, but then, I never had a good sense of timing, did I?'' She laughed.

''No, you didn't.''

Jen nodded. ''That's another thing I remember about you. Your honesty. You were always so dead straight. Anyway, I have to get this off my chest. For my new beginning, you understand.''

Leigh shrugged. She didn't have the faintest idea where the conversation was headed. One never knew with Jen.

''I know you've always thought I betrayed you. And I guess I did. But you had a chance to get Spencer back and you never took it.''

So this is where we're headed. Leigh glanced longingly at the door. ''It was all a long time ago, Jen. I've put it behind me.''

"I doubt it, Leigh. Because if the great egotistical Jen Logan couldn't put it away on a shelf, neither could the morally upright Leigh Randall."

Leigh's face stiffened. *Jen could always hit the bull's-eye.* "Well, I have," she said.

Jen waved a dismissive hand. "I know you better than you think I do, Randall. Just because I always acted the blond bimbo, don't think for a second I was one underneath."

"I've never thought that, Jen. You of all people should know."

There was a tense silence. "Yeah, you're right. I do know. Loyalty was your second name. I wasn't very good at that part of our friendship, was I?"

Leigh sensed Jen didn't want an answer to that. She kept silent.

"But there are some things I think you ought to know. I fell big for Spencer, too. I ate my heart out watching you with him, but I never made a move on him. I swear! Not until after you and he had that big fight about your going to Chapel Hill. You split up with him and I decided it was an open market."

"An open market," Leigh repeated, incredulous.

"Sure, let's call a spade a spade, okay? So I asked him to take me to the prom, and since he'd already heard you'd decided to go with Tony, he agreed. Not very eagerly, I might add. Anyhow, the day before the prom Mary Ann Burnett came to me with this note from you. She said you asked her to pass it on to Spence. I don't know why you didn't take it yourself."

"Because I'd offered to drive my father to his doctor's appointment in Hatteras, and I didn't have time to go looking for Spence. I told Tony I still wanted to go with Spence He…he was really great about it." Leigh's eyes filled. She had to stop.

"I figured something like that. So Mary Ann saw me first and showed me the note."

"Why?"

"I think she knew how crazy I was about Spence and that I wouldn't have a chance with you around. Anyway, you were heading off to Chapel Hill in September."

"Always the matchmaker," Leigh muttered.

"Huh?"

"Never mind. So you took the note and threw it away."

After a moment Jen replied, "Something like that. I read the note, saw that you asked Spence to meet you at the lighthouse. I threw it away and went over to his place to...kind of occupy him so he wouldn't be out walking in the village and bump into you later." She paused dramatically. "I was two months pregnant when you left Ocracoke in September."

Leigh was too stunned to speak.

"I'm sorry about that. It was a rotten thing to do."

Leigh cleared her throat. "I guess you managed to persuade Spencer I wasn't really interested in him."

"I thought I had. But the next night at the prom, he spent the whole evening following you around the dance floor with his eyes. He took me home early, said he had to go out fishing with his father the next morning. I knew he was lying."

"Instead, he drove around the island."

"Yup, and happened to be at the Creek when your boat capsized. You know the rest."

"I know the rest all right." Leigh massaged her temples. Her head was pounding. She looked across the room at Jen, sitting poised and comfortable in the rocking chair. The sweat and toil of confession had scarcely touched her.

Whereas Leigh was positive that, if she could see herself in a mirror right then, she'd appear seventy years old. She took a deep breath. "So why are you telling me all this now, Jen? It's a bit late, don't you think?"

"Late, yes. But I don't want to carry the burden of it around with me anymore, Leigh. I did a terrible thing to you—"

"My best friend!"

Jen's eyes flickered to her lap. When she raised her head, Leigh saw that her lower lip was trembling.

"Yes," Jen said in a hoarse whisper, "your best friend. That was my sacrifice fifteen years ago." She paused, averting her face from Leigh's. Finally she turned back and said, "I'm not asking forgiveness, Leigh. That wouldn't be fair. I only want to say I'm sorry for what happened. I saw a chance to be with Spencer and I gambled that it would all work out. I was wrong."

"But you had your chance," Leigh reminded her. "Just as you said I had my chance to patch things up with Spencer that night he drove up to Chapel Hill and I let him stand in the rain for an hour."

"You were there!" Jen chuckled. "Gawd, Leigh, I can see you hiding behind your curtain or something the whole time he's pounding on the door. You always were so...so hard. So stubborn."

"Not really, Jen. I just didn't parade my emotions the way you did."

Another chuckle. "Touché, Randall." She placed her hands on the armrests and pushed herself out of the rocking chair. "Guess I'd better return to my duties. I loved Sam, you know. He knew it, too. I was often a disappointment to him—" she lowered her head to smooth her dress "—but he always came first in my life, right after Jamie. I sent him money for years from whatever rinky-dink town Jamie and I were living in. It was damn hard."

"Yes, I think it must have been. I've often wondered what you were doing and how you were managing. My mother and then Grandpa Sam told me some things."

Jen's cool green eyes met hers. "Thanks, Leigh. I'll be

leaving tomorrow to go back to Charlotte. I've had a long talk with Spencer today.''

Leigh's ears perked up. She'd wondered where Spencer had been all morning.

Jen continued, ''You'll hear the whole story from Spence, but I've persuaded my husband to drop his adoption suit. I love Jamie and I want him to live with me all the time. But he needs to know his father, too.''

''Yes,'' Leigh agreed.

''We're going to see what we can work out.'' Jen moved toward the doorway. She halted a few feet from Leigh. ''I knew almost immediately after I said my wedding vows to Spence that I'd lost my gamble. He had that haunted look in his eyes. After Jamie was born, I couldn't bear to see that look anymore. I had to leave or I'd have ended up like…I don't know. Like nothing. I'd have lost my very soul. Spencer still loves you as much as he did fifteen years ago, Leigh. I hope this time you'll listen to him when he tells you.'' Then she walked out of the room.

Leigh picked up the pillow she'd been leaning against and hugged it, then closed her eyes and wept.

CHAPTER FIFTEEN

DAMAGE CONTROL following Jen's little chat was furtive and quick. Windswept Manor had only one bathroom, so there was a succession of discreet taps at the door while Leigh washed her face and reapplied mascara and lipstick. When she deemed herself acceptable, she strolled downstairs, replaced the cell phone in the kitchen, talked with a few people and avoided scanning the room for fear of making eye contact with someone she wanted to avoid. Like Spencer.

Then she made her way to the kitchen where she insisted on staying to help. Trish tried to push her into the other rooms.

"This is your house and you've just come back home. You should be out there meeting people."

But Leigh resisted. *Seems I have a reputation for stubbornness I may as well live up to.* Later, while guests began to leave, one of the women returned to the kitchen to inform Leigh that Spencer McKay was looking for her. Leigh took the opportunity to sneak upstairs and lock herself in the bathroom. The scene was eerily reminiscent of that night in Chapel Hill. Except this time Spencer wasn't sodden, but striding throughout the upper floor calling her name and stopping in front of the bathroom door. She held her breath, feeling more childish by the second as he tapped softly on the wood.

"Leigh? Are you in there?"

After a few seconds he walked away and Leigh scurried

across the hall to her bedroom. When she finally went back downstairs, everyone had left but the women in the kitchen.

Trish reproached her. "Where have you been? People were looking for you to thank you for hosting the reception. Spencer was especially upset that you couldn't be found."

Leigh ducked her head to pick up some dishes and mumbled, "I was exhausted. I took a quick nap."

When she glanced across the room, Trish's face looked doubtful. Then the woman said, "By the way, my sister's coming tomorrow. She was supposed to arrive Friday, but her plans were delayed a bit. Can we get together for iced tea and dessert at my place? Say, late afternoon?"

Leigh agreed and they continued the cleanup. When she finally closed the door behind the last person, Leigh headed straight to bed. It was only eight o'clock, but the emotional upheaval of the past two days had taken its toll. She'd just switched off her lamp when the telephone, which she'd left downstairs, began to ring, but nothing could induce her to get out of bed to answer it.

The aroma of coffee pulled her from bed next morning. Leigh took the stairs cautiously, tying the ends of her robe and wondering which of the many people who'd been in and out of her house over the past two weeks she was going to encounter now. The closer she got to the kitchen, the more she thought it would be Spencer. Her heart started to pick up speed and she paused in the hallway, steadying herself by holding on to the door handle for a minute. She inhaled, counted to five and walked into the kitchen.

Janet was standing at the counter, her back to the door. Leigh's heart fell to the pit of her stomach.

"Janet," she said.

The woman whirled around. Color seeped up her neck into her face, which broke into a huge smile. "You startled me!"

Ditto for me. "Why didn't you let me know you were coming?" Leigh asked.

"Oh, I tried to. I called several times, but there was never any answer."

"Yesterday?"

Janet frowned. "I did call yesterday, I'm sure of it. A strange person picked up the phone and I hung up, thinking I had the wrong number."

"Was that you who called last night?"

"Last night? I might have. Yes, I probably did. Are you all right, dear? You look rather wrung-out. Did you have a party? I noticed all the dishes stacked on the dining room table."

Leigh pulled out a chair and sat in it. She rubbed her eyes. "No, not a party. A funeral reception."

Janet clutched her bosom dramatically. "Good heavens! Not Spencer?"

An icy chill shot down Leigh's backbone. *Why does his name come to her lips first?* But before Leigh had a chance to respond, Janet asked, "Would you like coffee now?"

The non sequitur threw Leigh back into the never-never land of her very first conversation with Janet Bradley. "Please," she said. After Janet had placed the mug of coffee in front of her, Leigh said, "The funeral reception was for Sam Logan."

Janet's eyebrows furled. "Sam Logan?"

"Grandpa Sam! I told you about him."

"Ohhh." Janet clucked her tongue. "I'm so sorry. That's terrible. How devastated you must be."

The show of sympathy warmed Leigh. If yesterday's telephone discussion with the Bennington Agency hadn't been uppermost in her mind, she'd have been tempted to draw on Janet's sympathy. During the funeral she'd felt like an outsider even though Sam Logan had been like family to her.

She stirred her coffee, took a sip and then got down to

business. "Janet, yesterday I had a call from the Bennington Adoption Agency in Raleigh." The blank expression in Janet's face grated. Leigh hardened her voice. "You apparently telephoned there pretending to be Ellen."

Janet sagged into the chair across from Leigh. She covered her eyes with a hand that visibly shook. Leigh swallowed the remark perched on the tip of her tongue. The woman was obviously distraught.

Janet removed her hand to reach for the glass of water in the center of the table. "I had this a minute ago...for my pills," she explained.

Leigh said nothing, sensing that silence was the best response for Janet's labyrinthine conversational style.

Janet sipped the water and set it down, sloshing some onto the table. The eyes meeting Leigh's glistened. "It was a bad thing to do," she began.

I can think of more vivid adjectives. Leigh merely nodded.

"You have to understand that when I left here a few days ago, I was desperate. I knew you were beginning to doubt who I was and I couldn't bear to have that mistrust between us. I could see you drifting away from me. Moving to Spencer more every day."

Leigh tensed. Janet had a pretty good radar system, she thought. But something nagged at Leigh. "Why didn't you just tell me what you were feeling?"

Janet exhaled loudly. "I tried to. But with no real proof, how could I convince you?"

"But why the phone call to the agency?"

"I don't know what I was thinking. Sometimes I seem to get myself into these situations without knowing how or why. I did have to go back home to check on things. Before I left, I remembered your telling me about the letter the agency sent years ago. You said it was in the valise with the ducky blanket. I decided I would borrow it in case I needed it. I thought——" she stopped to sip more water "—I could use the letter to prove I was Ellen Randall. You see, I hoped to convince them to photocopy my original letter so I could bring it back to you and prove I really was your mother."

Leigh's head spun. "That doesn't make much sense."

Janet nodded vigorously. "I know it doesn't. That's how my mind works unfortunately. See, I never kept a copy of my letter. Why would I? I wrote it impulsively years ago. At the time I was married and my husband wasn't the kind to take to an illegitimate child. I had to hide everything about you. I even used a box number so the mail wouldn't come to my house. So the only proof I had was what I could tell you—you know, about the blanket and how you got your name and that."

Leigh said, "I still don't see what you hoped to achieve by pretending to be Ellen."

"But that's the crazy part!" Janet exclaimed, leaning forward in her chair. "The agency wouldn't give me my own proof to show you I'm your mother, but they *would* give me something if I were Ellen Randall. All I wanted was a copy of my letter. Then I could bring it to you and show you I...I really am your mother." Janet began to weep quietly, dabbing at her mouth and eyes with a handkerchief.

Leigh restrained herself from comforting the woman. She had to admit there was a kind of logic to the explanation. And certainly the evidence Janet had already given her was very convincing. Only a handful of those closest to her in Ocracoke knew about the blanket and the name. And yet she couldn't ignore the rational voice in her head. *Why keep everything so secretive?*

"Why did you use a phony name?" she asked.

Janet's eyebrows arched in surprise. "I changed my name years ago, dear. When I left my husband. He was abusive, you see."

When Leigh didn't respond, she went on, "I brought

something back for you. I'd forgotten all about it.'' She reached for her handbag on the table and rummaged through it, pulling out a creased photograph, which she handed to Leigh.

A very young Janet was standing on a semicircular paved drive that curved in front of a large plantation-style home. Cradled in her arms was a tiny baby, wrapped in a pale pastel blanket. Leigh brought the picture closer to her face. The colors had changed with time and exposure to light, so that everything was highlighted by a narrow chartreuse border.

It was definitely Janet—the large frame, high cheekbones and long dark hair. But the baby... Leigh squinted, straining her eyes. All she could see was a cap of raven hair and a small pinched reddish face.

"I had that taken the day I gave you away. That place is the home for unwed mothers where you were born. You can see I don't look very happy."

Leigh studied the picture again. Janet did indeed have a morose expression on her face.

"That blanket—the color's no good now, but it's the ducky blanket. I persuaded one of the nurses to take our picture. Of course—'' her voice fell to a hush ''—it's the only one I have of us.''

The bleakness in her voice touched Leigh. Her resolve to have it out with Janet, to get to the bottom of her story, began to dissolve. She no longer knew what to believe or whom. She placed the photo on the table and looked at Janet. *The answers to all my questions are right here,* she thought, *sitting across the table from me.*

"Would you like to stay for a few more days?" she asked.

Janet's face brightened. "I'd love to. And that photo is for you, dear. Put it somewhere safe."

"I will. By the way, Evan may have a buyer for the

house, so things may get a bit hectic the next couple of days. But I hope you won't mind the interruptions.''

''As long as I'm here with you, that's all that matters.'' She hesitated, then added, ''And Spencer? How are things with him and that son of his?''

Leigh peered down at her empty coffee mug. ''Oh, fine. Jamie will likely be cleared of arson charges. He finally explained what happened, but Sam's death interrupted the process. He and Spencer will be working things out with the judge in the next few days.''

''So we may not be seeing much of them?'' Janet asked softly.

Leigh stood up and carried her mug to the counter. ''Probably not,'' she said, keeping her voice as neutral as she could. She turned back to Janet. ''Where's your suitcase?''

Janet smiled. ''On the front porch.''

''Then you go get it and take it upstairs while I get showered and dressed. Later we'll think of a way to celebrate.''

Janet's eyes gleamed. ''That would be wonderful, darling. Simply wonderful.'' She walked over to Leigh and gave her an awkward but hearty embrace.

LEIGH REMEMBERED Trish's invitation for tea shortly after she and Janet had eaten a sandwich lunch in the shade of the front veranda. The morning had passed uneventfully. Leigh called Evan, but he was unavailable. She hesitated, wondering whether or not to tell him to go ahead with the offer on the house. But something held her back. When she put the cell phone down, she scolded herself for procrastinating yet again.

Face it, Randall. You just don't want to leave. It was a sentiment she'd been avoiding thinking about, especially after her quarrel with Spencer. *How can you leave when there's still unfinished business?*

When Leigh mentioned the tea invitation to see Trish and Faye, Janet looked away. "You go, dear. They're your friends and I'd feel out of place. Besides, this is my first day back and I'd just like to enjoy the sea air. I missed it in Elizabeth City."

Guilt tugged at Leigh, and since tea with Trish and Faye hadn't been at the top of her own list of things she wanted to do, she called Trish to beg off. The woman's disappointment was audible over the line, and so, without consulting Janet, Leigh agreed to make it lunch the next day.

By midafternoon, she'd decided that neither Spencer nor Evan was going to call. She was beginning to feel housebound.

"I think I'll go for a walk," she announced to Janet when she returned to the veranda. "Care to come?"

As Leigh had hoped, Janet shook her head. "Too hot for me, dear, if you don't mind. Don't forget your hat."

She's got to be a mother, Leigh thought.

She left by the back door, heading across the yard and the dunes beyond to the Sound side of the island. The walking was rougher, but she'd be alone. Few tourists ventured into the marshes in the middle of a hot summer day. And she did wear a hat. Not because Janet had reminded her, but because she'd grown up on the island. People who didn't wear hats didn't last long in the sun's glare. She also carried a small knapsack with her bathing suit, sunscreen lotion and a bottle of water.

The hike was a good idea, she decided once she was under way. She needed to be alone, to think about everything that had happened in two short weeks. *Two weeks!* She'd managed to be reunited with an old boyfriend, her birth mother and a former best friend.

Well, she amended, make that not quite a reunion but a patching up. Leigh stopped to catch her breath at the top of a dune that had been man-made years ago and was the highest point on Ocracoke. She could see the ocean on both sides of the island.

Is that Sam's cottage to the north? Losing Sam had been the worst part about coming home. Yet she was grateful to have had a chance to see and talk to him again. Leigh dug into her pack for the water bottle, took a long swallow and continued toward the shoreline beyond the salt marshes. She passed a section of fence that enclosed the ponies and peered through it, catching a glimpse of two standing dejectedly in the pitiful shade of a juniper tree. They were a hardy race of animals, however, accustomed to the tough wild grasses and brackish water of the Sound. When she reached the shore of Pamlico Sound, Leigh found a gnarled hunk of driftwood beneath a bush. If she crouched, she'd have enough shade to keep the sun from her.

Dropping the pack at her feet, she stretched out her legs and used her heels to lever her sneakers off her feet. Then she leaned over and pulled off her socks, wriggling her toes in satisfaction. It was midtide and the narrow beach, littered with clumps of dried eel grass and waving strands of beach grass, was alive with ghost crabs, sand hoppers and an assortment of shorebirds.

Leigh unbuttoned her denim cutoffs and loosened the zipper. She looked up and down the shore, but this part of the marsh jutted in and out in tiny sheltered coves fringed by bushes and other vegetation. Confident of privacy, Leigh yanked off her sweaty tank top and flung it aside. She pulled up her one-piece suit quickly, found the tube of sunscreen and lathered it all over her shoulders and back. Then she replaced the baseball cap on her head and waded into the shallow water.

It was warm, but still cooler than the sun and sand. She pranced back and forth, flicking sprays of water up into the air. Refreshed, but not completely cooled, Leigh ran farther into the surf and flung herself into the gently curling waves. She'd always been a skilled swimmer, and growing up on the island had instilled in her a healthy respect for riptides and undertows.

Leigh came up for air, rolled over and swam to shore. Wading through the shallows again, she pulled out the wet fabric of her suit, realizing she hadn't thought to bring a towel, but decided the sultry air would do the job quickly enough.

When she reached the shore, Leigh strolled along it to look for shells or interesting bits of driftwood. But the pastime she'd enjoyed so much as a child no longer held quite the same fascination. Or maybe it was simply that Spencer's face kept drifting before her mind's eye.

Leigh gathered up her things. She'd wear her wet bathing suit home, rather than carry it in her pack. On the way through the edge of the marsh and across the dunes leading to Windswept Manor, she went over a possible scenario for meeting Spencer again.

Their tiff over his investigation of Janet seemed almost silly now. Leigh didn't understand why she'd gotten so upset. Perhaps the idea that he'd done something so important without consulting her. Or perhaps her faith in Janet was indeed too trusting, as Spence had suggested. By the time she reached the center of the island, she'd decided to find Spencer and apologize. If she turned toward the harbor, she could find out if he was home. If he wasn't home, she'd simply turn back. The beauty of Ocracoke's smallness ensured that all distances were relatively short.

Yet by the time she'd reached the hummock of wild grass overlooking the tiny enclave where Spencer's house was, Leigh was ready for another swim. Wearing the bathing suit had kept her cool, but had also exposed her to mosquitos, scratches from the sharp edges of the grass and assorted scrapes from other bushes. The V at the front of her suit glistened with sweat, and tendrils of hair clung to the nape of her neck.

Everything at Spencer's looked closed and empty. Perhaps he and Jamie were at Sam's, packing up his things. Down the hummock in four long strides, she passed Spence's picnic table and dilapidated barbecue and headed along the side of the house to the front. The pickup sat in the driveway.

Leigh stopped, suddenly doubting her common sense. Why hadn't she just gone home and telephoned him? *Janet,* she thought. *That's why.*

Spencer was crouched at the rear of the truck. Leigh hesitated, then marched alongside the truck and stood behind him as he tinkered with one of the tires.

He almost fell over when she said, "Hi, Spence," but recovered quickly, bracing himself against the truck bumper as he stood up.

He looked her up and down before finding his voice. "Where did you come from? Or are you a mirage?"

"No mirage, unless they come with scratches and mosquito bites."

He still seemed dazed. "Were you at the beach?" he asked, referring to the public beach near the Creek.

"No, I came from the marsh." Leigh gestured with her head behind her.

"You were walking around the marsh in a bathing suit? No wonder you're all covered in—" he scanned her legs, his eyes pausing briefly midway up and then stopping at chest level "— bites."

Leigh wished she'd pulled on her tank top and shorts.

He managed to raise his eyes a bit higher then, squinting at her. "Is something wrong? Is that why you've walked over here, instead of driving or calling?"

"I went for a walk and a swim in that part of the marsh where Jen and I used to play. Remember? Behind my place? I was on my way home when I...well, I thought I'd like to see you."

She set her backpack down on the truck's bumper and zipped it open. "It's too sunny. I'd better put on my shirt."

"Why don't we go round back in the shade," he suggested. Cupping her elbow in his hand, he grabbed the pack and led her along the narrow path beside the house. Then he handed her the pack. "Put your shirt on if you like. I'll go get a couple of chairs."

"Look, I shouldn't have come. You're busy. We can arrange another time."

He stepped close to her, so close the front of his short-sleeved shirt brushed against her damp suit. "Leigh."

His voice was hoarse and sounded strained. He didn't take his eyes off hers, but raised his hand to her shoulder and deftly flicked off the strap of her bathing suit. "You're so beautiful," he whispered. "Coming out of the marsh like some kind of...of..."

"Swamp monster?"

He shook his head, letting his gaze drift down the hollow of her neck and to the moist darkness at the V of her suit. "More like goddess," he murmured, lowering his head to kiss the swelling of her breasts.

Leigh gasped. A rush of heat shot through her, and when his hand slipped off the other suit strap, she arched back. Her breasts tumbled loose from the suit and she heard his groan of pleasure as he cupped a hand around one and planted his mouth on the other. When he got down on one knee, moving his mouth in a line from breast to navel, she clutched his hair to stop him.

"No, Spence. Please. Not here. Jamie..."

He froze, waited a moment and then stood, pulling her to his chest. She could feel his desire. Finally, in a voice thick with frustration, he said, "Jamie's not here. We have to be in court again day after tomorrow. I let him go to a movie in Hatteras to thank him for his behavior yesterday. But you're right. Inside is safer."

Leigh lifted the straps of her suit. She fumbled in her pack for the tank top, which she quickly pulled over her head. When she turned around, Spencer looked disappointed.

"I should get back," she explained. "I really came here to talk to you—to tell you how sorry I was for treating you so badly at Sam's funeral reception." The expression in his face changed to puzzlement. "I was hiding in the bathroom when you were looking for me," she admitted.

He slumped onto the bench of the picnic table. She sat down on the edge next to him. "Why?" he finally asked.

She took a deep breath, sensing how lame the whole explanation would sound. "I'd just had a little chat with Jen and I was feeling...bad. I couldn't face you."

"What did she say?"

"A lot of stuff. Most of it self-serving. Some of it had to do with the mix-up about the prom. I guess it was her way of apologizing."

"Apologizing?"

"About throwing away the note."

"The note you told me about the other night? The one you gave Mary Ann?"

Leigh nodded.

"I might have known Jen was involved somehow. She was always so manipulative."

Leigh paused, then said, "She also told me how she kept you occupied while I waited for you at the lighthouse."

Spencer turned toward her. "I want you to know that was the only time I ever... You were the first one, Leigh. The first woman I ever made love to. Don't look at me like that. It's true. I know about all the rumors in the village. There were lots of girls around before I fell in love with you, but you were the very first one I ever actually made love to."

"And then there was Jen."

He rubbed his hands into his face and sighed. "Then there was Jen. I guess I should explain myself, but frankly," he said, turning back to her, "I can't. I fell for the oldest seduction in the book. As far as I knew, you no longer wanted me."

"And Jen was right there offering comfort."

He shook his head slowly, as if he could scarcely believe it himself.

Leigh placed her hand on his arm. "Spencer, it was a long time ago. We were all very foolish—proud and stubborn. Let's close the book on the whole thing. Right now."

Spencer clutched her hand in his, staring intently into her face. "Do you mean it, Leigh? Can you do that?"

She had to smile at his earnest expression. "I do. You know, saying that makes me feel so...light. So good!"

Spencer put his arm around her shoulders and pulled her closer. "And I can't tell you how great it feels to hear you say that. Put the past behind. Work on the present." He kissed the tip of her nose. "Hope for the future."

The future. Leigh thought of Janet, waiting for her at home. *Unfinished business yet.* "About the future—" she began.

He silenced her with his lips. "A second chance, Leigh," he whispered. "That's all I want." His fingers began to stroke her neck, working their way down the column of her throat. His mouth nibbled around the curve of her chin.

Leigh put up her hand, halting his hand from further exploration. He raised his head, a question in his eyes.

"Janet's come back," she murmured.

He dropped his arm from her shoulders so he could turn right around to face her. "When?"

"She arrived sometime this morning before I was awake."

"And?"

"And what?" she asked, playing dumb.

"Did you confront her with the phony-name thing?"

"Yes. She said she changed her name years ago to escape an abusive husband."

"Bull!"

"Why is it? Things like that happen all the time."

"That's why it's so damn convenient for her. She can pull out a ready-made story."

Leigh stood up and reached for her pack. "I don't understand why you're so biased against her. What does she have to do to prove to you she's my mother?"

His eyes narrowed. "You tell me what concrete proof she's been able to give you, Leigh. Come on. One thing."

She hoisted the pack onto her shoulders. She was so upset she was trembling. "I've gone through all this with you, Spence. Weren't you listening? The blanket? The story about my name? She even has a photo of herself with me the day she gave me up."

That stopped him for a second. Then he countered, "How can you tell it was you? All baby pictures look the same."

"Brother! I can't believe we're getting into this again."

"Because it hasn't been resolved, Leigh. You have to decide what you're going to do about her."

"She *must* be my mother. Where else could she have gotten those stories?"

He shrugged. "Everyone in Ocracoke probably knows those tales."

"They're not tales," she argued. "They're all I have to connect me to my real mother."

"Ellen was your real mother."

Leigh went still. When she spoke, her voice was dead calm. "This isn't about Ellen or Pete. Please don't imply that they'll ever be...supplanted by anyone. If they were here, they'd be encouraging me."

"I'm sorry, Leigh. I didn't mean your love for them wouldn't be the same. Gawd!" He stood up, placing his hands on her shoulders. "Just don't lose track of people who love you. Listen to me. Please!"

"I am listening," she whispered. She felt her chin tremble. Tears filled her eyes and she averted her face, pretending to fiddle with the strap of her pack. "Please, just let *me* worry about Janet Bradley. I'll sort everything out." She waited, then cracked, "I won't change my will in her favor or anything."

She didn't look at him, but heard him mutter, "That's not even funny, Leigh. Janet Bradley is a weirdo. A complete wing nut. I just hope you find that out before you get hurt."

After a long moment Leigh glanced at him. He was staring across the yard toward the harbor in the distance. She started to walk around to the front of the house.

"Wait," he said, his voice husky. "I'll drive you home."

"I'd rather walk, Spence. Clear my head, Really, it's okay. I'll take the easy route this time."

"Please," he said, "be careful. Janet could be anyone. She could be..."

"Crazy? Dangerous?" she scoffed. "Spencer, this is Ocracoke, not New York." Then she disappeared around the corner of the house.

CHAPTER SIXTEEN

LEIGH HUNG UP the phone. Evan was not happy, but he'd agreed to negotiate two more days from the people who wanted to buy her house.

"I hope after all this you're not going to turn around and inform me you are not selling at all," he'd sniffed.

And because that had been exactly the thought at the back of Leigh's mind, tucked away from reason and logic, she'd felt a pang of guilt that lasted at least half an hour. Until her discovery of Spencer's bandanna.

Midmorning she broached the subject of the missing adoption letter with Janet. Whatever the woman's reasons had been for "borrowing" it, Leigh wanted the letter returned.

"Oh, dear, I completely forgot about it. It's upstairs in my bedroom, most likely still in my purse. Shall I get it?"

But Leigh was on her way to the bathroom and insisted on getting it herself. Janet's handbag was lying on the unmade bed. Leigh glanced curiously about the room. Although she'd invited Janet for a few days, the woman hadn't set out any personal items on the night table or bureau. The Pullman suitcase stood in a corner of the room, still closed. There were no dresses or even a robe hanging from the hooks on the back of the bedroom door.

She picked up the hefty purse, surprised by its weight. It was the type of bag with two main compartments, each with its own gold clasp. The letter wasn't in the first section Leigh opened. There was a tattered wallet, a hairbrush, tube of lipstick, vial of a well-known brand of painkillers and the folded section of newspaper that Janet had shown Leigh the first day of her arrival last week. Leigh smiled, touched by the sentimentality that had stopped Janet from discarding the article.

Then she unclasped the other section, finding a folded road map of the Outer Banks, a ferry schedule, a minipack of tissues, a pocket novel, a package of mints and the white business envelope from the agency. When she pulled on it, a corner of the envelope failed to budge, caught on something at the bottom of the purse. Leigh pushed her hand in and felt soft fabric. She pulled out Spencer's red-and-black checked bandanna.

For a moment a peculiar disjointed sensation flowed over her. Like participating in a game without knowing you were playing. She sat on the edge of the bed, trying to recall when she'd last seen the bandanna. Ah, yes. The day she'd gone up to Hatteras with Spencer. She'd left it on the hall table to give it to him, but had forgotten. Sometime later, she'd discovered it was missing and had assumed he'd picked it up. Well, she thought, someone *had* picked it up. Janet. But why?

Leigh took the letter and, bandanna in hand, sought out Janet.

"Find it, dear?" Janet asked when Leigh walked into the kitchen. The woman was finishing washing up the breakfast dishes and had her back to the door.

"Yes, I did, Janet. And something else, too."

Janet turned around, curiosity in her face. She looked at Leigh, then at the cloth in her outstretched hand.

"Oh," was all she said.

"How did you get this, Janet?"

"Well, dear, it's not as bad as it looks." She wiped her hands on the towel hanging from the cupboard door and sat down at the table. "The day of the open house I arrived late. Of course, I didn't even know there was going to *be* an open house. I'd gotten your address from a clerk in one of those convenience stores in the village. When I found the house, there were cars and people coming and going. The Open House sign was up. I knew I couldn't barge in to see you for the first time with all those people around. That wouldn't have been right!''

''So you waited until everyone left?''

''Yes, but I had no idea you weren't home. I knocked and waited more than fifteen minutes. I thought maybe you were out in the yard. The door was unlocked and I opened it and called out. Of course, I soon realized no one was home.''

''And?''

Janet shook her head. ''I was so terribly disappointed. I can't tell you how long it took me to get up the nerve to go to your house, and then to find you gone! I stepped into the hall, thinking I'd write a note. But I dismissed that idea almost at once. You can't leave a note for your long-lost daughter.''

Leigh could merely agree with a nod of her head. She knew the story would get out, but found the retelling exhausting.

''When I realized I'd have to come back, I started to leave and I suddenly noticed that handkerchief on the hall table. I wanted some contact with you so badly I took it. Just to have something of yours!'' she cried. ''That night, I slept with it under my pillow. I meant to give it back, but after I came here, you were so nice to me I couldn't bear the thought of losing your respect. I didn't want you to know I'd taken it.''

Leigh didn't tell Janet the scarf was Spencer's, although a mischievous side of her wanted to. The explanation made sense, Leigh decided, but she still didn't like it. ''Did you come right into the rest of the house? Get coffee from the kitchen?''

Janet drew herself up in the chair. "Goodness, what do you take me for?"

And that was that. One part of Leigh wanted to believe her, and another part wanted to drop the whole thing.

"Janet, as you said, it's no big deal, but I hope you're not going to be afraid to tell me things in the future. I don't think it's a good idea to base a...a friendship on secrets."

"I agree completely, Leigh. I promise, no more secrets."

Leigh tucked the bandanna into her shirt pocket and headed for the door. "Oh, I almost forgot. Yesterday Trish invited us for luncheon to meet her sister, Faye. I've put her off before, so I really must go this time. We should leave about noon. Okay?"

Janet was busy cleaning the table with the dishrag. She didn't look up, but said, "Of course, dear."

Back in her room Leigh put the bandanna into her drawer. She remembered the day Spencer had given it to her and the sensitivity he'd shown about the episode with Laura's mother. It was a side of him that at nineteen hadn't yet evolved. Then she had a sudden memory of yesterday's argument with him about Janet. How could she have behaved so badly? So holier-than-thou. After finding the bandanna in Janet's purse, Leigh was beginning to realize that Spencer's suspicions about the woman were understandable. She peered at her reflection in the mirror.

What *was* the truth? Part of her could relate to Janet's plight. Fifteen years ago a number of people had thought they knew the truth about her role in the drownings, and even now the doubts hadn't been erased. Surely Janet deserved a chance to prove herself, too.

On the other hand, there were so many parts of Janet's story that raised questions in her mind. And of all the questions and what-ifs, the one that resounded the loudest was simply, *Why?*

Why would Janet Bradley step into her life and pretend to be her mother if she wasn't? What could she possibly gain from it, considering she hadn't once asked her for money? In fact, she'd even borrowed her car and returned it.

Granted, Janet was apparently someone who didn't always follow the norms of social behavior. She acted impulsively and secretively, but from the heart. That was the point Leigh needed to remember.

Now I just have to change Spencer's mind. If Leigh was going to accept Janet, Spencer would have to, as well. Because now—she stared hard at her reflection—she was going to make sure she took that second chance with him. The chance he was talking about yesterday.

Leigh thought of Sam's using what little strength he had to make her promise not to turn her back on Ocracoke and Spence again. *I'm not going to, Sam. I'm not going to let Spencer out of my life so easily this time.*

Leigh stepped back from the mirror. *Nothing like a good heart-to-heart with yourself,* she thought.

The phone was still on her night table from the talk with Evan. She dialed Spencer's house, crossing her fingers while the phone rang. Jamie answered.

"He's not here, Leigh."

"Oh." Disappointment flooded through her. "Out on charter?"

"No. He's at Grandpa's place packing up things and cleaning stuff. I'm supposed to go over and help later this afternoon. Want me to pass on a message?"

"No, it's okay, Jamie. I have to go out for lunch, but maybe I'll get a chance to pop over to Sam's later. How are you doing, by the way?"

"Great. Guess what? I'm not going to be adopted by my stepfather, after all. And Shane's admitted everything to the police, so my lawyer said charges have been dropped. We just have to sign papers."

"I'm very happy to hear that, Jamie."

A slight pause and then, "Thanks for everything you did for me, Leigh."

"Jamie, I didn't do anything."

"You listened to me."

"Well, I liked listening to you, Jamie, so it was no effort, and…and I hope we'll get to be good friends by the end of the summer."

"You mean, you might not be leaving right away?"

"That's what I've been thinking."

"Hey, cool! Wait'll I tell Dad. He'll be, like, totally happy." Another pause. "Oh, maybe I shouldn't have said that."

"I'm glad you did," Leigh said. "It gives me hope. Listen, have a great afternoon and I'll see you later."

"You bet. Oh, and Leigh?"

"Yes?"

"We already *are* friends," he said.

Leigh was smiling when she hung up.

"JANET?"

Leigh walked down the hall and hesitated outside the closed bedroom door. She'd called Janet more than half an hour ago on her way into the shower to remind her of their luncheon date and had assumed Janet had heard. She tapped quietly on the door.

"Janet? It's time to go." There was no response, so Leigh cracked open the door.

The room was in darkness, curtains drawn against the midday sun. The mound on the bed stirred.

"Janet? Are you all right?"

"Oh, is it time? I've got such a vicious headache," she whispered.

Leigh frowned. *Hasn't this happened before?* "Can I get you something?"

"No, dear. I've taken painkillers and the best thing is

simply to lie in a dark room. I'm so sorry to disappoint you again. I hope you won't put off your plans.''

"No." Leigh sighed. "I'd better not—not again. I won't be long." She started to close the door when Janet's reedy voice stopped her.

"Dear? Do me a big favor?"

"What?"

"I'd rather you didn't announce the news about me yet. You know, I'm not up to all those stares I'll be getting in the village. Privacy is very important to me. I think I'd rather you tell your friends about me after I've left the island.''

Leigh wished Janet would make up her mind. Only days ago the woman had been hurt because Leigh hadn't introduced her to Trish as her birth mother.

"Sure, Janet, whatever you say. Oh, and if Spencer should happen to come by—if you hear him at the door—could you tell him I'll see him at Sam's place later this afternoon? He's cleaning up there and I want to help him when I get back."

There was a brief silence before Janet mumbled, "Certainly. Bye, dear. Have a nice time."

When Leigh reached the downstairs hallway, she decided to leave a note for Spencer in case he arrived when Janet was still asleep. She taped it to the inside panel of the big glass door, leaving it ajar to let in the cooling ocean breeze. She'd drive to Trish's house in order to get home as quickly as possible after lunch. A thrill of excitement at the possibility of being with Spencer later prompted her to skip down the porch steps. Soon, when she could decently escape what would inevitably be a boring luncheon, she'd be in his arms again. *And this time, I won't be so eager to run off.*

SPENCER THREW the bucket of dirty water over the porch railing onto the sand. Sam had been one lousy housekeeper. *And he'd have been the first to admit it, too.* He propped the mop against the rail and left the bucket on the porch. Inside, he stood in the center of the living room, scanning it for any overlooked details. No doubt the cottage had never been cleaner. Still, given the choice, he'd rather have Sam back and the place looking like the storage room of a discount warehouse.

Spencer exhaled loudly. Lots of choices in life, he thought, but not about bringing back loved ones. That was why it was damn important not to lose them when they were still alive. And if you did...well, you'd better do whatever it took to get them back. He grinned. Spence McKay, philosopher. Then just as quickly, frowned. More like Spence McKay, king of fools.

Because only a damn fool, he reasoned, would have so unthinkingly jeopardized the opportunity he'd been given to be a normal human being again, instead of an automaton going through life without really connecting to anyone. *Not even your own kid.* It was a sobering thought.

How could he have jumped on Leigh for having such blind faith in Janet Bradley when she'd shown the same trust in his own son? If he could understand and accept it in the one case, why not the other?

Besides, the private investigation had only shown there was no evidence of someone with the name Janet Bradley. It hadn't proved she wasn't Leigh's birth mother. Maybe it was time he dropped his petty anxieties about competing with Janet for Leigh's attention. *That's what it boils down to, buddy, like it or not. You're jealous and don't like having to share her.*

Yet Leigh seemed to have no fears or questions about sharing him with Jamie. He felt certain of that, although it wasn't an issue they'd ever discussed. *Too busy discussing our own neurotic selves, that's why.* Damn. How had he let things get so out of control?

Just like the old days, he thought. *When you stepped*

outside the fray and watched, instead of taking charge of your life. How different it all might have been if— No, he wouldn't do that to himself. It was self-defeating and self-pitying. As he'd been saying all along to Leigh, the past is past. *Get on with the future.* Sound advice he really ought to take.

Decision made, Spencer felt free to take his time now. He'd stop in at Leigh's on the way home and make plans for the evening. They'd need some private quiet place. Maybe here, he thought, knowing Sam would heartily approve. And the rustic charm of the cottage was evident, now that it was cleaned.

Most of the knickknacks had been packed away. Lord knew what he'd do with them. Jamie would want some things; the rest they could donate to the local church for future bazaars. Lots of bazaars! Spencer grinned. Sam had been a pack rat of the first order. Still, it had been unexpectedly generous of him to leave his place and what little money he had in trust for Jamie.

And if Jamie, when he was eighteen, could work out a good deal with the National Park Service, he just might get enough out of the place to pay his way through college. At least, that was how Spencer hoped it would go. But one could never tell with teenagers. The irony of the thought brought another grin. *I think Jamie's got twice as much common sense at fourteen as I had at nineteen.*

Spence also realized that two weeks ago this realization probably would never have occurred to him. Amazing how much had changed in so short a time.

He closed the door behind him and headed for Leigh's place. Jamie should arrive anytime, but since the cleanup had been completed, Spencer left a note for him along with a tenner to go out with his friends. The kid deserved a break.

"She's not here?" he parroted foolishly moments later. Janet Bradley shook her head sympathetically. "I'm sorry, but she had a luncheon date with old friends in the village.''

''Do you know when she'll be back?''

''No, but she did say she had some business about the house to do up in Hatteras. If she had time, she planned to drive up to meet with her real-estate agent. I think she's had a good offer on the house.''

Spencer turned his head. He didn't want Janet to see what he was feeling—sick at heart. He swore silently. He didn't even have the agent's last name to call him, and Janet sure didn't seem to know much. How could he get hold of Leigh before she signed any papers on the house? He looked at Janet through the screen door again.

''So, she didn't leave me a note? I mean, it's not like her to just take off like that.''

''Was she expecting you to call?''

He shrugged, feeling like an idiot. Of course Leigh was *exactly* the kind of person to take off, especially if she was still upset with him. And why wouldn't she be? He hadn't called her. All he'd done was assume she'd be there— waiting as usual. The same thing he'd done fifteen years ago—assume she'd come around. Assume she'd see things his way in the end. Because she usually had—until the prom debacle. Spencer slammed his palm against the door frame.

Janet jumped back, covering her mouth with her hand. ''Goodness!'' she gasped.

Spencer took a deep breath. *Calm down, fella. Get a plan together and don't go berserk on the poor woman.* ''Sorry,'' he muttered. ''Look, do you know the last name of the real estate agent in Hatteras? That Evan guy?''

''Sorry, I don't.''

''Okay, then this is what I'm going to do, Janet. When Leigh gets home or if she phones, please tell her I want to meet her tonight at Sam's place. Say, about nine.'' He paused then, taking in Janet's expectant face. ''Uh, I'm planning a little, you know, romantic dinner for two. To make up for some things.''

She smiled. ''I understand.''

''So if she calls, tell her I'm heading up to Hatteras hoping to head her off at Evan's place—wherever it is. Tell her please not to sign any papers on the house until she talks to me. Tell her...tell her it's a matter of life and death.''

She frowned. ''It is?''

''Yeah, it is for me. Okay? Do you have all that? Should I write it down?''

''Oh, no, Spencer. Heavens, I can remember that.''

When he was climbing back into his truck, he couldn't shake the bad feeling he had about leaving such a complicated message with Janet. He shifted into reverse and was halfway down the drive when he squealed to a stop. *How can I have been so stupid?*

He stared at the For Sale sign on the front lawn, memorizing the Hatteras phone number. He briefly considered going back up to the house to simply telephone, but instinct told him not to waste precious time explaining any more to Janet.

THE TELEPHONE RANG just as Spencer's truck backed onto the main road. Janet closed the big glass door behind him and, tucking the note Leigh had left for him into her dress pocket, headed for the kitchen.

A youthful voice on the line asked for Leigh. ''I'm sorry, but she's at a luncheon.''

''Oh.'' The voice fell.

''Can I take a message?''

''Sure. Uh, this is Jamie McKay calling. Spencer McKay's son? Anyway, I want to leave a message for my dad, but I can't get hold of him at my Grandpa's place. No phone there.''

"Ah. Well, your father was here looking for Leigh. He just left."

"Did he say where he was going?"

"I believe he had some business to take care of in Hatteras."

"He did? Gee, I was supposed to meet him at Grandpa's about one-thirty."

Janet checked her watch. "Well, you're late. It's going on that now."

"I know, that's the problem. See, I had a call from our lawyer and he needs to see us today. I don't know what to do…"

"Maybe you can see the lawyer yourself."

"I guess so. If you see Dad again, could you tell him where I am? Or if Leigh shows up soon, could you tell her?"

"Yes, I can do that. So let me make sure I've got this right. You won't be going to your Grandpa's, after all."

"That's right. I'll wait at home for him."

"Fine. I'll pass that on."

When Janet placed the phone on the table, she was smiling. If she followed all the steps very carefully, things just might work out. Spencer was gone. Now Jamie was gone. Sam Logan had already left all on his own, and for that, she blessed him. Soon she'd have her daughter all to herself. *Just the way I wanted.*

LOOKING BACK, Leigh could almost pinpoint the moment she decided to break her promise to Janet.

Partway through the strawberry shortcake and iced coffee, she suddenly was tired of hearing both Trish and Faye rambling on about everyone who'd ever lived in or left Ocracoke. They'd ticked off the names of classmates in their years and, because Ocracoke School had been so small and included all the grades in one frame building, had started in on Leigh's class. She didn't mind that they did most of the talking, for it had given her the chance to daydream about Spencer. And she didn't object to their somewhat unsubtle references to "that terrible tragedy, dear," or poor old Sam Logan who'd died penniless.

Penniless but content. And she'd clenched her teeth and forced a smile when Trish gave her credit for forgiving Jen Logan.

"It was the talk of Ocracoke for some years, I tell you," Trish said. "Everyone knew she'd set her sights on Spencer. Didn't surprise me when I heard Mary Ann Burnett was up to her tricks there, too."

Guess I was the last to know, Leigh thought. The fact that she didn't care was reassuring. Faye hadn't done as much talking as Trish, filling in only on the reminiscing. But then, she'd been away from Ocracoke even longer than Leigh and had been oddly vague when questioned about her recent years.

Later, when Leigh was helping take dishes into the kitchen, Trish had told her, sotto voce, not to mind Faye. "She's had it tough. Maybe you haven't heard, but poor Faye's spent most of the past twenty years in and out of psychiatric hospitals."

Leigh had been genuinely shocked.

"Chronic depression, it seems. She always had what we used to call a flighty way about her. High-strung, you know." Trish bustled about the room. "We don't talk about it publicly. To spare her feelings, like. But she's been on some new medication the past year and we're hoping she won't have to go back."

"Will she stay here with you?"

Trish pulled her head back. "Lord, no! She has a nice little apartment in Elizabeth City, not too far from the hospital—just in case there's a relapse, you see."

They picked up their replenished tumblers of iced coffee and joined Faye on the veranda. Something in the older woman's pale face tugged at Leigh.

"Well, I have some rather unexpected news of my own," Leigh announced, sitting between the two sisters. And without thinking more than a second about Janet's request, she told them her story.

They were astonished and full of questions, which Leigh had to ward off eventually with a raised hand. "One at a time," she begged.

"So this is the woman you introduced as an old family friend the other day," Trish said. "And you say she has no proof?"

"No written proof. But the evidence she has is darn convincing. She knows some very personal details about my adoption—even about the blanket I was wrapped in."

"The ducky blanket," Faye murmured.

"You know about that, too?"

"You showed it to me once, when you were about six or seven."

"Was it in the leather valise?"

A frown wrinkled Faye's brow. "I don't remember where it was. I think it was just on a shelf. You still took it to bed with you in those days. Your mom and dad were trying to wean you away from it." She laughed. "I do recall one time your mother asked me to pretend I didn't know where it was. She said she'd washed it and put it away for you."

"Well, that blanket was from my birth mother. And Janet described it for me before I even pulled it out of the suitcase."

"What an amazing story!"

Leigh smiled at Trish's excitement. "I think so, too."

"Did she know the story about coming home from the hospital with your name pinned on your sleeper?" Faye asked.

"Heavens! *I* didn't know that story!" Trish exclaimed. "How did *you* know it, Faye?"

"Why, from Leigh of course. When I baby-sat her.

Sometimes we'd play 'adoption' together. Remember, Leigh?''

Leigh smiled and shook her head. "Not that part, though I suppose I must have told you lots of things. So you see," she continued, "although Janet doesn't actually have a piece of paper proving she's my mother, how else could she have known these things? I mean, she's never been to Ocracoke before. And even if she'd come as a tourist, no one in the village except for Faye and Jen even knew those things."

"So what are your plans now, Leigh? Are you still in a hurry to sell?" There was a twinkle in Trish's eye.

Now's your chance to let the whole village know at once. Save you a lot of explaining. "My plans aren't definite yet, Trish. But I want to get to know Janet much better. I have an apartment and a job in New York to take care of, but I'd like to spend the summer here at least. Pick up old friendships, you might say."

Trish clapped her on the shoulder. "Good for you. That's the spirit."

Faye smiled quietly and played with the spoon in her drink. "What does she look like, this Janet?"

Leigh thought for a minute. "She's tall like me and has my coloring, although we don't really have the same features at all."

"Maybe you take after your father," Trish said. "Has she talked about him?"

"No, she's never mentioned him at all. I mean, I know she was young when she got pregnant and she implied that her folks wanted nothing to do with her afterward. I haven't really wanted to press for too many details because we've only had a few days together. But I'll ask her soon."

"When can I meet her?" Faye asked.

"Why don't the two of you come for coffee in the morning? I'll make it a surprise." *Then there'll be no headaches,* Leigh thought. "Actually I have a photograph of her, Faye. But it's an old one. She's holding me in front of the home where I was born. It's in my wallet.''

Leigh reached down for her purse on the wooden floor of the veranda. "Ah, here it is. You can't see too much of me, but the shot of Janet is good. She looks much the same, only older.''

She passed the photo to Faye, then picked up her coffee, hoping she could gracefully make her exit now. All she could think about was Spencer, having his arms around her again, his lips on hers—

"I know her.''

Leigh stared at Faye. "What?''

"Her name isn't Janet Bradley, though.''

"I...I know it isn't," Leigh stammered. "She changed it years ago. But—''

"It's Mary Boone. That's her all right. I'd recognize her anywhere.''

"Oh, Faye!" A nervous laugh tinkled from Trish. "How could you know Leigh's mother?''

"'Cause she isn't Leigh's mother. She's Mary Boone and she shared a room at the hospital with me for almost three years. That's how I know she isn't Janet Bradley!'' Faye's voice rose indignantly with each word.

Leigh felt the veranda shift. Black spots flickered across her line of vision. She listened to the two sisters and tried to shape words with a mouth that wasn't cooperating.

"Leigh? Are you okay, honey?''

Trish's face swam before her. Leigh blinked and pulled herself up in the cushioned chair. "I don't understand,'' was all she could get out.

"You'd better explain this, Faye,'' Trish ordered.

"I knew Mary in the hospital. Like I said, we were roommates.''

"She could still be Leigh's mother,'' Trish insisted.

Faye shook her head. "No, because she told me the story about this picture a long time ago. Maybe she even showed it to me once. It looks familiar. She had a baby when she was seventeen and she'd planned to give it up for adoption.''

''See! It could be a strange coincidence.''

''No, Trish. The baby she gave up died when it was still an infant. Mary Boone never got over that tragedy, poor thing. That's what sent her into the hospital, I think. That and her parents.''

Leigh waited for the roaring in her head to fade. ''Then how...? Why...?''

Faye kept her face averted. ''I'm sorry. I had no idea. It didn't seem important at all, telling Mary about life in Ocracoke. She was fascinated by the island. And...and when I told her about the little girl I baby-sat for, who was adopted and had arrived wrapped in a blue blanket with yellow ducks on it from her own mother, Mary cried. She actually cried, Leigh!''

Leigh wanted to weep, too, but shock had blocked off all connections to important body functions—like thinking and speaking. She stared into Faye's pinched worried face.

''What else did you tell her?'' Trish demanded.

''The story about the note, too. And some things about the Randalls. All good, mind you.''

Of course, all good. Basically my whole life story. Leigh ran her tongue over her lips. ''So you told her everything you knew?''

Faye nodded miserably. ''I'm sorry, Leigh. I didn't mean for this to happen. It all came out in normal conversation. Just talk between two roommates. How could I know she was memorizing it all?''

And tucking it away for a rainy day?

''It doesn't make sense,'' Leigh whispered.

''Yes, it does,'' Trish put in. ''She gave up a baby girl and lost her. Maybe she blamed herself. Then she hears this tale about another girl who's been adopted. Did you tell her what Leigh looked like, Faye?''

"Only that she had black hair and eyes."

"General enough to do the job in a twisted mind."

Leigh looked at Trish. The woman's face was set and serious. She was a lot tougher inside than she appeared on the surface, Leigh thought. That led her to another realization. *You weren't any better at reading Janet than you were Trish. Or Spencer, for that matter. You only saw what you wanted to see.* Leigh slumped in her chair.

"You sure you're okay, Leigh?" Trish stood up. "Let me call Spencer for you."

Yes. Have Spencer come and make things all right for you. Especially when you were so certain he was wrong about Janet. "No! Trish, I'm fine. I'll go home now and find out why Janet has done this. She's—"

"A crazy woman!"

"Trish!" Faye sounded shocked.

Trish shot her an angry look. "Isn't she? Was she discharged, then, before you?"

Faye shook her head and stared down into her lap. "No," she whispered. "When I left, she was still there."

"How long ago was that?" Leigh asked, though part of her didn't really want to know.

"Three months ago," Faye mumbled.

Trish's eyes flashed. "You see! I bet she just walked out of the place. I bet they're looking for her right now. And if you're not going to let me call Spencer for you, honey, I hope you're going to let me call the hospital. I have to do *something*."

Leigh agreed to the latter and got to her feet. Faye was weeping quietly. Leigh patted her shoulder and murmured, "It wasn't your fault, Faye."

Faye didn't respond.

Leigh looked at Trish and said, "I'll come back later to talk to your sister. Right now I have to go. I'm sorry."

Trish accompanied her to the car. "Sure you're okay to drive? Now don't get into a fight with that woman. Who knows what state of mind she's in. Best to let her keep on thinking you don't suspect.''

"But she knew I was going to see Faye. That's why she had an excuse.''

Trish watched while Leigh pulled out of the driveway, then went inside to make her telephone call.

LEIGH SLOWED as her car approached Windswept Manor. She scanned the front veranda. No sign of Janet. *What did you expect? That she'd be rocking in her chair waiting to ask about my lunch?*

When she'd pulled out of Trish's drive, Leigh realized she couldn't go home. The only person she wanted to see was Spencer. She knew he'd come through for her this time. The knowledge made her smile, in spite of the churning in her stomach. She had faith in him. *About time.*

She passed Windswept Manor and headed for Sam's cottage. Spencer's truck wasn't there and Leigh hesitated, sitting in the car for a moment. Then she decided that even if Spencer had left, he'd come back. And Sam's would be as good a place as any to hide from Janet. The thought of facing the woman so soon made her want to throw up.

She ran up the stairs, almost knocking over a mop and bucket. The door was unlocked and she stepped inside.

"Spencer?'' Waited a heartbeat. "Jamie?'' Another beat.

Okay, sit down and make yourself at home. Sam would want you to.

Leigh sagged onto the sofa and plunked her purse on the floor beside her. She let her head roll against the back of the sofa and stretched her legs. Her head and stomach were still waging war with each other. She couldn't decide if she'd have to run for the bathroom or take a painkiller.

Painkiller. Again she thought of Janet and shivered. She closed her eyes and let the peacefulness of Sam's cottage soothe her. Then a voice came from behind.

"I thought you'd come here.''

CHAPTER SEVENTEEN

LEIGH DIDN'T MOVE. She swallowed the acid that had pumped into her mouth when she'd recognized that voice. Very slowly she raised her head and turned it slightly to her right. Janet was standing in the doorway to Sam's bedroom.

"Hello, Janet," she said in a tone more matter-of-fact than she'd have thought possible. "Why don't you come and sit down?"

Janet moved into the room. When she was standing in front of the sofa, Leigh was struck by the flatness of her demeanor. This unexpected meeting was no surprise to her, she thought. "Won't you sit down?"

And Janet did, pulling up the easy chair adjacent to the sofa as if she'd been living in the cottage all her life. "Did you have a nice lunch?" Janet asked.

Leigh felt another mouthful of bile work its way up from her stomach. *She really is crazy.* "Yes, I did. Trish and Faye were sorry you couldn't make it." Especially Faye, she wanted to add, but decided to let Janet take the initiative.

"Another time." Janet gave a small shrug, then leaned forward to whisper conspiratorially, "There *will* be another time, won't there?"

"If you like," she ventured.

It was the right answer. Janet smiled and leaned back in the chair. "I suppose you had a chat with Faye."

"I did. She told me all about her stay in the hospital."

"And the rest?"

"The rest, too."

"Are you angry with me? You said you didn't want any more secrets between us."

And this was definitely the mother lode of secrets. "Not angry. Disappointed, though."

"Because I don't look like the mother you expected?"

"I don't understand what you mean."

"You wanted a mother and I wanted a daughter. It's really quite simple."

She may be crazy, Leigh thought, *but she's not stupid.* "I guess you're right about that. But I wanted the truth, too."

A trace of a smile crossed Janet's face. "The truth? If only we knew the truth about anything, Leigh. The truth is I had a daughter years ago and I gave her up for adoption. The truth is I didn't want to, but my parents forced me to."

Leigh waited until she was sure Janet had finished. She didn't want to antagonize her. At the same time it was difficult to sit and listen. "The truth is—" Leigh paused "—your daughter died."

A flame sparked in Janet's eyes. Her voice rose in pitch. "My daughter didn't die! They told me that so I wouldn't continue with my lawsuit."

"Lawsuit?"

"To get her back. I took them all to court. My parents, the owners of the home where you were born, the parents who adopted her."

"The Randalls?"

Janet's eyes narrowed to slits. She tilted her head slightly, as if sensing a trap. "I know who the Randalls are. Pete and Ellen. They adopted you. They adopted my baby."

"Tell me more about the lawsuit," Leigh said. She wondered how much longer she'd have to continue this bizarre conversation.

"They were so scared I'd win, you see. In those days people were just starting to get certain rights. I had the right to change my mind."

"So you tried to get back your baby?"

"*You!* I tried to get you back, but they told me you'd died. Crib death. You were only four months old. But I didn't believe them. You were a healthy baby! They lied so I'd drop the lawsuit."

"And did you?"

Janet's voice fell to a whisper. "I had no choice. No money. Later, when I fought my parents about it, they put me in the hospital."

"Where you met Faye."

"She was nice to me. She told wonderful stories about life here. When I heard about you and the blanket, I knew you were the one. But I had to wait, see. Because the Randalls had taken you."

"So why didn't you try to get me back years ago?"

"Because every time I talked about you, they lied to me. Said you were dead. Or else they gave me shock treatment. Then pills. I lost so many days...years." She broke off, wiping her hand across her eyes.

It was a motion that wrenched at Leigh, in spite of the circumstances.

"Do you know where Spencer is?" Leigh asked.

Janet shook her head.

"Was he here when you arrived?"

"No one was here. There was a note for Jamie, telling him to go to a movie or somewhere. And a ten-dollar bill. I put that in my pocket for safekeeping. Spencer won't mind."

"No, I suppose not. Listen, are you hungry? Would you like to go out for dinner?"

"Dinner?" Janet smiled broadly. "It's only three

o'clock, Leigh. Besides, didn't you have a big lunch with Trish?"

"Well, then, I think we'd better go back home now." Leigh stood up.

"Don't go, Leigh."

Leigh stood in front of Janet. She reached for her purse and slung it over her shoulder. "It's time to go home, Janet."

"Where's home?"

"You know. My place."

"So you're not going to sell it, after all?"

"I don't think so."

"But you're not going to go off with Spencer, are you? It's just going to be you and me, together."

"Sure, Janet." *Just like the song.* "Come on. We'll have some iced tea on the veranda."

Janet rose from the chair, then stopped, wringing her hands. "I don't know. What if Spencer comes back? Or Jamie? Sam's gone, at least. He won't take you from me." She laughed aloud at the idea.

A chill rode up Leigh's spine. "Are you sure you haven't seen Spencer or Jamie?" Suddenly icy fear lodged itself in Leigh's chest. She felt herself begin to hyperventilate. *Calm down. Stay calm and controlled.*

Janet gave a quick cat-with-canary smile. "I might have."

Making her voice casual was the hardest thing Leigh had done since entering the cottage. "So where are they?"

Janet giggled. "Spencer's on his way to Hatteras, and Jamie—" she paused "—Jamie's at an important meeting with someone."

If only I could believe her, Leigh thought. She held out a hand. "Come on. It's stuffy in here. Iced tea and maybe a piece of that lemon cake we had yesterday. Sound good?"

Janet nodded. "It does sound good." She followed

Leigh to the door, but when Leigh placed her hand on the handle, she drew back.

"What is it?"

"I think I'd like to stay here a bit longer. Besides, I've left a little surprise for Spencer. He's coming back here later to fix dinner for you. I want to be sure he gets it." She giggled behind her hand.

The hairs rose on the back of Leigh's neck. "What kind of surprise?"

Janet's smile vanished. "I don't know that I trust you. I know what it's like to be in love. That's how I had you. I believed what he told me, but I was wrong about him. Just the way you were about Spencer years ago. I don't know the whole story, mind, but I do know you put your faith in him. And he betrayed you!" She was shouting now.

Leigh placed a hand on Janet's arm. "That's all in the past. Don't worry about it."

The woman shook her head. "I know he hurt you. Men are all the same. They can't be trusted. Even that boy of his. I heard about that fire. That's why I thought my little surprise would be so fitting."

Fear made speech impossible. Leigh waited until it subsided somewhat. In as calm a voice as she could manage, she said, "Why don't you show me the surprise? Maybe we can stay and enjoy it together."

Janet smiled coyly. "Maybe. But I think Spencer would be startled to find you here. It was meant just for him."

"What is it, then? Some special dinner?"

Janet's eyes narrowed again to slits. "Dinner? Why would I make dinner for him? I told you—he's planning a romantic dinner for you. That's what he said before I sent him off on that wild-goose chase to Hatteras." She laughed at the memory. "If you could've seen his truck tear out of your drive and off to the ferry."

"Maybe he'll be disappointed if I don't stay."

"Why should you care?" Janet's face flushed. She moved closer to Leigh. "Didn't you say that from now on it's going to be just you and me?"

Leigh backed away. "Of course, Janet, and I meant it. I have to tell Spencer, though, don't I? That it's all over between us?"

Janet chewed her lip and considered this question. When she looked up, there was triumph in her face. "You don't have to tell him at all, dear. When he gets the surprise, there'll be no need for any explanations."

Nausea rolled up from Leigh's stomach. Where was the help she was supposed to be getting? Then she realized that help, if it came, would be going to Windswept. She held out a hand to the back of the chair she was standing next to, steadying herself.

"Janet," she begged, "I'd really like to see the surprise. So I can share it with you later. Over iced tea on the veranda."

"Ahhh, that's sweet, darling. You're such a thoughtful daughter." Janet reached out a hand to pat Leigh's cheek.

Leigh fought to conceal her revulsion and smiled back. Her eyes never wavered from Janet's.

After a long moment Janet nodded. "All right, then. Come into the bedroom."

When Janet pushed open Sam's bedroom door, gasoline fumes wafted out. Leigh coughed, holding her hand across her nose and mouth. Before Janet slammed the door again, Leigh caught a glimpse of a jerrican of gasoline and Sam's bedding piled in a hummock on his bed.

"What have you done?" She turned to Janet, keeping her voice as neutral as she could.

Janet beamed. "After we've had our iced tea and chat, I'm going to come back here and wait for Spencer. He's expecting you at nine. When I arrive, of course he'll be disappointed and puzzled." She thought for a second. "I'll have to make some excuse to explain why you're not there.

Anyway, I plan to hit him on the head with something—maybe that conch shell over there—and when he's knocked out, I'll set the fire in the bedroom. Everyone will think it's an accident.''

Leigh shook her head. "Not with evidence of gasoline."

"It doesn't matter. That's what's so perfect about this, you see." Janet's smile became cagey. She linked her arm through Leigh's and drew her toward the screen door leading to the porch. "I found that jerrican outside in Sam's shed. The police will think Jamie set the fire. Hasn't he done it before?''

Leigh was so frightened she couldn't think straight. Her single goal was to get out of Sam's cottage before some spark accidentally ignited the fumes. She let Janet lead her out to the porch.

"What a pleasure to be going home with my daughter!" Janet squeezed her arm affectionately.

Leigh nodded. Her throat was too tight to speak. Partway down the porch stairs, she thought she heard the squeal of tires. Janet's fingers dug into her arm.

"Is that a car?''

"Probably someone braking for a rabbit or something on the highway. Don't worry. Come on, let's go home."

But someone was charging through the cypress trees behind Sam's cottage. There was a shout.

Janet ran back up the stairs to the landing. She shaded her eyes against the sun. The shout came again.

"Leigh!''

"It's Spencer!" Janet screamed from behind. She reached out a hand and grabbed the back of Leigh's shirt, clutching it like a drowning person.

Leigh tried to break loose, but Janet was holding on too tightly. She was afraid to pull away in case the older woman fell.

Spencer leaped over the crest of the dune fronting the cypress trees. Sprays of sand plumed into the air behind him. When he reached the bottom of the porch stairs, he was panting. He held on to the railing while he caught his breath.

"You're early!" Janet accused.

He frowned, looking first at Janet and then at Leigh.

Somehow Leigh found her voice. "Janet said you'd be back later to make dinner for me."

"What?"

Janet moved to the edge of the stair and pointed a finger at Spencer. "You told me to have Leigh come over about nine for a romantic dinner. That's what you called it. *A romantic dinner!* You men are all the same. Leading us on."

Spencer climbed the first step and held out a hand. "Why don't you come down here to talk, both of you? We can't carry on a conversation like this."

He stared at Leigh, but all she could do was nod her head vigorously.

"The three of us aren't having a conversation. My daughter and I are going home for our own little chat. But now that you're here, I don't see why you shouldn't come inside. I'll make you some tea."

"No!" Leigh cried. "He doesn't want anything, do you, Spencer? He has to get home for Jamie."

"Jamie's going to the lawyer's," Spencer said.

"How do you know that?" Janet asked.

Spencer shook his head. "Ladies, I'm finding this very confusing. Let me explain. I stopped in at your place before noon, Leigh, and Janet told me you'd gone to Hatteras to sign the papers on your house. I decided there was no way I'd let you do that without talking to you first." He looked up at her, a few steps above him.

When she didn't reply, he went on, "But when I got to the ferry dock, there was a huge line of traffic waiting to get on. I knew I wouldn't get on that ferry, so I called home to try and catch Jamie before he came here to clean.

That's when he told me he had to go to Hatteras himself to sign papers. So I knew that either way I'd have to go to Hatteras, but there was time to go back and get Jamie. As I passed Sam's just now, I noticed Leigh's car parked on the side of the highway. I couldn't figure out why she was here, but knew I had to stop her before she went on to Hatteras."

"How touching," Janet said. "One would almost think you really loved her."

Spence placed his foot on the bottom step. "I *do* love her, Janet." He shifted his gaze to Leigh. "I'm going to marry her."

"I don't think so," Janet said. "Come up here, though. I want to talk to the man who says he's going to marry my daughter."

Leigh held up a palm. "Don't go up there, Spencer. She's not my mother."

Janet shrieked and pulled Leigh backward against the landing. Leigh stumbled and fell onto her back. Spencer charged up the steps to Leigh while Janet rushed into the cottage.

"What the hell's going on? Are you all right?" He placed an arm underneath Leigh's head and raised her to a sitting position.

"She's set a trap in there—for you. A firetrap."

The words were scarcely out of her mouth when a resonant boom sent a burst of heat through the screen. Flames shot out of Sam's room. Spencer opened the screen.

"Don't go in there!" Leigh grabbed his pant leg.

The screaming inside the cottage made him push her aside. Leigh got to her feet to see him grab the afghan from the sofa and throw it over Janet, who was whirling about the living room, her dress afire. By the time he got Janet on the floor, the flames from Sam's room were spreading through the open door.

Spencer dragged Janet to the screen door, kicked it open and heaved her onto the landing.

Janet was moaning, "My daughter! Save my daughter."

Leigh closed her eyes and heard the faint wail of sirens.

LEIGH STOOD in the center of the highway, which was partly cordoned off by state troopers, and watched the ambulance door slam shut. She turned away to rest her head on Spencer's shoulder.

"Sure you're all right?" he asked.

She merely nodded, not yet trusting herself to speak.

"The paramedic guy said Janet would be all right. The burns aren't serious."

She burrowed her face deeper into the hollow between his chest and shoulder, aware of the sounds of movement behind her: the ambulance pulling away, the firefighters raveling hoses back onto their truck, everyone going about his or her tasks silently and efficiently. Some information had already been passed along to the troopers; the rest could be gathered tomorrow, they'd assured Leigh.

Spencer buried his face in her hair. "I love you so much. Gawd, I don't want to *think* about what might have happened."

When Leigh pulled her head back to look up into his face, she saw fear in his eyes. "She wouldn't have hurt me," she whispered. "Only you."

Spencer pressed her to him. "It's all over. Jamie's waiting for us at my place. Are you ready to go?"

She nodded and let him lead her to his truck. "I'll pick up your car later."

"I can do it," she murmured, climbing into the passenger seat of the pickup.

He shook his head. "Nah, I don't think so. I'm taking you home—to my house—and before I tuck you into bed, I'm feeding you a hearty bowl of soup."

Leigh nodded.

Spencer started the engine, shifted into gear and headed south.

"Did you mean what you said back there?" Leigh asked.

He turned to her, a frown on his face. "About loving you? Gawd, you know I do!"

"No. The other. What you said to Janet—about wanting to marry me."

The pickup zigzagged momentarily. His answer was a husky whisper. "Damn right I do." A painful pause. "If you'll have me."

Leigh extended her hand to his and squeezed hard. Tears brimmed her eyes. Then she laughed, a hoarse joyful laugh. "Yes, yes, yes!"

CHAPTER EIGHTEEN

THE SCREEN DOOR slammed shut behind Leigh. She hefted the picnic hamper onto one hip while she locked the door with her free hand. Three months ago she wouldn't have been doing this, she thought. *But life is different now.*

Tourist season was winding down in Ocracoke. In mid-September the highway was almost deserted after rush-hour traffic had departed for northbound or mainland ferries. Leigh had no trouble backing onto the road and headed toward the village. She pulled into the parking lot of the Ocracoke general store to buy cold drinks and fresh fruit for lunch.

After the bustle of the summer months, shopping with only a handful of locals was a pleasure. Leigh smiled, realizing she was already starting to think like an islander again. She headed to the cold section at the rear of the store and bumped into Trish Butterfield.

"Congratulations!" the woman cried, giving Leigh an impulsive hug. "Have you set a date yet?"

Everyone else in the store was looking her way and smiling. Leigh knew her face was burning. *No such thing as anonymity in Ocracoke. But I wouldn't have it any other way.*

"Well, not yet. I suggested the spring, but Spencer's a bit..."

"Impatient?"

Leigh grinned. "That's an understatement."

"You can't blame the man. I mean, he's been waiting fifteen years."

"That's what he says, too."

"And you want everything to be settled for the winter. It's been a long time since you've gone through an island winter, Leigh. Personally I think early October would be a great time for a wedding."

"Perhaps." Leigh shrugged.

Trish ducked her head closer to Leigh's. "Faye heard through a mutual friend that Janet is much better these days. They've put her on a new medication. Doesn't go off into her imaginary world so often."

Leigh tensed. She was grateful for the information, but mention of Janet still brought back unpleasant memories. "That's good to know. And how's Faye doing?"

"Oh, great. She may come down for Christmas. And what about young Jamie? Will he be here for Christmas?"

"We hope so, but nothing's definite yet. Jen's baby is due next month and we're not sure yet what she'll want to do. According to the agreement, Jamie is supposed to come every second holiday, and this would be the first. But Spence won't push it if Jen says she wants Jamie."

Trish clamped her lips together and shook her head. "Still the same old Jen, wanting to be in control."

Leigh surprised herself by defending Jen. "I don't think it's that, really. She's going to have a new baby and perhaps she wants all her family together for this first Christmas."

But Trish looked skeptical. "I think you're being too generous as usual. So where are you headed now?"

"I'm meeting Spencer at his office and we're having a picnic lunch."

"How romantic! Somewhere private?"

Leigh laughed. "That won't be hard in Ocracoke at this time of year."

Trish laughed, too, then said, "Say, I was talking to

Mary Ann Burnett the other day. She told me she asked you about writing an article on Janet and the rest of the story for the *Island Breeze*. Can you believe the woman?''

''Some people never change,'' Leigh murmured. She said goodbye to Trish, paid for her supplies and headed back out to the car. Mary Ann's telephone call a few days after the fire was still vivid in her mind.

''I've always felt so guilty,'' Mary Ann had confessed, ''for not delivering that note you gave me to Spencer. All I can say is that I was young and impressionable then myself. I figured you were going away to college and leaving Spencer behind. Jen was crazy about him and I thought...'' Mary Ann's voice trailed off without the prompt she was waiting for from Leigh.

Then she'd broached the topic of the feature article for the *Island Breeze*. ''Many people are seeking their birth parents, and vice versa of course. This would be a wonderful article about how something so important can go wrong.''

''No, Mary Ann,'' Leigh had replied. ''I don't think people need to know about something that personal. Besides, the major newspapers have already picked up the story.''

''But this would be from your perspective—how you felt, why you wanted to believe Janet's story so much...''

Leigh had managed to keep calm, but had hung up as soon as she could. *No, some people don't change at all.*

On the way to Spencer's office Leigh stopped at the post office to pick up her mail. Quitting her job—with the promise to do some contract work for Reg—and selling her apartment in New York—with the help of a friend of Evan's—had been so easy that Leigh questioned the quality of her life there the past seven years. *How can I just walk away from it all with absolutely no regrets?*

Spencer, of course. She thought back to that night Janet had been taken away. He'd driven Leigh home, made her soak in a hot bath, clothed her in a pair of his pajamas and tucked her into his bed. Then he'd lain on top of the covers and held her while she cried. He'd slept with her that night and every night since.

"Until you don't need me beside you," he'd promised.

"I'll always need you beside me," she said.

And later, when he'd asked her again to stay in Ocracoke as his wife, Leigh hadn't needed time to consider the question. She wouldn't let this second chance escape, she vowed, though a cautious voice deep inside begged her to wait. There were other feelings and opinions to consider—Jamie's and Jen's. Not to mention sorting out all the details from the summer.

Sam's cottage was restored and rented, the funds directed into a college fund for Jamie. Bill Cowan sold his share of the business to Spencer. There had been a small dilemma about Windswept Manor. Leigh knew Evan would still come through for her, but Spencer talked her out of selling.

"It's too original," he'd said. "How many places like that are left in Ocracoke? If you sell it, how can you guarantee that the new owners won't tear it down and rebuild some trendy monster cottage?"

Leigh had smiled at his phrase, but agreed with his point. In the end they'd decided to sell Spencer's house and live at Windswept. Evan would still get a commission and there'd be lots of room for little McKays. Or so Leigh reasoned privately. *But one step at a time—starting with the marriage.*

They'd seen Jamie off to school in Charlotte the week before. The new custody agreement allowed him to make more decisions about his living arrangements. He decided to spend winters in Charlotte, attending school. It was a decision that disappointed Spencer, but made him proud at the same time. There would be more educational opportunities in the city, and Jamie's agreement to take school more seriously was a welcome one. Alternate Christmas holidays and all summer holidays would be spent on Ocracoke.

Jamie had already chosen his new bedroom at Windswept—the gabled attic. The three of them had spent most of the summer cleaning and redecorating. When he'd left for school, Jamie had hugged Leigh fiercely.

"If you get married in October, Dad said I could take a few days off school. We can hike through the marshes again. Check out the ponies."

And Spencer had teased, "Are you crashing our honeymoon?" to which Leigh had added, "Not crashing. He's invited. We're family, right?"

Leigh paused to chat to some people on her way into the post office. She'd received many notes and wishes of congratulation about her engagement to Spencer. Over the summer she'd realized that deciding to stay in Ocracoke had not been the hurdle she'd expected. After their initial show of surprise and pleasure, people treated her as though she'd never left. And although Laura Marshall's mother still avoided her, Leigh knew the woman had stopped gossiping about her.

"Some of her friends set her straight," Trish had revealed to Leigh. "Suggested if she couldn't forgive and forget, then maybe she should just keep quiet."

Leigh shuffled through the stack of business envelopes, then reached for a small brown padded envelope wedged into the rear of the box. The postmark was Virginia City and there was no return address on the outside. Back in her car Leigh ripped open the envelope. Inside she found a small package wrapped in tissue paper and a folded letter.

She unfolded it and began to read.

Dear Ms. Randall,
I read about your story in our local newspaper and

my heart went out to you. Ever since I wrote to the Bennington Adoption Agency sixteen years ago, I have dreamed about this day. I am taking a chance that you may still be interested in finding your birth mother. If you are not, kindly disregard this letter. But I hope the contents of the package will persuade you to contact me when you feel you want to.

Because I never received a reply to my inquiry years ago, I never thought this opportunity to find you would happen. I have instructed the Bennington Agency to release the necessary information you will need to show that I am indeed your birth mother. Looking forward to meeting in the near future,

Lois Morley

The packet inside tumbled out onto Leigh's lap. Her fingers fumbled with the tape wrapped around it, finally tearing at the paper. The small remnant of powder blue fabric was the missing corner of her baby blanket.

"WELL, IT'S A LOT MORE convincing than Janet Bradley's story," Spencer said, tossing the square piece of blanket onto the desk. "How do you feel about it? What does your gut instinct tell you?"

Leigh had to smile. "You're trusting my gut instinct?"

Spencer reached out to clasp her hand. "I've always trusted your instincts, Leigh."

"To be honest I feel nervous and scared—but excited, too. I think I'm ready for this." She caught his eyes and grinned. "But we'll take it nice and slow, won't we?" She tucked the blanket remnant into her straw bag.

Spencer stood up, walked around the desk and tugged Leigh out of her chair. Then he pulled her toward him, dipping his head into the crook of her neck. "Mmm, you smell good. Like a fresh summer day." He kissed the spot behind her ear that drove her crazy. "What's this?" he murmured. "You're shivering. And it's such a warm sunny day."

"Spencer!" Leigh stepped backward, pushing gently against his chest. "This isn't quite the lunch I had in mind."

"It isn't? Then we're not on the same wavelength at all, lady, because it's exactly the one I pictured."

She leaned down to pick up the picnic hamper and her bag. "Let's go."

His halfhearted grumbling was an act, she knew. They locked up and walked down to the docks.

"Where are we going?" Leigh asked after she'd stowed the supplies on board.

"I thought it would be the perfect day to take a ride over to Portsmouth Island," he said. Before she could respond, he quickly added, "You up for it?"

Her eyes met his. She thought for mere seconds. "Yes, I'm up for it."

His smile spoke a thousand words.

"Okay," he said. "You start her up and I'll get the lines." When he hollered the go-ahead, he pushed off from the port side while Leigh thrust the lever into reverse and backed out of the slot. Spencer moved to the stern to give directions, but he knew she no longer needed them. She was turning into an adept pilot. *Just as well,* he thought, *if she's going to be my new business partner, as well as my wife.*

Once they were under way, Spence took over to steer out of the Creek into the Sound. "I was talking to my investment counselor the other day," he said.

Leigh turned her head, grinning. "Yeah? What'd she say?"

"That I'd get a tax break if I got married this fiscal year. And with the profits from the sale of my house and buying out Bill Cowan, I'll really need that tax break. So how about it?"

In spite of the teasing in his face, his eyes burned with determination. ''I think that's good advice,'' Leigh finally said.

''Then come here, counselor.'' Spencer pulled her to him with his free arm. Standing so close they seemed one, they steered the boat through the deep blue water of Ocracoke Sound toward Portsmouth Island.

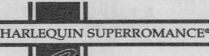

HARLEQUIN SUPERROMANCE®

Every now and then comes a book that
defies convention, breaks the rules and
still offers the reader all the excitement of
romance. Harlequin Superromance—a series
known for its innovation and variety—
is proud to add these books to our
already outstanding lineup.

There's more to the story...

RELUCTANT WITNESS (#785)
by Linda Markowiak

Attorney Brent McCade is used to dealing with *hostile*
witnesses. What he can't understand is Sarah Yoder's
reluctance to help him put away the man who has the power
to hurt her again.

Available in April 1998 wherever Harlequin books are sold.

Born in the USA

Look for these titles—
available at your favorite retail outlet!

January 1998
Renegade Son by Lisa Jackson
Danielle Summers had problems: a rebellious child
and unscrupulous enemies. In addition, her Montana
ranch was slowly being sabotaged. And then there was
Chase McEnroe—who admired her land and desired her
body. But Danielle feared he would invade more than just
her property—he'd trespass on her heart.

February 1998
The Heart's Yearning by Ginna Gray
Fourteen years ago Laura gave her baby up for adoption,
and not one day had passed that she didn't think about
him and agonize over her choice—so she finally followed
her heart to Texas to see her child. But the plan to watch
her son from afar doesn't quite happen that way, once the
boy's sexy—*single*—father takes a decided interest in *her*.

March 1998
First Things Last by Dixie Browning
One look into Chandler Harrington's dark eyes and
Belinda Massey could refuse the Virginia millionaire nothing.
So how could the no-nonsense nanny believe the rumors that
he had kidnapped his nephew—an adorable, healthy little boy
who crawled as easily into her heart as he did into her lap?

**BORN IN THE USA: Love, marriage—
and the pursuit of family!**

HARLEQUIN®   *Silhouette*®

Welcome to *Love Inspired*™

A brand-new series of contemporary inspirational love stories.

Join men and women as they learn valuable lessons about facing the challenges of today's world and about life, love and faith.

Look for the following March 1998 Love Inspired™ titles:

CHILD OF HER HEART
by Irene Brand

A FATHER'S LOVE
by Cheryl Wolverton

WITH BABY IN MIND
by Arlene James

Available in retail outlets in February 1998.

LIFT YOUR SPIRITS AND GLADDEN YOUR HEART
with *Love Inspired!*™

Steeple
Hill™

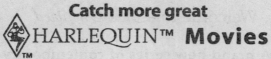

DEBBIE MACOMBER

invites you to the

HEART OF TEXAS

Join Debbie Macomber as she brings you the lives
and loves of the folks in the ranching community
of Promise, Texas.

If you loved Midnight Sons—don't miss
Heart of Texas! A brand-new six-book series
from Debbie Macomber.

Available in February 1998
at your favorite retail store.

Heart of Texas by Debbie Macomber

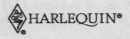

HARLEQUIN®

BESTSELLING AUTHORS
IN THE SPOTLIGHT

.WE'RE SHINING THE SPOTLIGHT ON SIX OF OUR STARS!

Harlequin and Silhouette have selected stories from several of their bestselling authors to give you six sensational reads. These star-powered romances are bound to please!

THERE'S A PRICE TO PAY FOR STARDOM... AND IT'S LOW

HARLEQUIN SUPERROMANCE®

Loving DANGEROUSLY

They're tall, dark and dangerous. Exciting. The kind of men who give women thrills—and chills. The women are daring, strong, compassionate—and willing to take a risk. Danger may threaten, but together the hero and heroine can face any challenges. Even the challenge of love.

Look for these upcoming *Loving Dangerously* books:

Available wherever Harlequin books are sold.